MAFIA SUMMER

MAFIA
SUMMER

A NOVEL

E. DUKE VINCENT

BLOOMSBURY

Published by Bloomsbury Publishing, New York and London
Distributed to the trade by Holtzbrinck Publishers

All papers used by Bloomsbury Publishing are natural, recyclable products made from wood grown in well-managed forests. The manufacturing processes conform to the environmental regulations of the country of origin.

Library of Congress Cataloging-in-Publication Data

Vincent, E. Duke
Mafia summer : a novel / E. Duke Vincent.—1st U.S. ed.
p. cm.
ISBN 1-58234-500-7 (hardcover)
ISBN-13 978-1-58234-500-0
1. Hell's Kitchen (New York, N.Y.)—Fiction. 2. Italian Americans—Fiction. 3. Jewish teenagers—Fiction. 4. Male friendship—Fiction. 5. Mafia—Fiction. 6. Gangs—Fiction.
I. Title

PS3622.I527M34 2005
813'.6—dc22
2004019490

First U.S. Edition 2005

1 3 5 7 9 10 8 6 4 2

Typeset by Hewer Text Ltd, Edinburgh
Printed in the United States of America by Quebecor World Fairfield

This book is dedicated to the inimitable Bob Smith. At one time or another during the past ten years, he insisted I tell this story and never lost faith. He is one of the brightest, bravest, most honorable men I have ever known. Sidney Butcher lives on in him . . .

And to the *boyus* . . . in the order that I met them:

Ed Snider, Barry DeVorzon, Herb Simon, Bob Smith, Bob Fell, Jeff Barbakow, Andy Granatelli, Mike "the Judge" Bonsignore, Len Freedman, Don Fareed, Jimmy Argyropoulos, Gene Montesano, and Peter Douglas.

Finally, to my irreplaceable, loving wife, "the Hens," without whom there would be no me.

Many thanks, dear brothers and dear love.

There is no such thing as the Mafia . . .
                    —J. Edgar Hoover

AUTHOR'S NOTE

All references to events such as the sinking of the *Normandie* at her pier in midtown Manhattan, the televised Kefauver hearings, and the beginning of the Korean War are historically accurate. The attitudes and desires of the Mafia leadership living at the time, as well as their relationships with one another, are also factual. Finally, the animosity between Frank Costello and Vito Genovese, the hatred Albert Anastasia had for Vincent Mangano, and the friendship between Costello and Anastasia is well documented and revisited in the novel. The remaining characters—the street gangs and their friends, relatives, and enemies—are composites of people I knew at the time or had heard about, and therefore, this is a work of fiction.

THE FIVE CRIME FAMILIES

From 1928 to 1931, Salvatore Maranzano and Joseph Masseria, the two most powerful Mob bosses in New York, clashed in a brutal and bloody power struggle known as the Castellammarese War. The war was named after Maranzano's hometown of Castellammare del Golfo, Sicily, and ended with Masseria dead and Maranzano proclaiming himself *capo de tutti capi*—"boss of all bosses." He then decreed that all gangsters, not just in New York but all over the country, would answer to a ruling body called the Commission. This Commission would consist of five families—Luciano, Mangano, Bonanno, Profaci, and Lucchese—each named for their leaders.

Following are the members of the two families and the street gangs that are the focal point of the story:

LUCIANO FAMILY
"Lucky" Luciano (capo, deported 1945)
Frank Costello (capo, replaced Luciano)
Vito Genovese (Costello's underboss)
Giorgio "Gee-gee" Petrone (caporegime)
"Touch" Grillo (Petrone's underboss)
Paul Drago (caporegime)
Carlo Ricci (Drago's underboss)
Chucky Law (soldier)
Joseph "Joe Adonis" Doto (caporegime)

MANGANO FAMILY
Vincent Mangano (capo)
Albert Anastasia (Mangano's underboss)
Gino Vesta (caporegime)
Angelo Maserelli (Vesta's underboss)
Matty Cavallo (soldier)
Dino Cavallo (soldier)
Bo Barbera (soldier)
Carlo Gambino (caporegime)

THE STREET GANGS

THE RATTLERS
Nick Colucci (leader)
Sal Russomano
Al Russomano
Pete "Stank" Stankovitch
Junior Heinkle

THE ICEMEN
Vinny Vesta (leader)
Dominick "Boychick" Delfina
Louis "Little Louie" Antonio
Benny Veal
Attillio "Stuff" Maserelli
Ralph "Red" O'Mara
Antonio "Bouncer" Camilli

CHAPTER ONE

SUMMER 1950

T H E   F I R S T   T I M E I laid eyes on the kid, he was sitting on his fire escape four stories above the street. It was almost midnight, and he was squinting through wire-rimmed glasses, holding a flashlight and reading a book. I had just crawled out onto my adjacent fourth-floor fire escape and was settling onto the mat my mother had placed on its steel grating. The kid was so focused on his book, he didn't seem to see or even hear me.

Our fire escapes were only three feet apart and were on the front of a tenement facing Eleventh Avenue at the corner of Thirty-sixth Street. If tenements were the dominant feature of Hell's Kitchen, then fire escapes were the dominant feature of the tenements. There was one outside every living room window on all the upper floors.

That night it was sweltering hot. Summer had hit New York in late May and turned the asphalt streets of Hell's Kitchen into the devil's anvil. By noon the temperatures sailed into the mid-nineties, the humidity matched the rise, and the Hudson River, one block away, didn't help. The tar on the streets had stopped bubbling by six, but at midnight the mercury still hadn't led with an eight. Inside the apartment it was worse, and the only hope for relief was the one-foot journey from the oppressive interior to the fire escape outside. It held the promise of a slight temperature drop, the hope of a wayward breeze.

Stripped down to jockey shorts and a T-shirt, I sat against the brick wall, pulled my knees up to my chest, and peered over at the skinny kid who had just moved into our building—Sidney Butcher. He was wearing pajamas and a yarmulke, and he was sitting on a pillow with his legs crossed. The book was resting on his thighs, and while one hand steadied it, the other aimed the flashlight. Completely unnoticed, I studied him in the reflected glow of the corner streetlight. He was so thin that he looked like a stick figure. I figured he might weigh a hundred pounds and was probably no more than five-two or -three. His black curly hair flowed over his ears, and his skin was very pale. In profile, his head seemed too large for his body and his slightly curved nose seemed too large for his face. It wasn't an unattractive face, but it was dramatically different from the swarthy Sicilian faces that dominated our building and the rest of the neighborhood. I would soon learn that he had just turned sixteen, had been sick most of his life, and was almost totally self-educated.

My curiosity finally got the better of me, and I said, "Hi."

Sidney was startled. He flinched and his head popped up. He stared straight ahead for several seconds—and then his head slowly swiveled toward me, his eyes focusing. They looked round and owlish behind the glasses, and he seemed puzzled. He finally managed to stammer, "Uhh . . . h-hi . . ." It was a thin voice, almost a whisper.

"So . . . what're you readin'?" I asked.

Sidney hesitated, then glanced down at the book and back up to me as if it should be obvious. "A book," he said.

"I can see that . . . ," I responded, then added, "You do this a lot— read in the dark?"

Sidney answered with a negative head shake and held out the flashlight. He seemed to be suggesting that since he had a flashlight, he wasn't actually reading in the dark. I decided not to pursue the technicality and indicated the book. "What's it about?"

"*The Odyssey.*"

That stopped me cold. *The Odyssey*, I'd heard of *The Odyssey* . . . Homer, but I never knew anybody who actually wanted to read it . . . and certainly not in the dark with a flashlight. I cocked my head and said, "You're shittin' me . . ."

Sidney responded with a pained expression and shook his head. "Uh-uh," he said. He sounded upset—like I didn't believe him. I thought I'd hurt the kid's feelings, so I stuck my hand through the steel grating and said, "Vinny . . . Vinny Vesta."

Sidney stared at my hand like he'd never seen one, then looked back up at me and shook it. The corners of his mouth turned up slightly and he said, "Sidney. Sidney Butcher."

Full on, I thought his face had a cherubic quality, which even then struck me as ridiculous, since everyone knows there's no such thing as a skinny cherub. Nonetheless, to me it seemed angelic. I smiled back and said, "Right. Well . . . nice to meet you."

"Me too," answered Sidney. His smile got wider, his grip tightened, and he pumped my hand a few times. There was something about the way he did it that gave me the feeling this kid was different—very different—and that it had nothing to do with the way he looked. My thought was interrupted by a woman's voice that came from inside Sidney's apartment. It had a warm, lightly Eastern European accent. "Sidney, who are you talking?"

"The boy next door," he answered.

"Talk tomorrow," she called out. "It's late."

"Okay, Mom," he responded over his shoulder, and looked back at me. "See you tomorrow?" he asked hopefully. It sounded more like a plea.

3

"Sure," I said automatically—not sure at all—and Sidney disappeared into his apartment. That was the way it started. That was the beginning. It was that simple.

I had just graduated from high school along with five other members of my street gang. We were known as the Icemen—five Sicilians, one black, and an Irishman. Five of us were eighteen; the sixth, who would be a senior in high school next fall, was seventeen; and the seventh didn't know how old he was since he had never had a birth certificate. I was their leader—not because we'd ever had an election, this was just the way it had always been. As we grew up together, I was always a bit taller and stronger than the others, and by the time I was sixteen I was a well-muscled six feet one and 188 pounds. I thought God must have loved me—I was blessed with my father's brawny body and his Sicilian features: dark complexion, black wavy hair, and an arrow-straight nose. My mother said I had a face that belonged on a Roman coin. She was prejudiced, but she may have been right—the girls liked me as much as I liked them.

Three of my gang's seven fathers were in the Mob, and a fourth was a perennial wannabe. The fifth and sixth were "civilians," and the seventh was a shell-shocked World War II vet. We had all grown up together and since our preteens had been doing what Mob kids and their friends do. We hit warehouses, stockyards, railroad terminals, the airport—anything that carried value and didn't move. Recently we had heard that LaGuardia's freight terminal was a prime target, so I put it on our list. It was the beginning of what I'd come to know as the Mafia Summer, but in the middle of June, all was quiet . . .

In Mob history, however, "quiet" is a relative term. If there were no screaming headlines about gang wars, or blood in the streets as the result of spectacular assassinations, then it was "quiet." As far as the public was concerned, the monster was sleeping. It wasn't—it was resting.

At the time, there were five organized crime families in New York—Luciano, Mangano, Lucchese, Profaci, and Bonanno—each named after its leader. They in turn were responsible to a Commission, which was their board of directors, made up of the leaders of the families. By far the largest and most powerful was the Luciano family, but its founder, Charles "Lucky" Luciano, had been deported to Italy in 1945, and he left control of the family to Frank Costello, the Mob's "inside man." Costello owned half the judges, politicians, and cops in New York and rented the rest. Everyone knew he was a mobster, but it didn't matter. He was a celebrity, and New Yorkers love celebrities—famous or infamous.

The one exception was Vito Genovese, a very powerful caporegime (crew captain) in the same family who felt Luciano should have chosen him as capo (boss) of the family. Genovese was almost universally disliked, but he was extremely clever and a heavyweight earner for the family, generating millions for his crew, a percentage of which was kicked upstairs to Costello and Luciano. Not only was Genovese jealous of Costello's relationship with Luciano, he couldn't bear the fact that he was disliked as much as Costello was respected. He vowed vengeance, and he had been plotting to overthrow Costello for five years. It hadn't happened yet because Costello was too powerful and too well entrenched, but in May 1950 Genovese saw a chance to move while the attention of the five families, law enforcement, and the entire nation was focused elsewhere.

In May 1950, Senator Estes Kefauver formed the Special Committee to Investigate Organized Crime in Interstate Commerce and announced he would hold hearings in fourteen major U.S. cities. There was to be a vast difference, however, between previous hearings and those held by Kefauver. The Kefauver hearings would be broadcast on a new medium called "television." For the first time, the nation would become aware of a juggernaught called organized crime that was cutting across almost every facet of their daily lives. The Mob was petrified of the upcoming electronic attention and the consequences, and the Commission issued an edict: Violence that would draw even *more* unwanted attention to the Mob would not be tolerated. Unfortunately, not only would this fail to stop Genovese, he would *use* it to eliminate Frank Costello and take over the Luciano crime family. Even more unfortunate, his plan involved using my father—and me.

I was present for almost all of the events that took place that summer and found out about those I didn't witness shortly thereafter: My father's immediate crew . . . my crew . . . Frank Costello, the capo of the Luciano family . . . spies and informers, a multitude of police reports, and, finally, "the civilians"—six nuns, a hooker, two doormen, a funeral director, two wives, and the mistress of one of the players—all had stories to tell about the maneuverings between my family and the rival Luciano family. Secret meetings were revealed. Private conversations reported. Sources divulged and motives uncovered. Although some would rather have left the details unknown, with help I prevailed. But even with all the information I garnered at the time, it would take several years before the real repercussions finally became clear: The leadership of the Mafia would change hands, and its future would be altered for the next quarter century.

But it all started with Sidney. Sidney's father was a tailor, and in an incredible twist of fate, at the end of May 1950, the Butchers, a Jewish family from Queens, moved into a Hell's Kitchen tenement directly across the hall from a Sicilian family in the Mob . . . us. At the time we met on our side-by-side fire escapes, it was unimaginable that we would become friends and inconceivable that the friendship would make us closer than brothers. It was a bond that would change both our lives, the lives of every member of my gang, and the lives of family, enemies, and lovers.

CHAPTER TWO

THAT NIGHT I went to bed a bit bemused. Sydney was interesting, not like anyone I had ever met, but since we seemed to have absolutely nothing in common, I didn't figure I'd be seeing much of him in spite of our proximity. I was wrong. At eleven the next morning, I walked out of our tenement and Sidney was sitting at the top of the staircase.

It was a typical Saturday. Four kids were playing stoopball against the steps of the building next door, and a few young girls were skipping rope farther down the sidewalk. On the Thirty-sixth Street side of the building, another bunch of teenagers were playing stickball, our street version of baseball. We used a broomstick for a bat, and the ball was a very old, very bald tennis ball. The "diamond" was the narrow alley in the middle of the street, flanked by parked cars on either side. Home plate was a manhole cover. On that day, first base was the fender of a 1936 Dodge, second base was a burlap bag, and third base was a battered Studebaker of indeterminate vintage. As in baseball, there was a pitcher and a catcher, but there was no budding Allie Reynolds on the mound. Instead of throwing a fastball, curve, or knuckler, the pitcher had to bounce the ball in front of the plate and one-hop it to the batter. There was no umpire, so there were no called balls and strikes—but a swing and a miss was a strike, and three strikes made you history. The rest of the rules remained normal except that a ground-rule double was called when you "fendered the ball." This meant you had bounced the tennis ball up over a tire and wedged it between the mud and metal on the underside of a fender. Usually it took some twisting and grunting for the fielder to get it the hell out of there—so while this was going on, you were held to a "ground-rule double" at the burlap bag. It made perfect sense to us, though to baseball purists we were probably considered both heretical and demented—but purists played on grass, and the closest suitable grass was in Central Park. It might as well have been in Poughkeepsie.

Sidney was totally engrossed in a noisy craps game being played at the bottom of the steps by three members of my crew: Dominick "Boychick" Delfina, Benny Veal, and Attillio "Stuff" Maserelli. Like me, they were all wearing chinos, T-shirts, and sneakers. At nine o'clock it was already ninety degrees, but Sidney was wearing a sweater over a long-sleeved, open-necked white shirt, well-pressed tan corduroy trousers, brown brogans, and his perennial yarmulke. If he had added a tie, he would be dressed for church, which, as it turned out, he was. He'd just returned from shul. His hand was resting on a stack of four books bound by a piece of clothesline. The shooters didn't notice me coming out of the building, but Sidney did. He looked up, timidly raised his hand, and said, "Hi."

I looked down, my eyes narrowing automatically, and said, "How're you doin' . . ."

He seemed glad that I remembered him and said, "Fine," then added, "You?"

"Okay," I said, and took out a pack of Lucky Strikes. I shook out a cigarette and indicated the sweater. "Aren't you hot?" I asked.

Sidney shook his head. "Uh-uh. My doctor says I have thin blood."

"Must be pure water," I commented, and lit a cigarette. I inhaled deeply, then shot a pair of smoke plumes through my nostrils. I nudged his books with my toe and asked, "What's with all the books?"

Sidney picked up the stack and held it out. "They're from the library. I'm taking them back."

"Oh," I said. Trafficking in library books was a foreign concept to me. I looked back down at the craps game.

Benny had just rolled the dice, and the point was eight. "Eight! Eight, the point!" he exclaimed in an intentionally clipped street accent. He threw down a five-dollar bill and added, "An ol' Abe says yes!" As he shook the dice next to his ear, his ebony skin glowed with a light sheen of perspiration. Benny was black as a raven and faster than a finger snap. Boychick was convinced he could outrun a bullet.

Stuff immediately threw down a dollar and said, "A buck on the hard eight." Stuff Maserelli was five feet five and had hit 200 pounds by his fifteenth birthday. By his eighteenth, he was 240. He had a round, swarthy face, dark brown hair, and eyes to match. No neck, no waist, and strong as a sumo.

"Yer covered," said Boychick, and he turned to Benny. "And I got yer fin." He slammed a single on top of Stuff's dollar and another five on top of Benny's five. Boychick was my number two. He got the name Boychick from his mother's Jewish family when he was a toddler. The moniker stuck, but the last time he'd seen the inside of a synagogue was when he was four. Everyone who met him was startled by his hatchet face and narrow-set black eyes. He had a hair-trigger temper and a pair of deadly fists that were making a name for him as an up-and-coming 146-pound welterweight.

"Comin' out," howled Benny, and threw the dice.

Stuff yelled, "Lemme see a pair a fours, baby!"

"Bad bet," said Sidney.

I looked down at him and said, "Huh?"

"The hard eight. It's a bad bet," Sidney repeated with all the confidence of Arnie Rothstein, the world-class gambler who reportedly fixed the 1919 World Series.

I was stunned. If anyone in my crew had made that observation, it would have been an obvious comment (anyone but Stuff, who was a notoriously bad crapshooter), but an emaciated kid in a yarmulke who read *The Odyssey*? No way.

"You're right," I said, eyes narrowing again. "But how do you know?"

Sidney got up, grabbed the stack of books by the end of the clothesline, and shrugged as if it were no big deal. "Hoyle. It's a book about all the games. Cards, dice, chess . . . I read it."

I shook my head in disbelief. "And you remember the odds in a crap game?"

"Uh-huh. It's really only math. Math is easy for me."

I looked at the books and back to Sidney. If math was easy, what else was easy? My father had a lot of axioms. His favorite was "Knowledge is power." Suddenly my impression of Sidney changed: The kid knew shit. I was about to ask what the rest of the library books were about when Benny exhorted the dice with a bellow.

"Five'n three, two'n six, come to papa!" He threw the ivories and rolled a five and three . . . eight—the point. "Hallelujah big time!" Benny chortled. He swept up Stuff's five, and Boychick scooped up the singles. Benny looked up and spotted me at the top of the steps.

"Hey, m'man, you like to donate to the cause before we head out?"

Before I could answer, Stuff noticed Sidney. His eyebrows shot up and he asked, "Who's he?"

"Uh . . . Sidney," I murmured. "Sidney Butcher. He just moved in across the hall."

The three of them gave Sidney a desultory wave, and Boychick said, "I'm starvin' over here. Let's get some chow."

"Right," I said. I turned back to Sidney and on an impulse asked, "You wanna come along? It's on the way to the library."

"Really? I mean . . . sure!" He followed me down the steps and across the sidewalk, where I held up my hands in a T and called out, "Time." In the street, the pitcher relaxed, the batter lowered his broomstick, and the rest of the players waved deferentially as we crossed their playing field. This was our turf. On it we were kings, and to the even younger kids we were gods. Growing up, I'd often heard the Kitchen referred to as a ghetto. It wasn't—not to me and not to my crew. It sure as hell wasn't Sutton Place, but it was ours, it was home. I stepped back up on the curb and waved to the kids, and we all proceeded on our way.

Our Saturday morning routine had been a tradition for us for as far back as I could remember—brunch at our favorite eatery on the corner of Eighth Avenue and Forty-first Street. We walked east on Thirty-sixth Street, turned north on Eighth Avenue, and passed the array of outdoor stands that lined both sides of the street. The stands stood in front of the stores and were packed with everything from fresh fruit to live chickens. Roll-down canvas awnings shielded the stands from the sun, and the air was alive with the fragrant aroma of freshly sprayed fruit and vegetables. The sidewalks were teeming with women who were picking, squeezing, and choosing the succulent ingredients that would make up elaborate weekend spreads—and then adding them to already overloaded shopping bags. The din of dozens of vendors hawking their wares was mixed with raucous haggling and punctuated by the relentless banging of metal bins that hung under round overhead scales.

On the way past a particularly dazzling display of ruby red apples, Stuff's hand shot out and retrieved a sample. Even if the vendor had been watching, he probably would have missed it. Benny may have had the fastest legs in Hell's Kitchen, but Stuff had the fastest hands and nimblest fingers. Boychick loved to say he could strip off your shorts while you were still wearing your pants. Stuff bit noisily into his purloined prize and nodded approvingly while we discussed the moves and countermoves in *The Asphalt Jungle*, a movie we had seen the night before. It was about a robbery, and the crew in the movie had set up a million-dollar score with a "planner," a "boxman," a "driver," and "muscle." We all loved it because this was what we did. We planned robberies and carried them out. Not million-dollar ones—but it was the same concept. In John Huston's film noir, Sterling Hayden's plan didn't work. I thought Sterling and his crew made stupid mistakes, which was why they had failed. I figured I could've made it work. Boychick was dubious, but Benny, who thought I was a genius, agreed that I would have come up with a better plan. Stuff was noncommittal. He thought the best thing about the movie was the music—and a blonde who had a bit part, name of Marilyn Monroe. Through all the back-and-forth, Sidney tried desperately to follow the conversation, but it was obvious he might as well have been listening to a bunch of aliens.

Eight blocks later, we arrived on the corner of Eighth Avenue and Forty-first Street opposite a huge construction site that would soon become the Port Authority Bus Terminal and walked up to Barney's Sabrett hot dog stand. Barney was a happy-go-lucky dwarf of uncertain age who sported a Hercule Poirot mustache, a goatee, and a face full of laugh lines. He'd been on the same corner for as long as anyone could remember and wore a chef's hat, a butcher's apron, and riding boots. His two-wheeled cart had a signature blue-and-yellow Sabrett umbrella, and he was standing on a three-legged stool high enough to let him oversee his culinary domain. As far as we were concerned, Barney had the best sauerkraut dogs in New York. Topped with relish, mustard, catsup, and onions, they were a gastronomic home run. Washed down with a chocolate Yoohoo, they were in the same league as sex.

Waiting for us at the cart were two more members of my crew: "Red" O'Mara, a stoic, fair-skinned Irishman who thought any sentence containing more than six words was a dissertation, and "Bouncer" Camilli, a naïve, well-meaning seventeen-year-old with sunken cheeks, a stutter, and a wispy body. We called him Bouncer because when he walked he kind of bounced along on the balls of his feet. He was my second cousin and part of the crew because I felt sorry for him. Red was in my crew because he was fearless, fiercely loyal, and had the instincts of a cobra. He had a habit of whittling wooden matchsticks with his switchblade knife—exactly what he was doing when we walked up.

We all greeted Red and Bouncer, but Red just stared at Sidney with a bewildered look that silently asked, "What the hell is that?" The eternally affable Bouncer, probably sensing a kindred spirit, stepped forward and extended his hand. "B-Bouncer . . . ," he said, "B-Bouncer Camilli."

Sidney took Bouncer's hand and shyly introduced himself.

"I see y-you're wearin' a yarmy-lukey," said Bouncer, proud that he knew the name of Sidney's little black skullcap.

"Yarmulke," Sidney corrected as gently as he could.

Boychick, his attention span stretched by the polite exchange, clapped his hands together and said, "Enough already. Let's do it." He turned to Barney and fired off his order. "A dog with the works, extra kraut, and a Yoohoo."

"Goin' along," chirped Benny.

Red held up the hand with the switchblade and said, "Also."

"Three with the works," Stuff said, "and two Yoohoos. Heavy on the kraut and onions, and don't spare the relish."

I turned to Sidney and asked, "Sidney?"

"Do they have cream soda?", he asked timidly.

"A dog, a Yoohoo, and a cream soda," I told Barney, who acknowledged with a nod. I pulled a roll of bills out of my pocket, peeled off a twenty, and handed it to Barney as the last member of my crew arrived.

13

"Little Louie" Antonio had light skin, was blue-eyed-handsome, and sported a Gable-like mustache. Little Louie wasn't actually little. He was six feet three inches tall and rail thin, but he had an older stepbrother who was also named Louie. The older stepbrother, who was five feet five, was called "Big Louie" because their father—the original Louie—was only five feet three. It got confusing only if you weren't from Hell's Kitchen. Louie greeted us all, then focused on Sidney. "What? A mascot?" he asked.

"Sidney Butcher," I explained. "He's on his way to the library."

"Oh," said Louie as if this made all the sense in the world. A born comic, Louie studied Sidney for a few seconds, then, failing to come up with one of his wisecracks, he stuck out his hand and settled for, "Hi, Sid."

Sidney took the extended hand, but nothing came out of his mouth. From the moment he had laid eyes on Louie, he had been completely speechless. Louie was dressed in a three-piece suit, a cuff-linked shirt, a broad tie, and wingtip shoes, all black. He looked like George Raft— one of Louie's heroes, along with Humphrey Bogart, Jimmy Cagney, or anyone else who played a wiseguy. Louie could imitate them all flawlessly, and he used his Cagney impression when he turned back to Barney and ordered. He rocked forward on his toes and pointed both index fingers at the smiling dwarf. Then he pursed his lips and sneered, "I want yoo . . . to get for meee . . . nnnnh . . . one fully loaded dog . . . nnnh . . . with extra kraut and a Yoohooo . . ."

Barney had heard it all before and he loved it, but he waved his arms in disapproval and chided, "What the hell are you still doing with these bums? I keep saying, 'Get an agent—take a shot,' you could make good bread with that act! What's the problem? What're you waiting for?"

Louie chuckled and dropped his act. "All in time, Barney." He leaned back, painted the sky with his palm theatrically, and announced, "Someday you'll see my name in lights, baby."

Sidney watched the exchange in complete fascination. Louie was standing in the sun, wearing an all-black outfit and not showing a drop of perspiration. Sidney looked up at me in awe and whispered, "He must have *really* thin blood. My doctor's never going to believe it."

Barney delivered the order to our waiting hands, and we devoured his creations like characters in *Oliver Twist*. Sidney finished his cream soda, thanked me, said good-bye to all of us, and headed crosstown toward the New York Public Library on Fifth Avenue and Forty-second Street, happily swinging four books tied to the end of a clothesline. I shook my head and tried to figure out why the hell anybody would want to go to a library on Saturday morning.

In four days I'd find out. In a week I'd be going with him.

CHAPTER THREE

THE SUMMER OF 1950 was destined to produce three more heat waves, astounding revelations from the Kefauver committee on organized crime, and a parade down Broadway because *trolley service in Buffalo* ended. (Go figure.) Meanwhile, somewhere in a place called Korea, a war started. But on the Saturday that Sidney first joined us for lunch at our favorite Sabrett stand, the opening of the Brooklyn Battery Tunnel was the talk of the town, and Louie was excited because he'd read that a new musical about gamblers was coming to Broadway—and since all the gamblers we knew were Mob guys, the show was about us. They were calling it *Guys and Dolls*.

Just before noon on Wednesday, the gang was waiting for me outside the tenement next to a 1941 Ford "woody" station wagon that belonged to Louie's father. A weak breeze had come up, but with the thermometer inching past ninety-three, all it did was taunt you. Everyone was wearing chinos, T-shirts, and sneakers—except Louie, who was in his standard black outfit. Stuff had made a run to Barney's and was carrying a pair of large bags that contained a dozen hot dogs and eight Yoohoos. We were about to leave for LaGuardia Airport to case a possible hit on its freight terminal. Stuff had computed the time factor and figured there was an outside chance we might have to skip lunch . . . unthinkable.

During the prior three days, I hadn't seen Sidney on the street or on the fire escape. He'd had an asthma attack and his mother had been keeping him indoors, but just as I left the tenements, I spotted him shuffling along the street, tears streaming down his face. His yarmulke was gone, his clothes were disheveled, and his eyes were glued to the sidewalk. He was clutching a few books in his arms as if they were a lifeline. He didn't seem to notice us until I called out, "Sidney! What the hell happened?" I ran down the steps to meet him, the rest of the guys gathering behind me.

Sidney stopped, looked up, and stammered, "I—I was on my way h-home from the l-library . . . ," he said. He choked up, took out a handkerchief, and wiped his nose.

"Sidney, for Christ's sake, relax. You sound like Bouncer. Just tell me what happened."

He nodded, calmed down a bit, and took a deep breath. "They tried to take my books . . ."

"They? Who, they?" I asked.

"They called me names and tried to take my books . . ."

"Sidney—what'd they look like?"

He shook his head. "I d-don't know. . . . There were three . . . I never saw them before . . ."

"What'd they look like?" I repeated, starting to get frustrated.

"They were older than me . . . and they pushed me down on the street . . . they kicked me when I wouldn't give them my books, so they stole my yarmulke."

I grabbed him by his arms and yelled, "Goddammit, Sidney, what'd they look like?"

His eyes seemed to focus and he said, "One was blond and a little bigger than you . . . and the other two looked like maybe they were brothers . . . the blond one had a gold tooth."

The gold tooth cinched it. I knew who they were. The blond with the gold tooth had to be Nick Colucci. He led the Rattlers, a street gang from Chelsea, and the two guys who looked like brothers were probably the Russomanos, two of his crew. To confirm it, I said, "The blond had a scarred chin."

Sidney thought for a second and then nodded. "He was the one who kept calling me names and stole my yarmulke . . ."

I felt the rage well up and balled my fists. Here was a kid who read Homer, could quote the odds in a craps game, and spent Saturday in the library. He was small, weak, obviously sick—he'd probably walk around an ant—but the bastards had beat him up. Clenching my teeth, I said, "Sidney, here's what I want you to do . . . Go upstairs and forget about this. The guys who pushed you around are punks. I'll deal with them and get your yarmulke back. It'll never happen again . . . I promise."

"Okay, Vinny. But I don't want you to get into trouble because of me . . . I mean, you don't have to—you hardly know me."

"I know you . . . leave it at that. Now go upstairs and forget about this."

He stared at me for several seconds and nodded, the corners of his mouth curving up in the barest trace of a smile. " 'Kay," he murmured, and walked up the tenement steps.

I turned to the guys and said, "Red and Benny, you're with me. We're goin' huntin' . . . The rest of you go back to Benny's and wait for us. When we get back we'll go to LaGuardia."

Boychick's eyes narrowed. He couldn't believe it. "You serious?"

"I'm serious."

"You thinkin' 'bout messin' up Colucci?" Benny asked.

"Maybe. It's up to him."

Louie glanced up the steps as Sidney disappeared through the door and said, "I don't get it."

"What?" I asked.

Louie held out his hands, palms up. "Like he said, you hardly know him."

Stuff shook his head. "I don't get it, either," he said.

I could see that they were all baffled. Why the hell would I want to go to war with Colucci's Rattlers over a scrawny kid in a yarmulke I'd just met? Everyone except Red was looking for a reason. Red had absolutely no sympathetic feelings for Sidney—he simply relished the thought of a fight. Violence was in his nature. He smiled and spoke his first and only words: "I love it."

Benny shook his head knowingly. When he looked back at me, he shrugged in a way that said, "If that's what you want." Red, Benny, and I turned and headed downtown. Boychick stood on the steps with Stuff, Louie, and Bouncer. He still couldn't believe what I was doing. "He hardly knows the kid!" he exclaimed. Stuff and Louie nodded in agreement.

Bouncer said, "I k-kinda l-like him."

The other three looked at him as if he had just grown antlers.

Though we were bitter rivals with Colucci and his gang, and attached to different families—they belonged to the Luciano family; we were with the Mangano family—we occasionally did business with each other. So I knew they belonged to a social club in Chelsea off Tenth Avenue and Seventeenth Street and usually had lunch at the hoagie shop next door. The three of us grabbed a cab and hopped out a block away on Eighteenth. I wanted time to check out the place while we strolled down to the shop. It had a small outdoor patio with several awning tables and a draft beer setup that was the talk of the neighborhood: a row of eight taps on a short portable bar that dispensed lagers from around the world. All of the tables were full, and there was quite a bit of foot traffic because of the lunch hour. Colucci and the

Russomanos were seated at an outdoor table, eating huge hoagies and sucking up oversize schooners of draft beer. The Russomanos were a pair of sneaky-quick brothers with ferretlike faces and pencil-thin mustaches who thought they were tougher than they were. Their hobby of choice was setting cats on fire. Their table was next to the sidewalk, but they didn't see us until we were right on top of them. When he saw me staring down at him, Nick's eyes widened, confusion spreading across his face.

"Enjoying your lunch?" I asked.

Nick slowly put down his sandwich and glanced over my shoulder at Benny and Red. He was too street smart to think this was about lunch.

"Yeah," he said, "why?"

"Because the kid you beat up this morning ain't enjoying his."

"I'm all choked up. What's it to ya?"

"He's a friend of mine."

"Since when you like Jews?" he scoffed.

"This one? About four days," I said.

Nick's father was Sicilian, but he had been killed when Nick was an infant, and his mother had moved in with her older brother, Fred Heinkle. She never remarried, and the Heinkle family had raised Nick. His mother as well as the entire family was first-generation German, and they were all fiercely pro-Nazi—before, during, and after World War II. The Heinkles were the only family Nick Colucci had ever known, and he was poisoned by their prejudices.

"What's yer point?" he asked.

"You stole his yarmulke. I want it back."

"Yer shittin' me!" Nick said in total disbelief.

I shook my head. "You can either give it to me or I can take it. Your call."

Nick stared at me for a few seconds and then at Benny and Red. He was weighing his options—"Get up or give in." He shot a look at the Russomanos, who had put down their hoagies and were leaning forward. Their beady eyes were dancing in their sockets, and their thin mustaches were twitching. Never had they looked more like ferrets. Nick looked back at me, and I could almost hear the wheels grinding in his head. The fight would be three against three . . . even. Nick didn't like even, he liked uneven—two or three to one was perfect. His shifty eyes darted around the crowded patio, and he must have realized that most of the customers were from the neighborhood. He knew them, and more important, they knew *him*. If he made a move and we took him down, he would lose face—something no crew leader could afford. As the tension in his eyes faded, I knew I'd won. He wasn't going to take the chance of being embarrassed over some "Jew-boy's fucking skullcap." It was what I'd figured, and the reason I'd chosen to confront him where it was crowded and he was well-known.

With an unpleasant grin he said, "Okay, pal . . . you can have it." He reached into his back pocket, pulled out the yarmulke, and handed it to me.

"Thanks, Nick . . . it's always a pleasure," I said, smiling down at him.

"Yer gonna live to regret this, Vesta."

"I look forward to it. In the meantime, if the Jew we're talkin' about ever comes back without his yarmulke again, first I'm gonna send you a very nice wheelchair—and then I'm gonna make sure you need it."

We took a cab back to my tenement, and I told Benny and Red to wait while I went upstairs. I knocked on Sidney's door. When he answered it, I held out the yarmulke. He stared at it in awe but didn't reach out to take it.

I pushed it toward him and said, "Take it. With the stealer's compliments. He said to tell you he's no longer interested in yarmulkes. It was a phase he was going through, and he said he's sorry."

"Wow," Sidney said.

"Please—take it . . . and then tell me why the hell you'd take a beating rather than give up a few library books."

He took the yarmulke and said, "They're books . . . books are important. My pop says they're the most important thing in the world. Everything that anybody ever learned is in them. My rabbi says so, too."

"Sidney, lemme explain something to you. This ain't Queens—it's the Kitchen. Here there's principle and there's practical. Principle may say to do the right thing, but *practical* says it could be the *last* thing you ever do. So I want you to think practical . . . okay?"

He nodded reluctantly. "Okay."

"Good. Go finish your books."

"You want to see them?"

"I gotta go meet the guys."

"Maybe later?"

At that moment, he looked so frail and needy that I couldn't shut him down, so I sighed and said, "Maybe later."

He broke into an incandescent grin, and I hurried back down the stairs. Benny and Red were waiting, and we turned north toward Benny Veal's latest pad, which was the basement-floor apartment of an old brownstone on West Thirty-seventh Street between Ninth and Tenth avenues.

In a typical arrangement, a short flight of stairs led to a doorway below sidewalk level, with three windows flanking the door. One half of the large front room was a seating area with overstuffed chairs, a pair of facing couches, and a coffee table made out of an old oak door. In the right front corner next to the windows, a heavy punching bag was suspended next to a speed bag. A deer horn chandelier hung overhead, throw rugs were positioned around the floor, and posters from gangster films decorated the walls. The back half of the room contained a player piano and an antique pool table. It was comfortable, and it doubled as our hangout.

Benny was probably eighteen or nineteen years old, but he didn't know for sure because he never had a birth certificate. He was an unwanted Depression baby born in the back room of a Harlem speakeasy, where his mother sang and his father was a bartender. During World War II, his father was drafted, and on D-Day he was in the first wave of landings on Omaha Beach. He was badly wounded, and when Benny's mother found out he was also severely shell-shocked, she divorced him. A month later she gave Benny to the state. Five years later, in the summer of 1950, his father was still a mentally incapacitated vet confined to a VA Hospital and his mother was a drugged-out singer in one of Harlem's lesser nightclubs. He knew who his parents were, but obviously neither one could tell him exactly when he was born. He was shuffled between relatives and Juvenile Hall as he grew up, then dropped out of high school and hit the streets when he was sixteen. I'd met him a few years earlier—recognized a street-smart, natural athlete—and made him a member of my crew.

When we got to Benny's, I noticed Louie's father's station wagon parked out front and saw Stuff coming from the opposite direction with Angie, his basset hound, at his side. We walked in together, and I went to the phone to call my father's office. He was due back from Las Vegas and I wanted to see if he'd returned. The player piano was banging out "Mr. Sandman."

Boychick was at the pool table, Bouncer and Louie were plopped on the couch—Bouncer reading a comic book and Louie perusing *Screen* magazine. As usual, Louie was dressed in his all-black outfit, and although he had taken off his jacket, his shirtsleeves were buttoned, his tie was cinched up tight, and his trousers held knife-edge creases. He looked up from his magazine, grimacing when he saw the basset hound at Stuff's heels. He held out his hand, but it didn't do any good. Without hesitation the mutt jumped up next to Louie and dropped her head on his lap. Louie yelped, bolted off the couch, and swiped his pants. Angie stayed on the couch.

"The mutt stinks! Don't you ever wash it?" Louie barked.

Stuff shrugged. "Angie don't like water."

Bouncer petted Angie and asked, "So how c-come Angie ain't got f-fleas if you never wash her?"

"That's why she ain't got fleas," Stuff replied. "Fleas love water."

"Who the hell told you that?" asked Louie.

"Has she got fleas?"

"No."

"See?"

The logic was irrefutable. Stuff went to the player piano, switched it off, and started ripping through an up-tempo rendition of Ellington's "Satin Doll." Stuff's musical talent was as big as his body. It never ceased to amaze us, because he'd never taken more than a few lessons while he was in grade school—but if he heard it, he could play it. If he'd been born anywhere in mid-America, his family would be preparing him for a scholarship to a conservatory, maybe even to Juilliard. I dialed the phone as Boychick put up his pool cue and called out: "Benny, spot me a sec."

"Right," said Benny, and went over to stand behind the heavy bag. He held it as Boychick unleashed a set of combinations.

"Gonna be fightin' more'n more now summer's comin'," said Benny.

"Yeah. They got me set for a smoker or two up in Harlem. Maybe more."

"Don't matter. Gonna kill 'em all."

"Naturally," said Boychick.

"How 'bout me for corner man?"

I heard the request as I hung up the phone and saw that Boychick had stopped punching. He looked a bit taken aback by the request and studied Benny for a beat to be sure it wasn't a joke.

"You think you can handle it?"

"Sure," said Benny. "Watched all your fights. Saw what they do, and I listen. Can't be no cut man or nothin' yet, but I could be your corner man."

"Why?"

"Jus' thinkin'," said Benny.

"What?"

Benny said, "At some point we best have some kinda legit thing goin', even if onny to cover where our money comes from. When you was a kid you did real good in the Golden Gloves. Now you doin' good fightin' smokers. Startin' to make some noise."

"Yeah . . . ?" said Boychick, having no idea where this was going.

"Pretty soon managers gonna be all over you. They handle you right, you got a shot at the welterweight title. You gonna need trainers and workout guys. There I'm tops. I get to be one of them, okay?" He looked expectantly, waiting for an answer.

We all thought that Benny was probably the best natural athlete we'd ever seen, and Boychick realized he could probably be a great trainer. It took less than two seconds for him to make a decision. He smiled, put his gloved hand on Benny's shoulder, and said, "Ya got it. When I get a manager, you're on the payroll. Permanent."

"Okay, let's do it," I called out, and they all followed me back up the stairs.

The seven of us piled into the old station wagon and drove out to LaGuardia Airport. We had heard through the grapevine that the cargo terminal at LaGuardia was pretty easy pickings, so I had decided to check it out. During our senior year in high school, we had been pulling two or three jobs a month, but with graduation behind us and the summer ahead, we figured we should be picking up the pace. The jobs were always carefully cased and planned, with a minimum of danger and an even smaller chance of getting caught. But the fact of the matter was, we pulled off only half the jobs I cased. I had been born with a genius for selecting targets, spotting their weaknesses, and then creating plans to knock them off. Some of the jobs, however, were either too big, too small, or too dicey for us, so I sold them to the other young crews on the West Side and earned us easy cash with little effort.

The other crews, including the asshole Colucci's crew, loved the plans because they were always successful and reaped them a lot of money—as much as half of which was kicked upstairs to the bosses for the right to work in their various territories. This made the crew members "earners." A good earner got noticed by the bosses and was marked as a "comer." A comer could eventually get the opportunity to be "made," and when you were made, you were formally inducted into the family as a "soldier." That was the dream, the end of the rainbow, the pot of gold.

When we got to LaGuardia, it didn't take me long to figure out that hitting the freight terminal was a bad idea. The terminal was wide open with no cover, had floodlights all over the place, six cameras, a ton of workers, and operated twenty-four hours a day. The airport was almost entirely surrounded on three sides by water, which meant there was only one way out—the way you came in. If you were spotted, you were trapped. I made a mental note of the layout—the fences, gates, guards, and security cameras—then told Louie to take us home. We dropped off Red, Benny, and Bouncer first, then pulled up in front of my building at six o'clock.

"What time you wanna meet?" asked Boychick.

"The show's on at ten, so maybe we meet outside at nine-thirty."

I got out of the car, leaned back into the passenger-side window, and said, "Suits and ties on everybody, and everybody looks sharp." I smiled and added, "We embarrass ourselves in any way and my ol' man will kill me—right before he kills you three."

Boychick laughed and gave me a slap on the back, and Louie drove off.

CHAPTER FOUR

I WALKED INTO OUR building and was immediately assailed by the lingering scent of garlic from earlier dinners prepared by the predominantly Italian tenants. I climbed the four flights of stairs, inhaled the powerful aroma that was the building's permanent perfume, and entered our right-front "railroad flat." It was one of four apartments on each floor—two in front, two in back. Long and narrow, it consisted of a living room in front, a kitchen-dining area in the middle, and a short hall that led to two bedrooms and a bath. Many of the tenements in the area had one common bath at the end of their hallways, but the flats in our building had private baths in each of them. We affectionately called them "luxury dumps."

I could tell by the simmering coffeepot on the stove that my mother had left to help out with bingo night at our church and my father hadn't returned yet. There was a note on the table.

Gino and Vincenzo,
If you're hungry, heat the pasta.
There's also salami and I got fresh bread.
You can make a sandwich.
                    M.

If my mother wrote the same note to both my father and me, she always signed it "M." "M." could either be Mama or Mickey (short for Michelena). This, she thought, would avoid confusion. My mother hated confusion.

I walked across the nicely furnished living room, where a pair of wing chairs with matching end tables faced a couch and Queen Anne coffee table. The group sat on a large Oriental rug in front of a fake fireplace, and on the wall opposite the fireplace there was a drop-leaf table flanked by side chairs—the side chairs were also Queen Anne. My mother loved Queen Anne, but my father thought it was too feminine for the tenement, so they compromised by making the wing chairs leather. I was pretty sure that neither of them thought it really worked, but I was too smart to get into it.

Our front living room window was open, but it didn't help. The room was stifling. There was no breeze, the temperature still hovered in the low nineties, and the air smelled of asphalt. I thought Sidney might be outside on his fire escape, so I leaned out the window and looked for him. Somewhere behind the warren of windows a baby was crying, and four stories below I saw a street-cleaning truck go by, but Sidney's fire escape was empty. A door opened and closed behind me. I ducked back inside and went into the kitchen. Standing at the kitchen table reading the note was my father, Gino.

He was six feet two inches tall, weighed 225 pounds, and very little of it was fat. He had raven eyes, a square jaw, and the arrow-straight nose that I had inherited. The combination gave him a dangerous, darkly handsome appearance. He was born in Sicily at the turn of the century and arrived at Ellis Island in 1928. Shortly thereafter he became a member of the Vincent Mangano family, one of New York's original five crime families. His mentor was Albert Anastasia, Mangano's underboss and probably the most violent killer in Mob history.

I greeted him with a warm, "Hi, Pop."

He was wearing a conservative suit, shirt, and tie, topped by a snap-brim hat. Except for his white shirt, the entire outfit was in complementary shades of tan. His wingtip shoes were the color of cocoa, and as always he looked sharp. He smiled at the note, looked up, removed his hat, and took off his suit coat. There was a .45 automatic in a shoulder holster under his left arm. He put the coat and hat on a chair and said, "Vincenzo—you hungry?" His voice was baritone, mellow, and moderately accented.

I shook my head and took a bottle of milk out of the fridge. "Uh-uh," I said. There was a set of mugs lined up in front of the round compressor on top of our old Kelvinator refrigerator, and I retrieved a pair. "How was your trip?"

My father sat at the table and said, "Las Vegas is hotter than New York. How people live there is a mystery."

"How was the Desert Inn?" I knew it had opened in April and was the reason for his trip.

"Loud," he said, and pointed to his ear and his eye. "Here and here."

"What do you think?" I asked.

He paused and then, in a gesture that was his trademark, thoughtfully caressed the side of his nose with his index finger. "The families think Vegas is the new golden goose." He shrugged and said, "Possible," then changed the subject. "And you?"

I poured coffee in the two mugs and said, "We cased LaGuardia's freight terminal today."

"Anything?"

I shook my head. "Too tight. We'd need an inside man—which we don't have."

He sipped his coffee. "Smart," he said, and removed a small white envelope from his shirt pocket. He handed it to me and said, "Enjoy."

As promised, my father had arranged for tickets to see Tony Bennett, our favorite singer, at the world-famous Copacabana on East Sixtieth Street. The Copa was a Mob-owned club, and my father was close to one of the silent partners, Frank Costello. That—added to the fact that Little Louie's father, the original Louis Antonio, was the maître d'— guaranteed us reservations and a prime table. There were just four tickets in the envelope, but Bouncer was still underage at seventeen, Benny couldn't get in because he was black, and Red wouldn't put on a suit for the pope. It would be Boychick, Louie, Stuff, and me.

I smiled gratefully and said, "Thanks, Pop. The guys've been *patzo* ever since I dropped it on 'em."

A moment later Angelo Maserelli came out of the hallway, zipping up his fly.

Angelo was the underboss of my father's crew, and he ran a stretch of the West Side docks for him. At five feet six and 260 pounds, he looked like a fireplug with a head: forty-eight inches around—chest, waist, and hips. His dark gray suit jacket was draped over his arm, and he was wearing an unbuttoned vest over a white-on-white shirt. A leather holster with a .45 automatic was jammed between his spine and his belt, his tie was loose, and the top button of his shirt was undone, but the collar still seemed to be choking him. Angelo looked like Stuff's father—and he was. He was married to a fiercely religious Catholic who went to Mass every day and Rosary Society every Thursday night, never ate meat on Friday, and was damn near as big as he was. Angelo never went to church, didn't own a rosary, and ate whatever he wanted. He was an atheist married to a saint.

"Hey, kid," Angelo said as he buttoned his vest and put on his jacket. "What's up?"

I shrugged and said, "A bust-out on LaGuardia, but we've got a line on a possible liquor truck heist."

"What's the setup?"

"We're still workin' on it."

Angelo looked at my father and smiled. "The kid's got a tight lip. That's good. What time you wanna be picked up?"

"Eight-thirty is good," he said.

"See ya then . . ." Angelo opened the door and grinned at me. "Take care, tight lips. Enjoy Tony." He waved and left.

My father asked, "Anything else since I've been gone?"

"Yeah, I met the kid next door."

"The Butchers' son . . . Sidney."

That stopped me cold. "How do you know him?" I asked.

He shook his head. "I don't. When I heard the apartment had been rented, I had them checked out. The man's a tailor. Honest. A good man. The son is in bad health, no?"

"Yeah. But he's a good kid. Smart. I like him."

"Try not to be a bad influence."

"No problem."

"*Bene. Grazie* . . ." He finished his coffee, we both got up, gave each other an *abbraccio*, and I went to change my clothes.

CHAPTER FIVE

A T NINE-THIRTY, we made our way through the usual crowd lined up outside the Copa. The entrance was cordoned off by a dozen brass stanchions linked together by red, velvet-covered chains, but when the bouncer out front spotted us, he immediately waved us to the head of the line and ushered us through the door. As soon as we were in the entryway, Louie's father left his maître d's station and came over to greet us.

Louis Antonio was five feet three inches tall, with a pencil-thin mustache and shiny, slicked-back hair. He reminded me of an Italian Adolphe Menjou. He was the maître d' at the Copa, but he also ran a "book" on the side, and while not really a member of my father's crew, he was a close associate.

"Gentlemen," he said graciously with a slight bow.

"Hi, Pop," said Louie, towering over his father.

"No 'Pop,'" Louis scolded. "Dignity!"

"Right," Louie said apologetically.

He smiled and looked at us. "Hello, boys."

I smiled back and said playfully, "Men . . . accuracy."

Louis laughed and said, "Point taken." He waved us toward the tables.

The club was packed, but since it was a weeknight the crowd was mostly tourists, businessmen, or conventioneers. Louie and I had been to the Copa on many occasions with our fathers, but it was the first time Boychick and Stuff had been there, and their eyes swept the room in amazement as we made our way to a ringside table.

We sat, and Louis snapped his fingers. A waiter immediately rushed over, and Louis said, "Take very good care of them and bring me the check. These"—he glanced at us and smiled—"men—are friends of mine."

Feeling mature, we decided against our usual beers: I ordered a Scotch and soda, Boychick ordered "two," and Louie politely requested a bourbon and branch water, something he had picked up in a Bogart movie. Stuff ordered cognac because he thought it was dignified. A few minutes later the waiter returned with our order, and we toasted each other and drank. Boychick, Louie, and I sipped our drinks and nodded approvingly, but Stuff, who had never heard of sipping anything, tossed his down and almost choked.

A minute later the lights dimmed—we heard a drumroll, and the orchestra began the first few bars of "Because of You," Tony's first million-record seller. The audience exploded into a chorus of cheers, whistles, and applause, and a backstage announcer thundered out, "Ladies and gentlemen, Tony Bennett!" It didn't seem possible, but the ovation got even louder as Tony walked onto the stage, picked up the mike, and bowed. When the audience finally began to quiet down, the orchestra returned to the top of "Because of You," and Tony started singing. Everyone was mesmerized for the next hour and a half.

After the show ended, I got up and headed backstage. My father had arranged for me to meet Tony. He knew how crowded the dressing room would be, so the plan was for me to go back alone and get autographs for the rest of the gang. As he predicted, the dressing room was packed with friends and celebrities, but Tony was very gracious and we chatted amiably while he signed seven photos for my crew and me.

I came out starry-eyed, ogling the photos, when I rounded the corner of a backstage hallway and collided head-on with a girl coming the other way. The collision sent us both to the floor like a pair of string-cut puppets. After a few awkward apologies, we grinned, untangled, and got up. There wasn't much light backstage, but there was no mistaking the fact that she was a knockout: candy apple lips, cascading honey blond hair, and ice blue eyes that were damn near level with mine. She was tall—showgirl tall—and I had been a sucker for showgirl types since the first time I had discovered Billy Minsky's Burlesque House. But this girl was light-years ahead of anything I'd ever seen on Billy's stage. I recognized her skimpy outfit with the plunging neckline, black fishnet stockings, and stiletto heels. Hatcheck girl, I thought, somewhere in her mid- to late twenties. Suddenly I realized that she was staring at *me*. I thought she might be sizing me up—maybe even trying to figure out how old *I* was—and became self-conscious about my age. I hoped she was just trying to figure out what I was doing backstage. She broke the silence with an incredibly sultry smile, suggesting she liked what she saw, and said, "Nice bumping into you."

I managed a stilted, "Ah . . . me too," as she walked away to begin her nine-p.m.-to-four-a.m. shift. I wasn't sure how long it had taken her to perfect that walk, but the end more than justified the means.

Just as she disappeared through the door at the end of the hall, I noticed a shiny object on the floor and bent to pick it up. It was a Ronson cigarette lighter inscribed "T.D.," and she must have lost it in the collision. It took me ten minutes to find out that "T.D." stood for Terry Dvorak and another ten for me to get her address from Louis Antonio: Seventy-sixth Street off Lexington—the Upper East Side. Impressive . . . and a universe away from Hell's Kitchen.

It was only eleven-thirty when we left the Copa, and since we were dressed for a night on the town, the four of us headed for Bop City to catch Billy Eckstine, went on to Birdland to hear Dizzy Gillespie blow the lacquer off his skyward-bent trumpet, then headed home.

My apartment felt like a pizza oven when I walked in at two-fifteen. I stripped to my shorts, climbed out onto the fire escape, and settled onto the mattress. Sidney was sitting on his adjacent fire escape, again reading a book by flashlight. The huge volume rested against his thighs, and he was wearing the same outfit he had worn the first time I had seen him: pajamas and a yarmulke.

"Hi, Vinny," he said as soon as I was comfortably seated with my back against the wall.

I leaned toward the iron sidebars and said, "You're still up? It's after two."

"I know. I've been waiting for you . . . this afternoon you said you might want to see my books later."

"Yeah, but—"

"My pop bought me a new book today," he said excitedly. "It's really good!"

"Sidney, you're either gonna go blind from readin' in the dark or broke from buyin' flashlight batteries."

Sidney ignored the comment and said, "It's about the Renaissance."

"Yeah?"

He leaned toward me conspiratorially and said, "It's got lots of nude pictures."

"No kiddin'," I said, a bit more interested. "Lemme see."

Sidney switched on his flashlight and held out the volume. It might have been new to him, but it was a very old book. About fifteen by twelve inches and two inches thick, it had the battered remains of a leather cover, and I could still make out the faded gold tooling that had once made it an expensive buy.

"Pop got it from his friend at the bookstore on Second Avenue," Sidney explained. "It cost a whole dollar, but his friend gave him ten cents off because they belong to the same temple." He opened it to a two-page spread of the Sistine ceiling and announced proudly, "Michelangelo!"

"Incredible," I murmured, awestruck. "My old man said he saw it once. Said it took Michelangelo years."

Sidney nodded as his flashlight flickered. His latest set of batteries was about to fade, and he closed the book. "If you want, tomorrow I could show you more—and maybe later you could come to the library with me."

He sounded so hopeful, I was forced to think about it. There was no question the kid fascinated me, and no question he might prove useful in the future. Besides that, I couldn't help liking the little guy. He was kind of like a stray puppy you find in the street and can't bring yourself to abandon. What the hell, I thought. "I'm gonna be busy tomorrow," I said. "But . . . maybe Friday."

"Really!"

"Really," I said.

"Wow! When?"

"I dunno . . . in the morning. Ten or eleven o'clock. Now get some sleep." I rolled over on my side and closed my eyes.

A few moments later he said, "Vinny . . . ?"

"Yeah . . ."

"Thanks for getting my yarmulke."

"No problem."

"Right . . . G'night, Vinny."

"G'night, Sidney."

That was the night I decided to go to the library with Sidney the first time—the night that changed everything.

CHAPTER SIX

THE NEXT AFTERNOON I was going on a mission, and I dressed to impress—gray gabardine slacks with a knife-edge crease, a black silk shirt, and spit-shined ebony loafers. I took a cab to the Upper East Side and showed up at Terry Dvorak's sixth-floor apartment at one p.m. with the lost lighter, ulterior motives, and high hopes. I knew she probably hadn't gotten to bed much before five in the morning, so I purposely allowed for eight hours' sleep before I pressed the button outside her door. I was surprised by a set of chimes that rang out the first eight notes of "Georgia on My Mind" and even more surprised when several seconds later the door opened. She was dressed in cobalt blue hip-hugging shorts, a white silk blouse, and tennis sneakers. If anything, she looked sexier than she had when wearing the fishnet stockings and stiletto heels. I had been practicing a few opening lines all morning, but they melted away when she scanned me from head to toe and flashed that sultry smile. The moment seemed suspended until she finally said, "Hi . . ." Her voice had a soft, lilting southern drawl that made "Hi" sound like "Hah." If I had closed my eyes, I could have been listening to Dinah Shore.

At that moment the best reply I could come up with was a simple "Hi . . ." I feebly held out the cigarette lighter.

She accepted it and said, "Thank you . . . I'd thought I'd lost it . . ."

"It was in the hallway," I managed, and then added unnecessarily, "Where we fell."

She chuckled at the memory and slipped the lighter into the back pocket of her shorts. Funny, I thought, she doesn't seem surprised to see me.

"I was about to go out for a bite of breakfast," she said, then raised an eyebrow and added, "Care to join me?"

"Sure," I said, unable to stop a million-dollar grin.

"I'll get my purse," she said, and walked toward her bedroom. I looked around and saw that the apartment was a typical Upper East Side one-bedroom affair . . . roomy, beautifully furnished, and expensive. The color palette was black and white—sofa and chairs in black; ebony coffee, end, and side tables; white wall-to-wall carpeting that swallowed your shoes—and lots of mirrors. It could have been a set in the Thin Man movies, with William Powell and Myrna Loy sipping straight-up martinis out of crystal stemware. It was obvious the girl who lived here made serious money.

She returned with her purse and took me to a small café on Third Avenue. Over a two-hour late breakfast we gently probed all the subjects that two people who are attracted to each other explore: backgrounds, feelings, thoughts, and ambitions. But through it all, our age difference never came up.

I learned that she was a grocer's daughter from Brunswick, Georgia, and had hitched a ride into the Big Apple right out of high school. She wanted to be "on Broadway"—in anything. Musical, comedy, drama, revue, it didn't matter. Chorus line, showgirl, or walk-on—she'd do it. The parts had been far between and short-lived, but she had gotten a few, and when she did, she'd send a picture taken with the cast back to her hometown paper to prove that she'd "made it." During the long stretches between acting parts, she had been a model, a waitress, a salesgirl, and ultimately a hatcheck girl at the world-famous Copacabana, the job that finally paid off.

The Copa was a Mob hangout, and the wiseguys loved to flash their bankrolls in front of the "three B's"—big, blond, and beautiful. Terry was all three, and at the age of twenty-nine she was at the height of her powers. I thought that she looked like Lana Turner, only taller—a lot taller—five feet nine without the spikes, and with them she topped six feet. She was formidable, but she said it was still all she could do to fend off the wandering fingers of the wiseguys who gleefully stuffed cash down the front of her costume's viciously plunging neckline.

At one point I commented that Dvorak was a pretty unusual name. She laughed and told me that everyone she met asked her if she was related to the composer. She said it used to drive her crazy, so she finally looked him up and found out he was Czechoslovakian, his name was Anton, and he was famous. She chuckled and added that from then on, she told everyone they were distant cousins. It seemed that in Terry's small-town insular world, fame was as important as life—even if it was only the false, reflected fame of a nonexistent relative.

We continued talking during a walk to Central Park and a stroll around the lake. At five o'clock we roamed through the zoo and split a giant pretzel with mustard from a food cart . . . magic.

I took her home at six.

She took me to bed at seven.

More magic.

By the time I was eighteen, I had been to bed with my share of girls, but this was a woman—a completely different animal . . . which was a pretty fair description of her sexual appetite. At eight o'clock we were still in bed, glistening with sweat from an intense round of what Terry called "party time"—but to me felt more like combat. The air-conditioning wasn't very efficient when the city topped ninety, and it was even less effective when challenged by the added heat of serious lust. I grabbed a handful of sheet and wiped my face.

Terry laughed, brushed my cheek with her lips, and slipped out of bed. "I've got to dress for work, sugah."

"Right," I said. "I'll move along."

She went into the bathroom, and I heard her turn on the shower. I got up to get dressed, and by the time I finished, she came back out in a robe and walked me to the door.

"Big day," I said.

"Very big day," she agreed.

I opened the door and said, "Tomorrow?"

"Call me, sugah."

"Right," I said.

She leaned in and kissed me, and I saw that stunning smile for the third time. She winked, then closed the door. I thought I'd fallen through a time warp to paradise.

I dropped by Benny's at nine and found him shooting pool with Red and Boychick. Bouncer had gone home, Louie was reading *Photoplay*, and Stuff was at the piano, thundering through Stan Kenton's "Artistry in Rhythm."

Louie looked up when I walked in and asked, "Where ya been all day?"

Stuff left the piano, and Benny, Red, and Boychick put up their pool cues and arrayed themselves around the sitting area.

"I had to drop off the lighter I found last night."

Louie cocked an eyebrow and said, "An all-day delivery? Where's this hatcheck live—in Buffalo?"

"We went for a walk in the park," I said defensively. I was being protective, and they immediately became suspicious.

"Yeah . . . so . . . ?" said Boychick, rotating his open hand, indicating he wanted me to continue.

"And we had a bite to eat," I said with a shrug.

"So . . . ," said Stuff, smiling expansively, "what we got is . . . a drop-off of a lighter, a walk in the park, and a bite to eat . . . for over eight hours with the sexiest hatcheck alive." He sniggered and looked at the guys.

Louie pulled his lips back in a broad, full-toothed grin, forced his eyes wide open, and in a perfect imitation of Burt Lancaster said, "Stuff, my boy, you have a very dirty mind! Yessir, I say—a very dirty mind!"

Benny looked at me admiringly and spat out, "I am impressed! And I ain't even seen the chippie!"

"Okay, knock it off," I said.

"That all ya got ta say?" Boychick objected.

"No," I said. "I'm gonna grab a bite and hit the sack." I got up and walked out, leaving them suspecting more than they knew, but knowing that what they suspected was true.

CHAPTER SEVEN

ON FRIDAY MORNING I got up late, took a cold shower to beat the heat, and put on chinos and a T-shirt. My parents had already left, so I made myself an onion omelet breakfast and turned on the radio. The announcer was rattling off the baseball scores, and it reminded me that Louie's father had promoted us tickets to Yankee Stadium. I had completely forgotten because of the mind-numbing interlude with Terry.

Bucky Harris was the Yankees manager, and when he came to the Copa, Louie's father had swapped a ringside table for a dozen ducats for the Yankees and Red Sox. It was going to be a great game: Yogi Berra was catching Whitey Ford; Joe DiMaggio was playing in spite of his bad heel; his brother Dom DiMaggio was playing against him for the Red Sox; and next to him in the outfield would be the great Ted Williams.

We had planned to meet in front of my place at eleven, go to the stadium early so we could watch batting practice, and, if we got lucky, maybe even grab a few autographs. I had more than an hour to kill before the meet, and since I knew that Red would be cleaning up his father's pub as he did every morning, I decided to pick him up.

O'Mara's Irish Pub was long and narrow, with a bar on one side, booths on the other, a few tables in the middle, and a pool table in the back. Red hated it. He'd hated it from the first time he was ordered to sweep it out, and he hated living with his parents in the apartment above it. The pub was between Forty-fourth and Forty-fifth streets and was one of many that lined Ninth Avenue and catered to clandestine nests of devoted IRA partisans.

I walked past five of the faithful who were sweltering in the morning heat while they waited for the opening bell and rounded the corner of Forty-fifth Street. There was a service alley behind the pub, and I used it to get to the pub's back door.

Red was taking one last lunge at the dirty sawdust on the floor when he saw me and offered a forlorn wave of his hand. I waved back, winced at the rancid smell of stale beer and cigarette butts, and picked up the shovel leaning against the bar. I scooped up a pile of the prior night's detritus, dumped the load into a garbage can, and carried it out to the back alley's Dumpster. I was about to go back in when I heard Colin O'Mara pounding down the rear stairs. Red's father hated my crew, so I stayed back and lingered at the door.

Colin was a powerfully built fifty-year-old bully with a jowled face, thick arms, and bristling eyebrows that matched his wild red hair. In another era he would have been a buccaneer. His two eldest sons were in Belfast with the IRA, fighting for "the cause," and his wife was a female firebrand for whom "the cause" was the holy grail. She insisted that all good Irish wives should withhold sex from their husbands until they contributed to it. Rounding out the immediate family were her two younger brothers, who were NYPD detectives. They were "on the take," but so were half the cops in the city.

"What's the problem, then?" roared Colin, tying on his apron. "Almost openin' time and the sawdust's not down yet!"

Red ignored the comment, picked up a bag of sawdust, and started flinging it across the floor. Always a man of few words, he was even more taciturn around his family. Colin thought that the hospital had accidentally mixed up two newborns at birth and switched Red with his real son. He had often tried to beat what he thought was some good old Irish sense into the boy as he grew up, but it didn't work. Red just took the strap and ignored him.

Colin continued an oft heard tirade as he moved to unlock the front door. He waved his arm like a conductor and growled, "Out half the bloody night with yer guinea mates. All of 'em hoods! Sleep half the a.m. so's the sawdust ain't even down yet and expect me to feed and put a roof over that good-for-nothin' head. Keep it up, boyo, and you'll be tastin' more of me strap!"

Colin opened the front door, and in the blink of an eye the scowl became a grin. He joyfully greeted the five thirsty men as they chatted in thick Irish brogues and made their way to their favorite stools, where they eagerly awaited the "first of the day." Colin moved behind the bar and simultaneously began drawing five tankards of ale while the men made small talk, interspersed with indecipherable Gallic asides. Colin guffawed at what must have been a joke and was still grinning when Red hurled a last handful of sawdust across the floor and started out. In another instant reversal, Colin's grin snapped back to a scowl. "And where the hell d'ya think you're goin'?" he snarled, dashing out from behind the bar.

Red pulled a cap out of his back pocket, tugged it on backward, and planted himself in front of his father. He was wearing a T-shirt, chinos, and loafers over bare feet that were spread to shoulder width. His fists were balled on his hips, and he looked as if it would take a truck to move him. Red wasn't big, he was average—but his five-foot-nine-inch frame was more tightly packed than a can of sardines, and his muscles were twisted rope. He spat on the floor, looked his father square in the eye, and said, "Out."

Colin lashed out with a sharp backhand to Red's face. Red's head snapped back and his eyes flared. Why the hell he didn't lash back was a bigger mystery to me than the Resurrection, but he just held his father in a deadly glare and touched his lip. The tip of his finger came back crimson. "Congratulations," he said, and again spat on the floor. Then he wheeled around and walked out the door.

Embarrassed in front of the men, Colin pointed his finger and roared, "I'll have yer hide, boyo—yours and yer wop friends! I'll have it, I tell ya!"

The men, having witnessed similar confrontations, ignored the latest one. Colin glared at the departing figure and went back behind the bar. I shook my head, walked through the alley to Forty-fourth Street, and met Red on the corner of Ninth Avenue.

Red put up with the abuse because he'd promised his mother he'd remain at home until he graduated from high school. But when he graduated in June, she begged him to stay until the end of the summer, when they were going to take a trip to Ireland. He loved his mother, so he figured if he could take his father's shit for eighteen years—what the hell were a few more months if it made her happy. Everyone in our gang had a reason for remaining at home. Boychick's was similar to Red's: His father had a habit of getting drunk and slapping his mother around, and he was determined not to leave the house until he could take her with him. Louie couldn't afford to leave his home because he spent all his money on clothes. And Stuff figured his mother's kitchen turned out the best food in the city, so why leave? Bouncer was still in school, Benny already had his own place, and I still hadn't figured out what the hell I was going to do with the rest of my life.

As we continued down Ninth Avenue, neither one of us mentioned any of the above. We were relishing the thought of Yankee Stadium.

When we got back to my tenement, Stuff was sitting on a car fender, flipping peanuts into the air and catching them in his mouth. Boychick and Benny were tossing a tennis ball back and forth, Louie was juggling a few lemons, and Bouncer had a portable radio next to his ear and—what else?—was bouncing to the music. As usual, they were dressed for the heat, except for Louie. None of them were paying any attention to the diminutive figure sitting at the top of the steps.

Sidney.

The library! I thought. Between the day with Terry and the excitement of the Yankees game, I had forgotten all about Sidney. He jumped to his feet when he saw me, nearly knocking over his stack of books. In spite of the heat he was wearing his standard shirt, sweater, and yarmulke combination. He gave me a shy wave and called out, "Hi, Vinny!"

The gang stopped what they were doing and turned toward the voice.

"Uh . . . hi, Sidney," I responded, silently weighing the prospect of seeing the Yanks take on the Sox against my promise to go to the library. It should have been an easy call. The Yanks! The problem was Sidney's innocent, hopeful, beaming face staring at me. I struggled for a few seconds, but it was futile.

"So . . . Sidney!" I said. "You ready to go to the library?"

"You bet!" he said.

The guys remained frozen as Sidney rushed down the steps, greeting them as he came down. I could see the confusion on their faces. It was only the third time that Sidney and my crew had seen each other, and they still didn't quite know what to make of him, but they were all as surprised as I was that Sidney remembered their names.

After the initial greetings, Boychick asked, "You wanna bring him to the game with us? We got enough tickets . . ."

"No. We're not going to the ball game."

"Why not?" asked Stuff.

"We're, um . . . going to the library."

"The what?" Boychick gasped.

46

"The library," I said sheepishly. "I promised Sidney."

Boychick couldn't believe it. "Look, yesterday we knew the hatcheck story was bullshit. But today ya say yer goin' ta the library? What's with ya?"

"Nothing. I just don't feel like a ball game today."

Boychick looked at Sidney and back to me. "Can I see ya a sec?"

"Sure," I said.

He took me by the arm and led me about twenty feet away. "Look, if the kid's got somethin' on ya, we can handle it."

"What?" I asked, taken aback.

"These guys stick together . . . his ol' man a friend of Lansky?"

"What the hell are you talkin' about?"

"About maybe they put the arm on his ol' man to get the kid to put the arm on you for some reason."

"Are you nuts! Where the hell did that come from?"

Boychick balled up his fist and snapped out his thumb and then his fingers as he made his points. "One! Outta nowhere you bring him to Sabrett. Two! You take on Colucci over a goddamn *skullcap*! And three! You're givin' up the New York Yankees for the New York fuckin' *Library*! The way you're actin', nothin' else make sense!"

I sighed, dropped my chin onto my chest, and shook my head. "Boychick . . . there's no conspiracy. My pop checked him out. He's a good kid . . . and smart. Maybe he can help us—"

"Help us? He looks half-dead, for chrissakes!"

I put my hand on Boychick's shoulder. "Go to the ball game. Nothin's up."

He nodded grudgingly and said, "You're sure . . ."

"I'm sure."

He slapped me on the arm, I followed him back to the gang, and he said casually, "Let's go to the ball game. Vinny's takin' Sidney to the library." They headed south for Penn Station and the subway to the Bronx, we headed east for the library.

The massive New York Public Library/Bryant Park complex between Fifth and Sixth avenues extends from Forty-second to Fortieth
Street north-south and is a national historic landmark. At the Fifth
Avenue entrance a pair of huge stone lions flank the lower section of a
massive staircase, and a pair of equally large stone urns flank it farther
up. As Sidney and I climbed the steps together for the first time, he
pointed at the lions and said, "They have names."

"The lions?"

He nodded and said, "Patience and Fortitude."

It was my turn to say, "Wow," but it was a mild response compared
with the reaction I had when Sidney led me into the main reading
room. Sidney told me it was a Beaux Arts masterpiece. There was no
doubt about it: The room was a masterpiece of intricately carved
woodwork—and was damn near as long as a football field. Its gilded
plaster ceiling was five stories above the floor, and there were over forty
lustrous wooden tables with bronze, green-shaded lamps for readers. I'd
never seen anything like it. He enjoyed my awe and waited patiently for
me to take it all in before he smiled and said, "Let's go find some
books!"

Since he had noticed that I seemed interested in his Renaissance
book, we started there—with how, why, and when it had come about.
The next two hours went by like two minutes; we grabbed a sandwich
and resumed. The next four hours went even faster. At five o'clock
Sidney checked out *The Prince* and *Mandragola*, and we reluctantly left
for the walk home.

On the way, Sidney told me that he had never been able to go to
school on a regular basis because scarlet fever had left him with a weak
heart and asthma had left him with weak lungs. He'd made the massive
building on Forty-second Street his classroom, and it was there that he
had gotten most of his education. For years he had been going to the
library and had checked out all the books he could carry. All his
knowledge had come from voracious reading and occasional tutors from

his temple, but he said that it always worked out that he was smarter than the tutors. Finally the rabbi decided to test him, and they found out he had an IQ of 160 . . . I thought, No wonder the odds in a craps game were a piece of cake.

Over the next few months I would find out that Sidney's scope was awesome, his range limitless, and his understanding astounding. Literature, art, and history were all fair game. He was a Houdini who unlocked puzzles—an Aladdin who deciphered literature—an Ali Baba whose "Open Sesame" parted the towering doors of New York's public library. But all this knowledge amounted to less than a flyspeck of "street smarts."

I had never paid much attention to any of the subjects that were taught in school because I figured what the hell difference did it make if Lee surrendered at Appomattox or Anacostia, if Monet or Manet painted *Lady with Parasol*, or if Shakespeare might be Marlowe or Bacon? It wasn't the kind of knowledge that could help you knock off a warehouse. But in one day Sidney had made me see knowledge as a hunt for hidden treasure, and I became fascinated with the game.

By the time we got back to the tenement, I had made up my mind that I wanted more. I thanked Sidney for a great day and said that maybe we could do it again the following week . . . maybe a couple of times . . . maybe on Monday and Wednesday. Sidney lit up like a sunburst, nodding with agreement. I knew nothing in particular was planned for those days, and I felt pretty good about being able to keep my crew cool. We said good-bye, he walked through his door, and I walked across the hall into mine.

I opened the refrigerator, popped open a beer, and decided to call Terry before she went to work. She answered on the third ring, "Terry he-ah." Her mellifluous southern voice made my heart jump to a higher gear.

"It's me," I said.

"Me? And who might 'me' be?"

"Vinny!" I said, then added stupidly, "From yesterday." How many goddamn Vinnys could there be from yesterday?

"Oh . . . Vinny. I'm sorry . . . how are you?"

"Fine. I'm fine," I said. "You said to call."

"I know, I—"

"I thought maybe we could see each other later."

There was a pause, and then she said, "I've been thinking, Vinny . . . I really like you . . . but maybe it's not such a good idea."

"What're you talking about? I thought we had a great time."

"We did, but . . . well, it doesn't feel right."

"I thought it felt great!"

"That part did, but . . . I mean, I'm a lot older than you, and—"

"We spent a whole day together. It never came up!"

"I know, but it'd be there . . . we can't help it."

"I can. I can forget about it. I want to see you, Terry."

There was a long silence on the other end of the phone, and she finally said, "I'll tell you what. Why don't we cool it for a few days, and talk next week."

"I want to see you."

"We'll see each other and talk next week, okay?"

"Okay."

"Be well, sugah . . . bye."

"You too, bye."

An hour later I still felt like I'd been kicked by a mule when Boychick called and said, "We're on!" It was the liquor heist caper we had been trying to set up for over a month.

Shipments of Canadian whiskey were regularly hauled across the border and down the East Coast by a variety of shipping companies. Boychick had found out that the drivers from a company called Lyons usually arrived across the Hudson River in Hackensack, New Jersey, around midnight on the day before they were to deliver the booze to their warehouse in Queens. Since the distributor's warehouse didn't open until eight in the morning, they used Harvey's—an all-night diner/truck stop across the river—for a bite to eat and some shut-eye before the morning delivery. While the drivers ate, the trucks sat in the parking lot unguarded. Boychick had met the son of one of the Lyons drivers at a Golden Gloves bout and they'd become friendly. He'd waited for what he thought was a good opening and asked if maybe the kid's father might like to pick up some spare change. He'd gotten his answer. The driver had called and said he'd be at Harvey's at ten-thirty in a truck loaded with three hundred cases of prime booze.

It took a couple of hours to round up the guys and drive across the river to Hackensack, where, as planned, we found the Lyons truck in the parking lot in the midst of a dozen other long haulers. Stuff, Red, and Benny stood lookout while Boychick and I hot-wired the ignition. Louie and Bouncer waited in the idling Ford woody, ready to drive us all out in case anything went tits up. Nothing did, and we were back across the river and through the tunnel to Queens by one a.m. We met our fence at a warehouse on Flushing Avenue and picked up four dollars a case for the haul—twelve hundred bucks total. When we got back to Benny's, I split off four hundred for the driver's cut and divided the remaining seven hundred seven ways . . . not bad for a night's work.

CHAPTER EIGHT

THE FOLLOWING MONDAY morning I walked out of the tenement and saw Sidney sitting on the steps in what I now realized was his permanent wardrobe: trousers, a sweater over a shirt and tie, and a yarmulke. That summer, no matter how hot it got, the only things that changed were the colors of his trousers, shirt, and tie. The yarmulke remained black. The books he had checked out the prior Friday were beside him, and it was obvious he'd been waiting for me.

"Ready to go?" he asked.

"Sure," I said. I had already called Benny and told him I'd see them all later.

He got up, and as we walked down the steps, he held out the books. "Wait until I tell you about *The Prince*," he said. "Machiavelli wrote it. He was a sixteenth-century guy, a political philosopher who worked for the Medicis and knew the Borgias—I'll tell you about them later. But the book's all about power." He waved off the second book with, "*Mandragola*'s a comedy—funny—if you want to read it."

"Maybe," I said, "I'll get a library card and check them out."

"Terrific, Vinny!" he said with pride.

The main reading room was already fairly crowded when we arrived, and we had to stand in line to return the books. I filled out an application for a library card, and we went into the stacks. Sidney had decided to continue with our Renaissance study but wanted to avoid politics until after I read *The Prince*, so we spent the day on the lives and works of three of its famous painters: Leonardo da Vinci, Raphael, and Michelangelo. Their work spoke for itself, but their lives were a terrific insight into the period.

The rest of the day would become our template for the library trips: We would spend a few hours poring over the books in the morning, have a quick lunch, return for a few more hours in the afternoon, then leave by five.

After I walked Sidney to the tenement, I stopped by Benny's. The gang had decided to go see Jimmy Cagney in *White Heat* one more time. It was one of Louie's favorite movies. We'd seen it twice when it opened the year before, but Louie had found a neighborhood theater in Queens where they were reshowing it. He had offered to spring for the tickets if everyone would go with him to the eight o'clock show. They all had agreed, and I'd said, "What the hell, why not? It's a good flick."

When I got home at six, I decided to try calling Terry. My parents were out celebrating their anniversary, and I knew they would be having an early dinner before they went on to Radio City. My mother had left a beautiful lasagna in the oven, so I took out the chafing dish and dialed the phone.

A few rings later I heard the familiar, "Terry he-ah . . ."

"Vinny *he*-ah."

She chuckled. "Hi, Vinny. I was just talking about you."

"You were?" I said happily.

"Uh-huh. To my girlfriend Jill. The club's dark tonight, so I'm going to have dinner with her and some of her friends."

"Good," I said for want of something better. "When can I see you?"

"That's what we were talking about. It seems you have a new friend. Jill thinks it's fine."

I felt a rush and blurted out, "Terrific! When?"

"Is tomorrow too soon?"

"Are you kidding? What time?"

"The dinner's out in Westhampton, so I expect we'll be home late. How about noon and we can have lunch."

"Great!" I said. "I'll be there."

"Looking forward to it, sugah. Bye now."

"Bye . . . and thank Jill for me."

After she hung up, I jumped in the air and clicked my heels. The only thing better would have been if I pulled off a duplicate of the million-dollar Brinks truck job. That night I don't think I heard a word of what Cagney or anyone else in the movie said. All I kept hearing was, "Is tomorrow too soon?"

When tomorrow finally came, I again dressed to impress, this time all in tan: slacks, silk shirt, and spit-shined loafers. I arrived at her sixth-floor apartment at 12:01, pushed her buzzer, and listened as "Georgia on My Mind" chimed out. A minute later Terry answered the door wearing a short white towel and a dazzling smile. She had just gotten out of the shower—she was still wet—and the towel wasn't concealing the fact that she was a natural blonde. "Good afternoon," she cooed.

I stood in the doorway and admired the view. "And a very good afternoon to you," I said.

Any reservations about seeing me had obviously disappeared, because she put her arms around my neck and her towel dropped off. She drew me in and said, "It's about to get a lot better, sugah."

Somewhere during a long, lingering kiss, an elegant, elderly man carrying a cane and wearing a homburg stepped out of the next apartment. When he saw us he froze. First his jaw dropped—and then his cane.

Terry had heard his door open, and without missing a beat she turned, gave him the full frontal picture, and greeted him with a cheery singsong, "Good afternoon, Mr. Hoffler, it's real nice to see you, *too* . . . You have yourself a real nice day, you he-ah?"

She pulled me into her apartment, back-kicked the door shut, and broke out laughing. The towel was still in the hallway, so I reopened the door and popped back out to retrieve it. Mr. Hoffler was rooted to the spot, glassy-eyed. I scooped up the towel, picked up the cane, handed it to Hoffler, and ducked back into the apartment. Terry had not stopped laughing. I put my arms around her and enjoyed another lingering kiss. Finally she pulled back a bit and put her index finger on my lips.

"Can you wait till I have a cup of coffee? I just got up."

"I'll suffer, but I'll try." I smiled and held out the towel. "Want the towel back?"

"The towel was for effect. I'll get a robe." She crossed the spacious living room and entered the bedroom. The bathroom door was ajar, and I watched her as she finished drying off in front of a full-length mirror. Her body was a thing of wonder: perfect upturned breasts, an hourglass figure, and legs that went on forever. I watched her dab a touch of Chanel No. 5 behind her ear and re-enter the living room wearing a white satin robe that clung like redundant skin. She crossed to the counter that separated the living room from the kitchen, set out a couple of mugs, and began preparing coffee.

I sat on a stool and asked, "So what did Jill say?"

"She said, 'You only live once . . . This is not the dress rehearsal, it's the show.' Things like that. Jill's from London. She went through the Blitz, so she has a tendency to be fatalistic."

"I get that. What about you?"

She leaned over, put her elbows on the counter and her face in her hands. "You're here . . . *that* about me."

"Point taken. Where'd you like to have lunch?" I asked.

Without removing her hands from under her chin, she flicked her index finger toward the bedroom and said, "In there."

After her mercifully short-lived guilt trip about "robbing the cradle," we saw each other nearly every day from then on. The one dark facet of our affair was Terry's constant paranoia that my father would discover it. She knew he couldn't possibly approve, and because his close associates owned the club, she was afraid he'd have her fired . . . or worse.

CHAPTER NINE

BY THE END OF JUNE, Sidney and I had established a routine of going to the library three days a week: Monday, Wednesday, and Friday. Between the library and Terry, my life had turned into a fabulous parlay, and I couldn't get enough of either one of them. The only negative was that the new relationships had slowed down my activities with my crew. Although I had cased a few possible targets during June, we hadn't pulled a caper since the liquor truck heist several weeks earlier. We had all discussed the reasons for the drought, and the guys had said they understood. We could get back to work as soon as I was ready.

On a happier front, Terry and Sidney had formed a mutual admiration society even though they'd never met. I had told them about each other and they loved everything they heard, so I set up lunch for the three of us. Because I thought Sidney might enjoy a trip to the silk stocking district, we met Terry at the same Third Avenue café that she had taken me to on the day I returned her lighter.

Unlikely as it seemed, they hit it off from first look.

"Sidney . . . I've heard *so* much about you," she cooed in her soft Georgia accent.

"Me too," said Sidney. "I mean, about you . . . you really *are* beautiful."

Terry glanced at me and smiled. "Vinny tells me you're the smartest man he's ever met."

Sidney looked at me happily and said, "He said that?"

"He sure did . . . and from what he told me about you, I can understand why."

"Thank you . . . I read a lot. Do you read?"

"Uh-huh . . . but mostly magazines . . . *Vogue, New Yorker, Vanity Fair* . . ."

"Oh," Sidney said noncommittally. "How about books?"

"Well, I really liked *I, the Jury*," she offered. Sidney gave her a blank stare, so she added, "Mickey Spillane?"

"Right," he answered, but I knew he hadn't a clue.

She sensed it and said, "Maybe you could make a list of books you think I should read."

His eyes got wider. "Really?"

"Uh-huh. And then maybe I could get a library card like Vinny and take out the books," she said enthusiastically. I chuckled to myself, knowing this would never happen.

"Would you like to come with us?" he asked.

That stopped her. She shot a glance at me and was about to come up with a shuck and jive when the waitress came over and asked if we were ready to order. I saved her with, "Sure! A Coke and a ham on rye, slaw on the side. How about you, Sidney?"

"A cream soda and a grilled cheese sandwich."

"Terry?" I asked.

"A Coke and a Caesar salad," she answered, and then she turned to Sidney and said, "And I'd be de*light*ed to come to the library with you, Sidney."

That stopped *me*. Sidney's face lit up, and Terry reached across the table and shook his hand to seal the deal. I laughed: If Sidney and I made an odd twosome, I couldn't wait to see the reaction we'd get when we walked into the library with Terry between us!

A week later, I got it. Terry actually came to the library with us and applied for a card. The pride on Sidney's smiling face as he walked between us was solar. Terry was wearing yellow polka-dot shorts, a matching halter, and a pair of white spiked heels. The reaction of the prudish, bespectacled librarian at the desk was classic. She got "the vapors," fanned herself, and almost fainted. There isn't any record of the readers' reactions in the main reading room, but there is no question that when they saw Terry, time stood still.

By early August, although I was still spending a lot of time with Sidney and Terry, I had managed to get my crew back into action with a pair of simple jobs—but the payoffs were small. Added to that was the fact that the money we had previously earned by selling plans to the other crews had dried up because I didn't have the time to case the targets.

In the summer of 1950 a gallon of gas was twenty cents, a new Ford sedan cost eighteen hundred bucks, and the average working stiff made a little over three thousand dollars a year. In the past twelve months each of us had made twice that. The hundred bucks apiece we had earned by hijacking the truck was a small fortune for just one night's work, but by August everyone was running out of cash . . . and we weren't the only ones.

Unbeknownst to me, the other crews on the West Side had gotten very pissed off because a big source of *their* cash flow had been cut off. I hadn't been supplying them with the detailed plans that made them "earners," and they were holding me responsible for their loss of income. The worst part of it was they had figured out that Sidney was the reason and had come to hate him.

So at the end of August, with New York staggering under the

onslaught of the summer's third crushing heat wave, I realized that I had better do something about generating some cash for all concerned. I had already been casing a couple of "possibles" when I got a call to carry off what seemed like an exceptionally simple but lucrative heist. I was asked to steal forty cases of sable pelts from an outdoor storage yard on the Lower West Side. At thirty bucks a case, we'd net twelve hundred bucks—a great payday—so I accepted the contract.

I cased the job with Boychick and set up the hit for the following Thursday night.

CHAPTER TEN
Thursday, August 24

I WATCHED BENNY SLOWLY ease his head around the corner of Seventeenth Street and look across Tenth Avenue. He was tracking a uniformed guard who was patrolling a block-long cyclone fence that surrounded an outdoor storage yard. The guard was big, maybe six feet two, 250 pounds, exactly what I was hoping to see. A guy that big couldn't be too fast, and Benny was the fastest guy in Hell's Kitchen.

At the south end of his beat the weary guard turned, wiped the sweat from his forehead, and started back up toward Eighteenth Street. He was in the last hour of his four-to-midnight shift, the temperature was still in the nineties, and the late August humidity didn't help. The Hudson River, as usual, made it worse.

In the dim light Benny's blue-black skin and dark clothes made him almost invisible—but I saw him, and he saw me. I was one block north, peeking around the corner of Eighteenth Street. At this hour the area was totally deserted: no traffic, no pedestrians, no beat cops, and no apartments with insomniac kibitzers to call the cops.

I ducked back around the corner and checked my watch: 11:28. Bouncer was standing behind me, fidgeting nervously and bouncing up and down on the balls of his feet. I turned and lightly backhanded his shoulder in exasperation. "Will you relax? In two minutes Benny makes his move."

"R-right," squeaked Bouncer, sounding like a trapped mouse.

Benny continued to watch the guard as he patrolled the storage yard. Multiple floodlights on twenty-foot stanchions created an island of ersatz daylight in the otherwise dark industrial area. The yard was a temporary overflow facility used by the New York Central Railroad for merchandise that had been off-loaded on the Hudson River piers a mere two blocks away. Above it was an elevated railroad trestle that came out of the third floor of the National Biscuit Company's building two blocks south on Fifteenth Street. The trestle crossed Tenth Avenue, traversed the storage yard, and disappeared into another building farther uptown.

Halfway between Seventeenth and Eighteenth streets, the guard leaned back against the depot's double-wide gates and lit a cigarette. I saw a train rumble slowly out of the National Biscuit Company's building and noticed Benny's attention momentarily distracted as he heard it, too. He looked south and tracked it as it passed overhead. Benny thought the elevated rail system in New York City was the eighth wonder of the world. He checked his watch, took out a book of matches, lit one, and held it out to his side. We had positioned Stuff about a block behind him in a two-and-a-half-ton bobtail truck and told him that when he saw the flame we'd all be in position. He saw it and started the engine.

I nodded to Bouncer and we walked around the corner of Eighteenth Street, crossed Tenth Avenue, and casually strolled south toward the guard. I nodded again and we started singing "White Christmas."

The guard turned toward us and frowned. He had to have been thinking, "White Christmas"? It's August, for chrissakes!

As soon as Benny heard us singing, he began sneaking up behind the guard. He unzipped his fly, stopped a foot behind the guard's back, and, while the guard was still distracted by our performance, started pissing on his shoe. It took a few seconds for it to register, but when it did, the guard turned, looked down, and refused to believe his eyes. For a moment he was paralyzed, but then he looked up—and Benny smiled. The guard's face contorted, and he reached for Benny's throat. All he got was air. Benny was halfway across Tenth Avenue and heading up to Eighteenth Street before the guard took a step. He bellowed, blew his whistle, and pursued Benny, who had already rounded the corner of Eighteenth Street. When the guard charged around the corner, he ran flush into Benny's fist. He was out before his knees buckled. Benny pulled him into a doorway and ran back to join me and Bouncer as the bobtail came roaring around the corner of Seventeenth Street and headed straight for the dock's metal gates.

Behind the wheel, Stuff braced his arms, floored the gas pedal, and adjusted his considerable bulk for the impact. I had made him the designated driver because of his well-padded 240 pounds. I figured when the truck hit the gates and his belly hit the steering wheel, he was the least likely to be hurt. He wasn't—the impact just knocked the wind out of him. But it also ripped the gates off their hinges.

Benny, Bouncer, and I ran up to the breach, clambered over the fallen gates, and rushed up to the truck. The rear doors popped open and Red, Boychick, and Louie scrambled out the back. I pointed to a seven-foot-high stack of pine crates that were six feet long and two feet square. "That's them! The long skinny boxes," I yelled. "Boychick, up top—hand them down. Red, in the truck. Louie, help me load. Benny, back to Eighteenth and check the guard. Bouncer, check on Stuff."

They scrambled as told, and all went well for about five minutes. And then we heard the distant wail of sirens. We froze. I listened for several seconds and determined that the sirens were getting closer. I had a gut feeling they were for us. What the hell was going on? I thought.

We had cased this yard—there were no alarms, no telltale wires, and the guard wasn't due to check in for half an hour. We had loaded only two crates into the truck, and there were eight more on the ground behind it waiting to be handed up to Red. "Shit!" I said. "Move! Now!" I grabbed one of the eight crates and thrust it up to Red. Boychick jumped off the stack, and with Louie we scrambled to get the remaining crates in the truck.

Bouncer was up front, trying to revive Stuff. He leaned out the cab's passenger window and yelled back to me, "S-Stuff's still out . . . he's s-stuck behind the wheel!"

"Pull 'im out," I barked.

"He weighs t-t-two forty," Bouncer objected.

"So roll 'im out! The truck ain't gonna drive itself!" I sighed, looked at Louie, and popped my head toward the cab. "Louie, help the putz!"

Louie ran up to the cab and the loading continued as the sirens got louder. A few seconds later Louie ran back and announced, "We pushed 'im to the middle of the seat, but we couldn't get 'im out . . . the fucker's too fat!"

"Forget it," I said. "Get in."

Louie jumped into the back of the truck, Boychick followed, and I ran forward and squeezed into the passenger seat. Bouncer slid behind the wheel, and we sandwiched Stuff in the middle.

"Up Tenth and don't slow down!" I shouted.

Bouncer leaned forward and turned to me, completely astonished. "The s-s-steerin' wheel's bent!"

"What are you, the six o'clock news?" I screamed. "Drive!"

Bouncer ground into reverse, spun gravel, and shot back out onto Tenth Ave. He shifted again, and as we sped forward toward Eighteenth Street, I leaned out the window and yelled, "Benny!"

With the truck still accelerating, Benny tore around the corner and paralleled it. I stuck out my arm, and Benny grabbed it, levered himself onto the running board, and punched the air with his fist. He had probably just run a four-second forty.

"Right on Eighteenth and head for the barn," I ordered, then tried to slap Stuff awake.

Stuff's eyes fluttered open and he moaned, "What happened?"

"Ya b-bent the steerin' wheel!" said Bouncer.

We took Eighteenth Street on the two right wheels as the first squad cars roared down Tenth Avenue—sirens screaming, gumball machines whirling. The cops had missed our getaway by mere seconds, but by the time they revived the guard and figured out what had happened, we were pulling our truck up to the steel overhead door of a warehouse in the garment district. Benny was still on the running board—and I was still trying to figure out what the hell went wrong.

CHAPTER ELEVEN

THE OLD WAREHOUSE in the garment district on Thirty-sixth Street between Eighth and Ninth avenues had nothing to do with garments but everything to do with warehousing—the warehousing of stolen goods: radios, refrigerators, washing machines . . . whiskey, caviar, perfume . . . Persian rugs, fur coats, fur pelts. You name it, it was already there—or on the way. The loot was lifted from airports, railroad depots, hijacked trucks, warehouses, and the New York City docks.

Bouncer tapped the horn and a "speakeasy window" in a pedestrian door opened. A pair of eyes scrutinized the truck, recognized us in the front seat, and the window closed. The steel overhead door rolled up and Bouncer pulled forward about thirty feet, where we were stopped by a wall-to-wall barrier of garment racks ten feet high, effectively blocking the interior from the street. Behind the truck the steel door started down, and as soon as it was completely closed, the garment racks in front of the truck parted like a biblical sea. Bouncer pulled forward into the main bay and parked. Scattered around the cavernous ware-house floor, other trucks were being loaded and unloaded by a dozen sweating workers. Stolen merchandise was stacked everywhere.

I jumped out of the truck and Benny, Stuff, and Louie followed me to the rear, where Boychick, Louie, and Red had already climbed out.

"Stack the crates next to the fur racks," I said, pointing toward a mass of hanging sable, mink, and chinchilla coats. "Stuff, get rid of the truck. Take Bouncer. I'll go collect our dough." I turned, headed toward a staircase, and called over my shoulder, "The rest of you wait outside."

I climbed the stairs to the offices on a second-floor balcony that ran across the back of the warehouse. All the offices had large windows overlooking the warehouse floor and were full of teams of busy men working at littered desks—giving any casual observer the impression that they were looking at the nerve center of a typical shipping complex.

I ambled into the last office in the row and headed toward the rear wall. I was greeted by a few casual waves, but most of the men stayed zeroed in on their work. They weren't actually wiseguys, although they knew they were working for the Mob. Basically they were bookkeepers whose jobs paid a helluva lot better than Macy's or GM, and they had the added perk of being able to buy stolen merchandise at knockdown prices. They wore green eyeshades and plastic pocket protectors and had ash-colored skin. They looked like they never saw the sun.

I stopped next to the rear wall in front of a large bulletin board that held bills of lading, receipts, and assorted paperwork pinned by multicolored thumbtacks. I pushed one of the blue thumbtacks, and a moment later the wall swung open and revealed a very large, very plush office. A suave, distinguished-looking man seated behind a massive desk looked up and cupped the phone he was using. "You're early," he said. He spoke without an accent, was prematurely gray and about forty years old; his wardrobe and manicure were impeccable. His name was Giorgio Petrone, and he looked like a successful Wall Street attorney—but he was a feared and brutal caporegime in the Luciano crime family.

"So were the cops," I responded, and nodded to a mirthless hulk who had a fat cigar clenched in his teeth and was leaning against a red leather sofa. I sat in a matching leather chair in front of the desk, and the wall closed behind me.

"The order left an hour ago," Petrone continued into the phone. "We'll have one of our representatives meet it on Tuesday. He'll handle the details and the transaction . . . Naturally . . . A pleasure, my friend . . . Ciao."

Giorgio Petrone's office conveyed an overdone elegance that reflected the man—Empire furniture, Persian rugs, oil paintings, and paneled walls. Giorgio's street name was "Gee-gee." You didn't fuck with Gee-gee . . . you did and you died. He hung up the phone, motioned to the hulk—who was also his underboss—and looked back at me. "So?" he asked, extending his hands palms up.

I shrugged and answered, "When the cops showed up we only had ten cases loaded."

Gee-gee's eyes narrowed unhappily. "And?"

"And we took off . . . they never saw us."

The hulk brought over a metal strongbox and set it on the desk. His name was "Touch" Grillo, and he had the neck and shoulders of a Brahman bull. He was six feet tall, looked to be in his mid-forties, wore his black hair in a military crew cut, and had deep-set cold gray eyes that gave his face a permanent scowl. Nobody knew if he had a real first name or not. Even his rap sheet said "Touch." The word was that if he touched you, you were dead. He had hands like spades and fingers like sausages. For fun he snapped bricks.

"All sable?" asked Gee-gee as he opened the box and took out a stack of tens.

I nodded. "Stenciled on the crates."

"Three hundred even," Gee-gee noted, and slid the cash across the desk.

I looked at the cash and thought, Ridiculous. I knew the ten crates of sable were worth ten times that on the black market, so I decided to challenge the price. I didn't expect to get anywhere, I just wanted him to know I wasn't stupid. "They're worth over two hundred each," I said matter-of-factly.

"To me . . . I know how to move them," Gee-gee responded.

I shrugged. "So? You're not the only game in town."

The corners of Gee-gee's mouth eased up, and a gleam appeared in his eye. He loved confrontation, reveled in it—probably because he seldom lost. He leaned back in his chair and asked, "Is that a threat?"

I smiled and said, "A thought."

Gee-gee played along and smiled back. I could smell his musky cologne all the way across the desk. He casually ran a hand through his full head of silver hair and said, "A dangerous thought."

I dipped my head in agreement. "I'll keep it in mind."

"Do that," Gee-gee responded. "In the meantime, think about where you're going to find thirty more cases of sable pelts."

"When do you need the stuff?" I asked.

"I needed it tonight!" Gee-gee said sternly. "Friday night is it."

I was taken aback. "The railroad yard's too hot!"

"I agree," said Gee-gee, "but I've been informed that another part of the same shipment was sent to the Federated."

The Federated? I thought, completely dumbfounded.

The Federated Warehouse belonged to Paul Drago, a caporegime in the Luciano family whose territory was the Chelsea waterfront. While it wasn't unusual to be hired by members of other families—my father and I belonged to the Mangano family—that was only to hit civilian targets (warehouses, stockyards, depots, airports). But to be hired to hit a family-owned operation—and even more incredible, one in your own family? Crazy!

"That's Drago's warehouse," I said as calmly as I could.

Gee-gee threw out a hand and waved me off nonchalantly. "My problem is an unfulfilled contract for forty cases of sable. Your problem is Drago. We had a contract, and my buyer is waiting." He paused and then added darkly, "Don't embarrass me, Vesta . . . or yourself."

A giant alarm bell went off in my brain, but I quickly decided that this was not the time to answer it. I studied Gee-gee for a few moments, then got up and swept the money off the table.

Gee-gee punched a button on his desk, and the wall behind me again swung open. I started out, but when I got to the opening I couldn't resist the urge to get off a parting shot. I turned at the entrance, made a pistol out of my index finger and thumb, and pointed it at Touch. Just before the wall closed I smiled, snapped down my thumb, and said, "Click."

When I came out of the pedestrian door, Boychick, Red, Benny, and Louie were "matching quarters"—a game where each player flipped a quarter, caught it, and slapped it onto the back of his hand. All four then revealed their coin, and the odd man won all the quarters. If there was no odd man, they flipped again. Boychick stopped the action the second he saw me and asked nervously, "Was Gee-gee pissed about only ten crates?"

"He wants his thirty more," I responded, and then added, "By Friday night."

Boychick's eyes widened and he exclaimed, "He wants us ta go back ta the rail yard?!"

I took out a pack of Luckies, popped one out, put it in my mouth, and lit it. "No," I said, "he wants us to hit Federated."

Benny, Red, and Louie exchanged puzzled glances. They knew that Gee-gee and Drago were both in the Luciano family, and they knew that asking us to hit a warehouse owned by a member of his own family made no sense.

Red took out his switchblade, snapped it open, and began whittling a wooden match.

"Mind tellin' us yer answer?" asked Benny.

I grinned. Louie drew back his lips, hooked his thumbs in his belt, and paraphrased one of Humphrey Bogart's famous lines in *Casablanca*, including the lisp: "Of all the warehoushes, on all the rivers, in this cockeyed world—"

"Shut up, Louie," said Boychick. "You really thinkin' about this, Vinny?"

I said, "I'm thinkin' we'll all sleep on it and meet in the mornin' at Bronko's Diner to look it over and talk about it."

"We can sleep on it for a week," Boychick objected, "but when we wake up it'll still be Drago's warehouse. It don't make sense!" he insisted. "Why the hell would he want us ta hit a warehouse owned by a guy in his own family?"

"That is what we gotta figure out," I said.

Boychick spread his arms in frustration. "How?"

"Probably by hitting the warehouse." I took a long drag on my Lucky and exhaled.

We headed back to Benny's to split up the cash, and nobody said a word. There was nothing more to say.

It was two-fifteen by the time I walked into our tenement on Thirty-sixth Street and Eleventh Avenue to be greeted by the perpetual scent of garlic. I climbed the four flights of stairs, opened our door, and was hit by a ferocious thermal punch. I stripped to my shorts, went through the open living room window to the fire escape, and settled onto the mattress. Sidney was on his adjacent fire escape in his usual position and wardrobe—but he wasn't reading.

"Hi, Vin," he said as soon as I was comfortably seated with my back against the wall.

I leaned toward the iron sidebars, rested on my elbow, and said, "No book?"

"My batteries died. But I've been waiting for you . . . I've been thinking."

"About what?" I asked.

"Well, we've spent the whole summer on classical . . ." He left the statement hanging.

I nodded. "Right . . . so?"

"So I thought that maybe we should spend some time with something more recent."

"Like what?"

"Like maybe some American writers . . . Scott Fitzgerald, for instance. *The Great Gatsby*. It's all about the twenties. I read about it in a book review."

"Fine," I said. "And put it on Terry's list."

"Okay," he said. "Will she want to come with us tomorrow?"

I shook my head apologetically. "I can't go to the library tomorrow, Sidney."

"But tomorrow's Friday," Sidney objected. "Every Monday, Wednesday, and Friday, all summer. You promised."

We hadn't missed a day since the beginning of the summer, but the debacle at the rail yard could make the following day a problem. "I'm sorry, Sidney," I said, "I really am. But somethin's come up and I gotta meet the guys."

"What about in the afternoon?"

"Maybe. But I gotta go see Terry around two."

"After that, maybe?"

"Maybe," I said. "I'll try—but it'll be later. Three-thirty or four." I heard the front door of my apartment open and said, "That's probably the old man and Angelo. We'll talk tomorrow."

"Okay," said Sidney, disappointed, "but promise."

"What?" I asked, getting up.

"You'll try," exhorted Sidney. "Even if it's later . . . I'll wait for you."

"Promise." I tapped him on the arm and ducked back into my flat.

As usual, my father was dressed meticulously in a conservative suit, shirt, and tie. When I entered the kitchen he was removing his jacket, revealing the .45 automatic in his shoulder holster that was as much a part of his wardrobe as his tie. He gestured to the simmering pot on the stove and greeted me with, "Vincenzo—coffee?"

I shook my head and took a bottle of milk out of the fridge while he retrieved a mug from the top of our old Kelvinator and poured the coffee.

"I heard there was trouble," he remarked.

"News travels fast," I replied, adding milk to his coffee.

My father smiled cynically and sat at the table. "Gee-gee could not wait to let me know something had gone bad for you. He had Touch Grillo call Angelo." He pointed toward the hall, where Angelo Maserelli was once again coming out of the bathroom, zipping up his fly.

Angelo nodded a greeting at me and grumbled, "It's gettin' worse. I gotta piss every two hours." Even with his jacket off, his vest unbuttoned, and his tie loosened, the collar of his dress shirt looked like a noose tightened around his nineteen-inch neck, and the .45 automatic jammed between his belt and his spine looked like a permanent extension of his back.

My father chuckled. "We're getting old, Angelo . . ."

He waved it off and turned to me. "The sawbones says it's my po— pro—pos—somethin' state. We heard there was trouble. You okay?"

"I'm good," I said, "thanks for asking."

Angelo buttoned his vest, put on his jacket, and pressed me with a gleam in his eye. "Anything we should know?"

I recognized the obvious probe and said, "Not for the moment."

Angelo looked at my father and grinned. "Like I say, the kid's got a tight lip. That's good. Eight-thirty?"

My father nodded. "Eight-thirty."

"See ya in the mornin' . . ." He opened the door. "Take care, tight lips." He waved and left.

73

My father sipped his coffee, looked up, and said, "He asked because he knows Attillio was with you."

I sat opposite my father. "If I'm there—Stuff's there."

He took another sip of coffee. "And now Gee-gee wants you to deliver the rest of the contract."

"That's what he wants—from Drago's warehouse."

My father's eyebrow shot up. "What?"

"I know," I said, "it doesn't make sense."

He sniffed and put down his cup. "I'll handle it!"

I shook my head and shot back, "No, Pop! Somethin's crazy. I don't know how or why, but there's gotta be a reason for him to order a hit on a family-owned operation."

My father angrily agreed. "No question! There has to be more to it—but what?"

"Look, Pop," I said, "I accepted a contract, and I have to deliver. He practically threatened me if I didn't carry it off . . . If you bail me out, we'll never find out what's behind this."

"And if Drago finds out you hit his warehouse, you buy a bull's-eye for a nose."

I shrugged. "Maybe . . . but it's that or we're in the dark."

My father's eyes narrowed, and he thought out loud. "He had to know you'd tell me. He knows it's crazy and he wants me to know. Why?"

"There's only one way to find out," I said. "Hit the warehouse."

He waved off the thought with a flick of his hand. I leaned forward and changed my tone. "How about . . . I do it, but make it look like somebody else did it?"

He shook his head. "Gee-gee will still know it was you."

"Not if I make it impossible for Gee-gee to do anything about it," I said. "I've got a plan."

My father sat back down and studied me. He slowly picked up the cup and finished his coffee. Then he caressed the side of his nose with

74

his index finger. He smiled and I felt his pride, but I also knew he was conflicted. He wanted answers but knew that getting them would be dangerous. "You think you can do this?" he asked.

I shrugged. I'd come up with what I thought was a pretty good plan, but it was tricky and I was pretty sure my father would object, so for the moment I decided to play it cool. I simply said, "It's got a good shot."

He pondered my answer a beat and said, "It's late. I want to think about this. Tomorrow we'll talk and decide."

"It'll be your call," I said.

He got up, grabbed his coat, and started out. I picked up the cup, went to the sink, and called over my shoulder, "G'night, Pop."

My father paused at the hallway and looked back. "You know, if something happens to you—your mother, she'll kill me."

I nodded and smiled. I was an only child. My birth had caused problems, and my mother could never have any more children. "I know . . . ," I said. "I'll be careful."

"G'night, V-cenz," he said, then turned and walked to his bedroom.

When I heard the door close, I washed out the mug and went into the living room. I picked up the phone, dragged the extension cord behind me, and carried it through the window. I dialed the Copacabana.

CHAPTER TWELVE

FRIDAY, AUGUST 25

DEPENDING ON WHO and when you asked, everything from Thirty-fourth to Thirteenth Street and from Sixth Avenue to the Hudson River was Chelsea . . . Drago territory. Drago's Federated Warehouse was on Twelfth Avenue opposite Twenty-fourth Street. A long four-story building, it extended over five hundred feet out into the river. Bronko's Diner was one block north, facing the river on Twenty-fifth Street.

Red and I were the first to arrive at Bronko's, an art deco neon-and-metal shoebox with a Runyonesque clientele and lethal coffee. It smelled of fried food and stale smoke. Booths, under waist-to-ceiling windows, ran the length of the diner, all of them with foot-high jukeboxes on their tables. A long Formica counter with forty Naugahyde stools ran opposite the booths, and spaced every six feet along the counter were more little jukeboxes. Behind the counter, short-order cooks worked at grills, deep-fat fryers, stoves, and multiple chopping blocks, but it was the coffee urns that dominated the back bar. They were stainless-steel cylinders that stood five feet high. The waitresses who made the coffee said they never washed them and were proud that by the end of the day you could stand a spoon in your cup—but the diner's real claim to fame was the Boston cream pie, which was first class.

Red and I walked in after the morning rush hour was over and eyed the few hangers-on at the counter and a pair of lingering foursomes in two booths. We took the booth closest to the door—well away from the other patrons—and an overweight waitress with a poised pencil trundled over. She was wearing tight shorts, a low-cut peasant blouse, and low-heeled boots—all white, a bad color for any overweight woman but for her a disaster. Her heart-shaped name tag read "Agnes."

I ordered, "A Coke and Boston cream pie."

Red said, "Coffee—black." Red was not only a man of few words, he was the only guy in the crew who had the guts to order the legendary coffee. Agnes gave him an approving nod, scribbled the order on her pad, and departed.

A few minutes later Boychick arrived. He saw Red and me and then spotted a man coming out of the men's room at the far end of the diner. The man sat in the last stool at the counter. Boychick patted the air, palm down, signaling us to stay put, then sauntered to the end of the diner and sat in the corner booth behind the man.

Agnes tracked Boychick's entrance from one of the towering coffee urns and shook her head distastefully. Boychick was wearing studded black jeans, lizardskin boots, a Golden Gloves T-shirt, and a scowl. His belt buckle was a death's-head, and there was a pack of Camels rolled up in the sleeve of his T-shirt. Everything about him screamed "street gang."

Agnes dropped off our Coke, coffee, and pie, then ambled down to Boychick. She threw out her hip, cocked her head, and poised her pencil above her pad. "What's your poison?" she asked derisively.

Boychick looked at her name tag and ordered, "Boston cream pie and a Coke."

"Anything else, big man?" she sniffed.

Boychick folded his hands on the table. "Yeah, Agnes—the phone number of your insurance agent. I wanna make sure your accident policy's paid up because you're about ta have one." Agnes turned up her nose and walked away.

The man seated at the counter opposite Boychick was in his late twenties and dressed flamboyantly in the be-bop style of the time—a powder blue suit with pegged pants and huge jacket lapels, a pastel pink shirt, and a wide matching necktie tied with an equally wide Windsor knot. His face was pockmarked, sallow, and pinched, and he wore his slicked-back raven hair parted on the left with a pompadour on the right. He watched Agnes through the mirror opposite him. When she was out of sight, he spun around on his stool and looked down at Boychick with an oily smile.

I immediately recognized Carlo Ricci, Paul Drago's underboss. It was obvious that Boychick had gone to the far end of the diner in an attempt to distract Carlo so that Red and I could slip out of the diner unnoticed. Boychick had no way of knowing that if Carlo spotted us, it wouldn't matter.

Carlo got up and slid into the booth opposite Boychick. He placed his hat on the table with exaggerated delicacy, and grinned without humor. Boychick said, "I didn't hear somebody say 'Sit down,' Carlo."

Carlo oozed phony camaraderie as he explained, "That's because you're too far away. Sound don't carry that easy from Hell's Kitchen all the way down here to Chelsea."

"You got somethin' on your mind, spit it. I'm a busy man," said Boychick.

"Now that's what I was wonderin'," said Carlo. "A busy man like you findin' time to come all the way down here out of his territory to eat pie. It don't figure . . ."

Boychick snorted. "Since when did ya start figurin'? Drago don't pay ya to figure. What I can't figure is how he's stupid enough ta pay ya at all."

Carlo's face dropped—then he smiled, got up, and put on his hat. "I'll be sure to tell him you think he's stupid. And when I do, you might think about callin' *your* insurance agent." He flicked the brim of his hat. "Ciao, big man."

Carlo noticed Red and me as he approached the door. Just as he was about to say something, the door opened and Benny entered, followed by Louie and Stuff. "My, my . . . it's a regular summit . . . Enjoy the pie." He emitted a mocking grunt and left.

Stuff and Red slid into the booth; Boychick pulled up a chair and sat at the end of the table.

Stuff jerked his thumb over his shoulder and asked, "What was that all about?"

Boychick waved it off with a disgusted toss of his hand. "Carlo bein' a wise-ass . . . only now Paul Drago's gonna know we were here."

There was no question that Carlo would report he saw us in their territory—one block from the warehouse we planned to hit that night—but again, with the plan I had in mind, it wouldn't matter.

Agnes returned and Stuff grabbed her wrist. He pointed at my pie and Coke and said, "The same for me—but twice." Benny and Louie ordered the Boston cream pie and Cokes. Red signaled a refill, snapped open his switchblade, and began whittling a wooden match. Agnes shot a look at Stuff's hand on her arm and was about to make a remark, but the sight of Red's switchblade made her think twice about being a smart-ass. She gingerly removed Stuff's hand and walked away.

"Where's Bouncer?" I asked.

Stuff raised an eyebrow and said, "He's takin' a singing lesson."

"A what?" I knew Bouncer's father was a singer—he sang in the chorus of the Metropolitan Opera House—but Bouncer?

Stuff shrugged and repeated, "He's takin' a singing lesson. Lately he thinks he wants to follow in his old man's footsteps."

Boychick was aghast. "He stutters, for chrissake! How the hell could he sing?"

"His old man thinks it could cure the stutter," Stuff said. "Then, if he could sing, maybe he could get Bouncer a job carrying a spear next to him . . . in the chorus at the Met."

"Opera? He's gonna sing opera?" asked Louie.

Stuff nodded wearily. "With a spear—next to his old man—in the chorus at the Met."

Boychick threw up his hands and said, "I heard everythin'."

"Good," I said, anxious to get on with it, "now maybe we can do some business." They all muttered and nodded their assent. "We're gonna knock off the Federated Warehouse."

"Oh, shit . . . ," said Stuff.

I said, "Yeah, but we've got no choice. We'll case it today and hit it tonight." I paused and waited for further comments, but there were none. "I think I know a way in, but it's complicated," I continued.

"What's the plan?" asked Boychick.

I didn't want to tell them what I had in mind quite yet. I thought my plan could work, but we'd never attempted anything like it before, and I was worried we were short on know-how. I wanted to spend the rest of the day trying to figure out something more conventional, and doing that meant we'd have to set up surveillance on the warehouse. I told Boychick to steal a van, park on the corner of Twenty-fourth Street opposite the Federated, and see if he could spot a weakness. I told Red and Benny to rotate the watch with Boychick. Stuff's job was to get inside the gates to check out the alarms and find out the guard's schedule. I told him to wait until noon and do the "Sabrett bit" when everyone at the warehouse broke for lunch. We'd used the Sabrett bit before because it was simple and incredibly effective. When he was finished, I'd meet him and Louie at Barlow's Tavern at five o'clock.

Barlow's was on the Lower East Side and a known hangout of Socks Lanza's crew. "Joe Zox" was the man who ran the notorious Fulton Fish

Market, which supplied New Yorkers with all of their fish and most of their hoods. Zox taxed every fish that came through the market; it was a cash cow with scales, and the Mob made a fortune. I knew Lanza's crew hung out in Barlow's after work, and I needed a wallet—one of theirs. The plan was to pick out a mark and, when the guy went into the toilet, send in Stuff and Louie to bracket him at the urinals. While Louie distracted him, Stuff would lift his wallet. Stuff could pick a pocket as easily as he could pick up a tune. One night when we had all returned to Benny's after a movie, he had tossed our six wallets on the oak-door table and gleefully taken a bow. None of us had felt a thing.

The minute I mentioned lifting the wallet, Boychick was all over it. "We're gonna plant it in the Federated?" he asked.

"Right," I said.

"It won't work," Boychick objected. "One: Gee-gee'll know *we* raided the warehouse. And two: The guy without the wallet'll probably have an alibi—a real one!"

"It won't matter," I said. "The wallet's for Drago's benefit. It gives him someone to go after. Gee-gee'll know the truth, but I'm gonna force 'im to clam up."

Louie offered his opinion with a Jimmy Cagney impression. "Nnnn . . . I never heard—nobody ever made—Gee-gee ever do—nothin' he didn't wanna do."

Benny shook his head. "Still don't get it."

"I called Terry last night," I explained. "She's got this actress girlfriend who's English. Her name's Jill. Jill has an apartment on the East Side—paid for by Touch Grillo."

Stuff shrugged. "So he's keepin' a broad in a pad. So what?"

I ignored him. "Every Friday night he loans it to Gee-gee so he can pop Danny Pisano's wife."

"Holy shit," said Boychick. "Pisano's a caporegime in Joe Bonanno's family!" He glanced around the table and then back at me, waiting for the other shoe to drop. They all knew "Joe Bananas" was the capo of one of New York's original five crime families. Only an idiot would intentionally anger him or any of his captains.

I nodded. "Exactly . . . so I figure when I blackmail Gee-gee with the pictures that Jill's gonna take of him porking Mrs. Pisano, Gee-gee will shut up about where the furs came from rather than start a war with Pisano and the Bonanno family."

They stared at me silently for a long beat, then exchanged glances. Finally all of them except Red murmured their approval. Red stopped whittling his match and asked, "Why?"

"Why what?" I responded.

"Jill," said Red.

Boychick was again the first to pick up the thought. "Yeah. What's her angle?"

"Revenge," I said. "Touch slaps her around and treats her like shit. She also hates him for makin' her let Gee-gee get laid in her bed."

Stuff broke into a broad grin. "It's beautiful!" he said.

It was beautiful, I thought . . . if Jill could get the pictures. The plan was for Jill's doorman to call her the minute Gee-gee showed up with Mrs. Pisano, at which point she'd pop into her bedroom closet. Gee-gee didn't figure to look in there, since he was interested in getting into Mrs. Pisano, not the closet. Jill would take the incriminating pictures and give them to Terry. Terry would give them to the photographer who took her acting shots. He would develop them and get them back to Terry, who would give them to me in the morning. The only thing I didn't tell them was how we were going to break into the warehouse if I didn't figure out something simpler during the day.

"Where're you gonna be?" asked Boychick.

"With you until one," I said. "Terry's after that, and then with Sidney for a couple of hours. I'll meet Louie and Stuff at Barlow's at five and catch up with you at the stakeout on Twenty-fourth after we get a wallet." I dropped a ten on the table and said, "That's it."

Boychick slammed a fist into his palm and said, "Let's do it!"

I shot out an open, palm-down hand. They repeated the motion and stacked their hands on top of mine. A second later Boychick said, "Yes!" and we broke the stack. It was a "unity" thing. We'd been doing it since grammar school.

As we left the diner, Boychick held me back. He put his hands in his pockets and casually opened a new subject as we walked behind the others. "You tell your ol' man about Terry?"

"Not yet."

"For chrissake, Vinny, he's gonna find out."

"And when he does he's gonna kill me."

"So get your mother ta talk to him."

"If my mother finds out, she's gonna kill *Terry*."

"Then buy a pair of caskets. What're ya thinkin'! The girl's a hatcheck at the goddamn Copa. Your old man hangs out at the Copa. She probably sells him his cigars! Half the Mob guys in there've probably jumped her. How do you know one of them ain't keepin' *her*?"

I shook my head. "She loves me. We love each other."

"She's old enough to be your mother!" cried Boychick.

"She's twenty-nine," I said.

"So? She coulda had you young. There's places inna world where they have kids at twelve."

"Stay out of it, Boychick," I said evenly, "I know what I'm doing."

Boychick shook his head. "Sure ya do. But just in case—buy a pair of caskets."

"Lay out, Boychick!" I snapped.

Boychick knew when to shut up. He held up his hands, cocked his head, and continued walking.

Since we had started seeing each other, Terry would sleep until I woke her up, swearing I was sexier than "any ol' alarm clock." I loved the arrangement. She'd answer the door still half-asleep—without makeup and wearing the eye-popping white satin robe that I never tired of. The rest was automatic.

About a minute after the chimes announced my arrival that morning, she let me in and put her arms around my neck. "Mmmm . . . ," she cooed.

I kissed her neck and said, "Mmmm, back."

She leaned back and playfully touched the tip of my nose with her index finger. "Don't lose your place," she said, then padded across to the counter that separated the living room from the kitchen and began preparing coffee.

I joined her at the counter and asked, "You get a chance to talk to Jill?"

She nodded. "Last night, right after you called she came in with Grillo. As usual, he made his entrance with her on his trophy arm and paraded her through the tables like a poodle in a dog show." Her voice rose in a lilt. "And then when they finally sat down . . . ?" She paused for effect. "He ignored her—got up and made the rounds of the Mob tables. A few minutes later she came over to say hi to me."

Terry put on the coffeepot, set out a pair of mugs, and sat opposite me.

"She cool?" I asked.

"It's all set for tonight," she said, enjoying the prospect immensely. "As soon as Gee-gee walks into the lobby, the doorman'll ring up her apartment and Jill'll pop right on into the bedroom closet."

"She knows Gee-gee's gonna figure out where the pictures came from," I warned.

"It won't matter, sugah. By tomorrow afternoon her little ol' plane'll be halfway to London. She's always wanted to go back to the West End. She's just been waitin' for her chance to get even and get out."

"Thanks, Terry," I said sincerely, "you saved my ass."

Terry leaned in and kissed me. "And a pretty ass it is."

I kissed her back and said, "I love you, Terry . . ."

84

Terry smiled. "What you're feelin', sugah, is what we Georgia peaches call lust."

"I know the difference," I said.

"You're too young to know the difference," she teased.

"Bet?"

She again touched the tip of my nose with her index finger. "How much, and for how long?"

I laughed. "As much as you want, for as long as it takes."

Terry grew quiet and shook her head. "Nothin's ever that long, sugah . . . the right nows are what we have and what we get to use." She got up and took my hand. "Come on—forget the coffee."

She smiled and led me into the bedroom. Again . . . magic.

CHAPTER THIRTEEN

I RETURNED TO OUR tenement at three o'clock and found Sidney waiting on the steps. It was the hottest part of the day, and there was no stickball, stoopball, or rope jumping, but the younger neighborhood kids had cranked open a fire hydrant and were cavorting under the eruption like a bunch of crazed elves. The kids were all nude—Sidney was wearing his sweater and yarmulke.

I called out his name as I approached, and his head popped up. He broke into a wide grin and rushed down the steps.

"You made it!" he cried out.

"Who could ignore a shot at Gatsby?"

I put my arm around him and was about to lead him away when Bouncer rounded the corner. He was singing—badly, but he was singing, "Do-re-me-fa-so-la-ti-do . . . Do-ti-la-so-fa-me-redoooo." Looking skyward, he had one hand over his heart and his other hand thrown out parallel to the ground, palm up, like he was singing an aria. He continued vocalizing until he spotted us and then stopped immediately. He looked a bit embarrassed, so I said, "Caruso! What's new at the Met?"

He took the comment as a compliment and broke into a grin. "Y-you like it?"

"You're gettin' there."

He smiled. "R-really?"

"Sure," I said, and turned to Sidney. "Right, Sidney?"

That stopped Sidney cold. He looked at me like I was nuts, but he wouldn't dream of hurting Bouncer's feelings, so he fumbled a bit and came up with, "Ah . . . right . . . it's like . . . cool. Right—cool."

Bouncer grinned and said, "Thanks, guys. My pop says opera is c-curing my s-stutter. W-what d'you think?"

Sidney's eyebrows shot up. How the hell would we answer that one? he seemed to be asking. "Anything's possible," I said, jumping in to help.

Bouncer turned to Sidney and asked, "You like opera?"

"Well, I've never been," said Sidney, "but my dad listens to it on the radio, so I've heard some. I like it."

"You wanna come with me t-tomorrow?"

"Where?" asked Sidney.

"The Saturday matinee at the M-Met," Bouncer answered proudly, "*Aida!* My dad has the guard s-sneak me in through the stage door."

"Wow. Sure—I'll ask Pop," said Sidney.

Bouncer turned to me. "How about you, Vinny?"

I shook my head. If we hit the Federated that night, we'd be delivering the goods on Saturday—but I didn't know when or what the repercussions might be. "Tomorrow's not good, Bouncer. Another time."

"Okay . . . you guys going to the library again?"

"On our way," I answered.

Bouncer bowed his head guiltily. "Vinny . . . about this morning. I'm sorry. Stuff picked me up and we almost made it out the d-door to meet you guys when my old man collared us. He fixed it so I could have a s-singing lesson this morning."

"I know. Stuff told us. No problem." He thanked me with a nod. "Lemme ask you a question," I continued. "You like this singin' thing?"

Bouncer began to fidget. "Well, n-no. I mean, I d-don't know—maybe. It's like I been th-thinking maybe I should be lookin' ahead, you know?" He continued almost apologetically, "You guys are out, b-but I've still got another year in school. I've never been too g-good at what we do—you know that, Vinny. If I could learn to s-sing by the time I graduate, maybe I c-could go straight. I wouldn't be b-big or anything like that, but maybe I could be like my ol' man. He makes a d-decent buck, and he raised us okay . . . you know wh-what I mean?"

I looked at my cousin and realized that everything he said made sense. He wasn't cut out for our kind of life. My feeling sorry for him and taking him into the gang had probably been a mistake. I didn't know if he could ever make a living as a singer, but he sure as hell wasn't going to make one as a wiseguy. I said, "Yeah, Bounce, I know what you mean. You keep on singin'. We'll talk later, okay?"

"Thanks, Vinny," said Bouncer, obviously relieved. "Whatever you say."

"Don't worry about it." I tapped Bouncer on the arm and sent him on his way. "See you later."

"R-right," he said, and took off down the street.

I turned to Sidney. "You ready to say hello to Gatsby?"

Sidney nodded eagerly and we headed east on Thirty-sixth Street. We ducked across the street to avoid being drenched by a gushing fire hydrant and waved at the frolicking kids. The fine mist at the edges of the geyser gave us a pretty good spritz, and the kids got a kick out of it. They jumped up and down gleefully and shouted for us to join them. It was a familiar scene, and I flashed back a dozen years to when I was a part of it. The world had definitely changed. A big war had ended in Europe, and a small one had started in Korea. Chuck Yeager had broken the sound barrier, and we heard that the latest phenomenon was something called computers. But New York, I thought, had basically remained the same. The Kitchen continued to be tough, ethnic, unforgiving, immutable, and filled with kids playing in the streets. I laughed and wiped the water off my face as we continued on our way toward Tenth Avenue, passing clusters of garbage cans awaiting their Friday morning pickup. When the trucks came, disappointed men who hated their lot in life would slam the corrugated metal cans against the concrete sidewalks to register their frustration. It was a metallic symphony that could raise the dead, and I always tried to miss it.

We stopped for the traffic light at the corner of Tenth Avenue and waited alongside a blonde wearing sling-back heels, pink hip-huggers, and a halter that was struggling to contain its contents. Sidney saw her give me a "come hither" smile, and he tugged at my T-shirt. "How's Terry?" he asked in an intentionally loud voice.

I realized what he was doing and chuckled. "Terry's good," I said. "The best. I told her I had to leave her early to meet you and she said fine and to say hello."

"That's great . . . and hello back," said Sidney. The light changed, and the blonde led us across Tenth Avenue. She threw another smile over her shoulder, and Sidney blurted out loudly, "Maybe later we could have dinner with your girlfriend."

"Sure," I answered, "I'll set it up." I shrugged at the blonde; she returned a good-natured shrug and turned north up Tenth.

When we got to the library and started up the enormous staircase on Fifth Avenue, I realized that in a few short months I'd come to love the climb. If knowledge was power, this staircase led to the generator. But later that summer, it would also lead to the scene that would change both our lives.

*   *   *

Sidney and I left the library just as the afternoon rush hour was beginning. At the bottom of the steps, we turned south and joined the gaggle of bodies that were scurrying to their Friday night rendezvous, some to a lonely evening with a book, others to a family dinner, and single hopefuls to their favorite TGIF watering holes. Their wardrobe marked most of them as low- or midlevel business types, the men in lightweight summer suits, some carrying their jackets over their arms to beat the heat, the women in sleeveless dresses or skirts and blouses. They had one thing in common: They were all staring straight ahead and ignoring one another. As they rushed to wherever they were going, they seemed to be concentrating on something just ahead but un-reachable. Civilians, I thought, working stiffs who seem oblivious to the world around them. If I had ever let Stuff's nimble fingers loose in a bunch like that, we'd be able to open a wallet mart. I actually felt sorry for them. They had no angle and a life without much upside. We, on the other hand, had upside to burn. We belonged to a special circle—we had "family."

Sidney continued his analysis as we crossed Forty-first Street and headed south toward Thirty-sixth, "So even though it's like a picture of America in the twenties, it tells the story of a guy who goes from rags to riches, but finds out that money can't buy what he really wants—class and status." He had his arms wrapped around a copy of *The Great Gatsby* like it was a newborn.

"He sounds like Giorgio Petrone," I commented.

"Who?"

"A guy who's also in a book—of mug shots. He's—" I cut off the explanation, caught Sidney's arm, and we both stopped. Up ahead, the pedestrians were parting left and right to make way for six toughs with an attitude. They were coming toward us with a cocky rolling gait and a smirking disrespect for the people giving them a wide berth. They were all in their late teens and were all in "uniform"—black T-shirts with cigarette packs rolled up in their left sleeves, pegged pants, pointed boots, and a rogue's gallery of tattoos. You had to be blind not to know they were a street gang, and you had to be a "civilian" not to know they were Nick Colucci and the Rattlers.

Along with Colucci, I recognized Sal and Al Russomano with their ferretlike faces and pencil-thin mustaches. There was a pair of new additions I hadn't seen before and, finally, Pete "Stank" Stankovitch. He looked like Rasputin, just as big and twice as tough. The gang looked completely out of place on Fifth Avenue, which was obvious from the disgusted reactions they were drawing from passersby.

When Colucci spotted us he slowed down, hooked his thumbs into his belt, and seemed exceptionally pleased. I hadn't seen him since forcing him to give back Sidney's stolen yarmulke, and as he ambled up with his crew in trail, it crossed my mind that he might have been waiting for us. He cut his eyes over to Sidney, then back to me. "So— Vinny," he said, "I see you been continuin' yer higher ed-jacation."

That was the first time I realized that he'd been tracking my relationship with Sidney. I figured it was because he was still pissed about my protecting a Jew, but there was more. He had been one of the gang leaders who had been buying the plans I sold, and as with the rest of the West Side crews, his earnings were down. They were pissed, but with Colucci it was personal—and now he liked the odds. Six to one and a half.

Sidney's eyes widened, then darted back and forth between Nick and me. He swallowed hard and clutched his book tighter. The foot traffic had parted into two streams of humanity, flowing around us as if we were a human boulder in the middle of a fast-moving river. No one even got close.

"You got a problem with that, Nick?" I asked.

"Ya know somethin', Vinny, I might . . . I just might," said Nick. He was smirking. Behind him, Sal and Al Russomano agreed. They chuckled and tapped each other's fists. Stankovich remained stone-faced.

Nick Colucci was about my size, but bulkier and older. His scraggly blond hair, gold front tooth, pockmarked face, and scarred chin usually intimidated his enemies. It didn't intimidate me, and he knew it—but he still had to look good in front of his crew.

"Then I got a problem with you, Nick," I intoned in the calmest voice I could muster. "I don't like you."

"Aww . . . really?" he responded sarcastically. He looked to his crew for approval, got it, then turned back to me with a frozen smile. He shrugged. "Why?"

I responded with absolutely no edge in my voice. "Because you're an asshole."

Nick's crew was stunned for an eye blink, then reacted and lurched toward me. Nick held out his arms to restrain them, his phony smile dissolving.

"And you're a wise-ass, Vinny. I hear people say so. People like Touch Grillo. They say ya got a habit of makin' the wrong enemies." He shot a disdainful look at Sidney. "And the wrong friends."

"Take a news flash back to Grillo," I said. "I happen to like my friends. And anyone who ain't one knows where to find me."

"Okay," Nick said, nodding slowly. "Now lemme give you a news flash, *Iceman*. One day you're gonna fuck up, and yer old man isn't gonna be around to wipe yer ass. On that day, someone's gonna plant ya and yer Jew boy under a parkin' lot."

I knew Nick was trying to get me to lose it. He had big-time backup, and I had Sidney clutching a goddamn book. Nick expected me to go batshit, but I did the opposite and went warm and fuzzy. I gave him an ingratiating smile and said, "My, my. I really do thank you for the warning, Nick—very helpful. I'll certainly try to duck parking lots for a while." I made a pistol out of my thumb and index finger, pointed it at Nick's nose, and said, "Click!" I paused a beat for a reaction but got none, so I said as casually as I could, "Nice day for a walk. Think I'll take one," and started off. It worked. Nick and his crew looked stunned—so did Sidney.

As we walked away, I decided to put Sidney at ease by completely ignoring the confrontation with Colucci. I tilted my head toward him and continued our conversation as if nothing had ever happened.

"So, you were saying this Gatsby guy couldn't buy class because people figured he came from a shady past . . . Do you suppose he had a crew?"

Sidney stared up at me, awestruck.

CHAPTER FOURTEEN

I DROPPED OFF SIDNEY at our tenement and met Louie and Stuff at Barlow's Tavern at exactly five p.m. Barlow's was a short stickball shot from the Fulton Fish Market, and its proximity to their meal ticket made it the natural hangout for Lanza's crew. The décor was Gay Nineties, the air-conditioning was ineffective, and the overhead fans merely rearranged the smoke. Most of the orders were "onna rocks" or "shot an' a beer," and it was crowded, steaming, and boisterous. Everybody was hot—everybody but Louie. For the occasion, Louie had added a snap-brim fedora to his all-black ensemble and an inch to his height by putting lifts in his wingtips. When we entered, I noticed a few customers look at Louie with disbelieving stares.

We elbowed our way to the bar through a clutch of blue-collar stiffs and their girlfriends. A bartender came over to take our order. Louie pushed his fedora a few inches higher up on his forehead and ordered, "A Manhattan."

The bartender screwed his face into a question mark and asked, "Are you kiddin'?"

Louie pulled back his lips in a Bogart sneer and hissed through his teeth, "If I wus kiddin', I woulda ordered a whish-key sour!"

The bartender looked over the six-foot-four-inch wraith in solid black and decided not to push the discussion any further. "A Manhattan—right. I'll look it up." Stuff and I both ordered a beer, and the bartender departed, shaking his head.

While we waited for our drinks, I looked around and tried to pick out a mark. Halfway down the bar there were several better-dressed customers standing with their female trophies. I figured the better-dressed guys were with Lanza's crew, but I couldn't be sure. I watched the bartender study a small book, then felt a tap on my shoulder and heard a raspy, whiskey-ravaged voice.

"Hey, Vinny—Louie—Stuff . . . whatchu guys doin' down here?"

We turned and looked down at a smallish man in his mid-forties. He was a head shorter than me—two heads shorter than Louie—and his wiry body was the polar opposite of Stuff's. He had rumpled hair and a drunk's vein-covered nose. He was dressed in army surplus khakis held up by plaid suspenders, and his name was Leo Delfina—Boychick Delfina's father.

"I might ask you the same question, Mr. D," I replied.

"*Leo!* We don't hafta be formal, Vinny," he said with a "hail fellow well met" attitude. "You're my son's buddies! Part of the family, you could say, right?"

"If you say so, Leo," I replied.

Stuff and Louie remained silent. They couldn't stand Leo. None of us could—including Boychick—and we all had good reasons. Leo Delfina had wanted to be a "made" man all of his life, ever since he was a teenager hanging around the docks and running numbers for the Mob. He was drafted during World War II and begged the army to send him to Europe during the invasion of Sicily because he figured he might make some Mafia contacts over there. He told his commanding officer that he spoke fluent Italian, which he did; but it didn't help. He was sent to the Pacific and wound up on Borneo.

When the war ended he wrangled a job as a longshoreman and begged to be taken in at the lowest level of the Mob—in any family, anywhere. He'd do anything: armed robbery, extortion, arson—even murder. Especially murder. That would be his dream. He could be "made." The problem was that Leo was a gambler, a drunk, and a loudmouth. A dangerous combination in any job, but in the Mob— fatal.

When my father took over the West Side docks, Leo tried to get close to him by using Boychick's friendship with me. It didn't work. Boychick had already frozen his father out—ever since the night he came home and caught Leo beating his mother. Boychick had hit Leo with a flurry of combinations that put him in bed for a week, and they'd barely spoken since.

"So," I continued, "what are you doin' on this side of town?"

"You know how it is"—Leo shrugged—"sometimes it's a little tough gettin' work on the West Side. Some of the guys around here take care a me, know what I mean?"

Leo had already had a few drinks, so I decided to probe a bit and see if his rep as a loudmouth was still a lock.

"Well, ya know, Leo, maybe I could talk to my ol' man."

Leo jumped on it like a hyena on carrion. "Gino—you could talk to Gino?"

"Well—you know, I can't promise anything, but . . ."

Leo pressed his opening. "If ya could talk to Gino, I'd do anythin'— anythin'! I asked Boychick. He won't talk ta me. His own father and he hates me!"

"Look, Leo, what I'll try is—" Before I could finish, I was interrupted.

"Hey there, Leo . . . how ya doon?"

The interrupter was a stocky runt with buckteeth and a wandering eye. He looked to be in his sixties, with a belly hanging over his belt and seedy khakis similar to Leo's. He had obviously seen better days.

"Hey, Carmine," Leo said, and the two exchanged a hug. "I wantcha ta meet some friends a mine from the West Side." He pointed us out as he made the introductions. "Vinny, Louie, Stuff . . . meet Carmine. Carmine . . . Vinny, Louie, an' Stuff." We all knew that in casual meetings, no last names were ever used.

"A pleasure, I'm sure," said Carmine, shaking hands with the three of us, then turning back to Leo. "Listen, Leo—about dat thing we talked about the other day—call me. It looks like a go." He turned back to us and waved. "Nice meetin' ya, kids."

As he left I said, "Seems like a nice guy . . ."

Wanting to impress us, Leo leaned in conspiratorially. "Yeah—but ya see da guy over there"—he pointed down the bar to the group I had observed earlier—"da one with the cardigan jacket, Billy Eckstine shirt, and white tie?"

We looked down the bar at a garishly dressed middle-aged man. Louie said, "How could we miss 'im?"

"That's Johnny DiCarlo. Carmine used ta work for him before he retired. He still gives Carmine a crumb or two fer old times' sake, and Carmine cuts me in . . ."

I feigned noninterest and said, "So?"

"DiCarlo's Socks Lanza's top earner," said Leo.

That got our attention. The bartender returned with a pair of beers and a Manhattan. As he set Louie's drink in front of him, he announced proudly, "A Manhattan!"

Louie was still looking at DiCarlo. "No kiddin'?"

"Yeah, no kiddin'!" said the bartender. "It's even got a cherry—from the kitchen!"

"Not you," said Louie, waving off the bartender and pointing at Leo, "him."

"Yeah," Leo said, "no kiddin'."

Louie smiled. I glanced at Stuff, who picked up his beer and held it out. Louie lifted his Manhattan, I raised my beer, and the three of us touched glasses.

"Perfect," I said.

We had our mark. Leo was clueless.

CHAPTER FIFTEEN

FTER BARLOW'S, Louie decided to go home and change clothes before the evening's activities. I told him to pick me up after dinner, and Stuff followed me up to a new-looking black-paneled van parked at the end of Twenty-fourth Street. Boychick and Benny were up front; Red and Bouncer were in the back, sitting on the van's bench seats. I squeezed into the front alongside Benny, and Stuff got into the rear and began eating a bag of peanuts. The van was facing the Federated Warehouse on Twelfth Avenue. Running lengthwise down both sides of the warehouse were wide concrete quays where oceangoing cargo ships could be tied up to metal bollards and off-loaded. Longshoremen with forklifts would then move the cargo into the warehouse, where it would await further shipment. A twelve-foot cyclone fence with double-wide gates ran along Twelfth Avenue in front of the warehouse. Inside the gates was a guard shack and a large parking area that ran from the fence to a pair of huge overhead doors in front of the building.

As we watched, a guard in a motorized cart came around the south corner of the building and joined a second guard in the shack. Boychick reported that they had come on at four, and Stuff had found out they would be relieved at midnight by a fresh pair.

Stuff was our infiltrator. At noon, when the longshoremen broke for lunch, Stuff, with Angie the basset hound at his heels, had merrily rolled a Sabrett hot dog cart through the gate. The cart was as hot as the dogs—Stuff and Louie had stolen it the minute its owner went into a public toilet to relieve himself. Stuff began selling his wares, chatting amiably with the longshoremen in the jargon of the docks. As the son of a man who ran a large chunk of docks controlled by my father, the jargon was second nature to him. As he gabbed, he checked out the warehouse, nothing that the loading-bay doors on both sides were wired into the guard shack out front—the last shift ended at midnight, and after that, the place was deserted except for the two guards out front. Once every hour one of them circled the outside of the building in the cart and checked all the doors and windows. The circuit took fifteen minutes.

Obviously this meant the only way in was from the back, from the river. I'd already suspected as much but had hoped we could come up with something less complicated. We hadn't, so I reluctantly gave them my proposal. My plan was to come at the warehouse from the river—by boat. Bouncer damn near had a heart attack, Boychick thought I was nuts, Stuff nearly choked on his peanuts, Benny figured I was brilliant, and Red, as usual, said nothing. Benny was the only one of us who'd ever even been on anything smaller than the Staten Island ferry, so I told him to take Red up to the Seventy-ninth Street Boat Basin and figure a way to steal a boat.

After they left we continued the surveillance, and I remarked to Boychick that the owner of the van he'd stolen must really be pissed that someone had jacked his new wheels. He said the owner didn't know because he had hot-wired the van in a police "repo" yard. I thought it sounded a bit dicey, but Boychick claimed it was worth the chance because there were always plenty of new wheels in the yard. He pointed out that a lot of people who bought on time found out they couldn't make the payments, so they had their vehicles repossessed. Better yet—because their vehicle was already gone, they had no way of knowing it had been stolen and therefore no way of reporting it. I had to admit, if nothing else, it was creative.

About an hour later, Benny and Red still hadn't returned. We all began to worry. Boychick sighed and said, "Whadda ya think?"

I shrugged. I was pretty sure they'd run into trouble but didn't want to admit it.

Boychick reached over his shoulder and snapped his fingers.

"O-on the way," Bouncer responded from the back of the van, and took a cold beer out of a cooler he had brought from home. He handed it over to Boychick and said, "It's t-taking too long. Why's it t-taking so long? Vinny, you want a beer?"

"No thanks," I said. Stuff took one and casually chugalugged half the can.

"They should be b-back by now," Bouncer insisted.

Stuff said, "They never stole a boat before. Benny can't swim and Red hates the water. They're probably goin' around in circles so tight they'll wind up each other's assholes." He giggled at the image.

"What the hell are you jokin' about?" Boychick snapped. "We got a situation here!"

I was used to the banter, and most of the time I enjoyed it, but it drove Boychick crazy. Stuff knew that, so he needled him every chance he got.

"Sorry," said Stuff, but he was still smiling.

"They're probably just bein' extra cool," said Boychick, but he didn't sound convinced. Stuff caught the nervous tone and dropped his smile.

He suddenly realized he might have cause for concern. "Suppose they can't heist a boat? Then what?" he asked.

"Get a pair of water wings," Boychick growled, "because we're goin' fer a dip."

"Holy shit! I don't swim that good," Stuff exclaimed.

"Are you kiddin'? With all that fat, you could float to *Cuba*."

"Ya know somethin', Boychick, sometimes you piss me off."

There was a light tap on the back door, and Bouncer slid back to open it. Benny and Red hopped in and sat down.

"What took you so long!" Boychick exclaimed.

"Got a problem," said Benny.

"What?" I asked.

"No boat?" said Stuff.

"There's boats," said Red, somewhat disgusted.

"But they went an' put a fence around the marina," Benny said sardonically, "an' a little shack thing by the gate. Must've done it lately. Seems like some dishonest folk been tryin' to steal shit."

"So take out the guard," Boychick said as if it were obvious.

Benny shook his head. "Tough. Fence sits next to the street—streetlamp next to the gate."

"Also traffic," added Red, "foot and car."

"Gotta have a diversion," said Benny. "Like last night, only quicker. Guard gets distracted—I slip through the gate and I'm gone like smoke."

"Okay," I said. "Stuff and Bouncer, you go with Benny. Wait until well after dark. After ten would be good—it'll be quieter then. You'll be the diversion."

"Us? H-how?" asked Bouncer, now even more worried.

"You'll walk up close to the shack and get the guard's attention," I said. "When you've got it—start an argument. Yell loud and make like you're beatin' the shit out of each other. Stuff, you grab him by the throat and take him down. Bouncer, you yell, 'Help, police! He's killin' me!' "

"S-suppose he d-don't come out?" asked Bouncer.

"He'll come out," Boychick said. "He'll feel sorry for ya. First he sees ya bouncin' up and down, then when he sees Stuff take ya down, he'll think he's savin' a faggot from bein' smothered by a blimp."

"Now you're really startin' to piss me off," Stuff growled.

"Good. Be mad at me, but take it out on Bouncer. It'll make it look good."

"Th-thanks a lot," said Bouncer.

I wanted a diversion at the marina, not in the van, so I hung my head and waited a few seconds for the banter to end. When it did I asked, "Are you through?" They grumbled but said nothing. "Okay," I said to Benny. "Once you jack the boat, run it down to the Christopher Street pier and wait."

From Christopher Street to the Federated at Twenty-fourth Street was a little over a mile. I figured half an hour would give us plenty of time. "We'll all meet there at eleven-thirty, leave at eleven forty-five, and motor up behind the Federated at twelve-fifteen—right after the guard finishes his twelve o'clock rounds. We'll have the place to ourselves for forty-five minutes."

"Except for the g-guards out front," said Bouncer.

"Will you stop with the negative shit!" said Boychick.

"And I'm worried about that marina g-guard, too," Bouncer protested.

"Don't worry, Bounce," said Boychick, "in a worst-case scenario— sing. That would raise the fuckin' dead. Now get the hell out of here and do some good . . ."

Bouncer and Stuff grumbled, got out, and followed Benny. Benny tried, but he couldn't stop laughing.

"You and Red stay here and keep your eyes peeled," I said. "I'll head back to my place and get the go-ahead from my old man."

"You sure he'll give it to us?" asked Boychick.

"He has to," I said, not nearly as confident as I sounded. "If we do nothing, we know nothing. We gotta find out why we were set up last night—there's gotta be more to it than the lousy furs."

CHAPTER SIXTEEN

I GOT BACK TO the house at eight, just in time for a typical "meatless Friday" dinner: broiled halibut, eggplant parmigiana, and a tomato, onion, and arugula salad. My father was not particularly religious, but my mother insisted on the basics of a Catholic household: no meat on Friday, Mass on Sunday, fasting during Lent, and an occasional trip to the Rosary Society on Thursday with her super-religious friend Lena Maserelli. Privately, my mother thought Stuff's mother was a bit of a fanatic, as did Stuff's father, who intentionally ignored all the basics. That made his wife crazy, which of course was the point. It was one of those relationships that could flourish only in turmoil.

My parents' relationship was the opposite. It could flourish only in peace and quiet—and it did. My father's lawless, sometimes violent life was kept well away from my mother, and although she was aware of it, it was never discussed.

They had met at a Christmas party given by Tommy Lucchese, the capo of one of New York's five families. My mother's father, Mario DiCairano, had been invited to the party since he was Lucchese's barber. My grandmother had died, so he brought his daughter—my mother, Mickey. At the time, she was seventeen, with olive skin, green eyes, an hourglass figure, and ebony hair that reached her shoulder blades. She was considered a knockout. From the time my father asked her to dance to the time he received Mario's blessings, a year had passed, and it was once again Christmas. They married on Christmas Day and had one son. They said they had loved each other from their first dance.

After dinner my mother was washing dishes and I was drying—still waiting anxiously for my father to broach the subject of the Federated. I wanted him to make the first move, but if he didn't, I'd have to look for the first natural opening. The phone rang, and while my father answered it, there was a soft knock at the door. My mother dried her hands and opened it.

Standing in the hall was a short, slightly built man in his fifties. He was pale and permanently stooped over from long hours at a sewing machine. He wore his glasses low on his nose, a shawl around his neck, a yarmulke on his head, and he held a newspaper under his arm. Sidney's father: Ira Butcher.

"Ah, Mr. Butcher," my mother said warmly in her lilting Sicilian accent, "come in. I just finished the espresso . . . Gino," she called out, "it's Mr. Butcher."

"Thank you, Mrs. Vesta. Espresso would be nice," Mr. Butcher replied in a distinct Eastern European accent. He then turned to me. "Sidney went to the movie with his mother . . . on Friday they give dishes . . ."

My father hung up the phone and rose to greet Mr. Butcher. He shook his hand and said, "Come and sit, Mr. Butcher."

Mr. Butcher turned back to me. "Sidney told us about today . . . Thank you, Vinny."

That stopped my father. "Something I should know about?" he asked.

It seemed like as good an opening as I was going to get. I shrugged dismissively and said, "Nick Colucci. Nothin' serious," then added quickly, "Can I see you for a second, Pop?"

My mother brought Mr. Butcher into the living room, gave him a cup of espresso, and I led my father toward the bedroom.

I lowered my voice and asked, "Well, Pop . . . is it a go?"

"You're sure you can get a boat?"

"Sure as I can be. My guys are good."

"And you're also sure you can put all your eggs in the 'Jill' basket?"

"She's got good reasons to get it right."

"Is that what Terry told you?"

I felt like a tree had just fallen on me. I was more than speechless; it was as if the air had been sucked out of my lungs. My father saw the unspoken question on my face and put me out of my misery. He pointed toward his face.

"I have two eyes here—and two hundred on the street. Also I'm not deaf. I hear things. Tomorrow you can tell me why I hear them." He paused and looked toward my mother and Mr. Butcher sitting in the living room. He caressed the side of his nose with his index finger, and when he had made his decision, he turned back to me. "That was Costello on the phone. He wants to meet me and Angelo at the Copa. He insisted. It could be about last night. I don't know. If it is, then we're right—something was behind the setup, and we have to find out what." He paused, took a deep breath, and slowly let it out. "To-night—be smart. Do it fast and get out. Watch for alarms and the guards—but the biggest danger is Gee-gee. If this Jill girl fails and there are no pictures of him in the morning—you pack a bag. You'll be on your way to your cousins in Palermo until things cool off."

"Right."

He tapped the side of my cheek, and I went back to drying the dishes. He walked into the living room, sat in a wing chair, and opened his newspaper. My mother and Mr. Butcher were sitting opposite him on the couch.

In the few short months since the beginning of summer, my father had become very fond of Mr. Butcher. He knew he was an extremely hardworking tailor and had tried to help him by offering cash for Sidney's "tutoring" of me—but Mr. Butcher would not hear of it. He was a proud man, and his family would make do on what he earned. He said the fact that my father had befriended him and I took care of Sidney was payment enough.

Mr. Butcher opened his newspaper, adjusted his glasses, and began what was now a ritual between him and my father. The *Forward* was the Jewish newspaper, and *Il Progresso* was the Italian newspaper. Both men religiously read their respective journals and constantly discussed opposing opinions. The subject matter changed, but the routine was invariable.

"It says here in the *Forward*," Mr. Butcher began, "that Mr. O'Dwyer might resign."

My father turned the pages of *Il Progresso* and found a similar article. "*Il Progresso* says the mayor wants to be an ambassador."

"Here, too," Mr. Butcher said, indicating his article. "It also says a Mr. Impellitteri then would be the new mayor."

"True," my father answered. "Vincent Impellitteri is head of the council. So he's next."

Mr. Butcher nodded thoughtfully, then said, "Is this good for the Jews?"

It was the question that Mr. Butcher asked whenever there was to be a change in politics, the economy, or anything else that might affect any aspect of Jewish life. My mother studied her husband while he pondered his answer. A few moments later he said, "If anything, Impellitteri is a corkscrew more crooked than O'Dwyer—but he's Italian . . ." He paused and smiled. "And that's always good for the Jews."

Mr. Butcher chuckled, slapped his hands together, and exclaimed, "Hah! It's good for the Jews."

My mother laughed and asked, "More espresso, Mr. Butcher?"

Mr. Butcher held out his cup and said, "Thank you, Mrs. Vesta. That would be nice."

My mother took the cup and went into the kitchen to refill it. Mr. Butcher adjusted his glasses while my father lit a cigarillo.

There was a knock at the door, and my mother went to answer it. Standing in the doorway was Louie, who'd changed into a jumpsuit, sneakers, watch cap, and gloves—all black. Around his neck was a bandanna, also black. My mother smiled knowingly and looked at me. "It's for you." She poured another demitasse cup of espresso for Mr. Butcher, and I went to the door.

"What's with the outfit?" I asked.

"I got tired of wrecking my suits."

"You bring it?" I asked, sure that he had but knowing it was important enough to check.

He held up Johnny DiCarlo's wallet, pulled his lips back over his teeth, and delivered a flawless Bogart: "Here'sh lookin' at you, kid." He smiled and added, "Anything else?"

"Yeah. Pray for a boat."

I slapped Louie on the arm, took the wallet, and called out, "G'night, all . . ."

CHAPTER SEVENTEEN

WHEN LOUIE AND I got back to the van, the river smelled like dead barnacles, the breeze couldn't move dust, and the lights on the Jersey shore were dancing in the haze. It looked peaceful . . . on that side. On this side, anything but.

As Louie got into the rear of the van, I settled into the passenger seat and asked, "Anything?"

Boychick answered, "Nothin'."

"Where's Red?"

"Went for sandwiches."

The Federated Warehouse was lit up like Times Square at midnight, and a large cargo ship was being unloaded on its north quay. Men operating shipboard cranes were lowering wooden crates in rope nets from deck to dock. Human gorillas with vicious hooks stabbed the crates and muscled them onto pallets, while forklift drivers hoisted them up and hustled them into the warehouse. The dockside looked like a traumatized anthill—a panorama of constant motion, growling engines, screeching machinery, and shouted orders. Most of the men were shirtless, and those who weren't had their shirts glued to them by sweat.

At eleven-forty I knew the racket would stop, the floodlights would die, and the men would start wrapping up for the evening. By midnight they'd be gone, and that was when we'd go to work . . . if Benny got the boat—if we could get in from the river—if we could get thirty crates of pelts loaded into the boat—and if the weight didn't sink it. If—if—if.

"You ever have nightmares?" asked Boychick.

"Sometimes . . . yeah," I said. "Why?"

"I had one last night. It was weird."

Red returned with the sandwiches and got in back with Louie. Boychick reached a hand over his shoulder, and Louie slapped a ham and cheese into it.

"What was it about?" I asked.

"I was tryin' ta beat the shit out of my ol' man."

"How come that's a nightmare?" I asked, knowing Boychick's relationship with his father.

"It wasn't. The nightmare part was that every time I knocked him down, he kept bouncin' back up like one of those goddamn plastic 'Shmoos' they got at Coney Island. He wouldn't stay down."

"You're right," agreed Red, "a nightmare."

Boychick unwrapped the waxed paper and took a bite out of his sandwich. He chewed a few times and asked Red, "You ever tried to beat the shit out of your ol' man?"

"No," said Red.

"Why? Ya told me he tries ta beat the shit out of you."

"Right."

"So?"

"If I ever let go, I'd kill him." His switchblade snapped open and he split his sandwich in two with a quick, murderous swipe of the blade.

I exchanged a glance with Louie. We all thought it was possible that Red was a borderline sociopath.

Boychick swallowed hard and murmured, "Jesus . . ."

Red acknowledged the comment with a simple, "Yeah . . ."

I turned back to the front and took a swig of beer. Boychick took another bite of his sandwich, thought for a moment, and said, "Ya know somethin', Red? In a perfect world you wouldn't have ta do nothin'. See, when your ol' man beats the shit out of you, I beat the shit out of my ol' man—and make him beat the shit out of your ol' man."

Red thought about it, then said, "Who beats the shit out of you?"

"Nobody. Like I said, it's a perfect world."

Boychick chuckled—then suddenly became alert. I followed his eyes. A black Chevy sedan had pulled up to the Federated gate and stopped. Two men got out and walked up to the guards. We heard a movement from the back, and Red's head abruptly popped up between Boychick's and mine.

"Fuck!" he growled.

"What?" I asked.

"Fuck! Fuck, and double fuck!"

"What, for chrissake!" Boychick snapped.

"It's my uncles!" said Red.

Danny and Robert Collins, Red's mother's younger brothers, were NYPD detectives who had been on the Mob's pad for years. By routinely allowing gambling, drugs, and prostitution in their precinct, they exploded their detective's salaries by a factor of ten. Their fanatical sister forced them to send some of their dirty money to Ireland, because she didn't care where it came from—she cared only about where it went: "the cause!"

"What the hell are they doin' here?" asked Boychick.

"I dunno . . . but I know they ain't on the job. They work out of the Eighteenth Precinct. And they work vice. This ain't the Eighteenth, and them guards ain't hookers." Red took a deep breath and slouched in the seat. He had just run off four consecutive sentences. For him it was a filibuster.

"Shit . . . so what d'ya figure?" asked Boychick.

"They're on the take. Somebody got to 'em," I said. "Probably Gee-gee."

"You think they're warning 'em there could be a hit tonight?" asked Louie.

"I dunno," I said, "but I don't like the odds against it."

Boychick nodded in agreement and sat silent for a moment. He watched Red's two uncles with the guards and said, "We gonna call it off?"

I thought about it: I'd already gotten a go-ahead from my father—we were both certain that we had to find out what the hell was going on—there was only a *chance* that the guards had been tipped, and maybe they wouldn't figure we'd be coming from the river. The plan had always been a long shot; now it was a little longer. We'd just have to be more careful.

"We can't. We go tonight," I said to Boychick. "Drop Louie and me off at the garage. We'll pick up a spare set of wheels and meet you at the Christopher Street pier. Stuff and Bouncer should be there by now, and Benny should be on the way with a boat."

I checked my watch. It was ten o'clock.

Boychick dropped Louie and me off at an unimpressive auto repair garage on Thirty-eighth Street off Eleventh Avenue. We walked down the alley between the garage and the building next to it. It smelled of old grease, gas fumes, and rust. I unlocked the alleyway door, and we walked in.

There were four cars in the shop. A green 1939 Buick was parked next to a black 1940 Ford—this one a four-door sedan. Both needed washing and were singularly inconspicuous. The Ford belonged to Angelo Maserelli. The Buick belonged to my father. These were their "street cars," the ones that wouldn't attract attention as they went about their daily business along the docks. In a cabinet along the wall, there was a drawer with a false bottom that hid an assortment of license plates for both cars—all of them registered to residents of Holy Cross Cemetery.

Behind the "street cars" were two other cars, a new Cadillac and a new Chrysler convertible—also belonging to my father and Angelo, respectively. These were the cars that came out when they knew they wouldn't be observed. They were used for drives to their luxurious homes outside the city—listed, of course, under their wives' maiden names. Although many Mob members lived dual lives to avoid drawing unwanted attention, to my father, pursuing anonymity was a religion. He had witnessed what the sting of notoriety had done to Luciano, and he stressed the lesson to everyone in his crew. Unlike the flamboyant Gee-gee Petrone and Joseph "Joe Adonis" Doto, or the equally well-known Costello, my father had set up an elaborate front and insisted his soldiers do the same. In my father's case, it was our tenement on Thirty-sixth Street that masked a six-figure income and a farm in Connecticut. For Angelo, it was the apartment on Thirty-sixth Street off Tenth Avenue that covered for a small mansion in Spring Lake, on the Jersey shore.

Louie went to the front of the garage and pulled up the overhead door while I made a quick phone call. Louie returned and we put an assortment of tools into a leather satchel. I made a final check of the shop, got into the Ford, and pulled out. Louie closed the overhead and got in beside me.

"It's set," I said. "Jill got the pictures, and Terry's friend will pick them up tonight. We'll have the prints in the morning . . . all that's left is the boat."

"What happens if we can't get a boat?"

"We go to plan B."

"What's plan B?" asked Louie.

"I have no fuckin' idea."

"Good. For a minute there I thought we could be in trouble."

Louie put the Ford in gear, and we headed for the Christopher Street pier.

CHAPTER EIGHTEEN

ABOUT THE TIME Louie and I were headed for our rendezvous at the pier, my father was entering the Copacabana at 10 East Sixtieth Street. It was almost eleven o'clock when he took off his hat and handed it to Terry.

"Good evening, Mr. Vesta," she said pleasantly, fighting to control her nerves.

My father smiled and nodded. "Terry . . ." He could see she was trying, but it was obvious she was tense.

Louis Antonio rushed over immediately. "Gino," he said, "your party's here. They're waiting for you."

The club was crowded for the first show on a typical Friday night. On stage, Jerry Vale was singing "Al Di La." Louis took my father aside and lowered his voice.

"Something's going on. With the kids. You know what's going on?"

"What did you hear?"

"Nothing, really. Except Louie left the house like he hit a four-way parlay. He's never that happy unless he's made a score."

"I know what it is," my father told him. "It should be fine."

"You sure?"

"I'm never sure," was my father's answer. "I trust my son."

Louis's head snapped down in a single nod of acceptance, and he led my father toward the tables, where he exchanged greetings with various members of all five New York families.

Friday nights at the Copa were "Mob's night out." Wives were unwelcome. Trophy girlfriends appeared and replaced them like pop-up dolls. It was a tradition that went back to the days of the old "Mustache Petes." On any given Friday night at the Copa, you would see some of the most beautiful women in the city on the arms of some of the most powerful wiseguys in the outfit. They were joined by politicians, movies stars, and sports figures—who all wanted to be seen in the company of the glamorous underworld.

Angelo had arrived ahead of my father and was seated with two sharply dressed men at a prime table. Angelo looked like a block of granite holding a wineglass. There were no women with them.

The three got up and greeted my father as he arrived. The older of the two men with Angelo was the acting capo of the Luciano family, Frank Costello. He had held the position for the last five years—ever since the notorious Lucky Luciano had been deported to Sicily after World War II. The second man was Joseph Doto, famous for his movie star looks and known to the world as "Joe Adonis." He also headed the gambling operations of the family and was one of the silent owners of the Copa.

The crowd erupted in applause as Jerry Vale finished "Al Di La" and began "On an Evening in Roma." Once they were seated and Adonis had poured my father a glass of red wine, Costello began.

"You heard about this Kefauver thing?"

My father acknowledged, "I read in the paper it was a committee."

"A goddamn organized crime committee," Adonis growled.

"The word is we're gonna take some heat," said Costello.

"It's happened before," said my father.

"Local. We can handle local. This thing's federal," said Costello.

My father looked at Adonis, then back to Costello. This wasn't a casual conversation. When they had called him unexpectedly and asked for the meeting, they said it was to "touch base." Not so. With the mention of Kefauver, he knew our suspicions were valid: Costello had heard that trouble might be brewing between him and Gee-gee Petrone. The conversation would reveal that they didn't yet know what it was—or about my failed hit on the railroad yard—but it became obvious that they had called the meeting to ward off a "family feud."

My father and Petrone were from two different families. Petrone was in Costello's family and reported to Costello's underboss, Vito Genovese. My father was in the Mangano family and reported to Mangano's underboss, Albert Anastasia. Costello hated Mangano but was a close friend of Anastasia's, and over the years Costello had become very fond of my father. Had it not been for his friendship and respect for Anastasia, Costello would have tried to lure him away. Because of this, my father knew that what was coming would be a friendly warning.

"Is there something I should know?" he asked.

Costello nodded to Adonis, and he explained, "We hear that there's bad blood between you and Gee-gee Petrone. Anastasia's in Europe, and we all know Mangano is a clueless pussy—so we're worried it might get out of hand. You gotta know if that happened, it would come at a bad time."

Costello leaned forward and clasped his hands on the table. "Gino . . . you know why the Commission is concerned. Right now even Hoover and the FBI deny we exist. But this committee thing is gonna get a lot of ink. Anything any of us do to draw more attention will be magnified ten times. Whatever your dispute with Petrone—and I don't care what it is, I hate the sonofabitch—for your own sake, you have to end it."

"I understand," my father said as evenly as he could. "And I thank you for your concern . . . I give you my word I will not make an unprovoked move on Petrone. But he has already made one on me, and I suspect there will be more."

Costello and Adonis exchanged glances. My father's use of the word *unprovoked* was not lost on them.

Costello sighed and said, "Protect yourself, Gino, but use your head. If it goes bad for you, neither Anastasia nor I will be able to protect you . . ." He leaned back in his chair. "In the meantime, the Commission will make it clear to Petrone that it is not in his best interest to provoke a confrontation."

"With all respect, I wish I shared your confidence that he will listen."

A waiter appeared, poured the last of the wine, and pointed to the bottle. Adonis signaled yes. The interruption allowed my father's attention to be drawn to the entryway.

A very sexy girl carrying a small suitcase was handing a package to Terry. He smiled to himself—it appeared that a vital part of my plan might have gone well—and enjoyed the prospect of Gee-gee Petrone's horror when he saw his bare ass hovering over Silvana Pisano's naked body.

As if to approve of his thought, the crowd erupted in applause and Jerry Vale took his bows.

CHAPTER NINETEEN

BOYCHICK WAS NERVOUSLY lighting a Camel when Louie and I drove onto the pier and got out. He was facing north, staring up the Hudson River. Red was sitting on the van's front fender, casually flipping his switchblade. But I didn't see Stuff, Bouncer, Benny, or a boat, and that worried me. "No sign yet?" I asked.

"Nothin'," said Boychick. He took another deep drag on his Camel and looked back upriver. At the end of the pier we were fairly isolated, but the streetlamps threw more light than I would have liked. The sky was overcast and the moon hidden, and I thought, Good . . . at least we caught a little break. The last thing we needed was a full moon while we were breaking into the back of the warehouse from a boat on the river.

Boychick turned to Red and asked, "What time ya got?"

Red didn't bother checking his watch. "Two minutes since last time. Eleven-thirty."

"What about Stuff and Bouncer?" I asked, becoming even more concerned.

"Same as Benny," Boychick answered.

"Something must've held them up," said Louie.

I nodded. There was still time, if Benny showed up soon.

"Whaddaya wanna do?" asked Boychick.

"Wait," I said.

"Ya think he'll make it?" Louie asked.

"He'll make it," said Boychick.

"Anybody can do it," I said, "he can."

Boychick decided he'd had enough of the Camel and flicked it out into the black water, where it died with a hiss.

"Yeah," he agreed, "Benny ain't one ta throw in the towel." He turned back to us. "Ya know, if I turn pro, he wants to be my trainer."

"So I heard," said Louie. "He thinks we should all have somethin' legit going. He's probably right."

"I think he just wants to be sure that whatever he does, it's with us," said Boychick. "We're all he's got."

Boychick turned and looked back upriver. Red and I moved alongside him, and I noticed Boychick's cigarette butt moving away from us. Good, I thought, the tide's coming in. It would be with us on the way to the Federated. I figured we'd caught another break.

Louie leaned against the van's fender and lit a cigarillo. No one said anything for a while.

Boychick popped his jaw upriver and asked, "You ever think about what it would be like to be Benny?"

I asked, "How so?"

"Bein' black and all. A father who's a basket case and a mother who's a druggie. Christ, it almost makes ya feel like we been lucky."

"He's fucked, but we ain't been lucky," said Red.

"Yeah . . ." Boychick thought for a moment and said, "Sometimes I wonder what it would be like ta be . . . like normal. Like in the flicks."

Our number one passion in those days before television came of age was the movies. Louie loved gangster movies, Stuff loved comedies,

Benny loved westerns, Bouncer loved biblical movies, I liked most of them, and Red hated most of them—but Boychick loved musicals. They painted the perfect world he had always dreamed about. He knew that world didn't exist—especially for him—but it didn't matter. He loved "Boy meets girl, boy loses girl, boy gets girl, and everyone lives happily ever after." He loved them all, from *42nd Street* to *Oklahoma!*— but he had one special favorite.

"Ya remember *Meet Me in St. Louis?*" he asked.

I nodded. "Sure. Judy Garland."

"Right . . . there was this great father and mother—kids—a nice house where everybody loved everybody else . . . and there's the guy who's the boy next door—who meets Judy onna trolley—and they fall in love . . . you know—it's kinda like what ya think heaven might be like . . ."

Red looked at Boychick as if he had just dropped in from Mars. "You okay?"

"Yeah . . . why?" asked Boychick.

"You sound like a fuckin' idiot."

Before Boychick could answer, Stuff's voice called out from the street. "Yo!" We turned and saw him jogging toward us with Bouncer lagging behind, trying to keep up. For a big man, Stuff moved pretty quickly, and like a lot of big men, he was light on his feet. We'd seen Jackie Gleason at the Adams Theater in Newark, and he immediately became Stuff's idol. He loved the way Gleason glided across the stage with an "Awaaay we go!" He could match the move—not as good, but damn near. They were both puffing and very agitated when they got to us. They were sweating, but Bouncer's clothes were soaking wet.

"He here yet?" asked Stuff, out of breath.

"No. What happened?" Boychick asked.

"You ain't gonna believe it," said Stuff, still trying to catch his breath.

"You didn't get the boat?" Boychick snapped.

"We got the boat," said Stuff.

"Then where the hell is it?" asked Boychick. He was getting frustrated, and so was I.

As calmly as possible, I asked, "Stuff . . . what happened?"

He took a deep breath and let it out. "We did the diversion—got the guard out and Benny in . . ." He took another breath. "He got a boat—started the outboard engine and headed out . . ."

Boychick exploded with, "Will ya get to it! What the hell happened?"

"The engine quit," Stuff replied.

"What?" yelled Boychick.

"The engine—it just died," said Stuff.

Bouncer confirmed the fact with vigorous nods of his head and kept bouncing on the balls of his feet. "D-died," he repeated, and snapped his fingers. "J-just like that."

Stuff said, "We saw Benny keep tryin' to restart it . . . pullin' the shit out of that little rope thing on top of the engine, but it won't start—and he's floatin' *up* the fuckin' river! The tide's got 'im!" So much for catching a break, I thought. Stuff took another deep breath and let it out. "We chased him halfway to the goddamn GW Bridge—all the way up Riverside Park. He was still pretty close to shore, so we figured there was a chance we could snag him. Once we almost did. I was anchorin' Bouncer from shore—their fingers were almost touchin' . . . then Bouncer let go of me and fell in."

"I a-almost h-had him," said Bouncer. Boychick threw him a look that could melt marble.

Stuff finished with, "Then he finally got the goddamn engine started and headed back downriver. We grabbed a cab and came back here."

"How long ago?" Boychick asked.

"About a half hour," said Stuff.

"It ain't that far," said Louie. "Where the hell is he?"

The answer came with the rumble of an outboard engine. We rushed to the edge of the pier and saw a white, thirty-two-foot sailboat pulling alongside. The sail was furled, and Benny was standing in the cockpit, ready to throw us a line. When the boat brushed a piling, Benny cut the outboard engine and threw the line. Red caught it and wrapped it around a cleat. Boychick was aghast.

"A sailboat! You stole a fuckin' sailboat?"

"Hey, man. Was all there was at the end of the dock," Benny yelled from the cockpit. "Where you think I got it—in a goddamn show-room, where I get to pick and choose?"

"It's white!"

"It was white when I got it! Where you think I got time to paint it?" said Benny, climbing out.

"And it's got a goddamn mast," said Boychick, pointing to it.

Benny put his hands on his hips and yelled back, "It's a goddamn sailboat! They all got a goddamn mast!"

"But it's stickin' up like a fuckin' beacon!" Boychick screamed. "They could see us pullin' up behind the warehouse!"

"M-maybe we could saw down the mast," said Bouncer, trying to be helpful.

"It's metal," said Benny.

"How's the engine?" I asked.

"Good, once I unflood the sucker."

I said, "The boat's too small for all of us and the furs, and I've been thinkin' we may need a truck to haul the crates . . . Boychick, take Red and Bouncer and do your repo yard number on a truck. The rest of us'll take the boat and hit the warehouse. We're in right after the guard finishes his midnight rounds, and out before he makes the one o'clock tour. Have the truck here by one-thirty . . ." I paused and scanned the group. "Any questions?"

They all exchanged glances and shook their heads. Boychick punched his palm with his fist and said, "Let's do it!"

I shoved out my palm-down hand; they stacked theirs on mine, and

Boychick yelled, "Yes!" We broke off the ritual, I picked up the satchel
and led Louie and Stuff down into the boat. Benny untied it, jumped
in, and started the engine. As we pulled away, the mast rocked back
and forth as if it were waving good-bye. Boychick still couldn't believe
it. He said, "A goddamn white sailboat. The way things are goin',
they'll hit a fuckin' coral reef in the middle of the river."

CHAPTER TWENTY

RATHER THAN CRUISING up the New York side
of the river, I had Benny cross closer to the Jersey side. When we
got directly across the river from the Federated Warehouse, we
turned and came straight in behind it. I figured the building would
block the telltale mast and we'd arrive unnoticed. Unfortunately, this
took longer than I'd planned. Louie saw me checking my watch and
asked, "We okay?"

"Twelve twenty-five," I said. "Not a disaster, but I figure at least ten
minutes behind."

The concrete walkway behind the warehouse was six feet off the
water and eight feet wide. It connected the loading docks on either side
of the building and allowed the guard to drive his cart completely
around the warehouse on his hourly rounds.

Benny cut the engine, and we coasted up to the walkway. I levered
myself onto it, then reached down and helped up Stuff and Louie.
Benny handed them the leather satchel and a line, and Louie tied off the

boat. I noted the mast sticking fifteen feet up above the walkway and shook my head. Anyone who came around either corner might miss the boat, but they would never miss the mast.

There was a row of casement windows across the back of the building four feet wide and three feet high. Each had a lever lock at the top and was hinged in the middle. That was the way we'd have to break in.

Stuff opened the bag and handed me a hammer and a flashlight. No one said anything as I carefully ran the light around the outer perimeter of the window, looking for telltale wires. Satisfied there were none, we all pulled on gloves and I held the light while Stuff got out a roll of tape and taped the glass directly under the lever lock. When he was finished I handed him the hammer, and he gave the taped window a quick, sharp blow. With the tape holding it in place, the glass shattered but didn't fall. Stuff carefully removed the shards, then reached in and unlocked the window. Louie, the thinnest of us, slithered through, and Benny handed him a pair of wrenches. Within minutes the hinges were history, and the three of us on the outside gingerly lifted out the window and leaned it against the building.

A few night-lights lit the dim interior, and we could make out long rows of containers in various sizes stacked on pallets. The rows extended all the way to the front of the warehouse. After a comparatively cool ride up the river, the heat inside the warehouse hammered us. It was stifling, and we immediately started to sweat. The time was 12:29 a.m.

"Spread out," I said. "When you see the fur crates . . . whistle."

We spread out and began walking down the long, parallel rows. Identifying the furs would be no problem—they would be in their six-by-two-by-two-foot crates. Finding them was a different story. Everything imaginable was in here: generators from England, whiskey from Scotland, furniture from Spain, and hopefully the sable pelts from wherever the hell they came from.

About ten minutes later I heard a low whistle from my left and quickly moved toward it, meeting Benny and Louie on the way. Two more whistles and we found Stuff ruefully staring up at a stack of the long, skinny crates. The stack was twelve feet high. There was no question these were the fur crates, but it would be a bitch getting them down, through the window, and into the boat.

I said, "Stuff, find a dolly. We'll put Benny up top." I pointed to a nearby stepladder. "Louie, you're in the middle—halfway up that ladder. Benny, you slide the crates down to Louie. Louie, you ease them down to me and I'll stack them until we get the dolly. We've got half an hour."

Stuff went off to search, Benny climbed to the top of the crates, and Louie retrieved the ladder. He climbed halfway up and reached out his hands. Benny tilted down the first of the crates, but he let it go before Louie had a good grip on it. Louie's hands slipped, and the crate slid down the front of his body, shot through my hands, and crashed between my legs. I quickly wrapped my arms around it before it could tilt over and crash a second time, but the racket from the initial impact sounded like a sledgehammer hitting a garbage can.

The three of us froze. Our eyes darted from side to side as the crash reverberated through the building. For several seconds there was no other sound—just a fading echo and then complete silence. None of us moved. We looked like a painting. A few moments later, I heard the sound of rollers and Stuff rounded the corner with a four-by-eight-foot dolly. He was livid.

"Assholes! What the fuck was that?"

"We dropped a crate," said Louie.

"You made me shit my pants!"

"Shhhhh! Keep it down!" Louie growled in a stage whisper.

"You want *me* to keep it down? You just woke the fuckin' dead!"

"Knock it off!" I said. "Stuff, run up front and see if the guards are movin'."

"Okay, but I gotta find a toilet."

"Go, goddamn it—we might all be in the toilet!"

Stuff grunted and took off in a kind of waddle. I looked up at Benny. "Okay, Benny . . . one more time. Carefully!" I checked my watch as the second crate started down. It was 12:35 . . . twenty-five minutes before the guard would round the back of the building, spot the mast, and discover the missing window. My heartbeat went from tango to samba.

When we had loaded the dolly with thirty crates stacked five feet high, there was still no sign of Stuff. Louie, Benny, and I pushed it up to the windowless opening, where Louie and Benny slipped out and I started handing Louie the crates. He passed them to Benny, who stacked them next to the boat. It was a bucket brigade with crates. I was handing out the last of them when Stuff rushed up behind me.

"Where the hell've you been?" I asked.

"Standing on a toilet," he gasped. "I got trapped in the stall when a guard came in to take a piss."

"I'm not gonna dignify that answer with another question," I said. "C'mon."

I made sure to drop DiCarlo's stolen wallet next to the window, and we crawled out. I jumped in the boat and again checked my watch: 12:52. "We've got less than ten minutes," I said. "Stuff, hit the corner and keep an eye out."

This time the crate brigade was from me to Louie to Benny, who stored them in the cabin. Stuff walked up next to me and watched for a moment. Louie looked up and sniffed the air. "You smell like shit," he said.

"*Now* I smell like shit. Before you dropped that goddamn crate I smelled fine!" He stalked off toward the corner of the building, then suddenly came running back, waving his arms frantically. "He's comin'! The guard's on his way!" he yelled.

"We need a couple more minutes," I barked. "Stop him."

"What? How?"

"How the fuck do I know? Sit on him—just stop him!"

We hurried the loading, and Stuff rushed back to the corner of the building and peeked around the edge. The guard was no more than twenty-five yards away and closing fast. Stuff plastered himself up against the wall, made the sign of the cross, and held his breath.

Just as the guard started to make the turn, Stuff jumped out in front of the cart, threw his arms in the air, and screeched like a banshee. The startled guard recoiled and instinctively swerved to avoid a collision—and a split second later he sailed off the narrow walkway and plunged into the murky water. He was screaming all the way to the splash.

I passed down the last of the crates and untied the boat as Stuff ran back and jumped to the deck. I followed him in. "Nice work," I said.

"Ditto," said Louie, and gave him a quick pat on the back—then sniggered and held his nose.

Benny giggled and started the outboard.

The infuriated guard had surfaced and resumed his screaming. He was so panicked, I'm not sure he saw us pulling away—or the mast waving its good-bye.

We turned downriver and headed back to the Christopher Street pier.

There were two men in a nondescript car who did see the mast. They were parked on the end of Twenty-fourth Street, facing the warehouse, in the same spot we had occupied during our stakeout. My father and Angelo Maserelli—they had been watching the guards at the Federated Warehouse since midnight. If the guards had reacted to a robbery in progress, our two fathers would have been across the street and into the building in a heartbeat.

The weather cooled and a light fog settled in as we passed Thirteenth Street. By the time we approached the pier on Christopher Street, I could barely make out the other boats on the river. I finally spotted Red, Boychick, and Bouncer anxiously peering upriver from about forty yards away and got ready to throw out a line.

"You get 'em?" Boychick called out.

"Thirty, count 'em, thirty," I called back, and threw Red the line.

"Bouncer, get the truck," said Boychick.

Benny cut the outboard engine, and we drifted the last few feet to the pier. Red tied off the bow, and I hopped out of the boat to tie off the stern. Benny immediately began hauling the crates out of the cabin and handing them to Louie, who handed them to me. Fascinated by the activity, Bouncer stood and stared until Boychick noticed he hadn't gone for the truck. "Bouncer, quit gawkin' and get the truck!" he yelled.

"I was just lookin'," Bouncer objected, hurt.

Boychick held up his hands and said gently, "Bouncer . . . I'm sorry. Just get the truck and back it up."

Bouncer still didn't move, "A-a-ll I w-w-was—"

"Will you please just get the goddamn truck!"

"Right," said Bouncer, and scurried back to the street.

Stuff climbed out of the boat to help with the unloading, and Boychick sniffed the air. "You smell like you shit your pants."

"I did shit my pants!" Stuff snarled, and pointed at Louie, Benny, and me. "You can ask them why!"

We continued unloading, and a few minutes later Bouncer backed up a two-and-a-half-ton bobtail truck. Both sides and the rear doors were emblazoned with the logo FRATELLO'S FRESH FISH.

"Christ!" exclaimed Louie, turning up his nose. "That truck smells worse than Stuff!"

"There was no *Chanel* truck available," Boychick said sarcastically.

Bouncer got out of the truck, opened the rear doors, and jumped in. Boychick handed him the first crate, and I said, "As soon as we're loaded, Benny'll push off the boat. Whoever finds it'll probably think it slipped its tie at the marina. The rest of you'll take the truck to the garage. Louie and I will take the car and meet you there. We'll paint out the fish logo, change the plates, and stash the truck there overnight.

Noon tomorrow we meet at Benny's. I'll have the pictures. We'll pick up the truck and deliver the furs and photos to Gee-gee and Touch."

"You figure maybe Gee-gee might try somethin' when he sees those pictures?" asked Boychick.

The million-dollar question. There was no way Gee-gee was going to go quietly into the gentle night.

"Sure," I said. "He'll try to kill me."

CHAPTER TWENTY-ONE

BY THE TIME I arrived back home, it was almost four a.m. I opened the door and reacted to the distinct aroma of a DiNapoli cigar. The famous Italian lung busters were narrow at both ends and fat in the middle. You cut them in half and lit the fat end. In a no-wind condition they announced your presence to anyone within a city block. In the unlit living room I could see the dim glow of the DiNapoli's tip and knew my father was waiting up for me.

He greeted me with, "So . . . it went well?"

"We got the thirty crates," I said.

"Good." He was sitting in his wing chair in his shirtsleeves with his cuffs rolled up and his tie pulled down. The .45 was on an end table next to the chair. "No problems?" he asked, and puffed his cigar.

"There was one thing . . . Red's two uncles—the cops—showed up at the warehouse about ten-thirty. It ain't their beat."

My father knew who Red's uncles were, and he knew they were dirty. "Gee-gee . . ." It was a flat, unambiguous statement.

"That's what we were thinkin'. It could be."

"It is. Those two are vice, in the Eighteenth. They're bought by Genovese, and Genovese owns Gee-gee. He tried to set you up— again!"

I shrugged. "It didn't work."

"Yet," he said. He ran his index finger along the side of his nose, thought for a few moments, and said, "But now we know. First he orders forty crates of fur pelts—then the cops show up before you can get them. A fluke? Maybe. Then he insists on the rest by tomorrow, from the only place they are available—Drago's warehouse. Another fluke? Possible. But then two dirty cops on Genovese's payroll show up. Three flukes? No. A very big setup—and not about a few crates of fur."

"Maybe it's like I said, he's tryin' to get to you?"

My father nodded and mused. "But why? Genovese doesn't care about me. He wants Costello. How does this help? And why now? Because Anastasia is in Italy? Maybe. What we do know is that he's coming at me—and he's using you."

"He made a mistake. Tomorrow I nail him with Silvana Pisano."

"Maybe . . . but I don't think so. He'll see the pictures, go wild— then figure a way out. Even if he has to whack her husband . . . like in the Bible."

"Huh?"

My father smiled. "David did it to Bathsheba's husband. He wanted the wife, so he killed the husband."

"Cute."

He nodded. "But effective. What we need is to jump one step ahead, then move before he gets to where we are."

"What about the furs?" I asked.

"Deliver them—with the pictures. Angelo and a few of the boys will go with you."

I started to object. "Pop . . ."

"They'll wait outside, but they'll make sure they're noticed," he said, overriding me. "You and the boys go in with the truck. Gee-gee will know Angelo's outside. That will stop him from doing something stupid."

"This is gonna get serious, isn't it."

"It could. I'm sure it's about Costello and Genovese. But somehow, we're in the middle."

"I'm sorry, Pop."

"Not your fault." He tried to console me. "If not this, then something else." He snubbed out the cigar and got up. "Later we talk about Terry. For now, go see your friend on the fire escape. He's been waiting for you all night."

"Thanks, Pop."

He got up and embraced me, "*Buona notte*—and remember what I said about your mother." He pinched my cheek and left.

I watched him walk toward the bedroom, then climbed out the window to the fire escape. The overcast sky had cleared and a bright moon threw a shaft of silver across the neighborhood. The fog had lifted and nothing was moving . . . no cars, no people. Even the pigeons were asleep. It was still in the low eighties, but Sidney had covered himself with a sheet and was lying on his back. He seemed to be asleep, so I decided not to wake him and started back inside.

"I'm awake," said Sidney. He got into a sitting position and slid over to the side of his fire escape.

I squatted next to the side of mine and said, "Christ, Sidney, it's four in the mornin'."

"I know," he said. "I couldn't sleep."

I sat and leaned against wall. "The asthma again?"

"Uh-uh. I've been worried."

I chuckled. "You're beginnin' to sound like the Bounce."

"That's what started it—what he told me," he said sadly.

"About what?" I asked.

"I asked him about what happened today," said Sidney, "When we came out of the library."

"Colucci?"

"He told me about why he's so mad at you. It's because of me."

I spun toward him and practically yelled out, "What!"

He turned his head to look at me. "You're not doing what you're supposed to because of all the time you're spending with me."

"He said that?" This time I was yelling.

"Don't be mad at him . . . he was just trying to help."

I couldn't believe it—no, actually, I could believe it. Bouncer was as clueless as Sidney was smart. If he wasn't my cousin, I would've throttled him . . . but then again, if he wasn't my cousin, he wouldn't be around in the first place. I held my breath and my temper. Whatever was done was done, and I couldn't reverse it. All I could do was try to set Sidney straight.

"Look, Sidney," I said as calmly as possible, "what happened with Nick Colucci was about me—not you. There's a lot going on right now. You heard me mention Touch Grillo. He's a bad guy—and I'm in a situation with him. It could be about that—I don't know. I do know the move today was supposed to scare us. If we're scared, he wins. You want him to win?"

"No. I just don't want you to lose."

"You really think he can take me?" I said, feigning astonishment.

"I don't want him to try. I know it's because of me. Even my pop knows. He said there have been Nick Coluccis around for centuries."

"Sidney, listen to me. You're my friend. You're not like any friend I ever had. You showed me things I never heard about and taught me things I never knew. Nobody—not Nick or a hundred Nicks—is gonna stop us hangin' out. Now that's the end of it, and we don't bring it up again."

Sidney started to tear up but made one final effort. "Okay, Vinny, if you say so—but maybe, just for a little while, we won't go to the library."

"Agreed!" I announced. "We won't go tomorrow!"

"Tomorrow's *Saturday*."

"I know that."

"We never go on Saturday."

"I know that, too."

Sidney stared at me a few moments as it sank in. Then the corners of his mouth curled up and he broke into a grin—then a chuckle—and then a full-blown laugh.

I joined him, and a few moments later lights started popping on in the adjacent windows.

CHAPTER TWENTY-TWO

SATURDAY, AUGUST 26

I WOKE UP EXHAUSTED. We hadn't finished removing the logo and repainting the fish truck until three a.m.—and after the talks with my father and Sidney, I hadn't slept worth a damn. I tossed and turned until eight, gave up, took an ice cold shower, and called Benny. He reported that he couldn't sleep, either, and that Boychick and Bouncer had shown up with fresh Danish at eight-thirty because *they* couldn't sleep. No word yet from Stuff or Louie, but I figured everyone was pretty stressed. The possible exception would be Red . . . nothing shook him. He'd probably sleep until noon. I told Benny I'd wake up Red, then round up Louie and Stuff, and we'd all meet around nine-thirty.

The large apartment above O'Mara's Irish Pub had a kitchen, a dining room, and a hallway off the living room that led to three bedrooms and two baths. At the end of the hallway there was a door that led to a back staircase and the alley. The apartment was comfortable and nicely furnished and reflected the fact that the pub was a successful business. Of course, Red hated it.

I wanted to avoid Red's father, so I took the back staircase up to the apartment and let myself in. The door was unlocked because Red's mother knew Red usually came home with the dawn and she didn't want him trouncing by their bedroom. Red's father was a light sleeper, and she wanted to avoid any confrontation.

As soon as I opened the door, I became aware of the pungent aroma of boiled cabbage and heard the sound of an alarm clock. The alarm was coming from Red's bedroom—the first door on the left. I opened it and saw Red spread-eagle on his back, snoring like an elephant. The alarm was loud enough to resurrect the dead, but Red kept snoring. He was in his shorts, the bed was disheveled, and a fan on the bedside table was slowly blowing back and forth across his sweaty body. Because Saturday was the pub's delivery day, Red had set the alarm for nine a.m., but he'd slept right through it. Like I figured, the prior night's events hadn't rattled him at all.

I shut off the alarm and shook him awake. He opened his eyes, taking a second to focus. I told him we were going to meet the gang at Benny's. He nodded, got up, and walked into the bathroom. No "Hello," no "How are ya," no reaction. I heard him turn on the shower and sat down to wait. There was a copy of *Guns and Ammo* on the bedside table. I picked it up and flicked through a few pages. A couple of minutes later Red came back out, drying himself off. I heard the sound of metal on the sidewalk and looked out the window. The liquor delivery truck was in the alley, and the driver was rolling aluminum beer kegs down the truck's metal ramp and lining them up next to the cellar stairs. The temperature was already in the high eighties, and the humidity wasn't far behind. It's going to be hell humping twenty beer kegs down into the cellar in this heat, I thought. The kegs were part of a typical Saturday morning delivery that also included several dozen cases of whiskey and soda.

Red had been wrestling them into the cellar ever since he was twelve. It was one more reason he hated the place.

I'd left the bedroom door open, and while Red threw on a T-shirt and slacks we heard his mother and father begin arguing in the kitchen. Molly O'Mara was in her late forties. She carried a bit more weight than she'd have liked, but you could see she had been, and still was, a very attractive woman. She had an oval face, strawberry blond hair, and startling green eyes that seemed to flash when she was angry. She also had a voice that could stop a truck.

Molly was on one of her tirades. It was about her favorite subject, and she was delivering it with fierce intensity. According to Red, even though his father knew it wouldn't work, he kept on trying to reason her.

"Molly," Colin said, "it's just the way yer goin' about it, that's—"

"I'll do whatever I damn please," she shouted, "and whatever it takes ta get those boys fightin' in Belfast what they need! And I don't need you tellin' me how ta do it!" We heard her fist slam down on the table.

"All I'm sayin' is—the customers are really gettin' pissed at yer tactics," said Colin, trying to placate her.

"They wouldn't have to be pissed if they'd do the right thing and spend less on the booze and more on the cause!"

"Ya can't go around tellin' their women it's a sin to go to bed with their husbands until they send some money to bloody Ireland!"

"The hell I can't, and the hell I won't!"

Colin yelled in frustration, "Does it ever dawn on you that the money they're *not* sendin' to Ireland they're *spendin'* downstairs?"

Red glanced at me and shrugged like it was no big deal. I didn't want to get into it with Colin, so I told him I'd wait for him in the bedroom, then help him hump the beer kegs into the cellar.

He nodded an okay and asked, "Coffee?"

"Black," I replied, and he nodded again. From the time I woke him up to the time he left the room, his entire conversation with me consisted of one word: "Coffee?" I peeked around his bedroom door and looked down the hallway, across the living room, and into the kitchen.

Colin and Molly were still yelling at each other when Red walked into the kitchen and started pouring coffee into a large paper cup. He didn't look at or say anything to either one of them. Colin saw him and shifted his anger from Molly to Red. "Ah! Another country heard from. And where the hell were you all night?"

He answered wearily, "It was hot. I went for a walk."

"A walk my ass!" said Colin.

"Watch yer language," said Molly.

"*My* language?" Colin screamed.

A very loud buzzer interrupted them. It was the front door, and it was insistent. Colin went to answer it. Standing on the landing were Danny and Robert Collins, Molly's brothers, the NYPD detectives. Both were in their mid-forties and wore suits with a bulge under their armpits, snap-brim hats, and brogans. Danny was bullnecked and overweight, and he had a flat nose. Robert had thick shoulders, long legs, and a flat belly. They shared their sister's strawberry blond hair and green eyes, but their green eyes had a mean look about them and they both were known as sadistic bastards. They had no use for Colin, and he had less for them.

"It's yer brothers," he said, stepping aside. "Why in the hell don't you get them to contribute more of their *not*-so-hard-earned money to the bloody cause and leave my damn customers alone."

The brothers crossed the living room and went into the kitchen without acknowledging either Colin or Molly. Red was pouring coffee into a second paper cup when Danny spun him around. Danny, who was the older and more callous of the two, got into Red's face and braced him. "Where were you last night?" he snapped.

"What's this about, then?" asked Molly.

"The Federated Warehouse was robbed last night," said Danny, still looking at Red. "We have it on good authority that your son and his mates were in the area."

"There it is!" Colin roared at Red. "I told ya no good would come of hangin' with those guinea hoods!"

Oh shit, I thought, we were right. When we saw them last night they were tipping off the guards . . . but why the hell didn't the guards buy it?

"I was shootin' pool," said Red, calm as a millpond.

"Where?" asked Robert.

"Benny Veal's place."

"Bullshit," Danny barked.

"I thought ya said ya went for a walk," said Colin.

"I did," said Red. "To Benny's."

Christ! I thought. Red says fuck-all, but what he says usually comes out smart-ass. He hands that to these two pricks, they'll tear him a new asshole.

"Who's Benny?" asked Molly.

"A nigger kid that's one of the Icemen—like your son," said Danny.

"Who was there?" asked Robert.

"All of us. It was a tournament."

"More bullshit," snarled Danny. "Look, kid"—he, leaned toward Red until they were nose to nose—"we're gonna nail your pals' asses to a wall. You got a choice. You go up on the wall with 'em or you tell us what went down last night."

"Okay," said Red. "I lost the tournament. To Benny . . . fuckin' nigger's really good."

Oh shit, I thought. There it was. He couldn't resist.

I felt the air get heavy, and the apartment suddenly got very quiet. I knew there was no way those two cops would ever take that kind of lip. I figured Red was gonna need some help, so I spun out of the bedroom. I started down the hallway for the kitchen just in time to see Danny's face go crimson as he launched himself at Red and grabbed his shirt.

Molly tried to stop him. *"Danny!"* she screamed.

Robert jumped in to separate them before it went any further, and I stopped before crossing the living room. Danny pushed his brother away and thrust his finger under Red's nose. "That's it for you, you wise-ass prick! From now on I don't know you. You're just another punk who needs to be squashed. I catch you in anythin'—*anythin'*— you're goin' down hard!"

He wheeled and stormed out of the kitchen, across the living room, and out the front door. Robert shook his head at Red, glanced at Molly, and left the kitchen. When Danny had crossed the living room, he hadn't seen me, but Robert had. He stopped, we locked eyes, and he gave me a bitter grin. He left without closing the door.

Great, I thought, one more nail in the coffin.

No one in the kitchen said anything for a few moments. Molly and Colin just stared at Red. Finally Colin growled, "Well? What have ya got ta say fer yerself?"

Red said, "The beer's in the sun." He picked up the paper cups and started out.

"That's it?" Colin shouted. "After bein' accused of a bloody robbery? *'The beer's in the sun'?*"

Red said, "Yeah . . . the kegs could explode." He walked out and left Colin and Molly staring at each other. He met me in the hall and handed me my coffee. Colin and Molly never saw me. As we walked out the back door, I heard Colin scream, "The hospital's the culprit—I'm sure of it! That ain't our real son! He was switched at birth with that lot!"

I silently helped Red store the beer and liquor in the pub's cellar. Then we picked up Louie and headed for Stuff's.

CHAPTER TWENTY-THREE

THE MASERELLIS' APARTMENT was in a building on Thirty-sixth Street between Ninth and Tenth avenues. It was a typical railroad flat except that their kitchen could have serviced a small restaurant. It reflected the Maserellis' love affair with food and included an industrial stove, a double-wide refrigerator, and a wide array of mixers, blenders, and shredders.

Lena Maserelli was a downsized version of her husband. She was five feet six inches tall and thirty-six inches around—chest, waist, and hips—but she wore floral print dresses that made her look even larger. She tied her hair in a bun, was proud of the fact that she never wore makeup, and was as strong as a bull and as religious as the pope. Her favorite topic was Angelo's certain road to hell, and her favorite name for him was "the heathen." When she wanted to make the point, as soon as he entered a room she would wave the back of her hand at him and say, "Ah! It's the heathen." Except it came out as: "Ah! Itsa da 'eathen."

Stuff had just finished dressing when he answered the door. He yawned and told us to come in. We followed him to the kitchen, where he decided to grab a quick snack before we left for Benny's. We declined his offer to join him and watched while he sawed twelve inches off the end of a loaf of Italian bread. He split it down the middle and then unloaded the refrigerator: prosciutto, salami, mortadella, capocollo, provolone, roasted peppers, lettuce, tomatoes, and an onion. He slavered the inside of the bread with olive oil, vinegar, and mustard, stuffed the loaf with the ingredients, and created a massive submarine sandwich. If it had been a real submarine, it would have been nuclear. It probably required a lifetime of training just to get your mouth around it. We sat and watched while he consumed his creation, marveling that not one morsel went anywhere but into his mouth.

There were about six inches of the submarine left when we were all startled by the sound of someone kicking the bottom of the door. Stuff went to answer it without letting go of his creation. When he opened the door, his mother was standing there, her fat arms wrapped around five large grocery bags and one skinny bag. The five large bags contained meats, fruits, vegetables, and pastries—the skinny one contained six long loaves of Italian bread. The contents would get them through the weekend . . . maybe. Lena pushed the bags toward her son and said, "Take da bags." It seemed impossible that she had carried them all.

Stuff bit into the remains of his submarine, holding it in his mouth while he took the five bags from his mother. As soon as he had them, she plucked the submarine out of his mouth, bit into it, and walked into the kitchen. Stuff followed her and put the bags on the kitchen counter. Lena was chewing vigorously and puffing with exertion when she noticed Red and Louie sitting at the kitchen table with me. Louie was in his usual all-black outfit, and she welcomed him with her usual greeting. "Who died?" she asked, then waved hello to me.

Louie was used to the gibe, so he smiled and said, "Hi, Mrs.

Maserelli." Then, trying to be nice, he added, "Havin' a little of Stuff's sandwich?"

"No," she said sarcastically, "I'm exercise a my teeth." She turned to me and jabbed her thumb at Louie. "He looks like the undertaker, and he's blind as the bodies." She plopped down at the table and took another large bite out of Stuff's sandwich. Watching his mother eat, Stuff figured he wasn't going to get his sandwich back, so he started making another one.

"What time you got home last night?" she asked through a mouthful of Stuff's masterpiece.

Stuff shrugged and tossed it off. "I dunno, it was pretty late."

"Your fatha' said it was four o'clock."

"How would he know?"

"He was waiting up!" she said as if it were obvious. "He was worried."

Stuff waved his hand dismissively. "Ah . . . nothin' to worry about."

"You know, your fatha' he's a heathen who's gonna spend eternity in hell. Why he's no excommunicated is a mystery and why I love him is two mysteries, but he also loves you and he worries."

"I know that, and I know he loves you, too, Mom." He took a bite out of the sandwich he was making, and they both continued to talk with their mouths full.

"*Ma*, sure he loves me. What's not to love? I'm the best cook in America. I should have been a big chef!" She took another large bite of her sandwich.

"Pop thinks you should have been a nun."

"Ah-ha! You see what I keep saying. He makes fun on the church."

"Sure he makes fun of it, it's the only thing you ever talk about."

She wagged her finger at him. "It's the only thing we *argue* about."

"Because it's the only thing you ever *talk* about."

Stuff finished making his sandwich, got up, and kissed his mother. "We gotta go meet the guys, Mom—be back in time for dinner." We all started out, but Stuff stopped and went back to sprinkle some more red pepper on his new creation.

Lena took another bite of the original, nodded approvingly, and observed, "Yew cud 'ave a fewtch, Attillio . . ."

Stuff smiled at the compliment and said, "Thanks, Mom," as we left. Red still hadn't said a word.

CHAPTER TWENTY-FOUR

WHEN LOUIE, Red, Stuff, and I got to Benny's, we found Boychick unenthusiastically tapping at the speed bag, Benny flipping through a comic book, and Bouncer distractedly playing solitaire. They were all wound tight because they thought that Gee-gee was capable of doing something crazy when we delivered the furs and I showed him the pictures Jill had taken. They insisted on going with me, citing "safety in numbers." I didn't think it would make a difference, but I didn't say so.

I left to pick up the photos at Terry's, and we agreed to rendezvous back at Benny's around noon. Since it was Saturday, the guys took a halfhearted walk to Barney's Sabrett stand for brunch. Even Stuff, who had just socked away an enormous sandwich, was up for dogs and a Yoohoo.

As I neared our tenement, I heard the screaming and yelling from two blocks away. Then I remembered: Today was the annual neighborhood stickball championship. The sidewalks on Thirty-sixth Street were jam-packed with roaring fans from Tenth Avenue straight across to Eleventh. Choice standing room on tenement steps was crammed with humanity, and parked cars had big kids sitting on fenders and small kids perched on roofs. The entire block was pulsating with a carnival atmosphere.

When I walked around the corner, Sidney was sitting on the fender of our Buick, and a six-year-old was bouncing up and down on the roof as if it were a trampoline. The game was in the third inning, tie score: Bombers 7, Bums 7. They were the Yankees and Dodgers of the streets, and a Bomber had just blasted a shot over the "center field wall"—an invisible barrier defined by a pair of upright broomsticks tied to car fenders on both sides of the street. Any ball that bounced on the far side of the broomsticks was a home run, and the kid's shot had just cleared the "goalposts" and was rolling toward Tenth Avenue, accompanied by an ovation.

Sidney launched himself off the fender and threw his fist in the air. "Eight–seven! Go, Bombers!" I'd never seen him so animated. When he saw me he grabbed my hand, pumped it, and yelled, "We're winning!" He was ecstatic . . . and then he started coughing. Too much excitement, I guessed, so I took his arm and led him around the corner of Eleventh Avenue and out of the crowd.

When he stopped coughing I said, "I had no idea you were a stickball fan."

"Just the Bombers. I love the Yankees but not the Dodgers, so I root for the Bombers when they play the Bums. Did you come back to watch?" he asked.

"No, I came back for the car . . . but with this crowd there's no way to get to it. I'm on my way to see Terry." I had to tell her that my father knew about us before she heard it from someone else, and I figured today was the day. The thought was depressing me.

Sidney caught my tone of voice and said, "You're always happy about seeing Terry . . . you don't seem happy."

"My father found out about us."

His eyes got a little wider and he said, "Oh boy."

"Yeah . . . I don't know how she's gonna take it, but 'whoopee' ain't in the cards."

"How can she be mad? It's not your fault."

"Not the point," I said.

Around the corner another roar went up. Somebody had scored, and the result was cheering mixed with groans. Two minutes earlier Sidney had been completely into the game. But now he wasn't reacting at all to the yelling and seemed to be pondering. Suddenly his face got brighter and he said, "Maybe I could talk to her first! She likes me, so she couldn't be mad when I tell her. But if she's mad, she's mad at me—not you. She 'shoots the messenger,' get it?"

I smiled—Sidney knew a lot about a lot of things, but women were under his radar. I said, "Thanks, pal, but I gotta handle this one . . . Go back to the game . . . I'll grab a cab."

I gave him a gentle tap on the arm and started walking uptown. There was a sudden howl from the stickball fans, and I began thinking about where the summer had brought me . . . I'd become a pawn in what looked like a brewing gang war, I had a girlfriend who was petrified of my father, six guys who would stand in front of a tank to protect me, a brilliant Jew trying to educate me . . . and no goddamn idea where it was all going.

Fifteen minutes later the cab dropped me off in front of Terry's apartment and I thought, Fifteen minutes and two miles from a stickball championship to the silk stocking district. Where else but in New York? To me, that was what the city was all about—rich, poor; black, white; happy, sad; brutal . . . and anything but boring.

Terry knew I'd be coming up early, so she'd left the door unlatched. I let myself in. The living room drapes were drawn and all the lights were out, so the apartment was dark. I heard the hum of the air conditioner coming from the bedroom and made the familiar cross to her bedroom door. I pushed it open and caught a hint of Chanel No. 5. She slept with a dim yellow night-light, and I could see she was lying on her stomach with her arms and legs stretched out, nude. I sat on the bed and kissed the back of her neck. She stirred, opened her eyes, and rolled over. She smiled and reached for me . . . and again, magic.

A half hour later I lit two cigarettes, handed one to her, and said, "I saw it in a movie once. A foreign guy did it for Bette Davis."

"Paul Henreid," said Terry.

"Who?"

"The foreign guy . . . Paul Henreid. The movie was *Now, Voyager*."

"Oh," I said. "After that movie came out, it took a year for the guys in my neighborhood to stop lighting cigarettes for every broad they met. I even saw a guy light a cigarette for another guy. *Faygelahs*."

Terry giggled and rolled on top of me. We were nose to nose. "You ever see that?" she asked.

"What?"

"A guy with another guy?"

"Are you kiddin'?" I said distastefully.

"How about a girl with a girl?"

"What? You're writing a book?"

"Just curious. How about a guy with two girls?"

"How about you let me up and we have some coffee? I gotta meet the guys."

"Okay, sugah, but if you wrap up early, stop by for hors d'oeuvres before I go to work." Terry rubbed noses with me and giggled, "Li'l ol' me's gonna be the featured delicacy."

She hopped out of bed and went to the kitchen. Not went—more like floated. She reminded me of a nymph I'd seen in Sidney's Renaissance book. I got up, went to the bathroom, and stepped into the glass-enclosed shower. I was half soaped up when Terry wrapped her arms around me from behind. "Need a back scrub, sailor?"

I handed a brush over my shoulder and leaned against the wall. Terry began scrubbing my back, and I figured this was as good a time as any to dive off the cliff. "Pop knows," I said without turning, and I felt her freeze. Two goddamn words and she knew exactly what I meant.

"What?" It was more of a gasp than a word.

"My father," I said, and turned to face her. "He knows about us."

Terry's eyes flared; she shook her head in disbelief and cried out, "Jesus Christ, Vinny!" She threw down the brush and dashed out of the shower. She angrily ripped a white terry-cloth robe off the hook behind the door and fumbled for the sleeves. I followed her out, grabbed a towel, and searched for the right words. None came, so I settled for a "Take it easy . . ."

She whirled on me and attempted to hold her voice down. "Easy? Easy . . . ? How?" The attempt failed, and her voice started to rise. "They'll fire me! I can't afford to lose my job!"

"You're not gonna lose your job," I said in another feeble attempt to calm her.

"It's the best job I ever had!" she blurted out, and started to get hysterical. "I know I'll never be an actress! I've tried for ten years! This is honest work, and it pays one whole helluva lot of money!"

"He hasn't said anything yet."

"What do you think he's gonna say, Vinny? 'Congratulations'? 'Y'all have a real nice life, yuh heah?'" The tears started to flow.

"I'll talk to him . . ."

Terry suddenly lost it. "And tell him what? What? That you want to marry a hatcheck girl from Georgia who's slept with half of his friends!"

The second it came out of her mouth she knew it was a mistake. She threw her hand over her mouth and her eyes got very wide. This time I froze. I leaned back against the wall for support, but after a few seconds my knees melted and I slid to the floor.

Terry sat on the side of the tub, crossed her arms, and hugged herself. "Oh, Vinny," she said, sobbing, "at some point I was going to tell you . . . but not like this. When I first came to town the only job I could get was serving burgers on roller skates at a drive-in in Queens. I did some modeling . . . nude stuff, but even that didn't pay all that well. On one of the shoots I met Jill—we became friends, and I moved in with her. She came from a small town like me—except hers was outside of London. She was trying to be an actress, too, but it didn't work very well for her, either, so in order to survive she became a call girl. She introduced me to some people . . ." She paused and shook her head in despair. "We both did it to live, Vinny. Whenever I got a part—I quit. But I always had to go back. Then I landed the job at the Copa. A guy I'd met set it up. Your father knew him . . ." She paused and shook her head slowly. "That's why I was so petrified that he'd find out about us . . . because he probably knows my whole story."

I was too stunned to say anything. I just sat there, shaking my head. My father probably knew the whole story, and most likely so did a lot of people . . . So they knew Gino Vesta's son was in love with a hooker . . . Christ! I'd become a goddamn embarrassment to him.

I finally got up, went into the bedroom, and dressed. As I was about to leave, Terry came out of the bathroom, leaned against the doorjamb, and said, "For what it's worth—I love you."

She was wrapped in a tattered terry-cloth robe, had wet, straggled hair, bloodshot eyes, no makeup—and was still beautiful. "I won't let them fire you," I said.

She smiled skeptically and said, "Thanks."

I picked up a tan envelope that contained the photos and started out. She followed me to the front door. I opened it and said, "For what it's worth—I love you, too." I closed the door and left.

CHAPTER TWENTY-FIVE

I PICKED UP THE Buick on my way to Benny's and was brought up to speed by one of the neighborhood kids—the Bombers had taken the day 18–15. Defense was never a feature of stickball.

I got to Benny's a bit past noon and saw the fish truck parked outside with its logo painted out. The temperature once again headed for the nineties, and the truck smelled worse than it had the night before. I parked behind the truck and walked down the stairs, still trying to tuck the scene with Terry into a remote pocket of my brain.

When I entered the room I was greeted by the usual activity, but the second they saw me, they all dropped what they were doing. I held up the tan envelope and said, "Okay, once more . . . I'll take the truck with Boychick and Red. Louie'll take the car with Benny, Bouncer, and Stuff."

"But only Boychick, Red, and you go in," said Louie.

"Right," I said, "just the truck. The rest of you stay outside. Give us about fifteen minutes, and if we don't come out . . ."

The front door opened before I could finish. Angelo Maserelli walked in. He was dressed in a dark suit and tie topped by the requisite snap-brim fedora: "working clothes." As usual, the top button of his shirt was loose. He ran a handkerchief around the inside of his collar and asked, "You guys ready to go?"

"Pop—what're you doin' here?" asked Stuff.

"Me and a couple of the guys are comin' along for the ride. You could call it insurance . . . you could also call it Gino's orders. Either way, you're right."

"But you don't come inside, right?" I said. I wanted it clear. This was *my* deal—I was at the pointy end of the spear. It had all started with me, and I wanted to finish it.

"Nah, nothin' like that," said Angelo, waving it off. "He just wants us to be seen—a kind of 'show the flag' thing. If Gee-gee's guys know we're in the area, it figures they don't make a move."

"Okay," I said, "it's a three-way caravan. Like I told the guys—we get there and just the truck goes in. Give us about fifteen minutes. If we're not out, come in after us."

"No problem," said Angelo.

Boychick slammed his fist into his palm and spat out, "Let's do it!"

My open hand popped out on cue—they built the stack, and Boychick yelled, "Yes!"

As we started out, Angelo held me back. "Kid—don't go in there alone. Bring Boychick. Tell 'im to watch Touch Grillo. Gee-gee won't dirty his hands, but Touch is gonna go crazier than Gee-gee when he sees those pictures came from his girlfriend's place. He's just wacky enough to do somethin' stupid. Watch 'im. *Capische?*"

"Got it," I said. "Thanks, Angelo."

"Forget it."

We walked out of Benny's apartment, and everyone got into their assigned vehicles. Angelo's old Ford was parked behind the Buick with three men in it—two in the back and one behind the wheel. All three wore dark suits, ties, and snap-brim hats. More "working clothes." The man up front was Bo Barbera, a Lee J. Cobb look-alike who was exactly what he seemed—muscle. The two in the back weren't anything like what they seemed. Dino and Matty Cavallo looked like a pair of mild-mannered schoolteachers, but they were as vicious as anyone in my father's crew. Born and raised in Detroit, they were full-blooded Sicilians, but they obviously had an unlikely ancestor somewhere in their distant past. They had light skin, blue eyes, and blond hair and were identical twins. Newly arrived in New York, they were unknown on the streets, and Angelo made a point never to let the twins be seen at the same time.

Angelo paused at the door of the fish truck and turned to me. "By the way, kid," he said, "your truck stinks."

By now I was resigned to the obvious. "Tell me about it," I said, and got behind the wheel.

Angelo got in the passenger seat of the Ford, and the unlikely three-vehicle caravan headed for the lion's den.

The last time we had driven up to Georgio Petrone's warehouse, it had been after midnight and the streets were deserted. But Saturday was a workday, and workdays in New York City's garment district could only be described as vehicular chaos. Although Monday through Friday might be more congested than Saturday, it would be like drawing a distinction between a mob and a horde. There were double-and triple-parked trucks loading and unloading and carts laden with apparel being pushed from point to point by an army of surging workers. Traffic jams were indigenous, horns blared, and people yelled, shouted, and cursed. If you threw in the late summer heat, it was a scene that Dante might have recognized.

Our caravan painstakingly weaved its way through the gridlock like a snake negotiating a maze until I finally pulled up to the warehouse. I stopped at the overhead door and tapped out three short blasts on the horn. Angelo parked on one side of the entrance, Boychick on the other, and we all waited. The small "speakeasy window" in the pedestrian door opened and revealed a familiar pair of eyes checking out the truck. Once again the watcher was satisfied that he recognized us, and the overhead door rolled up.

Two of Gee-gee's men flanked the entry, and as I started into the warehouse, Angelo and one of the twins made it a point to get out of their car and lean casually on the fender. When Angelo was sure the flankers recognized him, he smiled and delicately wiggled his fingers at them. They ducked back into the building, and the overhead door rolled back down.

Inside the warehouse, the great wall of racks parted and I drove the truck into the bay. "Boychick, you're with me," I said, and dismounted.

Boychick followed and said, "I got it. Touch makes a play—I'm all over him."

I handed him the envelope: "Hold on to this." Red joined us, and I told him to stay with the truck. "Make sure they count all thirty cases."

I noted that two men were already opening the rear doors of the truck. It was obvious we had been expected. Three other men were playing cards at a small table, but there was no other activity. I led Boychick up the stairs and through the empty office. When I punched the blue thumbtack and the wall opened with a soft *whoosh*, I could see that Boychick was impressed.

Gee-gee was seated behind his massive desk like an emperor on a throne. There was an elaborate and beautifully laid out lunch in front of him—complemented by Limoges porcelain, a silver place setting, and crystal stemware. He was sipping espresso from a demitasse cup and was about to enjoy a garlic-laden plate of zuppa di vongole. The office smelled like the kitchen of Mama Leone's restaurant. Touch was sitting across the room on a couch with an unlit cigar in his mouth. Both were in shirtsleeves, and Touch was wearing a .38 snub-nose in a shoulder holster that I figured was there to intimidate me.

"Ah, the young Mr. Vesta," said Gee-gee, smiling amiably. "Welcome . . . I see you've brought our aspiring welterweight with you. Were you expecting trouble?"

I smiled and said, "To be honest—yes."

The office suddenly went silent. The smile dropped from Gee-gee's face, and he glanced over at Touch. Touch's eyes darted back and forth from me to Boychick. Boychick's eyes never left Touch.

Gee-gee slowly put down his demitasse cup and said, "May I ask why?"

"You may," I said as affably as I could.

"Always the wise-ass," Touch said as ominously as he could.

I ignored him. "The way I figure it, you know we got the thirty crates of sable. You also know that the guards fucked up—even though they were tipped by the cops."

Touch leaned forward and exchanged a glance with Gee-gee. There was no question that I had their attention. I told Gee-gee that I was sure he'd call Drago and tell him I planted the wallet and stole his furs. Gee-gee would of course refuse to be my fence and generously offer to return the furs to Drago—which would force Drago to come after me.

Gee-gee leaned forward and nodded with begrudging admiration. "You clever little sonofabitch," he said. "You have it all figured out. Congratulations . . . but it changes nothing. Because you *know* what I'm about to do will in no way stop me from doing it."

"I think you'll change your mind," I said.

Gee-gee scoffed, "For a moment, I almost respected your intelligence. Now I'm having second thoughts."

I waved him off. "Have them, I don't mind."

Touch started to get off the couch, enraged by my attitude and what he considered gross disrespect for his boss. Gee-gee put up his hand and held him off. The room felt wired, but I continued as genially as I could, feigning indifference to the tense atmosphere.

"What I think you'll do is *not* tell him I stole his furs, keep them for yourself, tell Drago you believe that Joe Zox was behind the theft because of DiCarlo's wallet—and then let them fight it out."

There was another long moment of silence. Gee-gee was too smart to think that I would march into his office with such a ridiculous suggestion unless I had something to back it up. For the first time since I entered the room, I could tell he was wary.

"Why?" he asked.

"Ah!" I said, and held out my hand to Boychick. "The envelope, please."

Boychick handed me the envelope, and I presented it to Gee-gee. Touch got up, crossed behind the desk, and looked over Gee-gee's shoulder as he removed the photos. Gee-gee's face remained expressionless as he shuffled slowly through six eight-by-ten glossies. By the fifth photo, Touch began to realize where they were taken.

"Jill . . . ," he said in a hoarse growl, his disbelief turning to rage. He ripped the cigar out of his mouth and roared like a wounded animal. "The prick got to Jill!" He came around the desk, screaming, "You're dead, you motherfucker!"

For a big man Touch was fast, but Boychick was quicker. He sidestepped his bull rush and threw a flurry of punches into Touch's belly. It slowed him down but didn't stop him—he swatted at Boychick with the back of his spadelike hand and sent him flying onto the couch. I threw my best right cross into Touch's chin but succeeded only in breaking two of my knuckles. Touch barely winced. He came back at me with a straight right that I almost ducked—but not quite. It glanced off my shoulder into my chin. My left arm went numb, and I went down. Touch reared back to kick me in the face, but Boychick was up and jumped on his back. He wrapped his legs around the hulk's body and cinched his arms around his neck. Touch backpedaled and crushed Boychick between his body and the wall until Boychick dropped off like a burned leech. He raised his foot to finish off Boychick. Suddenly the wall swung open. Touch glanced up, distracted.

Standing in the doorway was Angelo Maserelli with a sawed-off shotgun pointed at Touch's belly. Behind him was Dino Cavallo, holding a tommy gun.

"Not a good idea," said Angelo, indicating Touch's foot.

Touch lowered his foot.

Boychick irreverently grabbed Touch's arm and pulled himself up. "You should watch where you put your foot. One day you're gonna step in some shit you can't handle." He ripped the gun out of Touch's holster, gave it to Angelo, and helped me to my feet.

"You okay?" asked Boychick.

"Terrific," I said, wincing. My chin was burning, my knuckles ached, and I couldn't feel my left arm.

"You shouldn't pick on kids, Grillo," said Angelo. "It really pisses off guys like me."

I smiled at him. "I thought you were gonna wait outside."

"I lied," said Angelo, and threw a thumb over his shoulder. "See you downstairs."

Boychick and I walked into the outer office but turned back to watch. Angelo had turned his attention to Gee-gee's lunch. "Zuppa di vongole . . . my favorite," he remarked. "Get up."

"What?" Gee-gee said a bit fearfully.

"Get up," Angelo repeated, more forceful this time. "Get over next to Grillo."

Gee-gee got up slowly, extending his palms toward Angelo. "Don't do something stupid, Angelo."

Boychick and I listened to the exchange and traded a fearful look. We knew Angelo was more than capable of pulling the trigger.

"Me? Nah," said Angelo. "If it were up ta me, I'd give you the left barrel and him the right, but it ain't. Gino says don't hurt nobody—just make sure you guys don't do nothin' stupid. Okay, but ya *did* do somethin' stupid. I gotta make sure ya remember not ta be stupid inna future."

He swung the shotgun over to the desk and unleashed both barrels. The top of the desk disintegrated in a cloud of debris, along with the food, silver, porcelain, and crystal. In the enclosed space the sound was deafening. Touch and Gee-gee recoiled, grabbing their ears in agony.

Angelo waited for them to recover—then took the cotton out of his ears. "Have a nice lunch," he said, and walked out, trailed by Dino. He beckoned us to follow him, and we all headed for the stairs.

In the office, Gee-gee and Touch were too stunned to react. Particles of debris were still floating down. Acrid smoke made their eyes water, and the aroma of garlic was replaced by the smell of cordite.

On the warehouse floor, Gee-gee's seven men were facing the wall, bent forward and leaning on their hands in what looked like the precursor to another St. Valentine's Day massacre. Bo Barbera and Matty Cavallo were covering them with Thompsons. Boychick and I got in the truck with Red. Angelo hit a button and the overhead door started up. When it was halfway up we drove the truck out and Angelo reversed the door. He, Barbera, and the Cavallo twins waited until the door was almost down, then ducked under it and were gone.

Fifteen minutes after we pulled the truck into the warehouse, we were again negotiating the gridlock on Thirty-sixth Street. The Ford and the Buick followed, all of us engulfed in a cacophony of blaring horns. Two blocks later, Angelo pulled up to a phone booth and called my father. He said only five words: "They're out, and they're fine." The rest of the story could come later.

Angelo took us all to Little Italy for a celebratory lunch, and then we split up. Red and Benny drove the stolen fish truck over to a parking lot in Coney Island, figuring it could be a month before anyone realized it was abandoned. Louie and Stuff followed in the Buick and picked them up. Angelo, Boychick, and I dropped off Bouncer at the tenement so he could pick up Sidney for their date with the opera. Then Angelo insisted Boychick and I have our injuries checked out at the clinic. We objected but lost the argument.

The facility was actually a small hospital in a brownstone. It was on Twenty-ninth Street between Eighth and Ninth avenues, but from the street there was absolutely no indication of what was inside. The entire staff was on Anastasia's payroll and included specialists in almost every field—many of them retirees bored with inactivity. It existed to handle the gunshot wounds and other injuries that occurred in the normal course of Mob activity. Like payoffs and bribes, it was considered just another cost of doing business.

We arrived at the clinic and Angelo made a doctor perform a head-to-toe. By then the feeling was coming back to my arm, and he quickly confirmed that there was no serious damage, only a pair of broken knuckles that he taped. Boychick's back was sore and his cheekbone looked like an overripe apple, but he'd survive.

After Angelo was satisfied that we were basically okay, we got back into his Ford and headed for my father's office. On the way, I noticed that the bruise on Boychick's cheek looked pretty raw . . . not good. In less than six hours he had a welterweight bout in Harlem.

CHAPTER TWENTY-SIX

MY FATHER'S OFFICE was on the corner of Twelfth Avenue and Fiftieth Street, facing the midtown piers—the section of piers from Thirtieth Street to Fifty-seventh Street—that made up his territory. If it walked, moved, or floated along that stretch, it came under the jurisdiction of the longshoremen's union. Albert Anastasia ran the union, and he had put my father in charge.

Vincent Mangano, the capo of our family, was in overall charge of New York's waterfront but had made Anastasia responsible for controlling it. Anastasia had then elevated my father to his present position.

Along with the simmering conflict between Costello and Genovese, there was a second war brewing between Mangano and his underboss, Anastasia. Because of the Kefauver hearings it had been put on hold, but it was festering just below the surface. Sooner or later, one of them would have to go . . . permanently.

My father's office was functional rather than elaborate, comfortable rather than spacious. "Martial" would best describe it, furnished with an oak desk, sofa, campaign chest coffee table, captain's chairs, and minibar. A large aerial photo of midtown's West Side covered the wall behind the desk, and the front windows overlooked the piers. The entrance on Fiftieth Street led into an outer office—usually occupied by Bo Barbera.

Angelo, Boychick, and I walked in at four-thirty, waved to Bo, and continued into my father's office. We were all sweating, but Angelo looked like he'd been hosed. He'd removed his jacket, but his shirt was soaked, and there were dark stains on the leather holster between his belt and his spine. We all gratefully sucked in the air-conditioned air and were greeted by the familiar scent of Hoppe's powder solvent. My father was sitting at his desk, swabbing out the barrel of his .45 with a soaked patch of the pungent fluid. It was a pleasant aroma that I ranked with garlic, oregano, and freshly baked bread. Boychick and I sat on the couch, and Angelo plopped into a chair in front of the desk.

"You expectin' trouble?" asked Angelo, indicating the gun.

"Maybe. I heard you had some." He glanced at Boychick and me.

"Nothin' serious," said Angelo, and waved it off. "Touch got a little frisky, so I decided to ruin Gee-gee's lunch. Who called?"

"Costello. He's pissed . . . I promised him there would be no trouble."

Angelo scoffed, "It didn't take Gee-gee long to squeal like a pricked pig, did it. He call Genovese?"

My father nodded. "And Genovese called Costello. This Kefauver thing has him wound up. He wants a sit-down."

"It don't figure," said Angelo. "Gee-gee knows we got the pictures. Is he gonna take a chance we show them to Costello? If anythin's gonna make the shit hit the fan, it's them pictures."

"I agree," said my father, "but somehow he seems to think they're not a threat."

"He's *patzo*," said Angelo, twirling his finger around his temple. "Danny Pisano sees Gee-gee porkin' his wife, he's not gonna ask permission to go after Gee-gee—he's gonna do it and Kefauver be fucked. Costello knows that."

"Unless Danny doesn't complain," said my father, one eyebrow raised.

"What the hell would stop him from . . . ?" Angelo stopped, realizing another possibility. So did I.

My father nodded. He cut his eyes toward me, then back to Angelo. "As I told Vincenzo . . . when King David fell in love with Bathsheba, he had to remove the obstacle of her husband. The king sent him into battle in the front rank so that he would be killed. He was. No more obstacle."

"But Danny's one of Joe Bonanno's captains, for chrissakes," Angelo objected. "If Gee-gee whacks Danny, Bonanno's gonna go nuts!"

"Not if Danny just disappears. Everyone would suspect, but there would be no body. Bonanno couldn't go to the Commission without proof."

"We could still show Costello the pictures," Angelo said.

"True," said my father. "But Danny would be gone, and Bonanno would have no proof he was dead. The last thing Costello wants is trouble. The Commission is too wound up about this Kefauver thing already. No—if Danny Pisano disappears, the pictures will be useless."

Christ, I thought. It's possible. Gee-gee might have outthought us.

"Can we warn him?" asked Angelo.

"Don't underestimate Gee-gee," said my father. "If he agreed to a meet, it's already too late . . . Danny is dead."

"When's the meet?" Angelo asked.

"Five o'clock," he said, shooting his eyes over to me. "And he wants me to bring you, since he was told you caused the problem. We'll stop at the house so you can put on a suit."

My father finished cleaning the .45 and inserted a clip into the grip. He paused a second and then slammed it shut.

The site of the five p.m. sit-down was Frank Costello's lavish apartment in the Majestic Towers on Central Park West. I was familiar with the apartment because I had been there a few times when Frank and Bobbie Costello had invited my family to attend one of their regal dinner parties. The enormous living room overlooked Central Park, and it was expensively and tastefully decorated in a way that reflected the lofty position of its occupant. The participants were limited to those caporegimes who ruled territories in the general area of midtown and the West Side. Costello believed that since they were closest to the belligerents, they would be more likely to help negotiate the dispute.

Gee-gee and Touch Grillo had arrived ahead of us, with their champion, Vito Genovese. When Angelo, my father, and I arrived and saw them, we realized that the threat of the photos had been removed. No one else in the room knew it yet, but Danny Pisano slept with the fishes.

Next to arrive were Paul Drago and Carlo Ricci. Drago was a no-nonsense ex-longshoreman who had taken out a dozen men on his trip to the top. He had a thick body, a square face, and a flattop crew cut that made him look like a marine drill sergeant.

Three other caporegimes and their underbosses followed Drago and Ricci. They were all dressed in business suits and chatted amiably while a uniformed waitress circulated an elaborate array of hors d'oeuvres. A tuxedoed bartender served drinks. After Costello was sure we had all been served and were relaxed, he asked us to follow him into the adjoining dining room.

A Louis XIV table with seating for twenty dominated the room, and there were matching chairs along the walls for the underbosses to sit behind their caporegimes. Costello sat at the head of the table, with Genovese to his right and my father to his left. Gee-gee and Drago sat next to Genovese. Angelo and I took seats behind my father; Touch sat behind Gee-gee; Carlo sat behind Drago.

Watching their body language, anyone could see there was animosity between Costello and Genovese. "I'll get right to the point," said Costello. "For some time bad feelings have been brewing between our friends Gino Vesta and Giorgio Petrone. I don't know what caused this, and I don't want to know. All I know is that these bad feelings have caused some escalations—one of which was today."

He paused and looked at both men as if to get their affirmation. Both nodded. "I've spoken to the other members of the Commission," Costello continued, "and we all agree. This must stop. You all know about the Kefauver hearings. Anything we do—*anything* that puts us in print while that's going on—is a disaster. What the Commission wants is our word that this dispute will not put Cosa Nostra in the spotlight. Now, in front of these witnesses . . . the word of both of you. Gino? Giorgio?"

Gee-gee was the first to speak. He held up his hands peaceably and spoke in his most placating manner. "What we've had is a misunderstanding. I'm sure neither one of us wanted it. Gino's very fine son, Vinny—for whom I have great respect—and I have had some business together. Unfortunately it didn't go well. The result was, my very expensive desk was blown up by Angelo Maserelli."

Angelo lurched forward to spit out an objection but immediately realized it was not his place to do so and held his tongue.

"*But*," said Gee-gee, "I hold no grudge. I want peace. Therefore, I will extend my hand to Gino and give my word that I will not be the one to start trouble."

Gee-gee sat back in his chair, very pleased with himself. He looked to Costello for approval. Costello nodded and turned to my father.

"Gino?" he said.

My father let the room wait in anticipation and then finally said, "As you all know, I have never wanted anything but peace, both within and without La Famiglia. This business between my son and Giorgio was, as he says, unfortunate. So . . . I will be happy to pay for Giorgio's desk, and I will overlook the cuts and bruises suffered by my son . . ." He paused. "For whom he has such great respect."

The jab was not missed by anyone, and Gee-gee shifted uncomfortably in his chair.

"I also hold no grudge," my father continued, "and I give my word that I will start no trouble . . ." He again paused and looked at everyone on the other side of the table. "However, I also give my word that if I or my family are attacked . . . I will respond—no matter what the consequences."

Costello's hand slapped the table. "And that is exactly what must not happen!" he said as he looked angrily from one to the other. "There will be no attack—there will be no response—and there will be no consequences! Anything less, and the Commission will act . . . quietly and with finality!"

Costello let his words sink in for a moment and then got up. Everyone rose with him. "Now," he said, holding out his hands to each of the belligerents, "take each other's hands in friendship, and the matter will be closed."

My father and Gee-gee leaned across the table and shook hands. The room erupted in applause. As we all filed back into the living room, I realized that Costello and Genovese hadn't uttered a word to each other during the entire proceedings, but now Genovese, Gee-gee, and Drago were whispering together conspiratorially. I indicated them to my father.

A humorless smile crossed his face. "As Mr. Butcher would say, 'This is not good for the Jews.'"

CHAPTER TWENTY-SEVEN

A LTHOUGH THE BUTCHERS seldom drank, at seven-thirty p.m. my mother served Ira and Sarah a vintage port in stemmed glasses. It was a festive occasion, and they were dressed for the evening. They had been invited to see a Broadway show as guests of the Vestas. *Gentlemen Prefer Blondes* was a smash hit musical playing at the Ziegfeld Theater, and good tickets were known to be somewhere between unavailable and impossible. The four tickets my father had managed to come by were "house seats" that belonged to the producers. They were given to him as a token of the producers' appreciation. No one asked, "In appreciation of what?"

I had come home to change out of my suit before going to pick up Boychick, and I stopped by my father's room to say good-bye. He was tying his tie when I popped my head in and said, "Enjoy the show, Pop . . ."

He said, "Thank you, V-cenz . . . I hear you're taking Sidney to the fights."

"Yeah. Bouncer took him to the opera today and tonight we'll take him to the fights. It may be culture shock, but he'd be alone tonight, so I asked him to come with us."

"Be careful with him, V-cenz. He's fragile. And he's not like your other friends." He tapped his temple. "He has a real brain and he knows how to use it. But the street—no. That he does not know."

"I've got him covered."

"Then have a good night," he said as he finished tying his tie and put on his jacket.

"Pop, about Terry . . . ," I began.

"Not now. When we have more time."

I pressed on anyway. "She's afraid you'll get her fired."

"I won't."

"I told her that. She doesn't believe it."

"Then you have a bigger problem than her past. If she has no respect that you are a man of your word, she will have no respect for anything else." He patted my face and said, *"Pericoloso, bambino."*

He went into the living room, and I followed him. Sarah was saying, "This is our first time. I can't believe it's going to happen!"

"Twenty-seven years we're in New York. Never to Broadway," said Mr. Butcher.

"Well, tonight we make history, no?" said my mother, and raised her glass in a toast. The three happily clinked their glasses and sipped the wine.

My father held up the tickets and announced proudly, "Orchestra—row eight—center."

The ladies clasped their hands joyfully. Sarah said, "Thank you, Mr. Vesta, I can't believe I'm to see Carol Channing."

"The pleasure is mine, Mrs. Butcher," my father said graciously. "What your son does for mine is priceless. This is a small repayment."

"They help each other, no?" asked Mr. Butcher.

"They do," my mother said, getting up. "We are all very lucky. Come, we don't want to miss the curtain."

I followed them down the stairs and out to the sidewalk, where my father had a final surprise waiting at the curb. He had ordered a limousine to take them to the theater. Mrs. Butcher gasped with delight and clamped her hands over her cheeks. Mr. Butcher nodded and smiled appreciatively at my father. As I watched the four happy people climb into the backseat, I immediately saw that even though my father was putting on a cheerful face, he was very concerned about the past two days. The man behind the wheel, in a chauffeur's uniform and cap, was Bo Barbera.

I waved good-bye and turned north to pick up Boychick.

Boychick Delfina lived in a fairly nice building on the corner of Thirty-fifth Street and Tenth Avenue. The building was managed by Leo Delfina, for which he received the basement apartment rent-free. Leo actually did nothing. Leo's wife, Vita, did whatever was necessary to keep the tenants quiet and the owners happy. This amounted to little more than collecting the rents, changing lightbulbs, and putting up with countless complaints regarding no hot water, broken banisters, and blown fuses.

What slight money Leo earned he got from running errands for Lanza's crew and occasional day work on the docks. Every day that dawned was a day he dreamed of being taken into the Mob.

Boychick had always suspected that Leo beat his mother, but his mother always denied it—until Boychick caught him in the act. Since then he hadn't spoken more than a dozen words to his father and refused to have anything to do with him. Leo was desperate to change that. Boychick was making a name for himself as a welterweight. If he turned pro, it could mean big money, and Leo wanted to be in position to feed at the trough.

When I got to the apartment I rang the buzzer and heard Leo yell out, "Come on in!" He was sitting at the kitchen table with Carmine, the has-been that used to work for Johnny DiCarlo. They were sharing a pint of Four Roses. Boychick's mother was out seeing a movie with her girlfriends—whenever Boychick was fighting, Vita Delfina had to do something to take her mind off the possibility that her son would be hurt. It didn't work, but she did it anyway.

I waved an unenthusiastic hello toward Leo and Carmine and went into Boychick's bedroom. He was packing a small bag with boxing gloves, tape, shoes, trunks, and the other paraphernalia he would need for his bout. I didn't like the way he looked. The right side of his face was still glowing, his right eye was bloodshot, and there was a puffy little pillow under it where Touch Grillo had whacked him. I leaned against the doorjamb to wait for him and watched Leo and Carmine in the kitchen. Carmine was reminding Leo of the "thing" that he had mentioned at Barlow's Tavern earlier in the day, and they obviously didn't care if we heard them.

"It's an easy gig," said Carmine. "All we gotta do is go across to Hoboken, switch the plates with the ones we bring, and drive the truck back here. A hunnert bucks."

"What's in the truck?" asked Leo.

"Who cares? It's a hunnert bucks!"

"When?"

"Any time after midnight."

"Okay, but I got somethin' I wanna do first." He took another long pull from the pint of Four Roses, slid the bottle into his back pocket, brushed by me, and walked into the bedroom. He slapped his hands together happily and said, "So, I hear you got a fight tonight."

Boychick continued packing without turning or acknowledging Leo's presence.

"I was thinkin'," Leo continued, "maybe I'd come see ya fight."

Boychick went to his bureau, took out a spare T-shirt, and slammed it into the bag without looking at Leo.

Undaunted, Leo pressed on. "I mean, we ain't talked much since—ya know—the little misunderstandin' with yer mother . . ."

Before Leo could finish, Boychick ripped the zipper closed and whirled on his father. "That little misunderstandin'," he growled, "knocked out two of her teeth!"

"Dominick," said Leo, trying to placate him, "I was drunk. Please—it was a accident."

"No, you sonofabitch! It was a mistake!" Boychick stuck his finger into Leo's chest. "It's over! You don't know me, you got that, *Leo?* It's *over!* And if you touch her again—so are you."

Boychick picked up his bags, shoved Leo aside, and stormed out of the room. As I followed Boychick out the door, I had never seen Leo look angrier.

CHAPTER TWENTY-EIGHT

SIDNEY WAS STANDING on the oak-door coffee table when Boychick and I walked into Benny's apartment. Red, Benny, Stuff, and Louie were gathered around him, sitting on the couch and overstuffed chairs, and Bouncer was sitting on the floor with Angie in his lap. Sidney was up on the table because Louie had asked him to "take the stage" while he regaled them with a very excited replay of *Aida*.

Sidney's father had told him that even though they would be behind the scenes, it was appropriate to dress for the opera, so he was wearing the yarmulke and black suit he had worn to temple earlier that morning. It made him look like a very short rabbi. Bouncer's father had also told him a suit was appropriate, so he had put on a gray sharkskin pinstripe. It made him look like a very skinny shill.

Sidney was gushing, "And so after the guard let us in—*he knew Bouncer by name!*—we shook hands and he told us where to sit." Sidney paused and looked to Bouncer for confirmation. Bouncer corroborated by nodding like a proud parent watching his son's commencement address.

Sidney rushed on. "It was on what they call a catwalk—way above this huge stage . . . we climbed up almost as high as our building . . . and when we sat down, right below us was Egypt! Ancient Egypt! It was tremendous!" He again turned to Bouncer for confirmation. "Wasn't it?"

Bouncer nodded sagely and agreed, "Tremendous."

"And then we heard the orchestra playing, and the curtain came up—right towards us! The opera started . . . and for the next four hours there was singing—dancing—and these huge painted scenery drapes going up and down all around us and the audience cheering—and encores—and curtain calls—and more cheering!" He paused to take a breath and said, "It was awesome . . ."

We all gave Sidney a round of applause and told him how happy we were that he had enjoyed the show. I clapped Bouncer on the back and thanked him for taking care of Sidney, and Bouncer admitted that he had enjoyed watching Sidney as much as he had enjoyed watching the opera.

When the room quieted down, Sidney gave Bouncer an admiring smile and said, "Just think . . . someday Bouncer could be singing there!"

Bouncer clasped his hands behind his neck and leaned back with a rapturous smile on his face. The rest of us exchanged wide-eyed looks. The concept was too catastrophic to contemplate. I let Bouncer float on cloud nine for a few seconds, then asked, "You guys ready to go?"

Sidney said, "Thanks for letting me come along, guys. First the opera—now the fights. I'm having a big day."

Louie, who towered over Sidney, rustled his hair and answered him as Edward G. Robinson's Little Caesar. "It's our pleasure, see—so don't you mention it, see—or I'll give it ta you like you gave it ta Sally Beanbags . . . yaaar."

We all chuckled, walked out, and started east on Thirty-seventh Street. A few short blocks away was the Pennsylvania Station, where we would follow Duke Ellington's legendary instructions and "Take the A Train"—to Harlem.

We got to Denbo's Hall during the final round of a light-heavyweight fight that appeared to be a one-sided slaughter. The crowd was on their feet screaming for more blood, in spite of the fact that there was nothing but blood flying in all directions. The two wannabes were both black, as was most of the crowd, but the face of the lighter-skinned fighter was smeared in red.

Most of the fighters didn't have managers and couldn't afford their own cut or corner men. The promoters hired the people who serviced them during the bouts, and the promoters wanted a show that would bring back the crowd. The health of the fighters was not their concern.

Viewing the action, a dispassionate onlooker would have wondered why the referee didn't stop the fight. He knew better—this was what the crowd came to see, and if he wanted to keep his job, he'd better let them see it.

Denbo's Hall was a multipurpose venue that could be used for anything from basketball games and boxing matches to swap meets and wedding receptions. For spectator events like tonight's boxing match, a set of graduated bleachers was rolled out from each of the four walls, creating a space not unlike a high school or small college basketball court. The facility had a kitchen, showers, a locker room, and several small dressing rooms.

In the final minute of the round, the lighter-skinned fighter refused to go down, and he paid the price. His opponent turned his face into an open wound. When the bell finally rang, the crowd was up, roaring, and the loser had to be helped into his corner. Boychick looked at Benny, shook his head, and they made their way toward the dressing rooms. Stuff, Louie, Bouncer, and Red squeezed into the remaining seats in the last row of the bleachers, while I followed Boychick and Benny. Boychick liked having me in his dressing room before a fight, and since this would be the first time Benny taped his hands, I figured I'd check it out.

We wound our way down a hallway crowded with fighters, relatives, and hangers-on. It was lined with doors, littered with debris, and smelled of rubbing alcohol and sweat. All the doors had a name on a sheet of paper tacked to them. The papers looked like they were torn out of a cheap blue-lined pad. We found the paper with "Delfina" scribbled on it and opened the door.

The room was a ten-by-ten cubicle with walls made of unpainted concrete blocks and a wire mesh fixture with a single lightbulb that glared down from the ceiling. The furnishings looked like they had gone through the landing on Omaha beach—two chairs, a rubdown table, and a locker with a battered terry-cloth robe in it. Boychick started to undress as Benny took the shoes, gloves, and tape out of his bag. He got a quizzical look on his face and began rooting around inside the bag. "You got no drops for the eyes?" he asked.

"I was gonna pick some up. I forgot."

"How you forget shit like that?"

"I had a fight with the ol' man."

I watched as Benny expertly taped Boychick's hands. No question—he had been watching, but he looked concerned. He said, "You best be puttin' your mind on this fight, m'man. They say this Porto Rican kid's good. He whacks you upside that big bruise, you gonna bleed like you been sliced. He whacks you good on that puffy eye—gonna close it. You keep your brain somewhere else, he gonna whup yo' ass."

Boychick knew he was right. He nodded, took a deep breath, hopped off the table, and put on his shorts. Someone in the hallway yelled out, "Delfina! Delfina's up next!" I slapped Boychick on the back and said, "Keep your left up." We tapped fists and I went back out into the congested hallway.

The guys had taken seats in the last row of the crowded bleachers, and I squeezed in beside them. Not ideal, but the place was small enough so that we wouldn't miss anything.

The crowd-pleasing light-heavyweight match had ended, and a pair of featherweights were in the second round of their bout. Neither was landing a single punch as they danced and ducked out of each other's reach. It was obvious they were both on the proverbial bicycle, but the fighter in the black trunks was clearly pedaling faster than the fighter in white. The crowd was booing wildly, and the ref was exhorting them to mix it up. The next time they clinched, the frustrated ref broke it up and stepped between them. He got into the face of the fighter in black trunks and rebuked him loudly. The fighter denied responsibility, shaking his head vigorously at the ref and pointing to the fighter in white trunks. He was still shaking his head when the white-trunked fighter blindsided him with a roundhouse right. It lifted his unwary opponent off his feet and set him on his ass. He was out. The crowd both cheered and jeered, but the ref had no intention of letting the farce go on. He lifted the standing fighter's hand. It was over—Boychick was next.

Boychick was introduced first, and we all cheered, clapped, and whistled our support. Benny shook hands with the cut man, exchanged a few words, and took his position in the corner.

Sidney, suddenly registering Benny's injuries, became concerned. "His eye," he said to me, "and his face . . ."

"I know. He's gonna have to make it short."

"Why is he doing this?" asked Sidney, obviously shocked. He had never witnessed anything like this, but he was smart enough to know that Boychick could be in real trouble.

"Because he said he'd take the fight," I explained. "No way he'd back down."

A trim, well-muscled Puerto Rican fighter was introduced as "Silver" Sanchez, and his supporters went wild. He looked a bit younger than Boychick, but he already had a mean-looking scar above his right eyebrow. He acknowledged the cheers and danced around the ring, exhibiting footwork worthy of Nijinsky. In their corner, Benny let out an admiring whistle and looked at Boychick. Boychick shrugged.

The referee signaled the fighters to come to center ring. He gave them his instructions, and the fighters returned to their corners.

"Gotta keep your left hand up and circle right," said Benny. "Stay clear of his right."

"Tell me about it."

"Check his eyebrow?"

Boychick nodded.

"You wait your shot, then hit it with the house, and pray."

Benny put the mouthpiece in. The bell rang.

Boychick came out fast and threw a quick combination to see how Silver would react. He danced away easily but immediately came back with a combination of his own. Boychick blocked it, and they circled each other.

Boychick again stepped in with the same left, right, left combination, and Silver responded with the same combination he had thrown previously. The final right grazed the welt on Boychick's cheek, and it began to bleed. Silver saw it and charged in. Boychick retreated under a barrage of punches, clinching repeatedly.

The crowd cheered and started screaming for blood. Boychick retreated to a corner and covered up. Silver flailed away wildly, pounding at Boychick's body, but he was unable to get at his face even though he must have thrown over forty punches.

With about a minute left in the round, Boychick bolted out of the corner. Silver came after him, but he was clearly showing signs of fatigue. As he came in, Boychick repeated the same combination he had used to start the fight and received the same response. But this time Silver was carrying his right hand low. It was exactly what Boychick

179

was looking for. He threw a thunderous left hook into Silver's right eye, the scar tissue parted, and blood gushed out of the ripped eyebrow.

Silver staggered back, pawing at his eye, and Boychick came in with a hook into his kidney. Silver's hands dropped and he winced in pain as Boychick measured him and unleashed another vicious hook into the damaged eye. Silver spun around, grabbed the ropes, and dropped to his knee, blood pouring out of his eye. The referee knelt to look at him and started counting. Silver tried to get up but again sank to his knee. The referee reached "ten" a second before the bell rang, and he raised Boychick's hand. The crowd cheered. We whistled and roared our approval, then rushed back to the dressing rooms.

We elbowed our way down the hallway, nearly tripping over a maintenance man who was on his knees with his back to us, repairing an electrical outlet next to Boychick's door. He had the cover off, the socket out, and was fiddling with the wires.

We all piled into the dressing room, but with eight of us in the cubicle, we couldn't close the door. We whooped it up, slapped Boychick and Benny on the back, and carried on like it was Mardi Gras.

Boychick was on the table, and Benny began unlacing his gloves. "Man! Told you 'hit him with the house,'" he said, giggling. "Ya threw in the garage!"

"It was survival, man. That Silver kid is quicksilver."

"Slowed him down just fine. Eye okay?"

"I'm good."

"Grillo mess you up pretty good with only one shot."

"The sonofabitch is an ox."

Benny finished unlacing the gloves, applied a styptic pencil to Boychick's cheek, and asked me, "Figure they ever gonna pay us for the thirty crates?"

"Not a chance," I said. "I figure he'll give 'em back to Drago."

"An' pin the robbery on DiCarlo?"

"I don't think so. I think he'll just keep his wallet and say nothing."

Benny shook his head and laughed. "Some mornin's it just don't pay to get up."

In the hallway, the "maintenance man" didn't even bother to replace the socket in the wall. He left it hanging, got up, and walked out of the hall unnoticed.

Carmine had just heard what he believed would earn him another payday.

CHAPTER TWENTY-NINE

W HEN WE LEFT Denbo's Hall it was only ten-fifteen. We were all hyped up, we were in Harlem, and it was still early on a sultry Saturday night. No one wanted to go home.

"How 'bout we grab a drink and some jazz," said Stuff.

"Yeah," Louie chimed in. "Benny, what's the hottest spot where we can get Bouncer and Sidney served?"

The legal drinking age in New York was eighteen. Bouncer was seventeen and Sidney was sixteen, but there weren't many clubs in the city that didn't serve underage clients.

"Th-that's okay, I'll just have a C-Coke or somethin'," said Bouncer.

"Me too," said Sidney. "I only drink a little wine on the holidays."

"Lotta good spots," Benny said a bit reluctantly. "One I can for sure get us in. The Rio Club."

"Ain't that where your mom used to work?" asked Boychick.

Benny shrugged uncomfortably. "Still does, far as I know."

"Look, Benny," I said, "if you don't feel right goin' there . . ."

"'S'okay . . . I ain't seen her in a while. Maybe she'll be glad to see me."

The Rio Club was in the basement of a brownstone on West 126th Street. A small neon sign pointed to a short staircase that ended at a thick oak door. In the thirties it had been a speakeasy, and there was still a "speakeasy window" in the middle of the door that had been used to identify customers during Prohibition.

The hippo-size black bouncer who opened the window recognized Benny and let us in. He had a shiny bald head that belonged in a bowling alley, and even though the place was packed he shouldered us toward a spot at the bar. The basement wall of the adjoining brownstone had been removed, effectively doubling the size of the club, but it was still jammed with an eclectic group of appreciative customers—and filled with enough smoke to fog up a small town.

About a quarter of the crowd were well-dressed "white folks" either slumming or enjoying some authentic jazz. On any given night, if you got lucky, you might catch legends like Dizzy Gillespie, Charlie Parker, or Teddy Wilson dropping by to "sit in." On a small stage a five-piece combo was backing a very attractive female vocalist. She looked to be fortyish and was wearing spiked heels and a low-cut red satin gown slit up to her thigh. She was singing "You've Changed" in a style reminiscent of Billie Holiday. Although she was billed as Ruby Carlisle, her real name was Lori Veal—Benny Veal's mother.

The song ended and the crowd gave her a standing ovation. Ruby took her bows and walked off backstage while the band rolled into a fiery rendition of "Green Dolphin Street." Spontaneous applause broke out immediately. A short, thin black man in his mid-twenties standing next to me was especially enthusiastic.

"Man, these guys are goood!" he remarked.

"It's my first time," I said. "Are they here all the time?"

"Depends," said the man. "They go on the road a lot, but I hear Ruby's been here a long time."

"You know her?" I asked.

"Not really," he answered, "but I dig her style. I been comin' to see her on my breaks for a couple of days, since I been workin' around the corner."

"Where's that?"

"The Apollo."

"No shit?" I said, impressed.

The man chuckled. "No shit."

"Are you somebody?"

"Well, everybody's somebody"—he grinned—"but I'm with the Will Mastin Trio." He stuck out his hand. "Sammy Davis Jr."

I took his hand and said, "Vinny Vesta."

He gave my hand a quick, short pump and said, "Nice to meet you, Vinny." His grin was infectious. "Come catch us," he continued, "we're there all next week."

"Thanks. I might do that."

"Have a good one," he said, and made his way through the crowd toward the door. All along the way people greeted him and shook his hand. He was obviously well-known and admired, and I decided I would make it a point to see his act.

Benny suddenly came up behind me and said quietly, "Goin' backstage. Come with me, okay? Be better with someone else around."

"You gonna try to talk to your mom?" I asked.

He nodded. "Yeah."

There wasn't a whole hell of a lot to "backstage" at the Rio. Most of the area was used for storage, but there were a couple of small dressing rooms, and one of them had a large star tacked to the door that read "Ruby Carlisle."

Benny hadn't seen his mother for over a year, and his last visit had been a disaster. She'd reminded Benny that she really didn't know him—or want to—and that she'd probably seen him only half a dozen times in her entire life. She couldn't help it—he was a stranger, and she felt nothing for him. If he wanted to do "touchy-feely" with family, he could go see her mother or her sisters, who'd raised him until he started moving in and out of Juvenile Hall. Or he could visit his father at the VA Hospital in L.A., although she doubted he would even recognize Benny.

Benny knocked gently on the door, and we waited for an answer. There was none, so he knocked again. We heard some rustling that sounded like his mother might still be inside. Benny sighed, summoned up his courage, and slowly pushed the door open.

Lori "Ruby Carlisle" Veal was lying on a Victorian divan with her eyes closed. On the table beside her was a spoon, a syringe, some matches, and an empty packet.

Benny shook his head and murmured, "Shit . . ."

We watched her shallow breathing for a few moments, then Benny went over and knelt beside the divan. His mother's eyes fluttered open, and she looked at him. Her pupils were dilated, the whites bloodshot. Her eyes narrowed—she seemed to be trying to remember something—but a moment later she closed them without a glimmer of recognition. He kissed her hand, then bent over and gently kissed her forehead.

We backed out of the room, and he stared at the star that read "Ruby Carlisle." He shook his head and closed the door. He turned to me and said, "That's it . . . never again."

CHAPTER THIRTY

ABOUT THE SAME time we were enjoying jazz at the Rio, Paul Drago and Chucky Law, his driver/bodyguard, entered the Copa. Chucky was a brawny, middle-aged thug with a blond crew cut, elephant ears, and the face of a Bavarian bartender. He was a relative of Dutch Schultz, whose real name was Arthur Flegenheimer. Chucky's real name was Charles Lipshitz. No one was confused about why they had changed their names.

After Dutch was gunned down in 1935, Chucky tried to make it on his own. All he made were mistakes. In 1938 he wound up being sentenced to ten years in Sing Sing for armed robbery. While in prison he ran into Angelo Maserelli, who was serving the last of a five-year sentence for assault during a labor dispute on the docks. Angelo saved Chucky's life during a prison riot, and Chucky owed him big time. After Chucky was released in 1948 and became Drago's driver body-guard, Angelo took repayment in the form of information. Having a set of eyes and ears in a rival family's camp had proved helpful on many occasions. In the current atmosphere, it was invaluable. We knew everything that Drago said or did before he did it.

The extended hand of Louis Antonio greeted Drago the second he entered the club. Although wiseguys were always seated at the best tables, it was still customary to pass a palmed fifty-dollar bill to the dapper little maître d' during the handshake. Louis took Drago's hand and, after two quick pumps, retrieved it. He slipped the fifty into his pocket with the expertise of an illusionist and unleashed a smile that could have lit up Broadway.

"So good to see you again, Mr. Drago. Just the two of you?" asked Louie in his smoothest, most obsequious voice.

"I'm supposed to meet Giorgio Petrone," Drago responded, looking out over the tables.

"Ah," said Louis, "he's already arrived." He snapped his fingers at a hovering captain and instructed, "Mr. Petrone's table for Mr. Drago." He bowed slightly as he passed Drago off to the captain, then dropped the smile and tracked Drago across the room.

The Saturday night atmosphere of the club was completely different from that of the prior evening. Gone were the gorgeous female trophies with their plunging necklines, the constant table-hopping and glad-handing, the blue haze of a hundred Cuban cigars. Terry was at her station and Jerry Vale was still performing, but for the most part he was singing "Femina" to wives, not mistresses— tourists, not locals.

"Paul, I'm delighted you could make it," said Gee-gee as Drago arrived. "You know Touch Grillo . . ." He waited while the two men shook hands, then asked, "Champagne?"

"Rye. Old Overholt," answered Drago. "Beer for Chucky."

Gee-gee looked at Touch, who snapped his fingers at a waiter and gave him the order.

"Ya said ya had information about my robbery," said Drago, preempting any small talk.

"As a matter of fact, I do," Gee-gee said pleasantly. "What would you say if I told you that your stolen furs are in my warehouse?"

"I'd say there better be a damn good reason for how they got there," answered Drago.

"I got them from Gino Vesta's son, Vinny," Gee-gee said in a smooth, offhand way. "Gino ordered the hit on your warehouse, and his son carried it out."

The waiter delivered the beer with a tall glass and a bottle of whiskey with a shot glass. He poured the beer and the shot and left. Gee-gee and Touch were silent. Chucky downed half his drink, and Drago contemplated his. When he finally looked up, he narrowed his eyes. "Vesta's too smart to pull a dumb stunt like that," he said.

"You would think so," Gee-gee concurred, "but I think this fur business is only the beginning. The Commission is distracted because of the Kefauver investigation. Vesta is testing the water to see how far he can go," he continued. It was a glib lie, he knew, and it was effortless. "If no one stops him, he'll push harder and start to take over more and more territory . . ." He leaned closer to Drago. "He's sniffing around my territory . . . and I happen to know he's definitely after yours."

Drago tossed down his shot and studied Gee-gee. Touch poured him another one. "Where'd ya get this from?" asked Drago.

"Does it matter? I know it's true, and I have the furs to prove Vesta's made his first move."

Drago didn't trust Gee-gee, and he didn't really buy it, but Gee-gee did claim to have his furs, so he decided to play along. "You say you got my stuff?"

"I have it. And as a gesture of our friendship, you can have it back."

Drago looked at Touch, then back to Gee-gee as he thought about the offer. "And what do you get out of this?"

"You have a kid called Nick Colucci working for you?"

Drago nodded, and Gee-gee continued in his silkiest voice. "I hear he hates the young Vesta. Have Nick teach him a lesson." He paused for effect. "Have him put the mighty Gino Vesta's son in the hospital."

Drago was not the brightest caporegime on the block, but he was wary. "What's that gonna accomplish?"

"Maybe nothing. But I think it will infuriate Gino into making a retaliatory move . . . a move strong enough to send you a message. If so, it will also be strong enough to enrage the Commission. They will have to solve our problem or look impotent."

Drago said nothing, and the four men remained seated while the crowd gave Jerry Vale a standing ovation. When the applause finally died down, Drago tossed back his second drink and got up. Chucky got up with him.

"I'll think about it," he said.

Louis Antonio watched Drago and Chucky leave the club, then went to a phone and dialed Gino Vesta. Chucky Law reported the conversation to Angelo Maserelli the very next morning.

CHAPTER THIRTY-ONE
SUNDAY, AUGUST 27

A T NINE O'CLOCK on Sunday morning, I walked into our kitchen wearing a blue blazer and gray slacks. My white shirt had a silver pin through its eyelet collar that lifted the knot of a blue-and-gray-striped tie. My mother was in her robe, putting on the coffee. She scanned me as I modeled the outfit with a quick spin. I thought my natty attire came off as Ivy League smart and said so. She snickered and said that with my black hair and dark Latin face I looked more like a stiletto salesman. In retrospect she was probably right. I poured myself a cup of coffee and waited while she left to dress. My father and I were about to give our weekly nod to religion by attending Sunday Mass with Mama.

I had just sat down when I heard the five-knock routine "shave and a haircut" at the door. The two finishing knocks representing "two bits" were eliminated. I smiled, went to the door, rapped out the final two knocks, and admitted Sidney.

"Wow," said Sidney, admiring my outfit, "pretty sharp."

"Thanks. You wanna come with me to Benny's this afternoon?"

"Sure. After lunch?" he asked.

"Yeah. It's gonna be brutal again." The temperature and humidity were already climbing toward the nineties, and in my church clothes I was beginning to wilt. "We might take a trip up to Central Park to cool off. Want some coffee?"

"Thanks," said Sidney, and sat at the table. I poured the coffee, set it in front of him, and sat down. He looked like he had something on his mind.

"You know, Bouncer really likes the opera . . ." He let the statement hang.

"Yeah, but I've heard him sing."

"Right. But if he works hard and studies, who knows?"

I studied him. I knew Sidney well enough to realize he had a hidden agenda, so I put down my cup and asked, "Where's this goin', Sidney?"

"Well . . . I don't think Bouncer knows how to say it, but he's been a little shaken up by what's been happening lately."

"And . . . ?"

"And if he could find a way to tell you without hurting your feelings, I think he would rather be left out of some of the—you know—stuff."

Sidney was one helluva smart kid and had spent a lot of time around us during the summer. He'd picked up a few remarks here and there that gave him a pretty good idea about what we were into. Plus, I was pretty sure Bouncer had shot off his mouth a few times too often. Sidney got the picture, but we'd never really discussed it.

I took a deep breath, exhaled, and nodded. "I've gotten the same feeling out of Bouncer all summer."

"I think he feels he's just not cut out for . . . you know . . . that sort of future."

I paused and poured more coffee. I stirred in a teaspoon of sugar, added some milk, and weighed my answer before I said, "I'm not sure any of us are."

"What?" asked Sidney, obviously taken aback.

The future had been on my mind lately—now more than ever. "Bouncer may be right . . . not only for him, but for all of us." I sipped my coffee. "There are other choices. Look at the rest of the guys: Boychick's got all the makings of a great boxer and wants to take Benny with him. Stuff plays one hell of a piano. If he put his mind to it, he could probably make a damn good living. Louie's a natural actor. He imitates everyone so good, he sounds better than the original. He could wind up playing the Copa someday . . . Red—I'm not sure about. But he grew up in the bar business. With a little stake, he could start his own place."

Sidney waited a beat and asked, "What about you?"

"I don't know. Sometimes I think I'd like to go to college—like my old man. He didn't finish and always regretted it. He wants me to go, but Mom says: 'You should follow in your father's footsteps and lead the union.'" I chuckled ironically. My mother knew better but insisted that my father was just a tough union leader—nothing more. His Mob connections were just a part of doing business. She denied the truth and didn't want to know different. It had been that way for as long as I could remember. It was ridiculous.

Sidney stared at me. "You're actually thinking about college?"

I shrugged and took another sip of coffee. "Mr. D'Augustino, my senior counselor, talked to me about it. He thinks I should go. I don't have the slightest idea what to think," I said. "What about you? You ever think about what you might want to do someday?"

Sidney seemed a bit hesitant to answer but finally said, "Not really. I mean, I used to when I was growing up. For a while I thought I'd like to be a rabbi—I have a cousin who's a rabbi. But lately when I think about the future, I think maybe it doesn't matter."

"What are you talkin' about? Of course it matters."

Sidney looked down at his hands. "Not if there's—I mean, not if I don't get there," he said.

"What are you talkin' about—not get there? You've got . . ." I suddenly realized the possibility. "Wait a minute. Is there somethin' I don't know?"

"Not really, Vinny. You know I've always been pretty sick. I can't remember when I wasn't, but now it feels like my heart keeps skipping. Like a flutter, you know? And it's getting harder and harder to breathe."

"For Christ's sake, Sidney—what does the doctor say?"

"He thinks the flutter could be because of the scarlet fever. And maybe my asthma is getting worse."

I blurted out, "This is crazy! There must be something we can do. I'll talk to my pop. He knows people. We'll find someone who can fix this stuff."

"Thanks, Vinny, I know you'll try."

"We won't try; we'll do it!" I said. "Whatever's bad, we'll fix it. You got me?" I paused and smiled. "And from now on, we don't think like the Bounce! We think nothing but positive, okay?"

"Okay," said Sidney, "but just so you know, these last few months were really special. The best in my life."

"Thanks, Sidney. Mine too." I stuck out my hand, and Sidney shook it. "And you can tell my cousin he can talk to me anytime he wants."

Bouncer wasn't the only one who wanted to talk—Carmine and Leo were desperate to get to Paul Drago and see if they couldn't come up with a big payday for the information they'd overheard at Boychick's fight. They finally reached him through the guards at the Federated, and he reluctantly agreed to meet them at Bronko's Diner.

Drago entered the diner at noon, flanked by Carlo Ricci and Chucky Law. They were all wearing suits and ties. Leo and Carmine, dressed in slacks and short-sleeved Hawaiian shirts, might have wondered how anyone could wear all that shit in the heat wave, but at the moment they were freezing their asses off. The overly air-conditioned diner was a meat locker.

Drago looked around at the fairly empty diner and immediately spotted the two men in their bright, tasteless shirts. That, plus the fact that they looked like they had just robbed a poor box, told Drago all he needed to know.

Chucky and Carlo followed Drago to the booth. He hovered over Leo and said, "Delfina?"

Leo smiled and held out his hand. "Leo. And this is Carmine."

Drago ignored the hand and sat opposite the two men. He didn't bother to take off his hat. Chucky and Carlo sat on counter stools, facing the threesome.

Leo cleared his throat and began, "It's really a great honor to—"

"Waddaya know about the robbery?" Drago cut in.

Leo nervously exchanged a look with Carmine. "Well . . . we thought what we found out could be worth somethin', an'—"

"I'll tell ya what it's worth when ya tell me what ya got. But if ya got me down here fer nothin', yer gonna walk outta here on yer knees."

"Right," said Leo. "Tell 'im, Carmine."

"What? Who, me?" exclaimed Carmine, looking like he had been just thrown in front of a train.

Leo nudged him with his elbow. "Tell 'im, fer chrissake! About last night."

Carmine shifted in his seat, glancing between Chucky, Carlo, and Drago. "Well," he began nervously, "Leo's got this kid who's a fighter, see . . ."

"I know who he is," said Drago.

"Well, last night he was fightin' up inna place in Harlem, an' he was wit dis udder guy who's black, and they was—"

"What the hell has that got ta do with my warehouse?" growled Drago, already reaching the end of his patience.

Leo jumped in and quickly spat out the facts. "My kid belongs to the Icemen—Vinny Vesta's gang. They're the ones that hit your warehouse. Carmine was outside the dressing room and heard 'em talkin' about it."

Drago studied him a moment. He knew who I was, and Carlo himself had told him he'd seen my gang here in Bronko's Diner on Saturday morning. His warehouse was a block away.

"How d'ya know it ain't just bullshit?" he asked.

"They said they planted a wallet there. If they didn't do it, and your guys found a wallet, how would they know about that?"

For the first time since he'd sat down, Drago was all ears. The two dummies guarding the warehouse on Saturday night had found a wallet. It belonged to Johnny DiCarlo. But Gee-gee had told him that Gino Vesta's son had made the hit. He'd thought about that possibility most of last night, wondering if Gee-gee was playing some kind of game with him. But Leo's knowledge of the wallet clinched it. Drago knew the only way my crew and I could have known about the wallet was if we had planted it in the warehouse. He also knew there was no way he could allow a bunch of kids to rip him off.

"Give 'im each a hunnert," said Drago to Carlo, and he slid out of the booth. "You don't know me, an' we never met," he said to Leo, and walked away.

Carlo peeled off two hundred-dollar bills from his roll and slid them across the table to Leo and Carmine. Chucky gave them a derisive snort. Angelo Maserelli would have these two jabeeps for breakfast. He got up and followed Carlo.

As they left, Drago turned to Chucky and said, "Tell Nick Colucci I wanna see 'im at the warehouse at noon."

"Got it," said Chucky.

That was Chucky's first call. His second was to Angelo to report this latest development—only the call didn't get through. Angelo had already left for church.

195

CHAPTER THIRTY-TWO

THE HOLY CROSS CHURCH was right in the middle of the theater district on Forty-second Street between Eighth and Ninth avenues. It catered to show business types, tourists, and local parishioners. Up until 1932, Father Duffy, the storied chaplain of New York's Fighting Sixty-ninth during World War I, was its pastor, and a bronze statue of him had been erected in Times Square in 1937.

The ten o'clock Mass ended, and I came out of the church with my mother, father, and Lena, Stuff's mother. Angelo and Stuff pulled up in my father's Cadillac wearing suits and ties, although neither of them had been to church. Like his father, Stuff was not a churchgoer, but on Sunday mornings he always put on a suit, left the apartment early, and told his mother he was going to the eight o'clock Mass. He actually went to have coffee at Benny's place. This kept a semblance of peace in the family, even though Lena didn't believe a word of it. The four of us piled into the car, and we drove down to Ferrara's Bakery in Little Italy for a Sunday morning tradition that went as far back as I could remember.

Ferrara's was a combination bakery and coffee shop and was to Little Italy what the Liberty Bell was to Philadelphia. Few could remember when it *wasn't* there. Our group was well-known to Ferrara's clientele, and we were welcomed with a warm series of greetings in both Italian and English as we were led to a table. The three Maserellis adjusted their considerable bulk into the wire-backed chairs, and a waitress came over to take our orders. Everyone wanted an assortment of Ferarra's famous pastries, but Lena was specific: *sfogliatelle*—her favorite. There was no need to order cappuccino; it was already on its way.

My father waited for the waitress to leave and then signaled to my mother with a slight incline of his head. She nodded and put her hand on Lena's.

"Lena, I have to go to the washroom. Come. Keep me company."

"Sure," said Lena. "Angelo, watch my purse."

As soon as the ladies departed, my father leaned in toward the table. We did the same. "Last night, there was a call from Louis," he said. "Drago came into the Copa and met Petrone . . . this morning before we left for church, Angelo heard from Chucky Law." He nodded to Angelo, who turned to me.

"Gee-gee told Drago that it was you who hit his warehouse," said Angelo.

"Oh shit," said Stuff through a mouthful of cannoli.

"He can't let that go," I said.

"No," said my father. "He'll come after you—in a way that can't be tied to him. He hopes to force us into making what will look like the first move."

"So, what?" said Angelo. "We stash away the kids awhile?"

My father shook his head. "It makes no sense to hide. We can't hide forever. We still have to play this out and find out what's behind it."

He turned to me. "Wait . . . he has to make a move. Be ready for it. Trust no one. Watch everyone. He'll come after you. Tell your boys— be ready."

"Got it," I said, but I knew it wouldn't be that easy.

Mickey and Lena returned from the ladies' room, Lena tucked into a beautiful *sfogliatelle*, and we continued to enjoy the pastries and cappuccino.

Just before noon, the Vestas and Maserellis departed for their weekly trip to my father's farm in Connecticut, where they would talk, swim, and entertain a few trusted and very special friends. After a sumptuous multicourse Sicilian dinner, they would return home in early evening and resume their alternate lives.

Before heading north on the West Side Highway, they dropped Stuff and me off at the Thirty-sixth Street tenement. I got into the old Buick parked outside the building and said, "I'm gonna run over to Terry's."

"What time you want to meet at Benny's?" asked Stuff.

"Two o'clock's fine. Pick up Sidney. I told him we'd take him to the park if we went."

"Right. Say hello to Terry."

I stopped off at a florist and bought Terry a peace offering of a dozen long-stemmed roses. I didn't think it would help, but it couldn't hurt. I rang the chimes at a little past noon, got "Georgia on My Mind," and waited. Nothing. About thirty seconds later I rang again. I was still waiting when I looked down and noticed a small white envelope protruding under the door. I picked it up, caught a whiff of Chanel No. 5, and opened it. It read:

Vinny,
Mr. Hoffler next door has something for you.
Terry

I slipped the note in my pocket and knocked at her neighbor's door. He answered and I said, "Terry said you had something for me."

"Come in," said Mr. Hoffler. "Here, let me take those for you." He took the roses, placed them on the entry table, and retrieved a small package and an envelope.

I opened the envelope first. Inside was a note that read:

Dearest Vinny,

I've thought about this for a long time . . . since way before yesterday when you told me about your dad. We could try, but in the end there would always be my past, and our age difference. We had three glorious months together, and I'll never forget them . . . or you.

By the time you read this, I'll be on my way to California. Mr. Podell at the Copa wrote me a great letter of recommendation to Ciro's in Hollywood. It's a real high-class club. Hopefully I can start a new life out there. Who knows, maybe some big shot movie producer will discover me . . . (ha-ha).

When I get all settled, I'll write. Please don't hate me for being a coward.

I love you,

Terry

P.S. I left a little piece of us to remember me by.

I folded the note, put it in my pocket, and opened the package. In it was a cigarette lighter, the one she'd lost the night we bumped into each other backstage at the Copa. That night seemed like a lifetime ago. I drew a deep breath and slipped the lighter into my pocket.

"Thank you, Mr. Hoffler," I said, and turned to leave.

"What about the flowers?" asked Mr. Hoffler.

"Put 'em in water," I said.

I don't remember leaving Hoffler's apartment, taking the elevator to the ground floor, or the ride back to Benny's.

CHAPTER THIRTY-THREE

NICK COLUCCI WAS still sleeping when he got the call from Chucky telling him to get his ass over to the Federated Warehouse by noon. He was in bed with a hooker, had only had six hours of sleep, and woke up with one hell of a hangover—but he made it by noon.

Drago was waiting in his Cadillac limo beside the Federated's guard shack when Nick drove up. It was one of the first cars equipped with factory air-conditioning, and Drago was so proud of it, he turned the interior into a four-wheeled igloo. Nick got out of his car, climbed into the backseat of the limo, sat opposite Drago, and shivered. Chucky was behind the wheel.

"What's up, boss?" asked Nick.

"Ya know the Vesta kid?"

"Sure. He's an asshole."

"Glad ta hear it. I want ya teach him a lesson."

"What's this about?" asked Nick.

"None of yer fuckin' business, but if ya hafta know, he knocked off my warehouse Friday night."

"Holy shit! The word on the street is it got hit and—"

"That's the goddamn point. It's only twenty-four hours and already I look like a fuckin' idiot! I want that asshole bent, and I want the street to know why!"

"What about his ol' man?"

"Fuck his ol' man. He's the one who set this up. Let 'im take it to the Commission. I'm the wronged party here, and I ain't goin' after him. I'm goin' after a bunch of young punks."

"What d'ya want done?"

"That's up ta you. But I want it done fast. Today would be good. You know their hangout?"

"Sure. Benny Veal's on Thirty-seventh."

"Fine. There's a grand in it fer ya. Now get outta here and bring me back some good news."

"Ya don't know what a pleasure this is gonna be . . ."

"Good. Go be pleased."

Chucky gripped the steering wheel and stared straight ahead. He knew that reaching Angelo was crucial—he'd already missed him once that day. What he didn't know was that it would be impossible. Angelo had already left for Connecticut.

Nick got out of the limo and headed south toward Greenwich Village. He already had the beginnings of a plan formulating in his sick head. Ten minutes later he pulled up to a pawnshop on West Houston Street. The sign above the three balls read:

Honest Fred's. We Buy and Sell Everything.
Open Seven Days

"Honest Fred" Heinkle was Nick's uncle—his mother's brother. He was actually *Fritz* Heinkle, but in post–World War II New

York, "Honest Fred" was obviously more desirable than "Honest Fritz."

Fred claimed he did a lot of business on Sundays—all the suckers who busted out on Saturday night needed cash on Sunday morning. This was true, but in addition to the shop's normal business, Honest Fred's could supply you with anything from a complete set of forged documents to a wide assortment of stolen firearms.

Nick's cousin Fred Jr. worked in the store when he wasn't running with Nick and the Rattlers. Junior was known for two things: One, he was as bald as a cue ball; and two, he had a maniacal laugh—a high-pitched giggle that could send chills through a statue. In the hands of an analyst, he would probably be diagnosed as a psychopath.

Junior was behind a glass case containing an array of jewelry and watches when Nick entered to the jingling of bells. It was twelve forty-five in the afternoon, but Junior knew his cousin's habits.

"Hey, Nick, whatcha doin' up so early?"

"Trouble, but good trouble."

"Yeah . . . what?"

"I got a gig from Drago."

"All riiight," said Junior, impressed. "You could be movin' up."

"Yeah, but I'm gonna need some help. You free?"

"My ol' man should be in any minute. Whaddaya need?"

"A bomb," said Nick.

"Holy shit," said Junior, his eyes widening.

"Somethin' I kin throw. A pipe bomb, maybe."

Junior thought for a few moments and said, "Yeah—okay. I got some stuff in back. I prolly kin make ya one."

"And I'm gonna need ya ta drive the car."

"When's this go down?" asked Junior.

"Soon as possible. Next coupla hours, I hope."

"Ya mind tellin' me who we're goin' after?"

"Vinny Vesta."

"No shit?"

"No shit."

Junior's maniacal giggle came to life, and he clapped his hands together. "I love it!"

Nick savored the moment with his cousin. He was clearly enjoying himself. "That smart-mouthed sonofabitch has had it comin' fer a long time."

"Yeah. Thinks he's hot shit," said Junior. "Asshole hangs out wit a Jew." He spat on the floor. "I think he does it just ta piss us off."

"How long's it gonna take?" asked Nick.

"Fer the bomb?" Junior shrugged. "Half hour, maybe." He opened a door to the back room and entered, followed by Nick. "What's the beef wit Drago?"

"Icemen was the crew that hit his warehouse."

"It was them? I heard there was a hit."

"That's what got him so pissed. He thinks everybody heard."

"So he tol' ya ta bomb 'im?"

"Uh-uh, the bomb's my idea. Their hangout is Veal's place—they got it fixed up real nice. They love it. We're gonna fuck it up."

"With them in it?"

"With them in it."

"Like I said—I love it!"

Junior again burst into a frenzied high-pitched giggle and set about making the bomb.

I was still driving back to Benny's when Nick and Junior found a parking space a half block away from the apartment and began their stakeout. It was one forty-five, and Benny was sitting on the steps with Stuff, who had changed into shorts and a T-shirt. Sidney was sitting next to them, wearing his usual sweater and yarmulke, and Angie was lying with her head in his lap.

Junior rubbed his hands together at the prospect of adding a Jew to their haul. It had taken him less than half an hour to make the bomb—a twelve-inch length of three-quarter-diameter pipe with a plug in one end and a fuse protruding from the other. It was filled with gunpowder. Not exactly a blockbuster, but in the right spot it could ruin your day. The logical plan would have been to wait until everyone was inside, then drive by and throw the bomb through one of the windows. The problem was that Benny's place was a basement apartment. The windows were just below sidewalk level, and there was a wrought-iron railing around the stairwell in front of them. The railing was there to prevent pedestrians from falling into the stairwell, but it would also prevent Nick from getting any kind of an angle during a drive-by. So they improvised: Junior would drive up and double-park. Nick would get out of the car, run across the sidewalk, lean over the railing, and backhand the bomb through one of the open windows. Not the easiest plan, but Nick was motivated—especially when he saw me pull into the last parking space on the block.

The street was fairly quiet, with most of the neighborhood either still at church or finishing up for lunch. Boychick walked up the street from the opposite direction, and we met at Benny's stoop. Benny took one look at Boychick's puffy eye and started berating him. "Dammit, Boychick, I tol' ya to *ice* that face."

"When I got home last night there was no ice. My ol' man must've used it all in drinks."

"He don't refill the trays?"

"Never."

"*You* didn't refill the trays?"

"I was too beat."

"You're hopeless, you know that? We ice it till the rest of the guys get here, then we all gonna take a nice cool walk in the park." He went down the stairs to his basement apartment. We followed. Angie lay down under the pool table, Stuff sat at the piano, and Benny went to retrieve some ice.

Sidney pointed to Boychick's eye and asked, "Does it hurt a lot?"

"Not as much as it could've," said Boychick. "I didn't catch it full on." He put up his fists and showed Sidney how to block and roll. "I blocked and rolled with it—like this."

Stuff started playing "We're Havin' a Heat Wave."

Boychick reacted after the first few bars. "Christ, Stuff! Do you have to play a 'hot' song? Ain't it hot enough?"

Without missing a beat, Stuff modulated directly into "The Cool, Cool, Cool of the Evening."

I was as depressed as I'd ever been. I hadn't said two words since I'd gotten there. I flopped into a chair and threw my leg over its arm. Sidney saw me moping and picked up my mood.

"Vinny," he asked uneasily, "is something wrong?"

I didn't answer; I just took out a Lucky and lit it with Terry's cigarette lighter.

Boychick walked over. Stuff sensed the tension, stopped playing, and joined him. Benny returned with a towel full of ice and handed it to Boychick. They all hovered over me.

"What . . . ?" asked Boychick as he pressed the ice to his face.

I took a deep drag on my cigarette and exhaled. "Terry," I said. "She's gone."

Boychick narrowed his eyes. "Whaddaya mean, gone—where?"

"Los Angeles," I said, and slipped the lighter into my shirt pocket.

"California? Shit, man. Gonna be a trip'n more ways than one," said Benny.

"She got scared . . . of my ol' man . . . of what would happen to her—to us. She packed and left. She's gone."

No one said anything. They all knew I loved Terry and figured I was on an Olympic downer.

Finally Boychick ventured a thought. "Vinny, look. Maybe—"

"Don't give me any of that 'maybe it's for the best' shit," I barked. "It ain't—it's the fuckin' worst!" I sucked another deep drag from the cigarette.

Suddenly Sidney jerked his head toward the front windows. I followed his look and saw the last part of a chin disappearing over the top of the middle sill. I also just made out a disembodied pair of legs and an arm . . . and there was something in the hand . . . what looked like a fuse burning in one end of a pipe. I saw it—and time slowed down. Boychick also saw it, screamed, "Bomb!" and dove for the floor under the pool table. Benny and Stuff followed him, but I was still in a semidaze about Terry and didn't react as quickly.

The bomb came through the window, but instead of sailing into the middle of the room, it hit a table lamp under the window and lost momentum. It fell short and wound up hitting the floor behind the sofa and rolling under it. My overstuffed chair was no more than twelve feet away, and Sidney was standing in front of me.

"Vinny!" Sidney screamed. He whirled around and launched himself into my chest with all the power his one hundred pounds could muster. The force of his rush tipped the chair over backward, with Sidney on top of me. We were almost to the floor when the bomb went off.

The couch jumped off the floor, filling the air with cloth, springs, splinters, and stuffing—but it also absorbed most of the blast. The bomb's remaining power peppered the posters and the wall map. The player piano and the pool table were covered with cotton stuffing and debris. The elk horn chandelier had a pillow impaled on it. The entire room looked like it had been hit by a cotton snowstorm. If it had been a stick of dynamite, we'd have all been dead. We were luckier than a gambler who'd filled an inside straight.

Out on the street, Nick ran back to his car and dove into the passenger seat. Junior looked past him and saw gouts of smoke pouring through the apartment windows. He burned rubber and sped off—laughing the whole way.

Around the corner, half a block away, Louie heard the explosion. He turned the corner, saw smoke, and broke into a sprint. He was running flat out when he watched someone dive into a double-parked car. He tried to get a license number as the car sped away, but he couldn't make it out. He did, however, make the car.

Louie coughed and gagged as he entered the smoke-filled apartment. The smoke burned his eyes, and he called out, "Hello . . . anybody . . . can ya hear me?"

I was too stunned to answer, and Sidney was out cold on top of me, but as the dust settled I saw bodies moving under the pool table. Louie rushed over and started to pull out the nearest one. "Benny," he said, choking, "are you guys okay?"

Benny nodded slowly, pointing to his ears. Stuff checked Angie, who seemed okay, and then crawled out, followed by Boychick. All of them looked confused, and none of them could hear. They tilted their heads and punched their temples like they were trying to get water out of their ears.

Louie looked around again and finally noticed the overturned chair. I was still dizzy, and Sydney was unconscious. Louie rolled Sidney over and stretched him out alongside me. There was blood all over his back. Benny went into the kitchen for water and towels. Boychick and Stuff knelt down and sat me up.

Just then Red walked into the apartment and gasped, "Christ! What happened?" Bouncer was standing behind him, wide-eyed and open-mouthed. He looked like a petrified stork.

"It must've been a bomb," Louie answered. "I saw two guys speed off right after the explosion."

That woke me up. "Jesus," I said, and then suddenly remembered. "Sidney!"

Boychick lifted up his shirt. His back was lacerated, probably from flying splinters, but most of the wounds weren't too deep. Benny returned with a pot of water and some towels.

Boychick took them and said, "We need some alcohol."

Benny left again while Boychick started cleaning up the blood. Sidney moaned.

I leaned next to his ear and said, "Sidney . . . can you hear me?"

"Uh-huh," came the weak response.

"He's awake," I said happily.

"You okay, Vinny?" asked Sidney. We could barely hear him.

"I'm good, Sidney. You saved my life!"

Sidney raised his head slightly and smiled. "No shit?"

Sidney never swore. He had to be punchy. "No shit," I said, and laughed.

"Wow," said Sidney. He was suddenly very proud of himself.

Bouncer had wandered over to Stuff. His eyes still held a "thousand-yard stare." Stuff waved his hands in front of Bouncer's face. "Bounce, you okay?" he asked.

Bouncer turned toward him but said nothing.

"I think he's shell-shocked," said Stuff.

Boychick looked up. "How the fuck could he be shell-shocked? He wasn't even in the room."

"I think I know who did it," said Louie.

"You make the guy?" asked Red.

"Yeah. I think it was Colucci," said Louie.

"You sure?" I said, and struggled to my feet.

"The guy who jumped in the car looked like he had scraggly blond hair, and the guy driving was bald—could've been his cousin Junior. The car was a black Dodge. If Colucci or Junior's got a black Dodge, it's them."

Sidney moaned as Benny began to clean his wounds, but they were soon drowned out by the scream of sirens. Someone had called in the explosion, and police and fire were responding.

"Okay," I said, "everybody listen up. They're gonna haul us all in for questioning. No matter what—nobody saw anythin', and nobody knows anythin'. Check?" I looked from one to the next and heard, "Check, check, check, check, check, check." Six checks. I nodded my approval and then heard one more.

"Check," murmured Sidney.

I looked down at him and back up at everyone else. They were all smiling. Sidney had just become an honorary member of the crew.

A fire truck and two police cars rolled up outside and disgorged their occupants. The cops led the firemen down the stairs, and they all scanned the room. The cops had their guns drawn.

Benny shook his head and said, "It gonna be a long day."

"Yeah," said Boychick. "So much fer a fuckin' walk in the park."

CHAPTER THIRTY-FOUR

EVERYONE BUT SIDNEY was taken to the Mid-town-South Precinct. The local police knew all the members of the Icemen, and Sidney didn't qualify. Since he was injured, they ordered him taken to Bellevue and notified the Butchers. Luckily, the Butchers were home and they rushed to the hospital. The rest of us were thrown into the "drunk tank" to await interrogation.

The police knew Red was the nephew of the Collins brothers, so they put in a call to Danny and Robert. But none of the other families were told their sons were in jail. The police definitely had an attitude about us. They had suspected for a long time that we were behind a host of break-in robberies but could never prove it. Some of their higher-ups who weren't on the pad berated the locals for not being able to nail us, so we were a constant pain in the ass to them. They couldn't bring any real charges against us for the bombing, so they held us for "questioning"—and were more than happy to make us as uncomfortable as possible.

It was almost five p.m. before Detectives Sasso and Burns finished grilling us. No one broke down, not even Bouncer, although it could be said that he was so out of it that he didn't know if he knew anything or not. The story was, no one saw anything, no one heard anything, and no one suspected anyone. The cops knew it was bullshit, but the story stuck.

I was the last to be questioned, and when I returned the rest of the gang was sulking in a claustrophobic fifteen-by-fifteen cell. Sasso opened the door and shoved me in. I tripped, fell on my face, and said, "Thanks, I needed that."

Sasso shook his head and slammed the door. The metallic clang made us all wince.

"You okay?" asked Boychick.

"A little sore from all the lovin' care," I said, "but okay. You?"

"All good," said Boychick. "Even Bouncer." And he slapped him on the back.

"Yeah, b-but, boy," said Bouncer, "is my old man gonna be p-pissed."

I turned to Louie. "You still think it was Nick and Junior?"

"No one else fits," said Louie.

I nodded in agreement. "But we gotta be sure of that—and of who ordered it." I ran my index finger along the side of my nose. "Drago fits, too, but somehow we gotta be sure."

Benny asked, "You thinkin' the fuzz bought our bullshit?"

"It don't matter," Stuff said confidently. "They can't prove squat." We all turned and looked at him. He blinked and lost his confidence. "Well, can they?"

"Not the point," said Red.

"Red's right," I said. "What they know is that somebody threw a bomb through our window. Not your average happenin' to your average citizen. It's like we put out a sign that says, 'We're involved in shit. Watch us.'"

"You got a plan?" asked Benny.

"Yeah, I'm gonna get some sleep," I said. "It's been a long day." I dropped down and curled up on the floor. It was the only thing that made sense.

I'd been asleep less than an hour when Boychick shook my arm—Sasso had shown up with Angelo and my father. Sasso unlocked the door and growled, "Come on, punks . . . you're outta here."

We all filed out, and I looked questioningly at my father. He answered, "You were on the six o'clock news. We heard it on the way back from Connecticut. They said you were being held." He smiled and added, "So we came and asked Detective Sasso to let you go . . ."

"That was it?" I asked, knowing it couldn't be that simple.

Angelo chuckled and said, "Gino mentioned that his friend Costello and the chief were *very* friendly . . . Sasso got the picture."

"Thanks, Pop . . . but Sidney got hurt. I'd like to go see how he is."

"*Bene.* Angelo and I will go with you."

The guys split up outside the police station, and my father, Angelo, and I headed for Bellevue Hospital. On the way I told them what Louie had seen outside Benny's apartment and that he was pretty sure it was Colucci and his cousin Junior. I also remembered that it had been Sidney's startled reaction that had drawn my attention to the window in Benny's apartment right before the bomb went off. All I had seen was the blur of a chin—but maybe Sidney had seen the face.

Sidney was propped up in bed and dozing when we entered his room. His eyes fluttered open and he smiled. There was a bandage on the back of his neck, and his eyes were bloodshot. He managed a timid wave of his hand.

"Hi, Mr. Vesta . . . Mr. Maserelli. Vinny—you just missed my mom and pop." The doctor in the ER had given him a painkiller, and he sounded drugged.

"Sidney," I said, "how do you feel?"

"Okay, I guess. My back is a little sore from the stitches, and I've got a headache, but they gave me something, so it's not too bad."

I sat on the end of the bed and Angelo remained at the door. My father pulled a chair up to the side of the bed, sat down, removed his hat, and crossed his legs. "They say it's a concussion," he said. "Observation for tonight, but you go home in the morning."

"I hate hospitals," said Sidney.

My father smiled. "Everyone does. Except maybe doctors."

Sidney looked at me. "Are you all right? My pop said they took everybody to jail."

"We're all fine and everybody's out," I said.

Sidney looked at my father and stated proudly, "Vinny said I saved his life."

"If he said it, it's true," said my father.

"There was a lot of smoke, and I was dizzy, but I heard him say it."

"You heard me right," I said, "and I meant it."

"This was after the explosion," said my father.

Sidney nodded. "Uh-huh . . . when Louie came in and then Red. Louie said he thought it was Nick Colucci . . . It was."

My father looked at Angelo. He crossed to the foot of the bed and asked, "You're sure?"

Sidney nodded. "I saw his face in the window . . . just before he threw the bomb."

"Why didn't you say so?" I asked.

Sidney looked confused by the question, then answered as if it were obvious. "Because Louie said so . . . I heard him."

My father got up and put on his hat. "Thank you, Sidney." He patted Sidney's hand. "And Sidney, you don't have to tell anyone we talked, okay?"

"Okay, Mr. Vesta."

"Good boy. Get some rest. As soon as you feel up to it, we'll go to Coney Island."

"Wow," said Sidney, becoming more animated. "Can we take my pop? He's never been."

"Sure!" answered my father. "We'll take everyone. We'll all go." He tousled his hair gently. "Good night, Sidney."

"Good night . . . thanks for coming, Vinny."

"No problem, Sidney. I'll see you tomorrow," I said, and followed my father and Angelo out of the room.

We walked to the elevators, punched the down button, and waited.

My father turned to Angelo and said, "I want you to find Colucci and Junior . . . tonight. Talk to them. We're sure they did it, but they didn't act on their own. Find out who gave the order."

"Junior works at his uncle's pawnshop," I said. "Honest Fred's in the Village."

The elevator door opened and we got in.

"You think it was Gee-gee?" asked Angelo

"Who ordered it—yes, but probably through Drago. If it was Drago, I want him to have our response before morning."

The elevator doors closed and we started down. We were all absolutely convinced that the fur robbery setup was just the first round of a coming confrontation between Costello and Genovese—but we still didn't know the reason or the plan.

CHAPTER THIRTY-FIVE

WHEN MY FATHER instructed Angelo to "talk to them," he was in fact ordering Angelo to beat the truth out of Nick and Junior. Angelo's interrogation techniques were well-known on the docks. It was said that he was as efficient as de Sade and twice as successful. On the few occasions when he did fail, it was because his subject had become unable to answer anything—ever again.

Angelo wanted the element of surprise when he located his quarries—Nick and Junior would recognize him on sight—so he brought along Dino and Matty Cavallo. When they pulled up to the pawnshop, Angelo sent Dino in to check it out.

Junior was about to turn off the lights in the back room when he heard the bells over the front door jingle. He walked out into the shop and was automatically on guard.

Dino knew that he looked harmless enough, but he saw Junior's eyes dance when he scrutinized his "working clothes": a dark suit and tie, snap-brim hat in his hand.

"What kin I do fer ya?" asked Junior, moving slowly behind the display cases toward the shotgun under the cash register.

Too slow. Dino's hat came up, revealing the gun he was holding alongside it. "Don't even think about it. Turn around." He pulled the shade down over the front door, quickly frisked Junior, and shoved him into the back room. Beads of sweat began to form on Junior's bald head.

Matty pulled the car up to the front of the shop. The shade coming down over the front door had been Angelo's signal to come in. Angelo got out of the car, lit a cigar, and entered the shop. He reversed the sign on the door from OPEN to CLOSED and turned out the lights.

In the back room, Junior heard the jingling of the bells again. "Look," he protested, "whaddaya want? Money? Take it." He was seated in a chair next to a workbench. Dino was leaning against the doorjamb, his .357 pointed casually at Junior's head. "There's more cash inna safe," Junior pleaded. "Guns? I got 'em. Just take what ya want and get the hell outta here. I kin get ya . . ." He stopped dead when Angelo walked in. "Maserelli . . . ? What the fuck? What're you doin' here?"

"Me? Nothin'. I just dropped by ta have a little—whatcha call it? 'Tête-à-tête.' "

Angelo opened a metal folding chair and placed its back up against the back of Junior's chair. He straddled the seat, rested his arms on the chair's back, and leaned forward. His mouth was six inches away from the back of Junior's bald head. "There's a coupla things I wanna know," he said. "How long it takes me ta find out is up to you. *Capische?*"

Junior eyed the .357 in Dino's hand. It was pointed at his chest, but he said nothing.

Angelo leaned forward to within an inch of Junior's ear and screamed out, *"Capische?"*

Junior cried out in pain, recoiled, and tried to jump up. Angelo slammed him back down and again leaned very close to his ear.

"I didn't hear you," Angelo said quietly.

A sheen began to form on Junior's cranium. He giggled nervously. "Sure . . . a talk. Whatever . . ."

"Good," said Angelo. "Now . . . first: Did you have a nice day?"

"What?"

"Today. Was it a nice day?"

"What the fuck're ya talkin' about?"

"Just answer the question."

"Christ! Yeah. It was fine. It was a nice day!"

"Good," Angelo said pleasantly. "What did you do?"

"I worked. I was here all day."

"And all day—while you were workin'—did you happen ta see Nick Colucci?"

Junior now had to have realized where this was going. He wouldn't have been quite sure how he had gotten there, but he would've been pretty certain he was in some very deep shit. He squirmed, eyes dancing. "No. I didn't see 'im. The fuck's dis about, Maserelli?"

"A bomb, Junior. The one that you and Nick delivered to Benny Veal's place."

"Yer nuts. I don't know nuttin' about no bomb. I was here all day."

"Where's Colucci?"

"How the fuck should I know!"

Angelo jammed the tip of his cigar into the back of Junior's neck. Junior screamed and rocketed out of the chair. Dino caught him and slammed him back into it. He put the .357 between his eyes.

"The man asked you a question," said Dino.

"I dunno where he is!" Junior shrieked. "He said he was goin' ta see some hooker in Brooklyn!"

"I thought ya said ya didn't see him," said Angelo.

"I didn't! He . . . he—called. He called and told me he was goin' ta Brooklyn."

"You know somethin', Junior? You're a shitty liar. A guy in our racket shouldn't be a shitty liar. Now what I'm gonna do is ask ya a question and count to one. If I don't get an answer, I'm gonna stuff the lit end of this cigar in your ear. Now—one more time. Did you and Nick bomb Benny Veal's place?"

"I told ya, goddammit, I don't know anythin' about—"

"One," said Angelo, and he shoved the cigar into Junior's ear. There was a bloodcurdling scream, and Junior tumbled forward onto the floor. He wrapped his arms around his head, curled up into the fetal position, and whimpered. Dino hauled him up and threw him back into the chair.

Once again Angelo leaned into him, this time toward his good ear. "Ya got one ear left ta listen with. After that ya ain't gonna be able ta hear what I'm askin'. That won't be good, because then you'll be worthless ta me. Anything that's worthless ta me, I get rid of. *Capische?*"

Junior nodded. His lips trembled and his eyes were running.

"Good," said Angelo. "Now—not if, but *when* you bombed Benny's place . . . who ordered it?"

Junior mumbled something unintelligible.

"The cigar's on its way to yer other ear, asshole!"

"Drago!" screamed Junior. "It was Drago . . ." He started whimpering again.

"I gotta be sure about this. Tell me again. With details." He put the tip of the cigar next to Junior's good ear. Junior could feel the heat.

Junior lurched away. "All right, goddammit!" He felt his scorched ear, winced, and tried to control his trembling. "Nick came here t'day and said he wanted me to make a bomb . . . to fuck up Vesta. I hate the prick and his Jew-boy buddy, so I said okay."

"Why'd Drago give the order?" asked Angelo.

"Drago told Nick to teach Vesta a lesson. The bomb was Nick's idea. He told me Vesta would show up at Veal's place, and I drove the car . . . we staked out Veal's, an' Nick tossed the bomb through the window. There, ya miserable prick! Are ya happy?"

"Actually I'm delighted. Thank you, Junior. It's always a pleasure chattin' with ya." Angelo looked at Dino. "Dino, tie this piece a shit up and throw him in the trunk."

"What're ya gonna do?"

"I dunno yet. Maybe I'll ask Vinny." Angelo got up and started toward the door. For a moment he was between Junior and Dino. He heard the chair suddenly scrape behind him, followed by a maniacal giggle.

Junior reached under the workbench and whipped out a snub-nosed revolver. He fired a shot into Angelo's back. Angelo lurched forward and cleared Junior. A split second later, Dino put a .357 round in Junior's forehead. It damn near tore his head off as he backflipped over the chair and into the wall.

Dino rushed to Angelo, who was lying facedown on the floor. Matty charged into the room with his gun drawn.

"What the fuck happened?" Matty yelled.

"Angelo's hit!" said Dino. He knelt down. "Angelo, where're you hit?"

"My back," Angelo groaned.

Dino lifted up Angelo's suit jacket. "Holy shit," said Dino. "Matty, look at this."

Matty knelt beside Dino. Angelo's .45 automatic was strapped to his belt in the small of his back. There was a hole in the leather holster, but the large gun had stopped the bullet.

"I'll be a sonofabitch," said Matty.

"Angelo, you're gonna be one black-and-blue sumbitch," said Dino, "but there ain't no serious damage."

Matty and Dino helped Angelo to his feet.

"I don't believe it," said Matty. "The forty-five stopped the slug. I were you, I'd light one helluva buncha candles."

"Yeah," said Angelo, stretching and rubbing his back.

"I'm sorry, Angelo," said Dino. "He pulled a gun from under the bench."

"Don't worry about it." He looked over at Junior. "Like I said, throw that piece a shit in the trunk, but ya kin forget about tyin' 'im up."

Angelo got to my father's office at nine o'clock. "What time is the reservation?" my father asked. He was on the phone with Louis Antonio, and he was wearing a tuxedo. "Good . . . No, that should be fine . . . Thank you, Louis." He hung up and turned to Angelo. "So . . . ?"

"It was like Sidney said: Colucci and Junior."

"Where are they?"

"Colucci, I dunno. Junior didn't survive our talk."

"Where is he?"

Angelo checked his watch. "Now? Probably in the belly of a thousand different rats. We buried him in the garbage dump in Secaucus."

"Drago?"

"He ordered the hit," said Angelo.

My father rubbed the side of his nose with his index finger. "Where are the twins?"

"Outside."

"*Bene*," he said, and smiled. "*Molto bene*. I want a fire to level the Federated Warehouse . . . an accident. Tonight."

"You want it should look natural."

My father nodded. "An electrical short—a broken gas line—a cigarette left burning. It must not look like arson. And I want the twins to set it up."

Angelo grinned. "That bomb is gonna be the most expensive mistake Drago ever made."

"Let's hope he learns from it, and it's his last."

"I doubt it, but . . ." Angelo shrugged. He pointed at the tux. "Why the penguin suit?"

"When the Federated starts to burn, I'll be at the Copa with the mayor. There's a testimonial for Captain Riley."

"He's the crookedest cop on the force!" blurted Angelo.

"That's why they're giving him a testimonial."

"No shit?"

My father smiled, shook his head, and got up. "He's retiring. I originally begged off when Costello invited me, but now I have a good reason to be conspicuous. You can drop me off."

Angelo followed Gino to the door. "What time you wanna be at the Copa?"

"Nine-thirty," said Gino.

"Good," said Angelo. "The Federated burns at ten—news at eleven."

CHAPTER THIRTY-SIX

AT 10:05 P.M., BO BARBERA intentionally smashed into Dino Cavallo's car, directly in front of the guard shack at the Federated Warehouse. Barbera then took off, making it look like a hit-and-run. Dino pulled his car to the curb and opened a bottle of tomato juice cut with water. When he lurched out of the front seat, "blood" was streaming down his face. He was wearing a white suit and a pink tie. The "blood" was ruining the suit.

The charade took place immediately after Dan, one of the two night-shift guards, departed for his tour around the perimeter of the building in a new golf cart. Marty—the guard who had sailed into the water with the old cart on Friday night—remained in the shack.

"Help me," Dino said as he lurched toward the gate.

Marty ran out and opened the gate. He put the injured man's arm around his neck, led him into the guard shack, and sat him down.

"Hold on, mister. I'll call an ambulance."

"Th-thanks," said Dino. "Did you get a license plate?"

"Too dark," said Marty. He turned and began to dial the phone.

Dino smiled, got up, and moved behind Marty. He put his arm around Marty's neck and slapped a chloroformed handkerchief across his face. Marty's knees sagged and he dropped the phone. Dino sat him at his desk and rested his head on his hands. He looked like he was sleeping. Dino then detached the key ring from Marty's belt and went back out to open the gate.

Angelo and Bo were waiting. They took the keys from Dino, ran to the warehouse door, unlocked it, and disappeared inside. Less than five minutes had passed from the time of the "accident."

Matty Cavallo had watched the entire episode from a block away. He checked his watch, noted that everything was on time, and entered Bronko's Diner. The place was almost empty.

Agnes was working a double shift and looked surprised to see the nice-looking young man wearing a white suit and a pink tie. If he hadn't been wearing such a gaudy outfit, he could have been a schoolteacher. He sat at the counter, and she went over to take his order.

"What can I getcha?" she asked.

Matty put his elbows on the counter, clasped his hands in front of his face, and rested his chin on them. "I just came from a wedding in the Village, and the food was terrible. I'm famished," he said, and fluttered his eyes. He watched the reaction on Agnes's face and could almost hear what she was thinking. *Famished? The Village? Uh-oh.* He fluttered his eyes and asked, "What's the house special?"

"Sundays it's goulash."

Matty dropped a limp wrist and said, "Love goulash . . . and a cup of tea."

Agnes looked at the wrist and raised her eyebrow. "Tea?" she asked.

"No tea? Coffee's fine—with skim milk."

"We don't have skim. Only regular," said Agnes, now obviously convinced that Matty was a three-dollar bill.

"Regular's fine."

Agnes started away, but Matty stopped her. "Excuse me," he said, indicating her name tag, "Agnes? Do you have the time? My watch seems to have gone south."

Matty could see it in her eyes. *That ain't the only thing*. She pointed to the clock on the wall behind him and said, "It's ten after ten."

Agnes went into the kitchen to retrieve the "house special," and Matty waited for the sound of fire engines.

One block south, Angelo and Bo came out of the warehouse and handed the key ring back to Dino. They had been inside less than ten minutes.

Marty was still out, his head resting on his hands. Dino reattached the keys to his belt, and the three men quickly left and closed the gate. It locked automatically behind them.

Dino got into his car and drove off. Angelo and Bo went to the corner of Twenty-fourth Street, retrieved Bo's car, and did the same.

Deep inside the warehouse, there was an open box of porcelain vases protected by cardboard and excelsior. A cigarette had been "carelessly" left on the lip of the box and had burned down until it dropped into the excelsior. A few seconds later, there was a burst of flame and the wooden box became a fiery torch.

Ninety-nine percent of the containers in the warehouse were made of wood. Many contained flammables. All of the warehouse's upright supports, as well as the roof's trestled beams, were made of wood. The building burned like a dried-out Christmas tree.

Dan came back from his rounds at 12:20 and found Marty passed out on the desk. Dan thought maybe he'd had a heart attack. He splashed some water on his face, and Marty came around. He seemed confused. He babbled something about an accident and a guy who slapped something over his face.

Marty and Dan went outside to look for the car. There was no car. Dan now considered whether or not Marty had had some kind of stroke.

It was then that they both smelled smoke. They ran to the warehouse and opened the door. They were stunned by what they saw. Flames were leaping toward the roof in the center of the building, and it was filling with smoke.

Dan pulled the fire alarm, and Marty rushed to the phone. He dialed Paul Drago's brownstone and said a silent prayer.

Matty, Agnes, and the few remaining customers rushed to the windows when the fire trucks came screaming by Bronko's Diner. They scrambled through the door and watched as they pulled up to the warehouse.

Matty could see that the flames had broken through the roof in the center of the building. A red glow began lighting up the parking lot. "Looks like it's a big one," Matty said.

"Yeah." Agnes sighed. "With all those cops and firemen down there wantin' coffee, it's gonna be a long night."

Agnes walked back into the diner. Matty got in his car and drove off.

When the police arrived at the warehouse, Dan told them that he had left for his rounds about ten o'clock, and when he returned twenty minutes later, he found his partner passed out. No, he didn't think Marty had been drinking. First he thought it was a heart attack. But the temperature was still in the nineties, so maybe it was heat stroke. He didn't know.

The scene was rapidly becoming chaotic as more and more firemen arrived and started pulling hoses in all directions.

A pair of cops took Marty across the street away from the conflagration and tried to get a statement. The cop asking the questions was a sergeant and had a name tag that read "Rowen." The other cop's tag said "Jablonski." He took notes.

"I wasn't drinking and I didn't faint," Marty told Rowen. "I must've been drugged."

"Drugged? How?" asked Rowen.

"I don't know. There was this accident. A hit-and-run. The driver of one of the cars was hurt. He was bleeding. I brought him in and tried to call for help. The next thing I know—I was drugged."

"But you don't know how," said Rowen, "that right?" He wasn't buying the story.

"No," said Marty, "but I got put out, and the guy who put me out may have started the fire."

"You got a lump on your head?" Jablonski asked.

"No, I told you. I was drugged, goddammit."

"Right," said Rowen. "What'd this guy look like?"

"He was wearin' a white suit with a pink tie," said Marty.

"A *white* suit and a pink tie?" Rowen asked, and looked at his partner.

"With blood all over it," said Marty.

"You get a lot of those around here?" asked Jablonski.

"No, goddammit! I know what I saw!" Marty insisted.

"How? You said you were drugged," said Rowen.

"That was later!" Marty was becoming more and more frustrated and flustered.

"Okay, we'll ask around the neighborhood," said Rowen. "Maybe somebody else saw something. Hang around," he instructed Marty. "I might have a few more questions."

Sergeant Rowen told Jablonski to canvas the neighborhood and find out if anyone had seen an accident or a man in a white suit and a pink tie with blood all over it.

Twenty minutes later, Jablonski returned and told him that the waitress in Bronko's Diner up the street had seen a guy in a white suit with a pink tie—no blood.

"What time?" asked Rowan.

Jablonski opened his notebook and read his notes. "The guy came into the diner about five after ten. She remembered because he asked her what time it was five minutes after he came in. It was ten-ten. Also, she said the guy was a queen."

"Why'd she think he was a queen?" asked Rowen.

"White suit, pink tie, limp wrist, and asked for tea."

"Figures," said Rowen. "So what we got is either a queen who can be in two places at the same time or a guard who's on somethin'. Maybe he saw the queen in the white suit when the queen was on his way to the diner. Maybe he's hallucinatin', so he thinks he sees an accident—thinks he tried to help the driver—and thinks he got drugged."

Jablonski shook his head. "Me, I go with the guard's on dope and he's tryin' to cover up."

"Yeah, me too," said Rowen, "but we'll see what the arson squad comes up with."

Drago's limousine roared up and skidded to a stop just in time for him to see the roof to his warehouse collapse. He stormed out, infuriated. He clenched his fists and marched toward the gaggle of fire trucks. Carlo and Chucky followed him, then Carlo spotted Marty and Dan leaning against a police car. He reached out, touched Drago's arm, and pointed. Drago recognized his two idiot guards and stormed toward them like an angry rhino. When the guards saw him, they cringed visibly.

Drago stopped just inches from them. He got into Dan's face and hissed, "Please don't tell me ya don't know what happened."

Dan was shaking. "I was on my rounds . . ."

"And . . . ?" growled Drago.

"And I came back and found Marty passed out on the desk."

"You prick!" Marty screamed. He whacked Dan across the back of his head. "I was drugged!"

Drago grabbed Marty's shirt with both hands and jerked him forward until they were nose to nose. "Drugged by who, Marty? Who?"

"A guy! Who was in the accident!"

"What accident?"

"The hit-and-run! Right in front of the guard shack! The guy was bleeding all over his white suit! I went out and tried to help him. I came in to call an ambulance and he drugged me!" Marty was in tears.

Drago stared into Marty's eyes and let his ranting slowly sink in.

"That's too absolutely, positively, fuckin' ridiculous ta be a lie," he said. He threw Marty against the car and stormed back toward his limo. Carlo and Chucky followed.

"Whadda ya think?" asked Carlo.

"That dumb sonofabitch couldn't make up a story like that in two lifetimes," Drago grumbled. "It was a setup. This was retaliation fer bombin' the kid's hangout." He paused at the limo's door and looked back at his collapsing building. "Vesta sendin' a message . . . Well, I got news—we're gonna send one back."

"What about Costello?"

"Fuck Costello."

CHAPTER THIRTY-SEVEN

MONDAY, AUGUST 28

THE SPECTACULAR WAREHOUSE fire on Sunday night made every radio station and newspaper in New York by Monday morning. A few of the stories reported that the warehouse was thought to be owned by Paul Drago, a reputed Mob figure, but all of the accounts stated that it was much too early to determine whether or not the fire was anything but accidental.

My father informed me otherwise. The image of one of the deadliest men in the city coming off as a white-suited *faygelah* brought me to my knees.

Earlier that morning he had sent some men over to clean up Benny's apartment. The bomb had destroyed one of the sofas, but most of the other furniture in the apartment was in fairly good shape. My father's cleaning crew had removed the debris, and while almost everything in the room had a few scars from flying fragments and still needed some cleaning up, the place was once again livable. He then told me that since my crew had been through a bombing, an interrogation, and a jail cell—and come through with flying colors—he thought it would be appropriate to congratulate us with a celebratory lunch at the Stage Delicatessen. He knew the "civilian" parents had probably been shaken up by the events, so he had also invited them and the Butchers, who would join us right after they picked up Sidney at Bellevue.

I rounded up the guys and we arrived at the famous restaurant on Seventh Avenue at noon. By then heat waves were radiating off the streets, the mercury had soared past ninety, the humidity imitated it, and New York felt like the Congo. We were met by a pack of fathers and one mother sweltering in the heat and waiting out front. The fathers were Gino Vesta, Angelo Maserelli, Louis Antonio, and Enrico Camilli—Bouncer's father. The one mother was Molly O'Mara. Leo Delfina, Boychick's father, wasn't there—he was sleeping off a hangover. And Benny's father was still in a VA Hospital three thousand miles away.

It was still early, but the deli was already overflowing and we had to wait outside until the crowd thinned out. A few minutes later Sidney and Mr. and Mrs. Butcher walked toward us, grinning like they had just hit the Irish sweepstakes. As they approached, Sidney called out, "Vinny, wait until you hear! Something wonderful happened!"

We all greeted one another, and then I asked, "What?"

Mr. Butcher said, "A miracle! The rabbi says everything has a reason. Now I know it's true."

"What? What's true?" I asked.

"Last night late, Sidney had a terrible asthma attack," said Mrs. Butcher, nodding as she looked around to all of us.

I said, "That's wonderful?"

"No . . ." Mrs. Butcher clasped her hands and looked toward heaven. "That's the miracle!"

Sidney read the confusion on our faces and explained. "Last night I had a really bad attack. I could hardly breathe. The nurse called for a doctor, and one came—"

"He was an intern," interrupted Mr. Butcher. He was beside himself. "From India!"

"He looked at me and asked me how often and when this happened," Sidney explained. "I told him, and he ordered the nurse to get some medicine, and—"

"And then he threw the pillows out of the room!" Mrs. Butcher jumped in.

"The nurse came back with the medicine," continued Sidney, holding up an atomizer, "and he sprayed my nose and throat . . . The attack stopped."

"It was the pillows!" said Mr. Butcher. "The feathers in the pillows! Not asthma! Allergy!"

"He got to the bottom," said Mrs. Butcher. "The intern from India! It came only at night. Not in the day. It was the pillows!" She hugged Sidney, delighted. "Sidney has an allergy!"

Everyone sang out their congratulations, and I balled my fist and gave him a gentle tap on the arm. "That's great, Sidney! You've got an allergy!"

"And he said maybe the stress of the attacks could cause my heart to skip! Think of it? I could almost be normal!"

I laughed, gave him another gentle tap, and said, "Why not? First thing ya know you'll be in the Olympics!"

"God works in strange ways, Vinny," said Mr. Butcher. "If Sidney doesn't meet you, he's not next to the bomb. If not there—not here. Not here—no miracle."

Everyone was once again registering their happiness with the outcome when the headwaiter ushered us in. We were greeted by the relief of the air-conditioned interior, the din of crashing plates, and a hundred shouted conversations. A few minutes later we were led to a table and seated, and one of the deli's legendary, and intentionally cantankerous, waiters came over to take our order. His name tag read "Manny."

"I'll take the corned beef," said Angelo.

"Me too," said Stuff.

"No good," said Manny, "too fatty."

"I like fatty," said Angelo.

"So do I," said Stuff.

Manny ignored him and asked Angelo, "You got ear trouble?"

"No," said Angelo.

"Then listen. The corned beef clogs your arteries. Take the pastrami."

"I want the corned beef," Angelo objected.

"I wouldn't sleep tonight," said Manny, and wrote down their order. "Two pastramis. Ya want slaw or fries with it?"

"Fries."

"Again with the fat. Have the slaw."

Angelo threw up his hands and surrendered. Stuff took one more shot. "Can I—"

"No," said Manny, and shifted his attention to his next victim. Everyone was laughing out loud by the time Manny went around the table and took the remaining orders. Anyone who frequented the Stage knew it was futile to argue with the waiters. If they didn't want you to order something, you didn't get it—no matter who you were, including the mayor, the governor, and, if he ever walked in, the president.

The lunch conversation turned to the Brooklyn Dodgers' Jackie Robinson. The prior year he had been the league's MVP—had won the batting title with a .342 average and led the Dodgers to a pennant. Was it possible he could do it again this year? Benny, the most avid of the avid Robinson fans, was willing to bet the farm on it. Everyone laughed, but no one took the bet. When the conversation finally got around to the catastrophic fire at the Federated Warehouse, my father and Angelo speculated that it was fortunate no one was injured in such a terrible accident. Enrico Camilli, Molly O'Mara, and the

Butchers agreed. Bouncer turned a pale gray, and everyone else had difficulty keeping a straight face.

When we were all full, Sidney said, "Pop, Mom—it's early. Do you suppose Vinny and I could stop by the library to celebrate on the way home?"

Mr. Butcher said, "As Vinny says, 'Why not?'"

"Good," I said. "We'll finish cleaning Benny's place, then go say hello to Steinbeck."

When we all left the deli to split up and go our separate ways, Mr. Butcher announced, "Tonight the Butchers take the Vestas for Chinese!"

I borrowed my father's Buick, the guys piled in, and we left. It was two-thirty.

The bookkeepers in Gee-gee's outer office cringed as Drago, Carlo, and Chucky thundered by their desks, leaving what felt like an earthquake tremor in their wake. Drago punched the blue thumbtack on the rear wall and stormed into Gee-gee's office. His arms were flailing and he was yelling. "That sonofabitch burned down my warehouse! I know goddamn well he did it!"

The chaos created by Angelo's shotgun blast had been cleaned up, but the office still smelled of cordite. Touch was perched on the arm of the couch, impassively chewing an unlit cigar. Gee-gee feigned sympathy from behind his new desk. "I'm truly sorry for your misfortune, Paul. You're sure it was arson?" he asked.

"Of course it was arson!" Drago bellowed. "It was retaliation for the move you told me to make on Vesta's kid!"

Gee-gee held up his hands. "Now wait a minute, Paul. I suggested you should teach young Vesta a little lesson—not blow up a building. The bomb was your idea."

"The bomb was Colucci's idea!"

Gino waved it off. "Touch, get Paul a little anisette."

"I don't want no fuckin' anisette! I want Vesta!"

"I know. Have some anisette. It will settle your stomach," Gee-gee insisted.

"I don't want my goddamn stomach settled, I want Vesta settled!"

Touch went to the bar and poured an anisette into a crystal cordial glass.

Gee-gee continued reasonably, "Look, Paul . . . what's done is done. *Finito.* However, I'm sure your warehouse was insured, so your loss will be covered. More important, perhaps we can turn this event to our advantage."

Drago looked at Gee-gee skeptically. Touch handed him the anisette.

"From what you've told me," continued Gee-gee, "this was very carefully set up."

"It was Vesta."

"Undoubtedly. So I doubt they'll find evidence of arson."

"I don't give a shit what they find, I'm goin' after Vesta!"

"No, Paul. The fire doesn't change our plans. What we still want is for Vesta to come after *you*. When he does, the Commission will take care of him for both of us. Will you listen to what I have in mind?"

Drago looked questioningly from Gee-gee to Touch, settled back in his chair, and sipped his anisette. He was prepared to listen.

After the bombing, Nick Colucci had spent the rest of Sunday afternoon and evening at the Brooklyn apartment of his sometime girlfriend, a hooker named Sherry. They started celebrating Nick's success early and spent the night alternately fucking and drinking. Gin for him, sherry for her. She was a tall, flaming redhead and liked to say, "Hi, I'm Sherry, and I drink sherry." She thought it was chic. They both finally passed out at four a.m.

Eleven hours later, a thunderous hammering on Sherry's door made Nick bolt upright in bed and damn near bounced Sherry out of it. He put his hands over his ears and moaned as someone violently twisted the doorknob. The door was locked, so the intruder hammered some more—harder. Then a voice started yelling, "Colucci! Get up, ya miserable sonofabitch, I know you're in there. Your piece-a-shit car's out front."

"Carlo?" Nick mumbled.

"Yeah, Carlo!" he said, and continued pounding. "Drago wants to see you. Open up or I'll break down the door and shove it up yer worthless ass!"

Nick staggered out of bed, opened the door, and faced Carlo and Chucky.

Carlo looked at him and winced. "Colucci," he said, "you are the sorriest excuse fer a *Homo*-fuckin'-*sapien* in the known world."

Nick moved his lips, but nothing came out. He covered his mouth, ran into the bathroom, and threw up. Sherry watched it all with a sheet pulled up to her chin.

Drago's limo was parked outside Sherry's apartment when Carlo and Chucky frog-marched Nick out of the building. A blast of heat and blinding sunshine buckled his knees, and Chucky shoved him into the backseat. Nick once again sat opposite Drago and shivered in the frigid interior. Carlo settled in beside Nick, and Chucky got behind the wheel. Drago was smoking a cigar and had a .38 on the seat next to him. Nick turned green and fought the urge to throw up all over the spotless upholstery.

"Hey, boss, how're ya do—"

"How the fuck can ya be so stupid?" asked Drago, typically eliminating small talk.

"What? Me? I don't know what you're—"

"I asked ya ta teach Vesta a lesson. Put 'im inna hospital, right?"

"Yeah . . . right, so . . . ?"

"So—ya dumb fuck, whaddaya do?" roared Drago. "Ya put a Jew inna hospital and Vesta in jail!"

"What?"

"That's right. They put Vesta and his crew inna tank. But not fer knockin' off my warehouse. No—fer gettin' his hair mussed by a fuckin' idiot wit a firecracker!"

"It was a pipe bomb," said Nick, completely confused.

"It was a piece of shit! They're all walkin' around free as a fart!"

"Junior . . ."

"Junior! Another fuckin' brain surgeon! I think I'm sendin' a pro ta do a simple job, and what'd I get? A psycho and a nitwit!"

Nick was beside himself. He had no idea what had happened but knew he'd better damn sure fix it or he was history.

"Look, boss, I'll make it right. Please—gimme another shot."

"You'll get another shot all right, but if ya fuck up again"—Drago pointed to the .38—"yer next shot's gonna come from that."

"Wh-when . . . ?" asked Nick, suddenly worried.

"When! Next year, ya stupid fuck," Drago responded. "Today!"

"Today?" murmured Nick, now really worried. He wasn't in any shape to do anything, much less take on another hit.

"Today! To fix what ya fucked up yesterday."

"Vesta again?"

"Not again. Still! Not da gang, not da Jew, Vesta! I want 'im hurt. Bad . . . bad enough ta drive his ol' man batshit. Not a bloody nose'r a split lip. Bad. Inna fuckin' hospital bad."

"T-today . . . ," stammered Nick once more.

"Today," Drago repeated. "Find 'im, and fuck 'im up but good. One more thing—I want ya to be damn sure he knows it was you."

"Okay . . . why?"

"None of yer fuckin' business. Do it right—there's three grand in it. Onny this time get some fuckin' help don't come outta a freak farm!"

"I'll get the Russomanos and Stankovitch. They're—"

"I don't give a rat's ass who ya get. Just don't tell 'em, or *anyone*, what it's about. Get it done before the sun goes down. I got a meetin' in

Atlantic City. By the time I get back tonight, I wanna hear it's done! This is yer last shot, Colucci. Before the sun goes down or you go down!"

Carlo pushed open the door and jerked his head toward the sidewalk. Nick got out, Carlo slammed the door, and Drago yelled, "Drive!"

Chucky put the Caddy in gear and took off, totally frustrated. He wouldn't be able to reach Angelo and warn him until they got to Atlantic City—four hours later.

After we finished cleaning out what was left of the debris at Benny's, we agreed to regroup after dinner—and Sidney and I headed east for the library. Louie and Red walked up Ninth Avenue to Thirty-ninth Street, where Louie turned east for Sixth Avenue. Red went on alone. He was a block away from the pub on Forty-fourth Street when a car suddenly pulled over to the curb in front of him—the doors flew open and the Collins brothers jumped out. His uncles each grabbed an arm and threw him over the hood of their car. Robert cuffed him, and Danny made an exaggerated charade of a pat-down for anyone on the street who happened to take notice. His hand came up flourishing a handful of betting slips he had hidden in his fist.

"So, ya little wise-ass," Danny crowed. "Ya been runnin' numbers, have ya?" He shoved the betting slips in front of Red's nose.

"Fuck you," said Red.

"That all ya got ta say fer yer miserable self?" Danny bellowed.

"No. Fuck you *and* him," said Red, indicating Robert.

Danny swatted Red with the back of his hand and split his lip. Robert restrained his brother and hissed, "We're on the street in broad daylight, for Christ's sake! Relax!"

Danny's eyes darted around, and he regained his composure.

"Right," he said unwillingly. He pushed Red into the backseat of the car and leaned in over him.

"We'll continue our little discussion at the precinct, boyo." He spat into both hands and rubbed them together. "I'll be real interested ta hear what *else* ya got ta say fer yerself." He slammed the door and got into the passenger seat, and Robert pulled away.

CHAPTER THIRTY-EIGHT

NICK COLUCCI PARKED on Forty-first Street at the corner of Fifth Avenue, directly across the front entrance of the New York Public Library. Sal and Al Russomano were in the backseat, Stankovich was up front. They'd watched Sidney and me climb the uptown side of the massive staircase and enter the building. Nick got out and tracked us into the reading room, where we began studying a book. Satisfied we would stay there awhile, he came back to the car and waited, complaining that his head was splitting and his whole body ached—in spite of the fact that he had taken half a dozen aspirin in the last five hours. He couldn't keep a spoonful of food down, the aspirin were eating a hole in his stomach, and he felt like he had ulcers.

After Nick had gotten his orders from Drago, he had tried to contact his cousin Junior. Junior wasn't at home or at the pawnshop, and his father, Honest Fred, hadn't seen him. He had finally given up on Junior and picked up the Russomano brothers and Stank Stankovich. Nick figured the four of them could easily take me out, and Sidney wasn't a factor—just an option. He had tracked us all summer and knew that we were at the library on Mondays, Wednesdays, and Fridays. But now they were getting nervous. Drago had said "before sundown," and it was getting late. He told his crew they'd have to take us out on the steps when we came out of the library. If we got to the street, it would be too crowded, and some asshole might try to be a hero.

Stankovitch checked his watch. "Two hours they been in that joint. What the hell they doin'?"

"Gettin' an ed-jacation," replied Nick. "But it ain't gonna do 'em any good."

"Not that I give a shit, but why now?" asked Stankovitch.

"Why now, what?" Nick responded.

"We hated the prick for years. How come now we're suddenly pissed off enough to whack 'im?"

"All ya gotta know is that you, Sal, and Al split two large."

"Ya want I should go check?" Sal asked from the rear seat. "Maybe they went out the back."

"Nah. They come out the front. I seen 'em lotsa times since he started spendin' time wit the Jew."

"Yer sure?" asked Stankovitch.

"His car's still there, so he's still inside." He thought for a moment and said, "Unless he thought he'd been tailed. In that case he might rabbit out the back into Bryant Park . . . Shit," he said, and smacked the steering wheel. "We'll take a look. Sal, stay inna car. Ya see 'em come out—start the engine. Stank, Al, and me'll hit 'em. Soon as you see our move, you pull across the street, pick us up, and we're gone. Got it?"

"Got it," said Sal.

The three-man hit team got out of the car and crossed Fifth Ave. Stankovitch had a tire iron hidden inside his pant leg. Nick and Al each had a thirty-inch length of steel chain in their pockets. They climbed the uptown side of the staircase, past the massive stone lion, and stopped behind the equally large stone urn farther up.

"Al, take a look inside and see if they're in there. Me 'n Stank'll wait here."

Al climbed the steps and went into the library. Five minutes later he came out. "They're still in there," he said.

"Okay," said Nick, "go back up the steps, an' when ya see 'im comin', signal us." He pointed to the columns that flanked the entry arch. "Then hide behind there. Me 'n Stank on one side, you on the other. When they go by, we jump 'em."

"Right," said Al, and went back up the stairs. Nick and Stankovitch followed him and watched the entrance.

Sidney and I returned a copy of *The Grapes of Wrath* to its shelf and started out of the massive reading room.

"So in *The Grapes of Wrath* and in *Of Mice and Men*," said Sidney, still excited, "John Steinbeck was writing about friendship and struggling to reach a goal. In *Grapes*, there was Tom Joad and Jim Casy trying to get to California. In *Mice and Men*, there was George and Lennie trying to buy a small farm."

"Yeah, but the relationships are different," I said.

"Right," said Sidney, pleased that I saw the similarity as well as the difference. "George and Lennie had a master/slave relationship that led to tragedy. Tom Joad and Jim Casy had a more equal friendship that led to salvation."

We came through the doors and walked toward the staircase. We were both too engrossed in our conversation to notice Al Russomano signal, then duck behind the uptown side of the entryway. We started down the stairs, and I nodded to a group of six nuns who passed us on their way up the staircase.

"Good stuff," I said. "What else did he write that we can read?"

"More good stuff. There's *Cannery Row* about migrant workers, and one I really like, *Tortilla Flat*, which is a kind of poor man's King Arthur and the Round Table."

I thought I heard scuffling footsteps behind me and instinctively turned toward the sound. I saw two men rushing down the steps at me. One of them was whirling a chain over his head—Nick Colucci! The other one was a bearded giant holding a cocked tire iron—Stankovitch! A third man was rushing Sidney. In the second it took Nick and Stankovitch to reach me, I realized I had only one chance. I took it and dove for their legs in a cross body block. It cut them down shin high, and Nick and Stankovitch flew over my back and tumbled down the stairs.

When I looked up I saw Al Russomano's chain tear across Sidney's face. Blood spurted from his nose, and he sank to his knees. I scrambled to my feet and rushed Al, but not in time to prevent a second whiplike blow across the top of Sidney's head that laid open his scalp.

I outweighed Al by thirty pounds, and when I bull-rushed him it drove him back into the stone urn. The air *whooshed* out of his lungs, and his eyes rolled up. I let him drop and picked up his chain.

Stankovitch had recovered and was charging back up the stairs. He held the tire iron low, like a knife fighter.

Nick seemed to be struggling. He was following Stankovitch up the stairs, but he was holding his stomach and retching. Somewhere behind me I heard the nuns screaming.

I lashed out with the chain and tried to rip the tire iron out of Stankovitch's hand. It didn't work. The chain wrapped around the tire iron, but instead of me pulling the iron loose, the bearded ape pulled the chain loose. He threw it into my face and swung the iron. I ducked the chain, and the tire iron missed my head but slammed into my shoulder.

For the second time in three days I felt my left side go numb. I lurched forward in desperation and wrapped my arms around Stankovitch in a boxer's clinch, then took a deep breath and shot my right knee into the big man's groin. I heard a bellow of pain, but Stankovitch broke my hold and pounded a forearm into my face. Three teeth came out—one through my cheek. Then the light in my world faded. I had blood in my mouth and jelly in my knees. I was aware of yelling and screaming, but nothing I could decipher. I went down, and my head slammed against the steps.

Stankovitch raised the tire iron over his head for the coup de grâce, but before he could deliver it, a sea of black swarmed over him. I saw fingers clawing at his face and heard a screeching that sounded like demented banshees. The nuns had attacked.

Nick must have gasped at the scene unfolding in front of him. The Jew was on the ground, bleeding. Al was choking and struggling to get to his feet. I was crumpled under Stankovitch, but Stankovitch was being assaulted by a bunch of . . . *nuns?* On top of that, a small crowd was gathering, and a few people were trying to help the nuns. I rolled away from the melee above me and saw a look of panic cross Nick's face. He grabbed his stomach, lurched over to Al, and pulled him up.

A few seconds later I saw Sal speed across Fifth Avenue, sideswipe two cars in the process, and skid to a halt at the curb. He jumped out and rushed up the stairs, swinging a chain over his head like a lariat. The nuns saw the new threat approaching and paused long enough for Stankovitch to break free. He ran back down the stairs and jumped in the car. Nick and Al piled in behind him, and Sal got behind the wheel. The drivers of the two sideswiped cars shook their fists in frustration, but Sal screeched into a U-turn and disappeared around the corner of Forty-second Street.

I started to get up, but an angelic face framed by a black habit kept me down. I crawled over to Sidney. He was lying in a pool of blood and looked like a broken doll. I put my ear on his chest and listened for a heartbeat. It was faint, but it was there.

One of the nuns took off her habit and placed it behind Sidney's head. In the distance I heard the bells of Saint Patrick's Cathedral. They were ringing out the five o'clock hour. They chimed three times before they merged with the sound of sirens, and I passed out.

CHAPTER THIRTY-NINE

ONCE AGAIN MY father heard about me on the six o'clock news. This time he was in his office with Angelo and Barbera. He called my mother, told her to get the Butchers and wait downstairs outside the tenement. Angelo called Lena and told her to phone the families and wait with Stuff outside their building. Ten minutes later they picked up everybody and drove to Bellevue.

Louis and Louie Antonio, Bouncer and Enrico Camilli, Lena and Stuff, Benny, and Boychick all arrived at the hospital almost simultaneously. Everyone figured Red was on his way. Bouncer was a basket case, and his father wasn't much better. All of his fears had become reality. The waiting room was a mob scene, and there were several cops in evidence since Sidney and I were two of the targets of the previous day's bombing.

The preliminary reports from the doctors were that I had several missing teeth, no feeling in my left arm, and a lacerated face where a tooth had ripped through my cheek. I also had a large lump on the back of my head and blurred vision, so it was possible that I had a concussion.

Sidney was in much more serious condition. He was in a coma and had lost a lot of blood. His head lacerations required forty-seven stitches, and the steel chain had fractured his skull. They were worried about possible brain damage. He was listed as critical, and for the moment no visitors were allowed.

Sarah Butcher collapsed into a chair when she heard the news. She started keening and rocking back and forth. Mr. Butcher, Lena, and my mother tried to comfort her, but with little success.

An Indian doctor, his name tag reading "Singh," entered the waiting room and asked my father if the Butchers had arrived. My father pointed at the group surrounding Sarah, and he went over and gently eased Mr. Butcher, Mickey, and Louis aside. He knelt in front of Sarah and took her hand.

"I am truly sorry, Mrs. Butcher," he said in his lilting Indian accent, "we are doing everything possible."

"Twice," she whimpered. "Twice, in two days . . . why? Please . . . why?"

"A terrible tragedy," said Dr. Singh.

"Yesterday he had only an allergy."

He patted her hand. "I know . . ."

"Just allergy. Now this . . . why?" She sobbed as another flood of tears burst forth.

"Sarah, please," said Mr. Butcher. "Dr. Singh—something to calm her, yes?"

"Of course. I'll send the nurse. And Mrs. Butcher . . . tonight I will stay with Sidney." He patted her hand and started back out.

Sarah again put her face in her hands and started rocking.

My father stopped Dr. Singh at the door. "Dr. Singh, my son is the other boy. The truth—how is he?"

"Ah, Mr. Vesta," said Dr. Singh. "The missing teeth and lacerations are not serious. The numbness in his arm could be nerve damage, and the blurred vision could be a concussion. We will keep him under observation overnight. If the feeling in his arm and his vision returns, we could release him tomorrow."

"I'd like to see him," said my father.

Dr. Singh shook his head regretfully. "Ah, but the police—they said they wished to question him before anyone else spoke to him."

"The police are interested in an assault," my father said reasonably. "My interest is my son."

Dr. Singh smiled. "I have become very fond of your son's friend."

"Sidney and Vincenzo have become very fond of each other," said my father.

Dr. Singh nodded. "Perhaps if you were to become lost on your way to the men's room and go past it—to the next door." He pointed to an EXIT sign. "Up the stairs to the third floor. Room three sixteen. It will be on your left. Good evening, Mr. Vesta."

The doctor left, and my father signaled Angelo. He walked over, and my father led him away from the group. "He's on the third floor. Room three sixteen. Put a man next to him. Make the arrangements with the hospital. Pay them whatever it takes. Then call Barbera and the twins. Have them pick up some men and spread out. Ask questions. Who gave the order?"

"Gotta be Drago again, no?"

"Confirm it. If so, he crossed the line. When we cross back over it, I want to find Petrone and Genovese on the other side. Find me the proof, Angelo."

My father left and walked toward the men's room. He passed it and went on to the door marked EXIT.

Louis Antonio watched him leave and then took his son aside. He was dressed in his tux. There was a private party at the Copa that night, and he'd been on his way to the club when he got the call from Lena.

"Louie," he said, "I try never to interfere with your life . . . but first the pipe bomb and now this. These are not kids you're playing with."

Louie nodded and said, "I know, Pop."

"You're old enough to make decisions, and I know you love Vinny as I love Gino—but think about where this is going! You have to talk to your friend!"

Louie looked down at his father. He towered over him. He wondered how a five-foot-three-inch man could have sired a six-foot-three-inch son. No one could figure it out, especially Louie, but the one thing he knew was that he loved the little guy. People said his father looked like a real movie star. Louie often wondered what it might be like to be a movie star's son, but he wouldn't trade in his father for Clark Gable.

Louie put his hand on his father's shoulder. "I'll talk to him, Pop. Promise."

Louis nodded and said, "Thank you, Louie. You're a good boy."

Louie knew his father was right. We weren't playing with kids, the episodes were escalating, and sooner or later someone was going to get killed.

An hour after I was put in my room, the Novocain wore off and it felt like the left side of my face was on fire. My vision was still blurred, but I saw the door open and a large out-of-focus man entered. I didn't recognize him until he spoke.

"Vincenzo."

"Pop?" It came out like I was talking through gauze.

"You don't look so good."

"I don't feel so good," I said.

He pulled a chair up to the side of a hospital bed, removed his hat, and crossed his legs. "Say a prayer. It could have been worse."

"Sidney?"

"Not so good."

"How not so good?"

"In a coma."

"Bastards."

"Who, V-cenz?"

"Colucci—with the Russomanos and Stankovitch."

"This Colucci is very determined."

"Yeah."

"And in broad daylight. He wanted you to know it was him." He stared off into space. "You were supposed to be careful. How did they take you?"

"I was stupid. Preoccupied with a goddamn bunch of books. They were waiting for us." I shook my head. "Sidney didn't have a chance. I should have never taken him to the library."

"Don't blame yourself. If not there, someplace else. If not then, later."

"Christ . . . how are the Butchers?" I asked.

"Rest now. I'll take care of them." He removed a snub-nosed .32 revolver from his jacket and slid it under my pillow. "Small, but for close work, good. In case someone else is 'determined.' Also, there will be someone here. Probably next door." He brushed back my hair and kissed my uninjured cheek. "*Ciao, bambino.*" He got up to leave, but I stopped him.

"Pop," I said, "Colucci's mine."

"*Capisco.*"

My father wasn't as blurred when he left the room; my eyes seemed to be clearing up. My last thoughts before I slept were of Nick Colucci, the Russomanos, and Stankovitch. Not if, but *how* I was going to make them pay.

A little after midnight I woke up to a soft rustling sound. I opened my eyes but saw only a shadow moving toward me. I slid my hand under the pillow and found the gun. I started to withdraw it when I smelled Chanel No. 5. I froze. I was either dreaming or hallucinating. A hand touched my arm.

"Vinny . . ." It was almost a whisper.

"Terry? How—"

"I heard what happened on the radio."

"But you're supposed to be on your way to—"

"My folks are on vacation in Miami. They get back to Georgia tomorrow. I wanted to see them before I left for California."

"Oh," I said, registering my disappointment. "I got your note."

"I'm sorry, Vinny, I thought it was the best way. I couldn't face it."

"Right."

"If it helps, I've been miserable the last two days."

"Yeah, I haven't been doin' so good, either. How'd you get in here?"

"I'm wearing a nurse's uniform." She flicked on the bedside light.

My eyes focused on a modern version of Florence Nightingale leaning over my bed. The vision of Terry in a nurse's uniform was stunning. For the first time in seven hours, I saw clearly and felt better. "Jesus," I said, "you look fantastic."

Terry chuckled. "I told you I used to be an actress. I picked up the uniform at a costume house. When the shift changed at midnight, I walked in like I owned the place, but when I got to your door one of your father's men put a gun in my back."

"Oh shit. Did he—"

"No problem. When I turned around he recognized me from the club. I talked him into letting me sneak in. He's in the next room."

"You're that good, you should've stayed an actress."

"Yeah," she said, then touched the bandage on my cheek. "They messed up your beautiful face."

"It'll be like a dueling scar. I'll be dashing."

"You were already dashing."

I shrugged. "So now I'll be more dashing."

We both laughed, and Terry sat on the bed. She took my hand. "What am I gonna do with you, tough guy?"

"You could start with a little friendlier 'hello.'"

Terry's mouth turned up in her sultry smile and she leaned down. She hovered over my face and brushed my lips with a feathery kiss. I put my arms around her, and she settled on top of me. When she tried to lean back, I stopped her.

"When's the next shift change?" I asked.

"Eight o'clock."

"Wouldn't be safe to leave before then."

"Vinny . . ."

"A person could get caught. Pretty serious charge—impersonatin' Florence Nightingale."

"I won't get cau—"

"A person might even get jail time."

"Vinny. I can't stay."

"You can't go."

"You're in no condition to—"

"You remember Howard Hughes?"

"What's he got to do with us?"

"He crashed his airplane in Beverly Hills. I read about it. In a swimming pool in somebody's yard. You read about that?"

"Uh-huh," said Terry.

"He was hurt real bad. They put him in the hospital. No visitors—like me."

"And . . ."

"And Katharine Hepburn got in."

"Impersonating a nurse?"

"Who knows? But she got in . . . and then so did he."

"You're serious."

"I'm a gladiator. 'Live tonight—tomorrow I may die.'"

"You're crazy, you know that?"

"About you. You know *that*."

She nodded. "I know that."

Terry reached over and shut off the light. In the darkness I could hear the whisper of clothes as she got out of her uniform. Moments later she slid into the bed and administered the ultimate painkiller.

CHAPTER FORTY

TUESDAY, AUGUST 29

BENNY, BOYCHICK, LOUIE, and Stuff waited with the gaggle of regulars for O'Mara's Irish Pub to open at ten o'clock. The temperature and humidity were once again in the low nineties, and when Colin opened the door the four of them followed the regulars into the air-conditioned interior and inhaled a refreshing breath of the cooler air.

The regulars took their seats at the bar, ignored the strangers, and smacked their lips in anticipation. Benny, Boychick, Louie, and Stuff sat at the end of the bar and folded their hands on it like a quartet of choirboys. Colin threw them a dirty look, angrily strode behind the bar, and proceeded to draw multiple tankards of beer. When all his regulars were served, he walked to the end of the bar and sneered. "Ya ain't welcome here," he said with all the distaste he could muster.

"Now that's a real shame," Boychick said, "'cause we came friendly-like."

"Get out!" snapped Colin.

Boychick dropped his chin to his chest and sighed. There would be no reasoning with this stubborn Irish bastard.

Stuff tried a different approach. "Look, Mr. O'Mara, we just came to see if Red's okay."

"Are ya blind? He ain't here."

"What about upstairs?"

Colin wasn't about to tell them anything, much less that he knew his brothers-in-law had picked up Red. "I ain't seen 'im since before he spent the day in jail—thanks to your lot."

"He didn't come home last night?"

"He don't come home a lotta nights. Ya oughta know that since it's *you* he's with!"

"He wasn't with us last night, and he didn't show up at Benny's this mornin'," said Stuff.

Colin leaned forward and stuck out his jaw. "Try puttin' 'im on a leash."

"So you haven't heard from him?" asked Stuff.

"Look now, ya fat guinea fuck, I told ya nice ya ain't welcome here. I wouldn't tell ya if I knew, and I wouldn't piss on ya if ya were on fire! Now, get out!"

Stuff's face flushed, and he moved forward involuntarily. Benny and Boychick grabbed his arms.

"Be calm, m'man," said Benny. "He ain't worth it."

Benny and Boychick backed Stuff toward the door. Louie hitched up his trousers, rocked forward on his toes, and pointed a finger at Colin. In an instant he became Jimmy Cagney.

"Nnnn . . . yew . . . you're gonna regret—yew ever said—anythin' like that—to that fat wop . . . nnnh . . . you dirty rat."

Colin picked up a beer mug and hurled it at Louie. He ducked, and it crashed through the front window.

"Ball four," said Louie, and darted out after his friends.

At the bar, the regulars were all frozen. They watched in awe as the last shards of jagged glass slowly broke away from the top of the window frame and crashed to the floor. They didn't quite realize the consequences until the first blast of hot air rushed through and hammered them.

Danny and Robert Collins had been interrogating Red since the prior afternoon at the Eighteenth Precinct. They were as exhausted as he was, and they'd gotten nothing. Red had resisted good cop, bad cop; no food, no water; solitary confinement; and a pretty good slapping around by Danny.

The morning newspapers had printed a description of the hoodlums given by the nuns, and the Collins bothers were fairly certain that Red would be able to identify them. They figured if he knew about the attack and who did it, it would shake him up. It was worth a shot.

They once again dragged him into an interrogation room. Robert pushed him into a chair, and they both sat on the table. Danny had a folded newspaper under his arm.

"Yer buddy's in the hospital," said Danny.

Red looked up at his uncle but said nothing. He face was bruised and puffy, and his eyes were bloodshot.

"He and the Jew kid got jumped on the library steps yesterday," Robert added.

"They say the Jew's critical," said Danny.

Red's eyes swung back and forth between them like a metronome.

"Ya don't believe us? Here . . ." Danny threw down an open newspaper. Red scanned it and spotted an article that described the attack. He immediately recognized the description of the bearded Russian. Stankovitch . . . who ran with Nick Colucci.

"I figure it's the same punks who tried to blow ya up," said Danny.

Red's face remained expressionless, and he pushed away the newspaper. The two brothers leaned in close to him. They suddenly became an extension of each other as they fired off a rapid-fire verbal barrage. Robert began.

"All we need is for you to finger Vesta."

"We don't even need the whole gang. Just Vesta!"

"This thing involves a lot of very dangerous people!"

"Yer mixed up with a bunch of punks whose leader's been marked!"

"He's goin' down! You wanna go with him?"

"I know ya hate yer father, but what about yer mother?"

"She's our sister. Suppose these pricks decide to throw a bomb at the pub?"

"I'm telling ya—ya give us Vesta and the bombs an' attacks stop!"

"Ya could be outta here in twenty minutes!"

"No charges, boyo!"

"A clean bill."

"All we want is Vesta!"

They were both breathing hard when they paused and leaned back. Danny finally caught his breath and leaned forward toward Red. Robert was still puffing.

"So. Whadda ya say?" asked Danny.

"I gotta take a piss," Red answered.

Danny couldn't help himself. He lashed out with a vicious backhand that somersaulted Red over the back of his chair.

At eleven o'clock, Detectives Sasso and Burns from Midtown-South arrived at the hospital and spent the better part of an hour questioning me about the attack on the library steps. For the second time in twenty-four hours, I told them nothing. I said I had no idea who attacked me and even less about who would *want* to attack me. They knew it was total bullshit, since the hospital had told them there was an armed guard in the next room. His name was Gus Chello, and he worked for Angelo Maserelli, who they knew was a labor racketeer. Obviously they also knew I was Gino Vesta's son, but for some reason there was no mention of my father. They had questioned Gus but had again gotten nowhere. Angelo's man had a permit for the gun, and he was paying for the room. Dead end.

They asked if I didn't think it was pretty goddamn unusual for a guy who had no enemies to be chain-whipped and bombed within twenty-four hours. I said, No . . . after all, we're in New York. They didn't like that. I then asked if they thought about the possibility of it being a bunch of anti-Semites—Sidney Butcher was a Jew, and he was at both scenes. If I'd been in an interrogation room, I'd have gotten the rubber hose for that suggestion.

The Collins brothers had told Sasso and Burns earlier that Red O'Mara had given up nothing, so the whole goddamn morning had been a waste of time. The detectives left, swearing that sooner or later they'd nail my balls to a wall next to those of my whole crew.

Louie had been waiting outside, and when the detectives left, he came in and told me about the conversation he'd had with his father. I told him I appreciated his concern but that it wouldn't be over until we evened the score with Nick Colucci. He said he understood and would be with me—but I knew it was out of loyalty, not conviction.

Bouncer arrived next and told me that *his* father had put his foot down and didn't want him hanging out with us anymore. Actually, I was relieved. If anybody was going to get hurt, it would probably be Bouncer, who couldn't stay out of his own way. It was one thing to let him hang around and be involved in a few of our simpler capers, but I knew there was no way he could handle what was coming. I told him I understood, released him from our crew, and said we would still be friends. Bouncer was so overwhelmed that it took him almost a minute to stutter out his "th-thanks."

Boychick, Benny, and Stuff arrived at noon with a dozen cannolis from Ferrara's Bakery. They hovered around my bed and asked how I felt. I told them the feeling in my arm had come back and my vision seemed to have cleared up overnight. I didn't tell them what I thought the cure had been.

What I did tell them was that Dr. Singh had checked on me after breakfast and said that if I was still okay by four p.m., I was free to go home. The swelling on my face had been reduced by ice packs, and Singh had removed the bandage covering the stitches. They noted the ten little knots above my jawline where a tooth had ripped through my cheek, but all things considered, they said I looked pretty good.

Stuff opened the box of cannolis and handed me one. "The kind you love," he said, passing out the pastries, "with nougats and crystallized fruit." He selected one for himself and blissfully bit it in half.

Benny leaned over my shoulder and peered at the newspaper on the bed beside me. It was folded to reveal a partially completed crossword puzzle. "Since when you inta crosswords?"

"Sidney got me started."

"Ya seen 'im yet?" asked Boychick.

I shook my head. "Not yet. He's still in a coma."

"Jesus," said Louie.

"You're lucky you're not in a coma," said Stuff.

"Your father told us it was Colucci again," said Boychick.

"With the Russomano brothers and Stankovitch," I answered. "We gotta find 'em."

"We're on it. So's yer old man."

"Good," I said, and then realized . . . "Where's Red?"

The four who had been to the pub that morning exchanged glances.

"Could be more bad news," said Boychick.

"How so?"

Boychick threw up his hands. "He disappeared. He wasn't here last night, he didn't show up this mornin', and his ol' man says he ain't seen 'im since Sunday."

"Shit," I said.

"Red don't just disappear. Not the type," Benny observed.

"After his father's act this morning, I wouldn't be surprised if he had him locked up," said Louie.

258

"You mean like in jail?" asked Stuff. He popped a second cannoli into his mouth and licked his fingers.

"Possible," I mused. "His uncles are cops."

The guys exchanged looks once again as they considered it. "Ya think they threw him back inna tank?" Boychick asked.

Bouncer offered a suggestion. "There's a soprano in the c-chorus with my pop. Her husband's a cop in Midtown-S-South. Maybe I could f-find out."

"Hey, Bounce!" said Boychick. "I thought you wanted out. Now ya wanna be a spy?"

"I'm just tryin' t-to help," Bouncer said sheepishly.

Thanks," I said, "but my ol' man knows more cops than your soprano—and Costello has more of 'em on his payroll than the commissioner. Between the two of 'em, we'll find out."

"Hey," said Benny, pointing, "what's with the lipstick onna pillow!"

The guys craned their necks, saw the red smudge, and looked back at me with arched eyebrows. There was no getting out of it. "Terry's back," I said.

"Yer kiddin'," said Boychick.

"Here? In the room?" asked Stuff.

"Last night, around midnight. She left this mornin' with the eight o'clock shift change."

Benny whistled, swept his hand toward me, and exclaimed, "Gentlemen . . . da man!"

"What happened?" asked Louie.

"The usual—cucumber sandwiches and a poetry reading," I said.

The guys stayed until they were shooed out by a nurse with a lunch cart. On the way out, Stuff passed the cart and without breaking stride swept a banana off a plate. It was an illusive, silken move that would have been admired by Houdini.

CHAPTER FORTY-ONE

FRANK COSTELLO WAS at the racetrack in Saratoga Springs, New York, when he heard about the attack on the library steps. He put it together with the warehouse fire, returned to Manhattan late Monday night, and called my father. He wanted to meet him for lunch at "21." Once again the invitation was friendly, but my father knew it was a command performance, and he was sure he knew why.

My father entered the club and found Costello and Joe Adonis sitting against the wall at a table in the bar area. As usual, the room was packed with the rich and famous enjoying three-martini lunches as they blew air kisses around the room to the equally rich and famous. In the midst of the hubbub and table-hopping, my father noticed that several fawning socialite types were hovering over Costello's table. He knew the socialites would later try to impress their friends by proudly announcing that they had met the notorious gangster who ran New York's shadow government. My father smiled at the hypocrisy of "civilians" and approached the table.

Costello dismissed his admirers, motioned my father into a seat, and said, "Thank you for coming, Gino."

My father sat down and greeted them. "Frank . . . Joe."

"You like a drink, Gino?" asked Costello.

"Soda water," he replied.

Adonis signaled a waiter and gave him the order. "We ordered you the chopped salad, Gino."

My father said, "*Grazie.*" It was his usual order at "21," and they knew it.

"Gino," Costello began in a reasonable voice, "I thought we had an understanding."

"We did, and we do. It seems that others don't."

Costello glanced at Adonis, then looked back at my father. He leaned forward, clasped his hands, and said somewhat apologetically, "A lot of people think you torched Drago's warehouse."

"And you, Frank. What do you think?"

Costello shrugged. "I think the same."

"I also think you know Drago had Nick Colucci attack my son . . . twice."

"Gino. I don't know. I suspect. The Commission is going crazy. You promised me the problem would stop—I promised them."

"I promised you I would not make an unprovoked move on Gee-gee Petrone. But it was Petrone who went to Drago, and it was Drago who sent Colucci against my son. First with a bomb—and again with three of his thugs at the library. His friend may die. Petrone was behind both, and I think you know why, Frank."

"Can you prove it?" asked Adonis.

"Not yet," said my father, "But . . ."

The three men waited while a waiter arrived and poured a glass of soda water. My father took a sip and put down the glass. "Frank," he said, "we know—in the end, this is not about me."

Adonis looked at Costello and said, "Genovese." It was a statement made in complete disgust.

My father nodded. "Through Petrone—who's using Drago—who's using Colucci." He paused and tapped his fingers on the table. "But at the top is Genovese."

"Why? How does coming after you help him?" asked Adonis.

My father rubbed his index finger along the side of his nose. "I've asked the same question, and I've only found one answer . . . Anastasia."

"Albert?" asked Adonis, mystified. "How?"

"You have to think like Machiavelli. You know him?" asked Gino.

"Medici's guy," said Costello, "Sixteenth century. He wrote *The Prince*. Lansky made me read it."

"I'm impressed," said Adonis, "but what the hell does this have to do with Anastasia?"

"I believe all this nonsense about the fur theft was designed to get me to retaliate against Petrone. That would allow the Commission to come after me. When Anastasia found out—*he'd* retaliate, and the Commission would go after him." He turned to Costello. "Genovese would not dare come after you with Anastasia still alive. But with your most powerful ally gone, he could try it." He leaned forward and folded his hands. "'First weaken your enemy—then destroy him.' Machiavelli, *The Prince*."

Adonis leaned back and pursed his lips as if to whistle, but no sound came out. He said, "Jesus Christ. The guy's a fuckin' corkscrew!"

Gino nodded. "And he'll do anything to take you out, Frank."

"I've been aware of that for a long time, my friend," said Costello. He continued firmly but with patience, "but I can't take suspicion to the Commission. I need proof."

"We know they want peace," said Adonis, "but if they think Genovese is trying to take you out without their approval, they'll act."

"Not without proof," Costello insisted.

"Genovese and Petrone are smart," explained my father. "Drago and Colucci are not. They'll do something stupid, and obvious. When they do, you'll have your proof." He raised his glass and said, *"Salute."*

The impressed socialite types who had been surreptitiously watching them shuddered. They probably thought they had just witnessed an assassination order. In the final analysis, they probably had.

CHAPTER FORTY-TWO

AT FOUR O'CLOCK, Dr. Singh gave me a final exam and said I could check out. Since my vision and the feeling in my shoulder had returned, he said the concussion was probably slight and there was no nerve damage. The shoulder and face would be sore but would heal normally. I asked about Sidney, and he said Sidney was still in the ICU. He'd come out of his coma and was doing better, but he was still critical . . . no visitors.

Earlier in the day, I'd asked Gus Chello to find out where the ICU was located. When Dr. Singh left I went into the next room and got the answer.

"This floor," he said, "right side of the intersection at the far end of the hall."

"Nurses' station?"

"On the left."

I told Gus to wait and I'd be right back. I walked to the intersection of the third-floor corridors and peeked around the corner at the nurses' station. A nurse was at the desk, her nose buried in paperwork. So far so good. There was a large set of double doors marked ICU on the other side of the intersection. I bolted across and through the doors, peeked through five curtains, and finally found Sidney behind the sixth. He was lying in bed attached to a maze of equipment. There was an oxygen mask and a couple of other lines plugged into beeping monitors. An IV drip was taped to his arm, and his head was swathed in bandages. I eased a chair over to the bed and watched Sidney's chest rise and fall in shallow breaths. I sat and took his hand. "Sidney," I whispered, "it's me."

His eyes fluttered open. "I've been waiting," he said, "I knew you'd come." His voice was as fragile as tissue.

"Jesus, Sidney, you scared the shit out of all of us. How do you feel?"

Sidney smiled weakly and said, "I've got a pretty good headache."

"Sidney, I'm sorry. I had my head up my ass. I never saw 'em comin'."

"It's okay, Vinny, it wasn't your fault."

I started to object and then figured it wouldn't do much good, so I changed the subject. "The doctor said you were in a coma."

"I know. I even knew when I was in it."

"The coma?"

"Uh-huh. It was beautiful. Kind of white and soft . . . and there was music."

"No kiddin'," I said. "In the coma?"

"Uh-huh. And you know something else?"

"What?"

"God."

I didn't quite know how to respond to that. "Eh . . . God?"

"Uh-huh. I didn't see Him . . . but it felt like He was there."

"Jesus," I said, and unconsciously crossed myself.

"Do you believe in God?" he asked.

"Well, sure. I mean, I guess so. I go to church an' all. I even went to the synagogue with you a couple of times."

"Not like that. Not like church. More like what you feel when see a billion, billion stars . . . and you think: Who could do that?"

I'd never looked at stars that way. "You make a good point."

"Vinny, would you promise me something?"

"Sure, Sidney, what?"

"You'll always be my friend."

That took me by surprise. "Jesus, of course I'll always be your friend! Why wouldn't I?"

"Promise?"

"Sure I promise. Now get some rest and I'll see you tomorrow—even if I have to sneak in again."

I patted Sidney's hand and headed out. I was almost out the door when I heard him say, "Love you . . ."

"Me too you, buddy."

Even though Sidney's head was swathed in bandages, I could see he was grinning from ear to ear.

I went back to pick up Gus and found my father and Angelo waiting for me. We left the building, and when we got to the parking lot I said I wanted to drop by Benny's place to see the guys. I asked if Gus could drop me off. My father and Angelo agreed I could remain in Gus's very capable hands, but my father wanted me home in time for dinner. I got into Gus's car and said, "Stop at a phone booth, I gotta make a call." Gus stopped at a booth on the next corner; I made my call and got back into the car.

"Benny's?" he asked.

"No . . . East Seventy-sixth Street."

I wanted to see Terry.

When we got to Terry's apartment, I told Gus to wait; I'd be out in an hour. The doorman said Terry had run out to pick something up and that I should go on up. He knew I had a key to the apartment.

I took the elevator, let myself in, and decided to have a little fun. I closed the drapes in the bedroom, turned on the yellow night-light, and left the bedroom door ajar. Then I got undressed and crawled into bed. Five minutes later I heard the front door open and close. Soft footsteps crossed the living room and became the click of high heels on the kitchen floor. The refrigerator opened and closed, followed by the distinctive sound of ice tumbling into a small metal bucket. More footsteps, this time coming toward the bedroom, and then Terry pushed open the door. She stopped, and the light from the living room silhouetted her as she peered into the darkened bedroom. She was carrying a bottle of champagne in an ice bucket. I quickly shut my eyes and started to snore. It had the desired effect. She put down the champagne bucket and placed her hands on her hips, exasperated.

"Men," she grumbled to herself. "All the same . . . young, old; rich, poor; wiseguys, legit . . . take everything for goddamn granted!" She finally sat on the bed, and I chuckled.

"You're early," I said.

"You're awake?"

"Uh-huh."

Again her hands went to her hips. "What was the snoring routine?"

"I wanted to see your reaction. It was good. The hips bit, the pout . . . good."

She slapped my arm with the back of her hand. "It wasn't a pout."

"No?"

"No. A little frown, maybe."

"You were pissed . . ."

"Bastard."

I laughed, pulled her down, and rolled on top of her. "I was just tryin' to get a rise out of you."

"I'm supposed to be the one who gets a rise out of you," she said, and grabbed me.

"Ouch!"

"While I have your attention, are there any more cute li'l moves you have in mind?"

"Just the one you're beginnin' to feel."

"That's a move a girl can identify with," she said, grinning.

"I just got out of the hospital. Wanna help me celebrate?"

"Why not?"

As usual, when Terry and I ravaged each other it was not without sound or frenzy. There was quite a bit of both, and suddenly we heard banging on the bedroom wall. It was coming from next door.

Mr. Hoffler.

We laughed and banged back. When we were finally satiated, exhausted, I lit a pair of cigarettes, and handed one to her, and we both lay back. We stared at the ceiling and smoked in silence for a few minutes, and then Terry broke the mood. "My folks got back from Miami yesterday . . ." She took a long drag on her cigarette and exhaled. "I'm leaving for Georgia in the mornin', sugah."

"Terry, you don't have to leave. We'll work it out . . ."

"It's no use, Vinny. Nothing's changed. I'm still me—you're still you."

"I'll talk to my father . . ."

She rolled toward me and caressed my cheek. "Vinny . . . don't you see, he can't let it happen. Maybe someday, maybe a few years from now while I'm out on the coast and everyone's forgotten about me . . . but not now."

She was right, and for the first time, I realized it. I got up and started to dress. "I have to meet the guys, and I haven't seen my mother since I got out of the hospital. I'll come back later . . . we'll celebrate our last night, okay?"

She smiled. "I'd like that."

I managed a smile and said, "Mr. Hoffler won't."

CHAPTER FORTY-THREE

FTER A FULL DAY of scouting for Nick Colucci, Boychick walked back to his basement apartment on Thirty-fifth Street and descended the stairs. He was about to open the door when he heard loud voices. It sounded like an argument between Leo and Carmine, and he thought he caught the name "Colucci." He quietly opened the door and listened.

"I'm tellin' ya," Carmine yelled, "I got it from a prime source! I know where Colucci's hidin'!"

"The fuck ya think's gonna believe ya?" Leo shot back.

"What's the problem?" asked Carmine.

"Us!" Leo responded. "We go to Vesta wit it an' he's gonna think it's a setup."

Boychick padded across the front room and paused outside the kitchen.

"Whyn't we tell 'im and let him decide?" Carmine pleaded. "It pans out, we'll be heroes! Gino might even take ya on his crew!"

"Ya think?"

"It could happen!"

"I dunno. If yer info ain't right . . ."

"I'm tellin' ya, it's gold!"

"I know, but . . ."

Boychick walked into the kitchen. Leo froze in midsentence. He and Carmine exchanged fearful glances.

"Where is he?" asked Boychick. His voice was brittle as glass.

Leo allowed his eyes to dart around. "What? Who?" he asked.

Boychick advanced on his father. Leo backed into the stove.

Boychick grabbed the front of Leo's shirt. "Stop with the bullshit. I heard ya."

"What? What didja hear?" Leo whimpered.

Boychick pulled Leo into a nose-to-nose. "Colucci! Where is he?"

"Boychick, wait," Carmine pleaded, and tried to separate them. "I know . . . let 'im go."

Boychick released Leo and turned to Carmine. "I'm waitin'."

"Look," Carmine said affably, "this is valuable information, ya know what I mean? We should get somethin' fer it. Maybe Gino could trow somethin' our way. It's onny fair."

"Gino ain't gonna take 'im on," said Boychick, tossing his thumb toward Leo.

"Maybe not. But why not let him decide? If not that, maybe somethin' else. Gino's fair. He'll be grateful. Take us to 'im."

Leo said, "Right . . . let Gino decide."

Boychick turned to Leo and held him with his cold gaze for what he hoped were the longest few seconds of Leo's life. Finally he said, "Tonight. Wait here. I'll tell you when."

He turned and walked toward the door, listening with disgust as the two grown men tripped over each other and lunged for the pint of Four Roses on the table at the same time. They fought a brief battle for control before Leo's shaking hand splashed the last of the whiskey into two tumblers.

At six o'clock, my mother and Mrs. Butcher were preparing supper in our kitchen. Mr. Butcher was in the living room with my father. My parents were determined to spend as much time as possible with the Butchers while Sidney was still on the critical list. Tonight, Sarah was preparing a side dish of kasha and bows while my mother made osso bucco.

When I walked in the door, the Butchers greeted me like the prodigal son. My mother threw her arms around me and cried happy tears. When I told them I had seen Sidney just a few hours earlier, they asked me a hundred questions. I couldn't answer most of them, but I convinced them that while he was not out of the woods, he was doing fine. They were visibly relieved.

My father informed me that he had found out Red was being held at Midtown-South on a numbers charge and he would get a writ in the morning. Then he and Mr. Butcher returned to reading *Il Progresso* and the *Forward* while my mother and Sarah resumed preparing dinner. I sat on the couch and picked up the sports section.

Mr. Butcher sighed and put down his paper.

My father looked up and asked, "You found something?"

"No," said Mr. Butcher. "I have no concentration. Nothing is important."

My father lowered his paper. "Mr. Butcher, you heard Vinny . . . Sidney is doing well." He smiled and said, "This is good for the Jews."

Mr. Butcher smiled back and nodded. "You're right. I need to take my mind off." He raised the paper. "I'll find something."

There was a knock at the door, and my mother went to answer it.

"Hi, Mrs. Vesta," said Boychick. "Can I see Vinny and Mr. Vesta a minute?"

"Sure. Come in." She stepped aside and held the door open.

"No," said Boychick. "I mean, could they come out?"

Mickey called out, "Gino! Vincenzo! Boychick would like to see you outside."

"*Scusi*, Mr. Butcher." My father and I got up, walked out into the hall, and closed the door. "A problem?" he asked.

"I dunno," said Boychick. "It could be a break. This friend of my ol' man's says he knows where Nick Colucci is holed up."

I said, "You gotta be kiddin' . . ."

My father's eyes narrowed. "He suddenly just brought you this?"

"No. Actually, I heard him and my ol' man arguin'.'"

"His name?" asked my father.

"Carmine somethin'. I think he used to be with Joe Zox, but I wouldn't trust him or Leo as far as I could piss in a hurricane."

"What'd you hear?" I asked.

Boychick explained what happened. My father and I listened attentively. Finally, he asked, "And they want to bring this only to me?"

"That's what they said."

"Pop," I objected. "You agreed. Colucci's mine."

"He'll still be yours," he said. "But first we have to take him."

My father's entire crew, as well as my guys, had been trying to smoke out Colucci's hiding place all day, to no avail. We had not yet heard from the twins, but we had no reason to believe they had fared any better. I knew he was very wary about Leo's information, but he probably felt he couldn't afford to ignore the opportunity.

My father said, "Pick up the Buick. Bring them to my office at ten o'clock."

"You trust them?" I asked.

"No," he responded, "but I have no choice."

"Right," said Boychick. "Anythin' else?"

"Call Angelo. Tell him to meet me at nine-thirty. My office."

"Right," said Boychick, and headed down the stairs.

We were about to begin the bloodiest night of the week.

CHAPTER FORTY-FOUR

BOYCHICK PICKED UP STUFF, then drove home to collect Leo and Carmine. They arrived at my father's office at the appointed hour of ten o'clock. I was sitting on the couch, drinking a Coke. My father was sitting behind his desk, and Angelo was sitting in front of it. They were both wearing dark suits, and I'd changed into a black shirt and slacks. We all looked like Louie.

Leo glanced around the office, noted its somewhat spartan nature, and tried to hide his disappointment. He must have imagined that a powerful caporegime's office would be plush, like in the movies. Carmine made no effort to hide his displeasure and grimaced at the surroundings. My father and Angelo did not miss either reaction.

Boychick sat in one of the captain's chairs and glared at his father. Stuff sat next to me and took out a bag of peanuts. No one moved or said anything while he noisily ripped open the package and began tossing the peanuts into his mouth. Leo finally got up the nerve to approach the desk while Carmine hung nervously by the door.

"I can't tell ya how glad I am ta be of some service ta ya, Gino," Leo gushed, extending his hand.

My father took it. "It's always a pleasure to see you, Leo," he said graciously.

"Hi there, Angelo," Leo said brightly. He moved toward Angelo and indicated Stuff. "That's some son ya got there, Angelo, a real chip off the ol' block." He again extended his hand. Angelo ignored it. Leo swallowed and murmured, "Heh-heh . . ." He indicated Carmine. "This here's my pal Carmine Pucci. He's the one what got the information."

"Whadda ya got for us, Carmine?" said Angelo, cutting to the chase.

"Well, ya see," said Carmine, "what it is, is I got dis pal works down at the Fulton Fish Market in Socks Lanza's crew. You know, Joe Zox?" He waited for an answer.

My father said, "I know him."

"Right. An' we wuz havin' a drink over at Barlow's Tavern, down by da market—ya know it?" He again waited for an answer.

"I know it."

"Right. So my pal, he says he knows a hooker who's got Nick Colucci shacked up at her place."

"This hooker—she got a name?" Angelo growled.

"Ah . . . ya see, I'm more than willin' ta tell ya, but it's onny fair we get somethin' in return," said Carmine, leaving the sentence hanging.

"What do you have in mind?" my father asked.

"Fer me? Nuttin'," said Carmine, holding out his palms. "But I'd like ya should do somethin' fer my friend."

My father looked at Leo. "Yes?"

Leo started to plead. "Gino . . . please, take me on. I'll do anythin'. I'll start onna bottom. Run numbers, do collections, drive—anythin'!" Leo pitched for all he was worth, which wasn't much, but his begging did sound sincere since he had rehearsed the plea in his mind for years. "I could be really good if I got a shot," he rambled on. "I'd even do a audition thing—you know, so's ya could try me out. It's my dream, Gino . . . please."

Leo finished his pitch, and the room went silent. Boychick looked at his father like he was something that should be scraped off the bottom of a shoe. He got up and left the room.

My father allowed a dramatic pause before he gave Leo his answer. "All right, Leo . . . you have what you ask."

Leo rushed forward and pumped my father's hand. "Thank you, Gino, thank you! You won't regret this."

"I sincerely hope not," my father said evenly.

"Now," said Angelo, "where's Colucci?"

"We'll take Gino to 'im," said Carmine, "but just Gino."

"What?" barked Angelo.

"The way it's gotta be," said Carmine. "Drago's got people protectin' Colucci. I know who they are and where they are. I kin get by 'em, but onny Gino, Leo, and me. It can't be no mob scene or we'll never get in."

Angelo threw up his hands. "Gino, this is nuts! It could be a setup, fer chrissake!"

"It could be, Angelo, but I don't think so. I listened to how Boychick came by the information. I think they can lead us to Colucci."

"Goddammit, Gino," Angelo pleaded, "ya could be walkin' into a—"

"*Basta!*" thundered my father. "Enough!" Leo and Carmine recoiled. "I know what I'm doing, Angelo." He got up and retrieved his hat from the standing hat rack. "You and the boys wait for us here." He put on his hat and said, "All right, Leo, take me to Colucci."

Leo and Carmine started out. At the door my father turned to Angelo and said, "Pick up Barbera and bring him here."

"Gino . . . ," pleaded Angelo.

"Pick up Barbera," my father repeated, and left. Carmine followed him.

"Be back in no time," said Leo. He smiled, waved good-bye, and quickly brushed past Boychick as he was coming back in.

Angelo shook his head and removed his hat from the hat rack. He put it on, took a deep breath, and slowly let it out. "See ya," he said, and left.

I took out a Lucky, lit it, and called Benny's apartment. I told him to pick up Louie and come to my father's office to await word. Stuff got three beers out of the minibar and handed one to me and one to Boychick. We popped the tops and found seats. Stuff leaned back into the couch, and a concerned look came over his face. "You think it could be a setup?" he asked.

Boychick shrugged. "I dunno. It's possible."

"I've never seen my father look that worried," Stuff said.

"What?" I asked. "You think he's rattled?"

"Him? Never. Worried, maybe—never rattled. He can handle anything."

Boychick contemplated his beer can. "You guys're pretty lucky, you know that?"

Stuff turned to Boychick "Us? How so?"

"Yer old man. You love him, he loves you." He looked at me. "You—the same."

"You're right," I said.

"Weird," said Boychick. "Fathers. How things lay out. When we were talkin ta Red the other night, he said he could kill his ol' man. Sometimes I think I should kill mine. And Benny's is a vegetable."

"Yeah," I said, "but Louie's good, I'm good, and so's Bouncer."

Boychick nodded, still staring at his can, "Yeah. Look at it that way, we're four for seven . . . battin' over four hundred. Too bad it ain't baseball."

Leo drove across the Manhattan Bridge and down Flatbush Avenue and parked his Mercury convertible near the corner of Atlantic Avenue. Sherry's apartment was in the small triangle made by the intersection of Atlantic, Flatbush, and Fourth Avenue. He told my father to hunker down in the backseat so that Drago's watchers wouldn't see him and to remain there while Carmine got out of the car and distracted them. "Carmine's gonna take out the guy in the De Soto watchin' the back entrance on Fourth," said Leo, "When he does, we're in. Colucci's onna second floor. We grab 'im, an' we're back out an' away in two minutes."

"Who will be with him?" asked Gino.

"Just da hook, Sherry somethin'. They're prolly both drunk."

Leo was right—at least about Sherry.

My father and Leo took the elevator to Sherry's second-floor apartment, and Leo eased open the door without knocking. The lights were out in the living room, but they could see across it and into the kitchen, where Nick Colucci was sitting at the kitchen table with a tall redhead. They were playing cards and drinking gin. The window air conditioner was turned off, and it was stifling. Sweat was running down Nick's face.

Leo paused and stopped my father. He held his index finger in front of his lips and gleefully watched the kitchen. He whispered to him that he wanted to take a minute to enjoy Nick's discomfort.

"Jeesh," Sherry groaned. "Turn on the goddamn air condishener." She had polished off her sherry and started on the gin. She was slurring her words and dropping her cards.

"It's too noisy."

"I'm burnin' up in here!" she snapped.

"So jump out the window!"

"Jeesh! Ya don't hafta get nashty."

"Just play a fuckin' card."

"I can't shee 'em."

"Oh, fer Christ sake, can't ya just . . ." He froze. In the living room, Carmine had arrived and Nick heard him shut the door. He stared through the kitchen doorway and trembled when he saw my father and Leo coming toward him. Leo pointed his gun at Nick and smiled.

"Hello, Nick. I brung a frienda yours."

Nick didn't answer; he just sat there, paralyzed, waiting. A moment later he got what he was waiting for. My father felt the touch of steel on his neck and heard the click of a hammer. Carmine said, "Okay, Gino, don't make a problem . . . This here ain't personal."

Leo swung his gun away from Nick and pointed it at my father. Nick relaxed, and the air rushed out of his lungs. Sherry's eyes darted drunkenly from Nick, to my father, to Leo. She hiccuped.

Carmine reached around, pulled the gun out of my father's shoulder holster, and said, "Now put yer hands in yer pockets and back up slow-like. You'n me're gonna take a little ride."

My father did as he was told and backed out of the kitchen. The charade was over.

CHAPTER FORTY-FIVE

NONE OF DRAGO'S neighbors heard the thuds, grunts, and moans that were coming from his brownstone. They probably wouldn't have reported them if they had. They knew who lived there. Carlo had been working on the Cavallo twins for almost two hours. They were tied to facing chairs in the den, stripped to their shorts and bleeding.

For the past forty-eight hours Carlo, Chucky, and Drago's entire crew had been on the street looking for a man who matched the description given to him by Marty, his dumbshit warehouse guard. The so-called blond who looked like a schoolteacher. The guy in the white suit. Drago was sure the guy was involved with the fire—and even surer when he had gotten a call from an associate named Stricker, who ran a local pool hall. Stricker told Drago that a guy had come into his place asking questions about Drago's friend Nick Colucci. Stricker had gotten suspicious and followed the guy to a house in Queens. Stricker said, "Coupla minutes later, *annuder* guy shows up who looks so much like the *first* guy that they hadda be twins. A pair a blonds who look like fuckin' schoolteachers, fer chrissakes!"

That did it. Drago put together the whole scenario for the night his warehouse was torched. He drove to the Queens address with Carlo and Chucky, and if the twins hadn't been so engrossed in watching their brand-new Dumont television set with an eight-inch tube, they probably would've heard the lock pick working on their back door. They were sitting on a couch with their backs to the living room door when Carlo put a bullet through the TV tube, blasting them both with a shower of glass confetti. Dino and Matty were so shocked, their assailants took them out like a pair of lambs.

Now, every fifteen minutes Carlo slowly donned a pair of leather gloves and beat one twin for about five minutes while the other one watched. He gave them fifteen minutes to think about giving him answers—and then repeated the process while the opposite twin watched. When they passed out, Chucky doused them with water. Their fair-skinned faces were bruised, swollen, and bloodied. Their spirit was not.

He had started with Dino. He was in the fourth go-round, and it was Matty's turn. "So," Carlo said to Matty, "you ready for a little conversation, or do I go on with the show?"

"By all means, go on," Matty answered through lacerated, swollen lips. "Dino," he called out, "fifty bucks says you talk before I do."

"You're on!" said Dino.

The exchange earned Matty a vicious backhand that knocked him out.

Carlo whirled around to Dino. "Goddammit, Dino, ya want me to kill your brother or what?"

"I dunno, Carlo," Dino muttered, running his tongue over broken teeth. "Matty dies hard."

"For what?" yelled Carlo. "A fuckin' warehouse? Admit Vesta told ya to burn it down an' we're done!"

"Are you nuts?"

"What the hell are ya talkin' about?" Carlo bellowed.

"I talk and I lose fifty bucks!"

Carlo punched out Dino and screamed in frustration. "Goddamn you two!"

Drago walked in. "Nothin'?" he asked.

"Not one fuckin' thing . . . unless ya count a bunch of wise-ass remarks."

The doorbell rang. "Must be Leo," said Drago, and walked into the front hall. Chucky followed him to the door and opened it. My father was standing there, flanked by Leo and Carmine.

"Nice of ya ta stop by, Vesta." Drago stepped aside and waved them in with an exaggerated sweep of his hand. "There's some friends a yours been waitin'. They'd be glad ta see ya . . . if they could see."

Drago led the group into the den just as Carlo was dumping a pitcher of water on Dino. He had already doused Matty, and they were both coming around.

Matty saw my father and managed a smile. "Hey, boss . . . sorry we didn't have time to dress."

My father looked from one to the other, noted the puddles under their chairs, and shook his head.

"They keep askin' about a fire . . ." Dino chuckled and spat out some blood. "We don't know nothin' 'bout no fire, nohow—no, sir!" He chuckled again, and Matty joined him. Carlo backhanded Dino.

"That's enough!" my father roared. "It's okay, boys," he added solemnly. "It's over." He turned to Drago. "I ordered the warehouse burned."

Drago stared at him for a few moments, then the corners of his mouth turned up and very slowly a smile formed. "Yer prepared to tell that ta the Commission?"

My father nodded. "I am."

Drago turned to Chucky. "Tie 'im up."

Chucky gestured Gino to a chair and did as he was told.

Drago went to his desk, opened it, and removed a thick brown envelope. He handed it to Leo, who hadn't moved since he entered the room. Carmine was standing next to him.

"There's five grand in there," said Drago. "I want you guys ta take a little vacation till dis blows over. Havana, Bermuda—wherever. A coupla weeks. Have a good time. When ya get back I'll have somethin' permanent fer ya."

Leo beamed, grabbed Drago's hand, and pumped it. "Jeez, boss, I can't tell ya how good that makes me feel. Ya won't regret this. I promise. Me'n Carmine'll really do good fer ya, right, Carmine?"

"Right," Carmine said enthusiastically, "really good."

"Chucky, take 'em home inna limo. They deserve it. They did good work tonight." He slapped Leo on the back.

Chucky gave a last tug to the ropes holding my father and headed out the door.

"I got my car," said Leo.

"No problem. I'll put it in my garage till ya get back," said Drago, and ushered them to the door.

"Gee, that's great, boss. Again just lemme say—"

Drago cut him off. "Don't mention it," he said, and shooed them down the steps after Chucky. Then, as an afterthought, he called out, "Carlo, go wit Chucky, I'm outta cigars."

Carlo took off his gloves and retrieved his hat. He put it on, started out, and then turned back to the three prisoners. "A pleasure doin' business witcha!" He tipped his hat and left.

Drago came back into the den, smiled at my father, and lit a cigar.

Leo and Carmine settled joyfully into the back of the limo and rubbed their hands over the plush leather seats. Carlo sat facing them, then called over his shoulder to Chucky, "Stop by Sheffield's on Fourteenth, I gotta pick up cigars fer the boss."

Chucky nodded and pulled out. Carlo poured two tumblers of Canadian Club and handed them to Leo and Carmine. He poured one for himself and raised it in a toast.

"To the future," said Carlo. "*Salute.*"

Leo and Carmine raised their glasses. "*P' cent anni*," they responded, and drank. They both savored the flavor and nodded appreciatively. They were not used to premium whiskey.

"Great stuff," said Leo, smacking his lips.

"Onny da best from now on," Carmine agreed. He clinked his tumbler against Leo's and finished his drink.

Leo glanced out the window and said, "Hey, Chucky, ya missed Fourteenth Street."

Chucky looked in his rearview mirror. He heard a *pfffft!* and saw Leo's left eye disappear. A moment later he heard another *pfffft!* and Carmine slumped into Leo. Carmine had a small hole in the middle of his forehead, but the backs of both their heads were blown open—Carlo was using dum-dums. He unscrewed the silencer of his .22 and finished his drink while Chucky drove to a landfill in Sheepshead Bay. They crossed the Manhattan Bridge, headed down Flatbush Avenue, and drove right past Sherry's apartment. It was the same route Leo and Carmine had taken less than an hour before.

CHAPTER FORTY-SIX

I HADN'T KNOWN IT, but the scene between Leo, Carmine, Angelo, and my father at his office was pure theater—on both sides. Chucky had gotten through to Angelo a half hour before Leo and Carmine had showed up, letting him know that Drago was setting a trap using Leo Delfina. When I found out, I thought Angelo's performance was worthy of Louie.

My father had instructed Angelo to take Barbera and follow him to his meeting with Nick Colucci. They had done as ordered, trailing them to Brooklyn and then back to Drago's brownstone. When they got to Drago's, Barbera went to a phone booth, called Costello, then called Boychick and me. He told us to take a cab to Drago's brownstone on Thirty-eighth Street. We arrived twenty minutes later. Costello and Adonis pulled up in their limo a little after midnight. Everyone got out of their cars and looked toward Drago's brownstone half a block away. Angelo told Costello and Adonis what had happened in the past two hours while Boychick and I remained silent. These were the big guys. If they wanted to hear from us, they'd say so.

"They still inside?" asked Costello.

Angelo said, "Chucky and Carlo left with Leo Delfina and Carmine Pucci. Drago answered the door when Gino got here, so he's still inside. Who else, I don't know."

"You're sure Gino didn't come here of his own free will?" asked Costello.

"Leo had a gun in his back," Angelo said.

I saw Boychick's fists ball up, but he remained quiet.

Costello nodded thoughtfully. "If Drago had Gino kidnapped, I'll nail his ass. This time we're witnesses."

"It still won't give us Genovese," Adonis observed.

"It will after Angelo gets through with him," said Costello.

"We ring the bell, he could rabbit," said Angelo.

"He could also come out blazin'," said Adonis.

"Barbera, you got your tool kit?" Costello asked.

"Always," said Bo. He removed a small leather case from his inside jacket pocket.

"Pick the lock," said Costello. "Carlo and Chucky are gone. With any luck, he could be alone, and we'll surprise him." He looked at Boychick and me. "When we get inside, you two stay back."

Boychick and I nodded, and the six of us crossed the street. When we got to the brownstone, we climbed the steps and shielded Barbera while he went to work on the lock. In the dim light it looked as if the six of us were waiting for someone to answer the door. A minute later, Bo quietly eased the door open and we entered. The hallway was dark, but we could see light coming from the den. We smelled cigar smoke and heard voices. There was no question: The voices belonged to my father and Drago.

Costello put his finger on his lips. He motioned for Adonis and Barbera to stay with Boychick and me and guard the door. He and

Angelo moved down the hallway. They paused just outside the den and listened to what was obviously the middle of a conversation.

My father was saying, ". . . and that's when Petrone came to you."

"What the hell does it matter?" Drago shot back. He was seated behind his desk, chewing on a cigar. My father and the twins were still strapped to the chairs.

"Because he set you up. It was Petrone who told my son to raid your warehouse."

"You're fulla shit. Why would he do that?"

"Who told you Vinny had your furs?"

Drago thought for a moment and said, "Petrone."

"How would he know?" asked my father.

Drago frowned as he thought about that.

"He knew because he ordered the raid," my father continued.

"The fuck is this about, Vesta?"

"You ordered Colucci to hit my son. What did Petrone tell you I would do?"

Drago again frowned. My father knew that Petrone had probably told Drago that he would retaliate. And he had. He had burned down the Federated. The look on Drago's face told my father he was starting to put it together. It was possible that he had been set up.

My father continued without waiting for an answer. "He told you I would go after Colucci . . ." He paused and said, "And what did I do?"

That did it. Drago's face flushed. His teeth clenched, and he bit his cigar in half. He ripped the phone out of its cradle and emitted a low growl.

"Put it down, Paul," said Costello.

Drago looked up. Costello was standing in the doorway with Angelo deferentially standing slightly behind him. "The fuck are ya doin' here?" he barked.

"I might ask the same about him," answered Costello, indicating my father. "Interesting conversation you were having."

Drago's eyes darted between the two men. My father said you could almost hear his mind racing: There was no way out. He had to know that Costello and Angelo were probably holding, but their guns weren't out, so he obviously decided to take his chances.

His fingers closed around a sawed-off shotgun hidden under the desk. He jerked it out and was bringing it up when Angelo's .45 roared. Drago took the bullet in the middle of his chest and was blown back into the bay window. It shattered, the shotgun went off, and the blast brought down the chandelier along with a cascade of plaster.

Costello got up and brushed himself off. When Drago had brought up the shotgun, Costello had dropped to the floor and Angelo had fired over his head—he had hidden his .45 behind Costello's back.

Adonis, Barbera, Boychick, and I rushed into the room. The floor was covered in plaster, and the chandelier was a twisted mass of metal and broken glass. Drago was on the window seat, jammed into the shattered bay window. His ass was thrust outside, but the rest of his body—his head between his knees and his arms and legs extended forward—was still inside. He looked like a folded-over, broken doll.

"Holy shit!" said Adonis. "What happened?"

"He pulled a shotgun," said Angelo.

Boychick and I ran over to my father and began untying him. Barbera and Adonis did the same for the twins.

"Where the hell ya been?" asked Dino. "We only coulda taken three or four more hours of this shit."

We finished untying my father. "*Grazie*," he said, and turned to Costello. "You heard?"

"Enough," answered Costello. "With this we'll take Petrone to the Commission."

"We could, Frank," my father agreed, "but he's not who we want. We still have nothing to tie this to Genovese."

"He's right," said Adonis. "And what the hell do we do with this mess?"

"Leave it," said my father. "When Carlo and Chucky get back, they'll have to clean it up."

"They'll call Petrone," said Adonis. "They'll want their next move."

My father nodded. "And Petrone will call Genovese."

"I like it," said Costello. "Whatever Petrone does, it will be Genovese behind it."

"If you don't mind a suggestion," Angelo said nervously, "I think we should get the hell outta here before Carlo and Chucky get back."

CHAPTER FORTY-SEVEN

WE DROPPED OFF the twins at the clinic and left Barbera with them. My father had the night staff wake up Dr. Gennaro, their chief of staff, and Dr. Sissle, a first-rate dentist. When he was satisfied the twins would be fine, we left.

It was one-thirty by the time Boychick and I got back to the office. Benny, Stuff, and Louie were still playing poker. When we explained what had happened, they couldn't believe we had been gone only three and a half hours. I told my father that Terry was leaving in the morning and I wanted to spend the night with her. He wasn't happy about it, or my going back out after the night's events, so he had Angelo call Gus Chello. An hour later Gus showed up and everyone left. Gus and I stopped to pick up a large container of coffee for him, and he drove me back to East Seventy-sixth Street.

We parked outside Terry's apartment, and I apologized to Gus for having to baby-sit me again. He laughed and said he was getting used to it. I got out and went into the building. Neither one of us saw Touch

Grillo, Carlo Ricci, or Chucky Law in the car parked halfway down the block.

Nick Colucci wasn't the only one who had been tracking my movements that summer. Genovese had had me watched ever since the goddamn fur scam. He knew Terry—knew her history—and knew I'd been seeing her. When she came up missing on Saturday night, he'd asked the Copa's manager, Jules Podell, where she was. He said she'd quit, that she was leaving for the West Coast. A talk with her unsuspecting doorman revealed she'd be leaving on Wednesday. Genovese was certain that if Tuesday was Terry's last night in town, I was sure to show up. He was right.

I entered Terry's building, waved to the doorman, and took the elevator to the sixth floor. Quietly I let myself into the apartment. By the glow of the night-light in the bedroom, I could tell that Terry was asleep. I didn't want to wake her, so I crossed into the bedroom, got undressed, and slipped into bed. I was pretty exhausted myself, and I wanted to be ready for some energetic good-byes in the morning. Terry didn't stir. I was asleep as soon as my head hit the pillow—which was why I didn't hear the scratching at the lock on the hallway door.

Chucky had parked in the alley behind Terry's building, eliminating the problem of Gus Chello, and Carlo had expertly picked the lock on the basement door. Then they had all taken the fire stairs to the sixth floor so the doorman wouldn't see the lights above the elevator going up or down.

Outside Terry's apartment, the tumblers fell into line and Carlo gingerly opened the door. Touch and Chucky followed him in, and they peered across the dark living room. They saw the glow of the night-light in the bedroom and crossed to the half-open door. Carlo could just make out two distinct shapes in the bed. He grabbed Touch's arm. "There's someone in the bed wit 'im!" he whispered. Carlo hadn't heard anything about a double snatch.

"So what?" whispered Touch.

"So what?" said Carlo, exasperated. "*Now* what the fuck do we do?"

"We take 'em both."

"Are you nuts?" Carlo objected. "We don't even know who the fuck it is!"

"Keep yer goddamn voice down," Touch hissed. "I know who it is, and there ain't no way to grab one witout da udder."

"This whole fuckin' day's been a disaster," Carlo moaned. It had taken them over an hour to extract Drago from the window and make a second trip to the Brooklyn landfill. And now *this*. "What the fuck's next!"

"What's next is ya stop bitchin' and we get the fuck on wit it." He took out a blackjack. "I'll take the kid, you take da udder one."

Carlo nodded dismally and took out his blackjack. He eased open the door, and the two men padded into the room.

Terry was curled up in my arms with her back to me, both of us sleeping soundly. Touch and Carlo took up positions on either side of the bed—Touch signaled Carlo, and they simultaneously brought down their blackjacks. Touch ripped off the sheets and levered me into a sitting position. Carlo did the same with Terry.

"Holy shit!" Carlo exclaimed. "It's the broad from the Copa! The hatcheck!"

"Who gives a shit? Pick 'er up an' we're outta here!"

"Un-fuckin'-believable," muttered Carlo, and hoisted Terry over his shoulder.

Touch shouldered me, and they both shuffled out with our two naked bodies. Carlo handed Terry to Chucky, and they left the way they came—down six flights of stairs and into the basement. By the time they got there, they were sucking air as if they'd never get another gulp. There was a laundry bin in the basement, and they decided to use it. They dumped us into the bin and rolled it out to the alley.

I had come to right when they dumped me into the bin. I waited until they lifted me out, then jerked my right leg out of Touch's hand and slammed my foot into his throat. Touch was totally unprepared for it. He gagged, lurched back, and bounced off the trunk. Chucky froze—he still had me under the armpits. He obviously wanted to help me, but there was nothing he could do without revealing that he was one of ours. I couldn't blow his cover, so I threw my head back into his face. I heard the crunch and knew Chucky's nose was broken.

Carlo was still reeling from the day's events and was fumbling with the gun in his shoulder holster. He got it out a split second before I drove my head into his stomach. He flew backward, tripped over Touch, and slammed into the trunk. The gun went off with a *pfffft!* and I pummeled him until he slumped into the open trunk.

Touch still wasn't moving, and Chucky was bent over on his knees, holding his smashed nose and groaning. Blood was pouring through his fingers.

I reached into the bin and attempted to lift Terry out. When I tried to stand her up, she moaned and her eyes fluttered open. Blood began seeping through her lips, and I noticed blood all over her stomach.

"Oh God, no," I whispered. "Terry . . ." There was a small bullet hole in her left side and a large exit wound on the right. Carlo's bullet had ripped through her stomach and torn up her insides. I lowered her back down and caressed her face. She tried to say something and reached her hand up to me, but a moment later her eyes rolled back and froze.

I sank to my knees and sobbed. That was the last thing I remembered, because Touch had recovered sufficiently to crawl up behind me and deliver his second blackjack blow of the evening.

When Carlo was revived and told he'd killed Terry, he was catatonic. Touch told him to put the bin back in the basement and then put Terry in the trunk. I was bound, gagged, and tossed into the backseat. Chucky got behind the wheel and wondered how the fuck he was going to explain this to Angelo. He held a handkerchief over his nose and once again headed for the Brooklyn landfill. When Carlo looked out the window and realized where they were headed for the third time in one night, he shook his head and muttered, "Un-fuckin'-believable."

My father told me later he thought Tuesday was one of the worst days of his life.

Wednesday would make it look like a picnic.

CHAPTER FORTY-EIGHT
WEDNESDAY, AUGUST 30

MY FATHER HADN'T gotten to bed until two, so my mother didn't wake him until ten. He showered, dressed in a lightweight tan suit, white shirt, and muted tie, then strapped on his shoulder holster and put on his jacket. The aroma of frying sausage and olive oil drifted in from the kitchen, and he smiled. My mother was preparing his favorite breakfast—sausage and eggs, home fries sautéed with cherry peppers, and very strong coffee. He walked into the kitchen, sat at the table, and my mother filled his cup. She thought he looked unusually stressed but knew better than to ask why, so she sipped her coffee and settled on a less problematic subject. "Red is still in jail?" she ventured.

"I don't think so," he said.

"You got him out?" she asked.

He nodded. "This morning Mark Perrault will go with a writ."

"Vinny didn't come home yet," she said.

"He stayed at Benny's," he lied. "He'll be along."

There was a knock on the door. My mother answered it and let Angelo in. "You had breakfast?" she asked.

"I'll take some coffee . . ." He sat at the table. Angelo waited until my mother finished pouring, then asked, "Mickey, ya mind if I talk to Gino alone for a minute?"

"Sure. I'll make the bed." She smiled, walked down the hallway, and closed the bedroom door.

"Touch Grillo called a half hour ago . . . he says he's got Vinny."

My father slowly lowered his fork, leaned back in his chair, and waited for Angelo to continue.

"I called Terry's apartment. No answer. I went over there and Gus was still waiting outside the building. The doorman said Vinny came in at three o'clock but never came out. Neither did Terry. Then I made the doorman open her apartment. Nothin'. I figured if Vinny and Terry got taken out, it had to be the back way, so I went down to check the alley door in the basement. There was a laundry bin in there with blood on it. I went out the alley door and saw some more blood next to the building. That's the way they took 'em out."

My father nodded slowly as he acknowledged the obvious. "We now know what Genovese ordered . . ."

"Whaddaya wanna do?"

"Nothing for now. They don't care about Vinny. If they wanted him dead, they could have killed him. No . . . they kidnapped him because they want something in exchange for him. They'll call with what it is." He got up and walked down the hall. He knocked on the bedroom door, and my mother opened it. He kissed her and said, "Vinny has disappeared."

My mother gasped and covered her mouth with her hand.

My father patted her cheek and kissed her again. "I'll bring him back."

By ten-fifteen the guys had all drifted into Benny's apartment. Boychick was working the speed bag, and Stuff was at the piano ripping through "April in Paris." Benny, Boychick, and Louie were shooting pool, and Bouncer was obeying his father by staying away.

Red walked in the door, and they all rushed over to greet him. After the hugs, backslaps, and handshakes, they sat down and Boychick pointed at Red's face.

"Christ," said Boychick, "ya look like ya been ziggin' when ya shoulda been zaggin'."

"A family misunderstandin'," said Red.

"Your uncles?" asked Louie.

Red nodded. "They wanted me to give up Vinny."

"About the warehouse?" Stuff asked.

Red again nodded. "Yeah."

Benny asked, "But you got out?"

"Gino's lawyer sprung me . . . Where's Vinny?"

"Out," said Boychick. "Spent the night at Terry's. He should be here any minute."

"And then we all spreadin' out to keep lookin' for Colucci," said Benny.

"There was a guy in the cell with me," said Red. "He saw Stankovitch's name in the paper. He knew him."

They all leaned forward a bit. "Anythin'?" asked Boychick.

"The guy had a girlfriend. Said Stankovitch stole her."

"This guy know where Stankovitch holed up?" asked Benny.

Red shook his head. "But the girl works waitress at the Mandarin on Fourteenth. Gloria Wong. She's Chinese."

My father entered with Angelo, and everyone got up to greet them. My father held up his hand and without preamble said, "Vinny's been picked up by Gee-gee Petrone." They gazed at him, stunned. They had a hundred questions, but before they could ask any of them, he continued. "They will call me and tell me what they want. It won't be long. Wait here until I find out." He turned to leave but was stopped by Boychick.

"Red got a possible lead on Stankovitch," he said.

My father paused at the door, contemplated, and said, "Good. Two of you follow it. The rest wait here. We'll be at my office."

At eleven-thirty my father was sitting at his desk sipping a cup of espresso, Bo Barbera was on the couch reading the racing form, and Angelo was looking out the window at the *Queen Mary* berthed at its Forty-ninth Street pier. They all had their jackets off and were impatiently awaiting Touch Grillo's call. A few minutes later a sharp knocking at the door interrupted the quiet. Bo got up to answer it, and a messenger handed him a shoebox wrapped in brown paper and tied with twine. He brought it to my father and put it on the desk.

Angelo walked over and said, "No note? *Sta corta*," he said. He knew it could be another bomb, so he told my father to take care.

Bo pulled the tool kit out of his jacket pocket and removed a razor blade. He leaned over the shoebox and carefully sliced open a six-inch flap in its side. My father handed him a flashlight and he peered inside. "It looks like a telephone," he said.

The three men traded looks, and then my father took Bo's razor blade and cut the twine. He pulled off the paper and removed the top of the shoebox. Bo was right: It was the receiver of a telephone. Attached to it was one of Chucky Law's elephant ears. Next to it there was a note. My father picked up the note and read it.

When we got home last night your "ear" made
a telephone call to his friend. He got
the friend's wife. We got him. His other
ear is with what's left of the rest of him.

"Christ," said Angelo. "Like I told ya—when I got home last night Lena said I had a call. No name, so I figured it was Chucky and he'd call back. He didn't. This is why. They caught him makin' the call."

My father replaced the top and handed the box to Bo. "Get rid of it," he said.

Bo started out, then stopped when the phone on my dad's desk rang. My father answered it on the third ring. "Vesta," he said, then listened for a full minute before saying, "We'll be there." He hung up. "Petrone. We have half an hour."

"He didn't leave us much time."

My father nodded. "To give us no time for a plan of our own."

"Where's the meet?" asked Angelo.

"Central Park. The zoo at noon. Next to the lion cage. Open, public, and crowded. He will bring only Grillo. I will bring you," he said, and went into the bathroom. He opened the medicine cabinet and released a hidden latch. The whole cabinet swung out from the wall and revealed a wall safe. He dialed the combination, opened it, and removed a hand-size package. It measured about four by four by two inches. He closed the safe and cabinet and went back into his office.

"I want you to go to the zoo," he said to Barbera. "There's a food stand across from the lion cage." He handed Barbera the package. "Give this, and a hundred-dollar bill, to whoever runs the stand." He looked at Angelo. "Tell him a fat man wearing a brown suit and a tie will ask for it around noon. When he delivers the package he will get another hundred dollars. *Capische?*"

"*Capisco*," said Barbera. "Anything else?"

"After the zoo, go to Benny's and tell the boys to keep searching for Colucci."

Barbera nodded and left. My father removed his shoulder holster. "Leave your gun," he instructed Angelo. "No one will carry. When we get there, Touch will pat us down and you will pat them down."

"You trust them?"

"They chose a very public place, and they want something. I think they'll do no more than to tell us what."

Angelo took off his coat and removed a new shoulder holster. His back was still sore from Junior's bullet, and he couldn't carry his .45 in its usual place in the small of his spine. My father put the guns in a desk drawer.

"Any idea what he's gonna want?" Angelo asked as they headed to the door.

"Me," said my father, and they walked out of the air-conditioned office into a vicious blast of heat and humidity.

CHAPTER FORTY-NINE

AS EXPECTED, by noon the Central Park Zoo was crowded with visitors and tourists from all over the tristate area. Just steps off Fifth Avenue, they were immersed in everything from rare monkeys to tropical reptiles and amphibians to polar bears and penguins in an icy Antarctic habitat. Many schools hosted tours for their students, and at the food stand, across from the lion cage, a few teachers struggled to wrangle a large group of pesky children who were prancing about and acting like a large group of pesky children.

Angelo spotted Gee-gee Petrone the moment he walked down the steps of the Sixty-fourth Street entrance with Touch Grillo. Gee-gee was wearing an impeccable chalk-striped gray suit and a matching homburg. Touch wore a jade sharkskin suit and a snap-brim hat, and he had the unlit stub of a cigar clenched in the corner of his mouth. Gee-gee was dry as sand. Touch was dripping. The pair looked like a diplomat being shadowed by a Doberman.

Angelo tapped my father on the arm and pointed them out. A moment later Gee-gee noticed Angelo and my father. He sauntered over with Touch in trail.

"Well, Angelo," said Gee-gee, his voice dripping with syrup, "we meet again. This time will hopefully be a bit more civilized than the last."

"I got nothin' to say to ya, Petrone," said Angelo. He looked at Touch and spread his arms slightly. "Let's get on with it."

Touch quickly patted him down and chuckled. "Enjoy yer new telephone, Maserelli?"

"I can't wait to return the call," Angelo replied, deadpan.

Touch patted down my father, and Angelo repeated the process with Gee-gee and Touch. Neither frisk was done with any degree of thoroughness since weapons weren't thought to be an issue. Angelo took a handkerchief out of his breast pocket.

"'Scuse me," he said, wiping his brow, "but I'm dyin' here. I gotta get a drink." He started toward the food stand before anyone could object and called over his shoulder, "Anyone else want a drink?"

They all declined by shaking their heads, and Angelo went to the stand. Gee-gee studied my father for a few moments and then asked, "How did you manage it, Gino?"

"It?"

"Drago. He had you and he had the twins," he continued with grudging admiration in his voice. "Yet you managed to slip through his fingers. *Bravissimo!*"

My father said, "I have no idea what you're talking about."

"Of course not. Nor, I am sure, do you know that Drago was found jammed into his own window with a bullet in his chest."

"Drago must have some very powerful enemies," said my father.

Gee-gee answered with an oily smile, "No one is in a better position to know that than you, my dear Vesta."

My father ignored the barb as Angelo returned from the food stand with a frosted bottle of Pepsi. He got right to the point. "You have my son."

"I do," replied Gee-gee.

"What is it you want?"

"I want to give you an opportunity."

"Go on," said my father, his voice emotionless.

"I will return your son, if"—Gee-gee paused dramatically—"you 'retire.'"

"'Retire,'" said my father.

"Yes," responded Gee-gee. "You will give me and the Commission your word of honor that you will leave the city, the state, and 'our thing' . . . and never return."

"And what will be my reason?"

"You will tell the Commission that you wanted to take over Drago's territory. He resisted, so you burned down his warehouse. Drago couldn't prove it, so he came to me for help—he knew Costello would never take his word against yours. I will tell the Commission I agreed to help Drago, but then last night he disappeared. I will say I suspected you were behind it, but again there was no proof. So . . . I kidnapped your son to get you to confess your plot." Gee-gee grinned and indicated "the end" by pretending to play a pair of cymbals. He brushed one palm against the other and said, "*Finito!*"

My father shook his head. "And you think Costello and the Commission will believe these lies?"

"They will . . . because the moment you agree to leave town rather than fight, they will be convinced."

"And when Anastasia returns?"

"The Commission will explain that you became greedy in his absence."

"He'll never believe it."

"That will be of no concern to you, my dear Gino, since by then you will have 'retired.'"

"And how will you explain Drago's 'disappearance'?"

"I don't think it will be necessary, but if it becomes an issue, Carlo Pucci will tell the Commission that last night he saw you and Angelo leaving Drago's house with his body. He followed you to Brooklyn and watched you dispose of the body in a landfill. He will then lead them to the landfill to prove what he saw . . ."

Gee-gee didn't know that this was an idle threat since Costello was there when Drago was killed. Gee-gee fluttered his hand as if he were shooing away an insect and added pompously, "I would like to hold this back because it sounds fortuitous and Carlo would be thought to have a reason to lie. No—your plot against a caporegime from another family in the face of the edict from the Commission will be enough to ensure your exile."

"And you thought of this all by yourself," said my father. It was a flat statement with just a hint of sarcasm.

Gee-gee smiled. "I'm a very clever man, Gino."

"That may be, but someone far more clever pulls your strings."

Gee-gee reddened at the suggestion. "I don't need a puppeteer to take you down, Vesta," he growled. "I've hated you and your arrogance for years. Fortunately everyone knows that, so they will have no trouble believing why I helped Drago."

"When do I get my son?"

"After you give your word to the Commission and leave the city, I will tell Angelo where to find him."

"And if I come back?"

"The Commission will order your *permanent* retirement."

My father looked off into the middle distance as though he were contemplating his options. When he looked back at Gee-gee, he nodded. "Agreed."

"I thought you would. I asked for a meeting at five o'clock. Costello's apartment."

My father acknowledged the appointment with a nod and walked away. Angelo followed him.

Gee-gee watched them depart and turned to Touch. A triumphant smile crossed his face.

CHAPTER FIFTY

WHEN I CAME TO, I was handcuffed to a water pipe under a large commercial sink. I was still naked, and thirsty, and the back of my head was throbbing. I didn't have to touch it to know there was one hell of a lump. A little light was coming in under the door. I could make out mops and buckets, so I figured it was a cleaning closet. The smell of rancid rags confirmed it.

I had recognized Touch Grillo in the alley behind Terry's apartment and could now hear the rumble of large trucks down below. I guessed I was probably in Petrone's warehouse. I tried to dislodge the drainpipe but succeeded only in bruising my wrists. I looked at my watch, and I could barely make it out in the dim light. It was ten after twelve.

Gradually I started to put together the night before: the parking lot . . . the fight . . . Terry. She was dead. I felt my eyes get wet and began to think about revenge. A few moments later, the door opened. The light blinded me for a moment, and then I saw a backlit man carrying a tray. He was wearing a pink shirt, a yellow tie that was four inches wide, and seersucker trousers held up by red suspenders.

His name was Beppo Palmieri, and he was Gee-gee's driver. He was also Gee-gee's brother-in-law, which was the only reason Gee-gee kept him around. Beppo was a middle-aged flunky with a relentless motor mouth. When he spoke, the words babbled out of him in a steady, unending stream.

"I got yer lunch—ya like hot dogs? Don't matter—ya got two of 'em an' a Coke—me, I like Pepsi—I told 'em Pepsi, but they went an' got ya a Coke anyway—go figure."

He put the tray on the floor next to me and released one of my hands. The other remained handcuffed to the pipe. Then he reached up and swept a pair of blue jeans, a shirt, and a pair of old shoes off the countertop above me. Everything landed in my lap. There were no shorts or socks.

He got up and spurted out, "Ya could get dressed if ya want, but ya don't hafta, it's up to you—me, I could care less, but like I said, ya could if ya wanna."

"How am I supposed to put on a shirt?" I asked, indicating my handcuffed wrist.

"What—ya goin' ta a fashion show? Put it half on an' let it dangle— who knows, ya could set a trend. Bone-appa-teet—if ya need anythin', just yell 'Beppo'—that's me. It won't do no good, but ya could do it anyway—see ya." He closed the door, and the closet was plunged into semidarkness.

"Shit," I said, and reached for a Coke.

Boychick and Red joined the lunch crowd at the Mandarin on Fourteenth Street at twelve-thirty. They were seated at a small table. Boychick perused the menu.

"Whatcha want?" asked Boychick.

Red grimaced and said, "I hate Chinese."

"Since when?"

"Since always."

"Ya never said."

"Ya never asked."

"What're you, some kinda freak? Nobody hates Chinese."

Boychick ignored him and ordered egg rolls, hot-and-sour soup, kung pao chicken, and white rice for both of them.

The Mandarin was a fairly large restaurant with about fifty tables. It catered to a mixed crowd of Caucasians and Asians, businessmen and blue-collar types. There were four waitresses, three older and one younger, all Asian. An older woman served them, but they spotted a very attractive Chinese girl serving the next set of tables who was wearing a name tag that read "Gloria." It had to be Stankovitch's girlfriend.

When he finished eating, Boychick noticed that Red had eaten everything on his plate.

"I thought ya hated Chinese," said Boychick.

Red shrugged. "I was hungry."

Boychick paid the bill, and they returned to Angelo's old Ford. It was parked across the street from the restaurant in a perfect position to watch the door. By two o'clock the lunch crowd was gone, and ten minutes later they saw two of the older waitresses leave.

"Probably off till the dinner rush," said Boychick.

Red pointed. "There she is."

Gloria came out of the restaurant carrying several takeout containers of food. She walked down the street, then stopped by a car, unlocked the door, and got in.

"Holy shit!" said Boychick. "It's a black Dodge!"

"Colucci's—gotta be," said Red.

Gloria pulled out, and Boychick followed. She drove west on Fourteenth, then south on the West Side Highway, and entered the Holland Tunnel.

"The hell's she goin'?" exclaimed Boychick.

"Hoboken," said Red.

"Colucci don't live in Hoboken. None of 'em do! Who the hell lives in Hoboken?" asked Boychick.

"Probably her," said Red.

They came out of the tunnel in Hoboken and followed Gloria west on Twelfth Street, then south again until she finally pulled up to a house a block away from Hamilton Park. There was a sign on the postage-stamp front lawn that read:

For Sale or Lease
Atlas Realty
279–4232

Gloria got out carrying the food and entered the two-story clapboard house.

"Whadda ya think? They in there?" asked Boychick.

"That or she's got a helluva appetite."

"Ain't a bad place ta hole up," observed Boychick. "Who the fuck would think ta look in Hoboken?"

"We gotta get a phone," said Red.

"Right. She figures to be in there for a while, and they don't figure ta come out if they got her deliverin' food."

Boychick pulled out and headed back to Benny's.

My father and Angelo walked through the lobby of the Majestic at three o'clock. As soon as he had left Central Park, my father had called Costello and asked for the meeting. Now the doorman rang Costello's apartment and was told to send them up. Angelo took off his jacket to enjoy the air-conditioned interior while they rode up to the penthouse.

Costello met them at the elevator and noticed Angelo's damp shirt and sweat-stained shoulder holster. "You want something cold?" he asked.

"Gin and tonic would be good," said Angelo.

"Gino?"

"Soda water."

Costello nodded and led them through the living room and into his den. It was lined with bookshelves and was as elegantly furnished as the rest of the apartment. The view of the park was spectacular. He opened a seven-by-seven-foot section of bookshelves, which was actually a set of double doors concealing the bar.

While Costello made the drinks, Angelo removed the device he had retrieved from the food stand and placed it on the leather surface of a beautiful burled walnut coffee table. He had been carrying it in the small of his back. Costello returned with the drinks, and they sat down on a sofa and wing chairs framed by a picture window. They all held up their glasses and together said, "*Salute.*" They drank, and then Costello picked up the four-by-four-by-two-inch metal device on the table. He examined it and read the manufacturer's name on the case: Webcor. It was a wire recorder.

"I never seen one this small," said Costello.

"This is the newest," said my father. "They started making them for the navy during the war. Since then they've been getting smaller. Two months ago, they came out with this. It's small enough to hide on your body."

"The cops even have an expression for it," Angelo said, chuckling. "They call it 'wearin' a wire.'"

"Where the hell did you get it?" asked Costello.

"You remember when the navy came to us during the war?"

"Sure. They were worried about Nazi sabotage." Costello chuckled. "We made sure they had something to worry about."

In February 1942, less than three months after America declared war on Germany, the French luxury liner *Normandie* mysteriously caught fire and sank at its West Side pier. The sinking was immediately attributed to Nazi sabotage. It *was* sabotage—but it wasn't the Nazis. It was the Mob. Costello and Meyer Lansky were behind the sinking, the first move in a plan to spring Lucky Luciano out of the "Siberia" of Dannemora Prison and into more civilized quarters where they would have access to him. Albert Anastasia was given the order to execute the masterstroke, and the *Normandie* went down.

When the *Normandie* sank five blocks from Times Square, in the middle of the midtown docks, it convinced the navy that they needed the Mob to protect the waterfront from saboteurs. The Mob ruled the longshoremen, and the longshoremen ruled the waterfront. But the navy was told there would be a price—the transfer of Luciano from Dannemora to the "country club" of Great Meadows, where he would be installed in a very comfortable open cell. Costello and Lansky negotiated the deal, and Luciano was transferred.

During the next four years, there were occasional "Luciano sightings" in the Big Apple—which the police denied as impossible—but there was also no further "sabotage" on the New York waterfront for the remainder of World War II.

"I kept contact with the navy guys," said my father. "They keep me up-to-date. Last month they told me about this, and I ordered one." He switched on the recorder, and they listened without comment to the entire conversation between Gee-gee and my father in Central Park. When it was over, Costello leaned back in his chair and lit a cigarette.

"We still don't have Genovese," said Costello.

"No," my father agreed.

Costello got up, went to the picture window, and looked down at the park. He remained there, apparently lost in thought, then turned back to his guests.

"I think what we do is bring Petrone here at four . . . an hour before the meeting."

He went to the bar, made himself a drink, and explained his plan.

*   *   *

At three-thirty I got another visit from Beppo. I hadn't called him, but he apparently couldn't find anyone to listen to his babble. Everyone in the warehouse shut him off the minute he turned himself on—sometimes by whacking him alongside his head. I was handcuffed to a goddamn sink, so he probably figured he was safe.

He entered the closet jabbering, "Hi, kid—I came ta see how you wuz doon because I know ya must be uncom'table what wit the handcuffs an' all, right? How wuz the hot dogs an' the Coke—which I know ain't as good as Pepsi, but like they say, 'Teech 'is own.' You want anything?"

"Yeah," I said, "I want to get out of here."

"Now dat, as they say, could be a bit prob-a-matical, because ya see Touch brought ya in, so's onny Touch could bring ya out—me personally, I hate the sonofabitch, but my brudder-in-law—that's Gee-gee—he thinks he's hot shit, so I gotta drive 'im all over town like a goddamn choffer and put up wit his shit, if ya get my drift."

"Why do you hate him?" I asked, more just to get a word in edgewise than because I really cared.

"Why? Why! What's not ta hate? He makes fun a me, fun a da way I talk, fun a da fact dat I'm onny here 'cause Gee-gee's my brudder-in-law—an' he even makes fun a my clothes if ya can believe it!"

I could. He was still wearing the pink, yellow, and red combination with the seersucker pants. "Well . . . ," I said, but he didn't want an answer, he wanted to keep babbling.

"Like, fer instance, the udder day at the station house, when we wuz talkin' ta the loot and the loot compl'ents me on my treads, and I say, 'Thank you very much, Loot, I'm glad ya like 'em'—an' all of a sudden Touch is all over me like flies on shit 'cause he says I'm so stupid I don't know the loot is pullin' my chain. Kin ya believe it? Why would the loot wanna pull my chain, I ask ya?"

"No reason," I said, and managed to get in, "What were you talkin' about?"

And he told me, chapter and verse, top to bottom, about it—and all the other times he'd been with Touch and been embarrassed, including Touch's tirade about Gino burning down Drago's warehouse. He must have figured I'd never get out of there alive, or else he just needed someone to listen to him. Either way, he was a babbling treasure trove.

CHAPTER FIFTY-ONE

THE DOORMAN WATCHED the familiar face of Gee-gee Petrone as he got out of his limo and rang Costello's apartment. Five minutes later Costello met him at the elevator and ushered him through the living room and into his den. "You still take Scotch?" he asked.

"With a splash of water," replied Gee-gee. "A lemon twist if you have it."

"Of course." Costello opened his bar and prepared a drink for his guest and one for himself. "A beautiful suit," he remarked.

"Thank you. Brooks Brothers."

"Very conservative," said Costello, thinking that Gee-gee was anything but. He returned with the drinks, and they sat in the facing leather wing chairs framed by the picture window. Between them was the burled walnut coffee table; there was a large crystal bowl on it, capped by a silver cover.

"*Salute*," said Costello, and extended his glass.

"*Per cento anni*," Gee-gee responded, and repeated the motion.

"As you must know, this Vesta business is very difficult for me," Costello began.

"I know he is an old friend. I'm sorry."

"Thank you." Costello sipped his drink. "You said the reason for all this misfortune was greed."

"He will tell you so himself."

"Will he tell me because you kidnapped his son?"

Gee-gee undoubtedly knew that Costello had been told that I'd been kidnapped and was prepared for the question. "I had no choice. We had a cancer in our midst, and it was growing in spite of your orders."

"And the son—he's safe?"

"He is. I will make the call to release him the moment Gino confesses his sins and agrees to leave us forever."

"And you'll insist on nothing more?"

"Nothing."

Costello reached out to the crystal bowl and removed its cover. "Tell me, Giorgio, do you know what this is?"

Gee-gee leaned forward and studied the wire recorder. He had never seen anything like it before.

"An electrical device?" he ventured.

"Yes," said Costello. "Battery-powered, actually." He reached down and turned it on.

For a few moments, Gee-gee was utterly confused. His own voice seemed to be coming from the small metal case. Then almost immediately he recognized my father's voice and the beginning of their conversation in the park. The blood drained from his face. It was impossible. He could not fathom how anything that small could be capable of recording a conversation . . . *his* conversation with Gino— and yet he was hearing it. Every word.

He looked up at Costello, whose face was completely expressionless.

Bewildered, Gee-gee looked back at the metal case. He was mesmerized. The conversation seemed to go on for an eternity.

Finally Gee-gee heard himself say, *The Commission will order your permanent retirement.*

And Gino replying, *Agreed.*

And finally, *I thought you would . . . I asked for the meeting at five o'clock. Costello's apartment.*

Costello reached down and turned off the recorder.

"Well, Gee-gee, what do you have to say for yourself?"

Gee-gee seemed to have gone into shock. He worked his mouth like a gasping fish and loosened his tie. He looked down and saw his hand was shaking. The ice cubes in his glass were rattling, beating out what sounded like an accusatory tattoo. He put the glass to his lips, closed his eyes, and threw down the last of the Scotch. When he opened his eyes he received the final shock.

Standing above him, next to the coffee table, was Albert Anastasia.

Gee-gee felt icicles crawl from the base of his spine up to the nape of his neck. His stomach turned, and he shivered involuntarily.

"You got five seconds to pick up the phone," said Anastasia. His voice could have frozen lava, and his eyes were dead—shark eyes. It was a chilling reminder of why Anastasia was called a stone-cold killer.

"Albert, I—"

"Four seconds." A silenced .38 appeared in his hand.

Gee-gee lurched out of his chair and dove for the phone. It was all he could do to get his trembling index finger into the dial. Rivulets of sweat were creeping down his forehead. The beautiful chalk-striped suit suddenly looked ill fitting and rumpled.

Angelo appeared in the doorway. My father came in behind him. "Where is he?" he asked, walking toward Anastasia.

Gee-gee closed his eyes and pinched the bridge of his nose. "My warehouse," he said, and finished dialing.

My father turned and tilted his head toward the door. "Angelo . . ."

315

Angelo nodded and quickly disappeared.

"Touch," Gee-gee said into the phone, his voice cracking, "let the kid go . . . Yes, I'm fine—let the kid go . . . I know, I'm coming down with something—Maserelli will pick him up . . . I know—I'm changing the plan . . . Listen, goddamn it! Let the fucking kid go!" He slammed down the phone, staggered back to his chair, and buried his face in his hands.

"Very good," said Anastasia. "Now tell us about Genovese."

Gee-gee looked up at Costello sitting across from him. "Frank, you have to help me . . . for old times' sake."

"Forget Frank, you sniveling prick!" Anastasia spat out.

Gee-gee held out his hands in supplication. They were vibrating. "Frank . . . please . . ."

Costello responded quietly, "Tell him about Genovese, Gee-gee."

Gee-gee's eyes began to dart among his three antagonists. Costello—Anastasia—my father—back to Costello. He appeared disoriented. Then he began to choke. His face twisted in agony. He clawed for his inside jacket pocket and pulled out a small pill bottle. Before he could open it, he let out a gargling sound and pitched forward onto the coffee table. His legs twitched a few times and he was still. Anastasia rolled him onto the floor. He knelt on one knee and checked his neck for a pulse. "The sonofabitch is dead!" he said.

My father picked up the pill bottle, examined it, and then gave it to Anastasia. "Nitroglycerin . . . for a bad heart."

Anastasia threw the bottle across the room, completely disgusted. "The prick didn't even give us the pleasure of whackin' 'im!"

Costello nodded thoughtfully and stared at the dead body. "He also didn't give us Genovese."

CHAPTER FIFTY-TWO

I HAD JUST DRESSED, with only one arm in my shirt, when the closet door slammed open and Beppo entered, babbling away as if he had never stopped.

"Good news," said Beppo, squatting next to me. "Yer gonna get outta here—ya know what they say—all good things come ta a end—so I figure all bad things also gotta come ta a end, too—like now." He inserted a key into the handcuffs and popped them open. "Although I gotta admit I didn't think this pie-tic-a-lar bad thing would end for ya this quick—if ya get my drift—'cause Touch hates yer ass an' wuz lookin' fo'ward ta seein' ya rot a while. Know what I mean? . . . No? Don't matter, yer outta here."

"How come?" I asked, and struggled stiffly to my feet.

"How come what?"

"How come I'm getting out?" I rubbed my chafed wrists.

"Whaddaya—some kinda dumbshit who looks inna mouth of a gift horse? 'Cause what's the difference how come—Touch says you're gettin' out so you're gettin' out—so put on the rest of yer shirt and let's get on wit it."

Beppo continued to chatter as he led me out of the storage closet and down the steps to the warehouse floor. There was a good deal of activity in the main bay as various trucks were off- or on-loaded. We passed through the overhead clothes racks that shielded the interior and into the area between the racks and the front entrance. Touch Grillo was waiting next to the access door in the overhead roll-down.

I stopped dead, clenched my fists, and fought for control. Grillo was the reason Terry was dead. I wanted to tear him apart. I lunged forward—then stopped. My father always said, "An intelligent retreat is better than a stupid attack." There were thirty feet between us, but when I again moved forward, it seemed like three hundred.

"So, asshole," said Touch, "yer ol' man bailed ya out." He chuckled and unlatched the door. "I were you, I'd pack a bag. Warm shit. Arizona's a bitch this time a year." He laughed and shoved me through the exit.

I stumbled across the sidewalk and winced at the sudden blaze of sunlight. I put my hand on the fender of a parked truck to steady myself and immediately pulled back scorched fingers. The sun had turned the fender into a griddle.

The street was packed with the usual array of garment district traffic, and it reverberated with dissonant sounds. A horn blared insistently from a car double-parked across the street, and when I looked at it I saw Angelo rolling down the passenger window. Bo Barbera was parked behind him in a Chevy sedan. Angelo seldom went anywhere without backup.

"Vinny! Over here!" he called out.

I maneuvered around the traffic and got into the car.

"You okay?" asked Angelo, looking over his shoulder to see if he could squeeze into the traffic. A few seconds later he realized he hadn't gotten an answer, so he turned back to me. I was staring straight ahead miserably.

"Vinny, what's wrong?" he asked.

"Terry's dead."

Angelo's head popped back. "The hatcheck? What happened?"

"Last night, when they grabbed me. She got in the way."

"Jeez, I'm sorry, kid. I knew ya liked her."

"Yeah . . . I liked her."

"I thought she left."

"She did. She came back. To see me."

"Christ . . . We got a lot to talk about."

"Yeah . . . a lot."

Angelo stuck out his hand, ignored the angry air horn of a semi, and cut him off.

An unmarked van drove up to the Majestic at five p.m. and parked in the passenger-loading zone directly in front of the building. Two men wearing brown coveralls got out and entered the lobby.

"Benson and Hedges for Mr. Costello," said the burlier of the two.

The doorman looked them over, cocking his eyebrow at the obviously phony names. Earlier in the day he had been told to expect several groups of men at five p.m., and as usual, he had been given a list of names. The names were all aliases, but the doorman knew that. He had occasionally seen their real names under their photographs in New York's tabloids. However, he was later told *not* to expect the men on his list and instead was given the names "Benson and Hedges"—two men who were supposedly from a rug company. They had a "dolly" with them, but none of the usual identifying logos on their coveralls. Since it was unwise to speculate about why visitors came and went to the Costello apartment, the doorman just smiled and dialed. A moment later he nodded and said, "Yes, sir." He put down the phone and pointed toward the elevators. "Go right on up."

In his den, Costello hung up the phone and said, "They're on their way up."

"The cocksucker sure knew his cigars," said Anastasia, blowing out a cloud of blue smoke. He admired one of the Panatelas he had removed from Gee-gee's cigar case and rolled it between his fingers. Anastasia was sitting in one of the wing chairs next to the picture window. His jacket was off and his feet were on the coffee table. My father sat opposite him.

Anastasia looked at Costello. "You gonna call Grillo?" he asked.

"As soon as they get him out of here," said Costello, indicating the rug rolled up in the middle of the floor. In it was Gee-gee Petrone.

Minutes after Petrone died, Costello had called the Commission members and canceled the meeting. He told them that Gee-gee had dropped dead of a heart attack before he had a chance to reveal his problem. God had resolved the issue. He decided to have the body secretly removed from his apartment and brought to Renaldi's Funeral Home. He would then call Touch Grillo, tell him what happened and where he would find the body. Touch could notify Gee-gee's wife and the others to make the necessary arrangements.

My father said, "I'm sorry I had to ruin your vacation, Albert."

Anastasia waved it off. "No problem. I was gettin' bored anyway."

Costello asked, "How do you think we should handle Genovese?"

"Whack the sonofabitch and tell the Commission to go fuck themselves," said Anastasia, then added quickly, "Except for you, Frank."

"Thank you, Albert," Costello said wryly. "I appreciate your sensitivity. I still sit at the head of that table, but I only have one vote. They won't stand for it."

"Where is Mangano with all this?" asked my father.

"Him? In left field," Anastasia said scornfully. It was no secret that Anastasia hated Mangano. Even though Mangano was the boss and Anastasia the underboss of our family, both my father and Anastasia admired and supported Costello, the boss of the rival Luciano family.

"He knows less about what's goin' on than a street punk! All he gives a shit about is politics and hangin' out with Camarda."

Emil Camarda was vice president of the International Longshoremen's Association, and he and Mangano had started the City Democratic Club. Anastasia had no use for either man and had been looking for an excuse to eliminate them. The Kefauver investigations had thwarted him temporarily.

"I still say we take our chances," said Anastasia. "Whack Genovese and get it over with. If that connivin' prick stays alive, we're all gonna wind up dead!"

"True, Albert," said Costello, "but we do nothing while the hearings are still on television." The chimes sounded and he got up.

"Fucking Kefauver," Anastasia groused.

"Unfortunately," said Costello, "it's Kefauver who's fucking us." And he left to let in the "rug company."

Anastasia turned to my father and asked, "What d'ya think?"

He shook his head. "Too many loose ends. Grillo won't believe how Petrone died. He'll react badly. Carlo Ricci knows everything and is still out there. Then there is the matter of Colucci; my son won't let that go. And finally, we have Genovese."

"You know that we're gonna have ta whack that fuck or he's gonna whack us. It's far from over."

My father nodded solemnly. "I know."

Costello returned with the two men in brown coveralls and indicated the rug. They lifted it onto the dolly and rolled it out without saying a word. He then went to the phone, dialed, and a few seconds later said, "Touch, it's Frank . . . Yes, he was here . . . No, he was just taken out . . . Yes, I said taken out . . . I have some bad news, Touch. Did you know Gee-gee had a bad heart? . . . Yes, we saw the pills . . . He tried, but he died before he could take them . . . ," Costello was silent for several moments, then said, "Touch? Are you there?" He listened a beat and nodded. "I had him taken to Renaldi's Funeral Home, you know it? . . . A few minutes ago . . . Yes—I'm sorry, Touch." He hung up the phone and poured himself a tumbler of Scotch. Anastasia and Gino watched as he tossed it down in one gulp.

"Well?" asked Anastasia.

"He didn't believe a word I said."

My father looked at Anastasia. He was right: It was far from over.

Boychick was the first to notice me when I walked in the door of Benny's apartment. "Yes!" he bellowed, and threw a vicious punch at the speed bag that sent it into a thundering series of ricochets. He rushed to embrace me and was immediately joined by the others, including Bouncer. He had decided to disobey his father and had dropped by Benny's to see if there was any news about me. They all but buried me under an avalanche of hugs and backslaps.

Angelo and my father watched the jubilant reunion from the door. We had picked him up at the Majestic on the way to Benny's. When the greetings subsided, Boychick noticed them standing at the door and cried out exuberantly, "Ya got 'im!" he said.

My father smiled and walked in. "Yes," he said, "we had good luck."

Boychick turned back to me. "What happened?"

I took in a deep breath, then let it out. "Last night Touch and Carlo grabbed me and Terry in her apartment," I said simply and without emotion. "They killed her."

"Christ . . ." said Boychick.

"Jesus, Vinny, we're sorry," said Stuff.

"Where is she?" asked Red.

"Grillo must have taken her. I don't know where," I said.

"C-can't we c-call the cops?" asked Bouncer.

"No," my father said. "For the moment, we do nothing. Angelo and I will deal with Touch and Carlo."

"We found Colucci in Hoboken," said Red.

"We think Stankovitch and the Russomanos are with 'im," Boychick added.

That got my attention. I snapped out of my sullen mood and said, "You're sure?"

Red nodded. "Sure."

"Okay," I said. "We go after them tonight before they can make another move."

"No," said my father.

I turned to face him. "Pop—"

"It makes no sense to storm a house with the three of them inside. Too much could go wrong."

I started to object again, but he held up his hand. "This is what I want you to do. Take the cars. Go back and watch the house. If they leave, follow them. I'll tell Costello to call his friends downtown. Sometime after dark you'll see the police arrest them."

"How?" I asked. "They have no jurisdiction."

"Downtown will call the Hoboken police. They will be told there are fugitives wanted in New York hiding in their city."

"That leaves them in New Jersey," I objected.

"No," said my father. "Costello will see to it that they are brought back and held here. Tomorrow the nuns will identify them, and they'll be charged with assault. You all do nothing but what I have said, *capische?*"

We nodded our understanding and gave my father the Hoboken address. He left with Angelo. Boychick noticed that I hadn't said a word.

"You okay?" asked Boychick.

"Tomorrow will be a week," I said.

"What?"

"Since we raided the rail yard and picked up ten crates of fur pelts."

"Yeah, I guess so," said Boychick. "Why?"

"Everything that happened: Drago, Junior, Petrone setting us up,

Sidney in the hospital, and Terry dead. All in one week. One goddamn week."

"We didn't start it, Vinny," Boychick said.

"No. But we'll finish it," I said, and headed for he door. "C'mon, I wanna shower and change. We'll stop and see Sidney on the way to Hoboken."

Everyone filed out but Boychick. He stopped me at the door. "Whadda ya mean, 'finish it'?" he asked. "How?"

"There's no doubt that Carlo or Touch will spring Colucci. He knows too much. I want Benny and Red to stake out the precinct and follow him."

"But ya heard yer ol' man," Boychick said.

"I heard him," I said, and walked out. Boychick shook his head and followed me out.

CHAPTER FIFTY-THREE

EVEN THOUGH BOUNCER had "retired," he insisted on coming with us to the hospital to see Sidney, so I sent him ahead with Benny and Red in the Ford. Boychick, Stuff, Louie, and I took the Buick. We stopped at my place so I could change clothes and then met them in the Bellevue parking lot—in the middle of a raging thunderstorm. No one had thought to bring umbrellas, so we covered our heads with newspapers and dashed out of the car. By the time we reached the lobby our shoes were squeaking and our clothes were damp—all except Louie's. Somehow his black suit looked like it had just been pressed.

Boychick couldn't believe it. He squeegeed his arms and grumbled, "He's dry! How the fuck does he do it?"

Stuff chortled and said, "He runs between the drops. You oughta try it."

"I will, but if you try it, the drops'll hafta be a block apart."

"When are you gonna stop with the fat jokes?"

"When you stop bein' a wise-ass."

Benny, Red, and Bouncer were waiting for us in the lobby. They had been told visiting hours didn't begin until seven. I said, "Okay, wait in the cars. I know where he is. I'll sneak up and see him—and then we go to Hoboken. Benny and Red, go ahead and stake it out. Bouncer, you can stay with us or grab a cab home."

"I'll s-stay with you," he said.

"You sure?"

"I'm s-sure," he said. He didn't sound sure, but he stayed.

The biggest problem would be getting past the reception area and to the elevators. I decided that the solution was not to try it. I retrieved my wet newspaper, ducked back into the rain, and ran into the Emergency entrance. As usual, it was controlled chaos. I weaved my way through the area holding my left arm in my right hand as if I were creating a makeshift sling. No one stopped me. I got into the elevator and punched "3."

With the exception of two preoccupied ladies in white who were at the nurses' station, the third-floor area was quiet. I waited until the nurses turned their backs, then darted across the corridor and into the ICU. When I entered Sidney's room I stopped cold. He was sitting up in bed, reading a book. He had attachments plugged into beeping monitors, an IV drip in his arm, and his head swathed in bandages, but when he saw me he grinned from ear to ear.

"Hi, Vin," he said. "I heard you checked out yesterday."

"Right," I said. I didn't want to depress Sidney by telling him what else had happened, so I changed the subject. "You look like you're feeling better."

"I am. The doctors are still worried, but I can tell I'll be okay."

"That's great, Sidney. The guys said to say hello."

Sidney smiled. "How are they?"

"Fine. They're downstairs. It's not visiting hours yet."

"Tell them I'm glad they came anyway . . ." He fiddled with his hands and seemed to struggle with the next question. I pulled up a chair and sat next to the bed. Sidney finally looked at me and asked, "Did the police catch the guys who beat us up?"

"Not yet, but they'll get caught. I promise."

"It was Colucci again, wasn't it."

"Yeah, and three other guys," I said automatically.

"I'm sorry, Vinny . . ."

"For what?"

"It's my fault."

"What are you talkin' about?"

"Colucci."

"What? Colucci?" I suddenly realized I'd made a mistake by confirming Sidney's suspicion. "Are you crazy? Colucci had nothing to do with you!"

"With us," said Sidney, and his expression wilted. "About going to the library. Just like Bouncer said."

"Sidney . . ." I paused, trying to figure out how to be patient and firm at the same time. "We've already been through that . . . Listen to me. Compared to what this is about, we're smaller than the balls on a gnat. It's about my father and Costello—and Petrone and Anastasia—and Genovese, and Christ knows who-all else! But you've gotta believe me, Sidney—don't blame yourself, because it's not about us!"

Sidney searched my face for several seconds, then finally nodded. "Okay, Vinny . . . if you say so."

"I say so."

"Okay," he said, and gave me a tentative smile.

I relaxed and returned a broad grin. "Don't mention it," I said, and clasped Sidney's hand. "I gotta go now. The guys and I have an appointment. I'll come back in the morning."

"Okay, Vinny. Be careful."

"Always. You too."

"Always," repeated Sidney, and waved as I left the room.

By the time we left Bellevue and headed for the Holland Tunnel, the thunderstorm had passed. The heat was back and the moisture had turned the city into a steaming swamp. We crossed under the Hudson into Hoboken at dusk and raced for Hamilton Park.

Benny and Red had parked the Ford fifty yards from the house with the Atlas Realty sign out front. We pulled up behind them. Benny got out of the Ford, and I met him halfway.

"Anything?" I asked.

"Gloria came back 'bout ten minutes ago. Carryin' a bunch of them white boxes wit the wire handles."

"More Chinese takeout. They're still in there," I said. "Sit tight. The raid'll probably come right after dark." We got back into our cars and waited.

Five cigarettes later, four patrol cars pulled up to the house. Two officers went around back, two covered the sides, and four went up the front steps. Even from a block away, we could hear a cop banging his billy club on the door and shouting, "Colucci! Police! Open up and come out with mitts in the air!"

There were a few more exchanges before the door opened, but then Nick Colucci walked out with his hands up. He was bitching and moaning the entire time he was being handcuffed. Two cops entered the house, and a minute later Stankovitch and the two Russomanos were led out. They were all in cuffs. The captives were loaded into cars and driven away. The whole operation had taken less than five minutes.

"Now what?" asked Boychick.

"Now it gets interesting," I said. "We meet at your place at nine o'clock tomorrow morning. Let's go home."

I blinked the Buick's headlights twice, made a U-turn, and headed back for the tunnel. The Ford followed.

Wednesday had ended with me back on the street, Gee-gee and Chucky dead, Touch vowing revenge, Anastasia back from Italy, and Colucci, Stankovitch, and the Russomanos in custody—but we still didn't have Genovese.

CHAPTER FIFTY-FOUR

THURSDAY, AUGUST 31

T HE EARLY TABLOIDS were ablaze with the news of Giorgio Petrone's sudden death. HEART ATTACK TAKES PE-TRONE, they screamed. "Reputed Mob leader dies of natural causes . . . wife and family shocked and distraught . . . Longtime 'associate' and spokesman for the family, 'Touch' Grillo, said viewing of the body would take place at five o'clock at Renaldi's Funeral Home in Queens."

The story was the talk of every police precinct in New York, but especially so at Midtown-South, since Petrone's headquarters was on their beat. The other event that had the precinct chuckling was an illegal extradition that had occurred in Hoboken the prior evening, with the four suspects winding up in their lockup.

When Detective Sasso checked in at eight o'clock, he looked in on the four men in custody. No question—they matched the nuns' description of the library assailants. He called the Eighteenth Precinct, thinking Danny Collins might be interested in the men they had in custody. After they'd exchanged thoughts on Petrone's untimely death, Sasso told Danny that the four perps they were holding could be the same ones who bombed Benny Veal's place; there would be a lineup at four that afternoon. Sasso then said, "Fine, I'll see both of you at the lineup."

Lieutenant McRae, our Midtown-South informant, called Angelo and reported Sasso's call five minutes after Sasso hung up.

Benny got up early, put the coffee on, and went out to get a dozen Danish at the local bakery. As agreed, the gang assembled at nine o'clock. Angie the basset hound padded in, followed by Stuff. He arrived with a dozen jelly doughnuts, took one look at the Danish Benny was laying out, and shouted, "What's with the Danish? Today was *my* day." The crew always alternated buying the breakfast pastries, and Stuff obviously thought Benny had bought out of sequence.

"Bum memory!" said Benny. "I dis-*tinct*-ly remember it was me what said, 'I get the Danish.' "

Stuff got in Benny's face and said, "Benny, I promise you, I never forget *nothin'* havin' *anything* to do with food!"

Benny thought about it for a moment and said, "Good point. I stand corrected. Accusation withdrawn." He grinned and chomped down on a jelly doughnut. A stream of strawberry jam squirted into Stuff's eye.

"Christ!" Stuff squealed, hurtling back and pawing his eye. "Ya blinded me!"

Benny ran to the sink and soaked a towel in hot water. "Hang in, m'man, help's onna way." He rushed back to Stuff and slapped the steaming towel over his eye.

"Owww!" Stuff yelled. "That's worse, you prick!" He pulled the towel out of Benny's hand, waved it frantically to cool it down, and dabbed at his eye again.

"Who said buy jelly doughnuts?" Benny groused. "Never woulda happened with a Danish."

"Excuse me," I said. It amazed me that no matter what was going on—or how serious—the bickering always returned. Stuff and Benny looked at me. "Are you through?" I asked.

They shrugged, then nodded their heads sheepishly. The rest of the crew, including Angie, all turned to me. Red stopped whittling a match, closed his switchblade, and looked up.

"Good," I said, putting down my coffee cup. "This morning I overheard Angelo tell my old man that the nuns are being brought in to identify Colucci, Stankovitch, and the Russomanos at four o'clock."

"They'll make 'em," said Boychick.

"Right," I agreed. "He also called Costello and said he wanted a judge there for an immediate arraignment so that bail could be set."

Stuff was incredulous. "Why's he doin' *them* a favor?"

"He's not . . . he's keeping Colucci away from me. He wants Perrault—our lawyer—to spring him, and then he wants Angelo to pick him up and stash him where I can't get to him." I paused to light a Lucky, then continued. "Benny and Red will stake out the precinct. When Angelo makes the pickup, you follow him to see where he takes Colucci. The rest of you wait and see if anyone springs Stankovitch and the Russomanos. If so, you split up and follow them. I want to know where all these bastards are located."

"Where're you gonna be?" asked Boychick.

"Here," I said. "The old man made me promise I'd sit tight today because he might have a job for me. I think it's bullshit—he just wants me out of the way until he makes Colucci disappear. But just in case, I'll stay here and wait to hear from the rest of you."

I noticed Bouncer's eyes flitting around nervously and took him off the hook. "Bounce, you're with me. We guard the fort."

"R-right, Vinny," said Bouncer, relieved.

"What do we do when we find where Colucci's at?" asked Benny.

"Nothing. You just tell me."

"And . . . ?" asked Red.

"And tonight we'll pay him a visit."

Red smiled and snapped open his switchblade.

"Whoa," said Stuff, "let's talk about this!"

"Talk," I said.

"I know how ya feel," said Stuff, "we all do, but your old man said do nothin'. We ain't never gone against the family before!"

"I know," I said.

"We move and he's gonna go batshit," said Louie.

"What're ya gonna tell 'im?" asked Benny.

"Nothing," I replied. "I'll handle it. At the end, I'm doin' this solo."

Since I had already told Boychick my intentions, he'd remained silent, but this was a new twist.

"Solo?" he asked. "The hell's that supposed ta mean?"

"Alone," I said. "I don't want any of you involved."

"That ain't right," said Boychick.

"It's the way I want it," I said.

Boychick yelled, "Vinny, goddamn it . . . !"

"It's the way I want it!" I barked back. It was the first time I had raised my voice throughout the entire exchange.

They stared at me, silent. Nothing like what I was planning had ever happened before. It was the first time since we'd been together that we'd be going against the family—the first time that I would be doing something without them—and the first time that a murder seemed inevitable.

CHAPTER FIFTY-FIVE

ENALDI'S FUNERAL HOME in Queens was a
well-known departure point for members of the Mob about to be
fitted for a marble apartment. It would be Gee-gee Petrone's last
curtain call before he was ensconced in St. John's Cemetery, the Mob's
preferred necropolis. Aldo Mari, the home's proprietor, had done a
landslide business during the Castellammarese War and several other
lesser-known but equally deadly conflicts. Through the years, Aldo had
often had special requests from his clientele, and he was always ready to
accommodate them. Therefore, when Frank Costello had asked him to
dress two of his employees in coveralls and pick up a body in a rug, he'd
thought nothing of it. And when Touch asked for an autopsy, Aldo
happily supplied a retired coroner to do the honors. The results bore out
the fact that Gee-gee had died of a heart attack, natural causes, but
Touch wasn't satisfied. He left in disgust, muttering, "Yeah, but
natural causes caused by that prick Costello!"

That Thursday afternoon, the street in front of Renaldi's was gridlocked. Two entire blocks were jammed with limos, cars, and crowds of curious onlookers. Law enforcement personnel took pictures from conspicuous vehicles that were supposed to be inconspicuous, and gawkers took snapshots of their favorite Mob heroes. Even more bizarre was a tour bus filled with a Hadassah group stuck in the middle of the jam-up. They were headed to a Broadway show, but their little detour was probably giving them a better show than the one they were going to see. All in all, the scene was a circus that made Barnum & Bailey look like a small-town carnival.

Inside the funeral parlor, dark-suited representatives of all five New York families filed by the casket to pay their last respects and check the position of their flower arrangements—the closer to the casket, the more respected the sender. There were over a hundred large wreaths, all swathed in black ribbon and mounted on steps elevated behind the coffin. It was a floral shrine that reached the ceiling. The aroma was overwhelming.

Bo Barbera dropped off my father, who entered and surveyed the scene from the back of the viewing room. It was understood that the bosses wouldn't show up until just before the funeral, but in all cases their respective underbosses arrived at the wake earlier and represented them—except for the Mangano family. Anastasia wasn't there because Costello didn't want it known that he had returned from Italy. His return, coinciding with Petrone's death, could only complicate matters.

My father offered his condolences to a veiled Mrs. Petrone, then noticed Genovese, who was there representing Costello. Genovese got into the queue that was filing past the casket, and my father slipped in behind him. Genovese looked over his shoulder and they made eye contact, but Genovese quickly turned away. He had no intention of talking. My father did. He wanted to get a sense of Genovese's mood. "I'm sorry for your loss," he said sympathetically.

"My loss?" asked Genovese, raising an eyebrow.

"For a close friend."

"A business associate."

"Ah . . . I was misinformed."

"Really. About what?"

"Your relationship."

"Which was . . . ?"

"More conspiratorial."

Genovese snapped his head around. His eyes were ice, and he spat out his words in a stage whisper. "Be careful, Vesta. Anastasia does not make you immune."

Genovese turned back, took a final step to the casket, and genuflected. He mouthed a perfunctory silent prayer, crossed himself, and hurried away. My father had his answer: Genovese was wound tight; he had overreacted. Not only had he stiffened when a conspiracy was mentioned, but with his next sentence he had brought up Anastasia. My father thought it was a guilt reflex. He approached the casket, repeated Genovese's routine, and followed him. He caught a glimpse of a knot of men surrounding Touch Grillo and Carlo Ricci. They were in an alcove off to one side, and Genovese joined them. My father figured he was spooked because his plan had been blown by Petrone's untimely death. He began paying his respects to a number of longtime associates, but out of the corner of his eye he watched Genovese take Grillo by the elbow and lead him aside.

My father was right about Genovese being spooked. But he was wrong about Genovese's plan being blown. It was altered—not blown.

The stakeout at the precinct began at three-thirty with Benny and Red in the Buick, Boychick and Stuff in the Ford, and Louie in the woody. They were spread out and parked a block away from the station because they knew Angelo would recognize the cars. At four-fifteen it was ninety-two in the shade, the nuns still hadn't shown up, and everyone looked like they'd been under a shower.

In the Buick, Benny slapped the wheel in frustration. "Goddamn, it's hot! The hell are they?"

Red was as stoic as ever. He whittled at a match and said, "You got a date somewhere?"

"Nooo," Benny said sarcastically, "Just tired a bein' parboiled over here!"

Ten minutes later the police van that had picked up the six "vigilante nuns" (as they had been dubbed by the tabloids) arrived at Midtown-South. There was a bit of commotion outside the precinct when the nuns got out, and flashbulbs began popping. A few reporters rushed forward and yelled questions at them, but Detectives Sasso and Burns quickly began herding the nuns into the building. They seemed to be enjoying the unusual attention and smiled at the cameras, but they said nothing.

Benny wiped his forehead and shook his head. "Lookit 'em. How they take this heat wearin' all that black?"

"Must be related to Louie," said Red.

"Uh-uh," said Benny, shaking his head, "Louie ain't related to any human. He a iguana."

"A what?"

"A iguana—a lizardlike thing—from the Galá-pagos."

"You shittin' me?"

"No, man, they're islands. Dude name of Darwin found 'em."

Red was astonished. "How d'ya know that shit?"

"I read some," said Benny, somewhat offended. "Not like Vinny and Sidney, but I got moments. When I did time in Juv-e Hall they had *National G-graphic*. Good pictures. The Galá-pagos . . . iguanas." He shrugged.

"You're amazing," said Red, meaning it.

"I agree," said Benny, also meaning it.

After refusing a cup of welcoming coffee, the nuns were escorted by Detectives Sasso and Burns, along with Lieutenants McRae and Naspo, to a room where they could view a lineup of suspects through a one-way window.

The first suspect was Stankovitch. In the adjoining room, he as well as five other large, bearded men who looked a bit like him were brought in. They were told to face left, right, back, and forward. Before they got halfway through the routine, Sister Angelica, the oldest nun and obviously the most senior, pointed at Stankovitch. "That's him," she said. "The one on the left."

"You're sure?" asked Sasso.

"I'd recognize him on a moonless night," answered Sister Angelica, and thrust her index finger at him. "He's the spitting image of that Russian heathen Rasputin!"

"Thank you, Sister." He turned to the others. "So say you all?"

The five other nuns nodded vigorously and murmured their agreement.

Sasso leaned into a microphone. "Next!"

Stankovitch and his group were led out, and another group of men who vaguely resembled the Russomanos was led in. Sasso started to repeat the instructions, but Sister Angelica stopped the routine before he finished.

"Those," she said. "The two in the middle. The sneaky, ferret-looking ones!"

Sasso wondered if Sister Angelica had an image for everyone. "You're sure?"

"As there's a God in heaven!"

He turned to the others. "So say you all?"

Again he got the same result. He leaned back to the microphone. "Next!"

Nick Colucci's group was brought in, but before they even got into position, Sister Angelica pointed him out.

"Him!" she said triumphantly. "With the pocked face and the scarred chin!" She turned to her fellow nuns and gave a victorious nod of her head. They softly applauded Sister Angelica and then nodded in unison to Sasso.

"Who does he remind you of?" Sasso asked Sister Angelica.

"Not a soul on the face of this earth!" she said with finality.

Sasso thanked them, and they were driven back to their parish.

Colucci, Stankovitch, and the Russomanos were taken back upstairs and immediately arraigned by Costello's judge. They were charged with "assault with a deadly weapon" (the tire iron and chains) as well as "felony hit-and-run" (the sideswiped cars at the scene). The judge set bail at five thousand dollars each, they were thrown back into the tank, and Lieutenants McRae and Naspo dutifully reported the results to Angelo and Touch.

Danny and Robert Collins were waiting at the coffee urn when Sasso, Burns, and McRae returned from the lineup.

"So?" asked Danny.

"They made 'em," said Sasso.

"All four?" asked Robert.

"All four," said Burns.

"Shit!" said Danny, and rubbed his chin with his knuckles.

"That a problem?" asked Sasso.

"Huh?" said Danny, and then realized it shouldn't be. He glanced at the lieutenant and covered with, "No, no problem. I was just thinkin' you're right. They're probably the same boyos that bombed Veal's place."

Sasso shrugged. "Makes sense," he said.

"Yeah, right," said Danny. "Thanks—nice work. Ya nailed 'em good." He shook their hands and started out.

"See ya," said Robert, and followed his brother.

The Collins brothers left the precinct and walked up to their unmarked car, where Danny put his arms on the roof and rested his head in his arms.

Robert walked up behind him. "So?" he asked.

"This ain't good," Danny muttered.

"Tell me about it," Robert snapped. "Colucci knows Drago got him to hit the Vesta kid because the kid's old man burned down Drago's warehouse. If he talks, it could lead back to the guards. And they can identify us as the detectives who told them about the robbery *before* it happened." He paused, leaned next to his brother's head, and yelled, "If we had bribed them with the lousy thousand bucks Grillo gave us, none a this might've happened!"

Danny tried to wave it off. "Who knew?"

"I knew!" barked Robert. "Shit!" He pounded the roof of their car.

"Stop bitchin', we gotta call Touch."

My father was leaving Renaldi's when the funeral director pulled him aside and said, "Signore Vesta, there's a call for you."

"*Grazie*, Aldo," he said. Mari led him into his office, then indicated the phone and left discreetly.

The call was from McRae at Midtown-South. After getting the news, my father called Mark Perrault. "Mark," he said, "a punk named Colucci is at Midtown-South. Bail is five thousand. Get over there and get him out. Angelo will meet you . . . Oh? When can you get there? . . . No, an hour more or less won't make a difference."

His next call was to Angelo. "Meet Perrault at the precinct," he said. "Five-fifteen. Wait for him outside. When he springs Colucci, pick him up and take him to the clinic. I'll meet you there at seven and decide what to do with Colucci."

I had guessed right: My father was going to bail out Colucci and hide him because he knew I would probably kill him, and he didn't want a murder hanging over my head before I was even nineteen. Somehow he would figure out a way to protect me and then make sure Colucci was put away for a very long time.

Touch got his call from Naspo at the precinct at about the same time Angelo got his call from McRae. Touch called Don Jeffries—Petrone's lawyer—and told him to spring Colucci, take him to his office, and wait for a call sometime after five-thirty, no later than six. The lawyer said he was on his way.

Right after the nuns came out of Midtown-South, Red and Benny saw a man wearing a pin-striped suit and a homburg enter the precinct. Red smiled, snapped open his switchblade, and began whittling a new match. "Gotta be him," he said.

"Onny a lawyer'd be seen in that rig," Benny agreed.

Red nodded. "Gino's lawyer . . ."

It wasn't. It was Jeffries, Petrone's lawyer, but neither one of them could have possibly known that.

"See Angelo?" asked Benny.

Red shook his head. His eyes narrowed and he said, "He's late." He sensed something might have changed, but all they could do was wait.

Ten minutes later, Nick Colucci and Don Jeffries came out of the building. They got into the lawyer's car and headed east.

"Still no Angelo?" asked Benny.

Red scanned the street and said, "No . . ." He snapped his switchblade shut and said, "Follow 'em."

Benny pulled out and stayed within two car lengths of his quarry.

Angelo would miss them by five minutes.

CHAPTER FIFTY-SIX

I'D BEEN WAITING all afternoon for word from Red and Benny. None had come, and it was getting late. Louie, Boychick, Stuff, and Bouncer had returned after Nick Colucci was released, and Red and Benny left to follow him. With Stankovitch and the Russomanos remaining in jail, there hadn't been any reason to stick around.

They were shooting an uninspired game of pool when the phone rang. I swept it up. "Good, stay with him," I said. "When he moves again, call back here." I hung up the phone and saw that everyone was staring at me in anticipation. "They followed Colucci and the lawyer to his office."

"He's not gonna hole up there," said Boychick. "He'll make another move."

"Right. And when he does, Red and Benny will call back and tell us where. Stuff, stay with Bouncer and take the call. If my ol' man calls, tell 'im I went out for a bite."

"Where're you headed?" asked Stuff.

"I'm tired of sittin' around. I'm gonna see how Sidney's doin'. Boychick and Louie, you're with me," I said, and started out. "We'll keep checkin' in."

"Right," Louie answered.

"Let's do it!" barked Boychick.

My hand shot out and we all stacked hands.

As Bouncer watched us leave, Stuff went to the piano and started noodling the keys with his index finger. Angie put her head on his lap.

"He's g-gonna do it, ain't he," Bouncer said.

"What?" asked Stuff, and kept on noodling.

"It. He's g-gonna kill Nick Colucci."

"Yeah," said Stuff. He stopped noodling and began to play Gershwin's "Summertime."

As we approached Bellevue, Boychick said, "It ain't visitin' hours again." He was driving the old Ford, Louie was riding shotgun, and I was in the backseat, thinking about Colucci.

"No problem," I said. "Pull into the Emergency entrance."

Louie parked beside an ambulance, and I entered the waiting room. The controlled chaos of the prior night was still going on. Once again I went into my "broken arm" routine; no one gave me a second look. I rode the elevator to the third floor, ducked around the nurses' station, and slipped into Sidney's room in the ICU. It was empty. The bed wasn't made up, and the array of monitors and drips that had been attached to Sidney was still all around it. They probably took him out for some more tests, I thought. A medical chart remained hanging at the foot of the bed. I looked at it and saw that the attending physician was Dr. Singh. I left the room and found a wall phone at the end of the corridor.

"Dr. Singh," I told the operator. A few moments later I heard the PA system announce: *"Paging Dr. Singh—Dr. Jawaharlal Singh."* I waited another minute, and the mellifluous voice of Dr. Singh came on the line.

"Yes," he said. "Dr. Singh."

"This is a friend of Sidney Butcher's. I'm callin' to find out how he is."

"And you are?"

"Vesta. Vinny Vesta. I was with him when we were jumped. You examined me."

"Ah, yes. Yours was the first name he spoke when he came out of the coma. Where are you now?"

"I'm . . ." I hesitated. "In a phone booth."

"I don't think so, Mr. Vesta. The line you are calling on is an interior hospital line."

I saw no point in continuing the charade; it was obvious the doctor knew I was in the hospital. "I'm in the ICU—by Sidney's room."

"Stay there, Mr. Vesta, I'll come right up."

I hung up the phone, wandered to the end of the hall, and looked out the window. There was a tourist boat circling Manhattan on the East River, but little other traffic. Tourists, I thought, a thousand people from a hundred places who come to see the Big Apple . . . "civilians." I wondered if any of them were like us—or could ever have our kinds of problems. I'd have to ask Sidney what he thought.

"Mr. Vesta?" said Dr. Singh.

I turned, Dr. Singh extended his hand, and I shook it. "Hi," I said, "I snuck in."

He smiled and said, "I know," then added, "You just arrived?"

"Five minutes ago."

"Ah." He nodded. "I see . . ."

"What?" I asked.

"It was very sudden."

"What?" I asked, becoming alarmed. "What was sudden?"

"Mr. Vesta, I'm sorry . . . your friend has passed on."

344

I didn't believe I'd heard him correctly. "Passed on?" My voice rose uncontrollably. "Passed on? You mean died?"

"Yes," he said sadly. "Less than a half hour ago."

"That's impossible! I was here last night! He was sitting up in bed!"

"I know," said Singh.

I started barking out words. "He felt good! He told me! 'Good,' he said! He was—"

"Mr. Vesta, please," Singh interrupted. "We think it was an aneurysm. A blood clot from the beating. It went to his brain."

As the words slowly sank in, it felt like all the air was being sucked out of my lungs. My face flushed and my eyes started to glaze. I leaned against the windowsill and bowed my head. For some stupid reason I didn't want a doctor to see me cry. "Do his mother and father know?" I asked.

"I called them five minutes ago. They were not in. I'll try again every ten minutes until I reach them."

I took a deep breath and faced Singh. "When you see them, tell them I know, and that my family will do anything . . . anything."

"I understand," said Singh.

I took off down the stairs. I didn't want to wait for the elevator. I walked back to the car and slid into the backseat.

Boychick and Louie twisted around and looked at me. "How is he?" asked Boychick.

"He wasn't awake," I said. It wasn't exactly the truth, but it wasn't exactly a lie. I didn't want them to know yet. There was work to do.

"I checked in with Stuff," said Louie. "Red called. Colucci left the lawyer's office. They followed him to Brooklyn—corner of Flatbush and Atlantic. It's where Leo took your father. It's his girlfriend's place. A hooker named Sherry."

"Drive," I said.

CHAPTER FIFTY-SEVEN

THE NORMALLY BUSY corner where Flatbush met Atlantic Avenue was fairly quiet. Rush hour was over, but there were still a few pedestrians on the sidewalks trying to beat the heat. No breeze—ninety-five degrees with humidity to match.

Red watched several customers, including Benny, sidle up to a stand on the corner. They were purchasing paper cones filled with crushed ice that was showered with syrup, an "Italian ice." They were refreshing, but you needed a quick tongue to prevent the concoction from melting all over you. No easy task in the withering early evening heat.

Benny and Red had been watching Sherry's building for almost an hour. Colucci had arrived, and they had called Benny's apartment and reported in to Stuff. But since then, nothing.

Benny rushed back to the Buick and handed Red a strawberry ice. "A redhead an' you get strawberry," he noted. "There a message in that?"

"What'd you get?" asked Red.

"Choc'let," said Benny.

"Case closed," said Red.

A minute later they drank the last of the melted liquid at the bottom of the paper cones, crushed them, and threw them out the window.

"Whaddaya thinkin' he's gonna do?" asked Benny.

Red knew exactly what he was talking about. "Take 'im out."

"Jus' like that?"

"How else?"

"Dunno . . . seem's kinda final, don't it?"

"Problem with that?" asked Red.

"No, it jus' seem's like . . . well, we done a lot of shit, but we ain't never killed nobody."

"Yet," Red said indifferently.

"You *like* it?" asked Benny.

"Nothin' to like or not like. The way it is."

"You a cold sumbitch, you know that?"

"Thanks," said Red, leaning forward. He pointed at a black Cadillac that had pulled up and double-parked in front of Sherry's building. A tall redhead carrying an oversize purse jumped out of the backseat and entered the building. The driver remained parked.

Benny said, "Sherry . . . Gino said a tall, flamin' redhead. Can't be two like that in one buildin'."

"Yeah," said Red, "and with a car and driver."

"Figure she comin' back out?"

Red nodded and stated the obvious: "The driver ain't leavin'."

A few minutes later Benny glanced up at the rearview mirror and said, "Vinny . . ."

Boychick double-parked our car alongside Benny's, and Benny leaned out of his window. I leaned out of mine and asked, "He still in there?"

"Yeah," said Benny, "and the hook jus' got here." He pointed at the Cadillac. "Got a driver waitin' . . ."

I looked ahead and saw Sherry come running out of the building with a small suitcase. She hopped back into the Cadillac and it pulled away.

Benny said, "Prob'ly nailed a big daddy for an all-nighter."

"Wait here and watch the front," I said, then tapped Boychick on the shoulder. "Pull around back."

We pulled around the corner and parked on Fourth Avenue, next to the back entrance of Sherry's building. We all got out and I turned my back to the building. I faced the car, stepped in close, and took a .32 snub-nose out of my waistband.

Red watched me check the cylinder and gave me a sadistic smile. "Sure you don't want company?"

"Uh-uh . . . I want it to be just the two of us," I said, and went into the building.

I climbed the stairs to the second floor and listened outside of Sherry's door. I heard a radio and tried the door. It was unlocked, and I slowly pushed it open with my revolver.

Nick Colucci was lying on the couch with an ice-filled towel over his eyes. His shirt and shoes were off, and he was listening to a Dodgers twi-night doubleheader. I quietly closed the door, crossed the room, and shoved the muzzle of my gun into Colucci's nostril. Colucci shrieked and tore away the towel. He saw the gun, held out his hands, and arched away from the barrel.

"The fuck!" he cried out. His eyes focused and got very wide. "Vesta! Wh-whaddaya want?"

I shut off the radio and said, "We have unfinished business, Nick."

I could almost hear the synapses arcing as he gradually realized why I was there. He began to panic and cried out, "It was orders, Vesta—orders! I had ta do it! It was Drago made me! Because of his warehouse!" His voice went up an octave. "Orders, Vesta—not personal! Orders!"

It was tough, but faced with that answer I still managed to keep my voice even when I said, "Orders . . ."

"Right!" Colucci nodded rapidly. "Orders!"

"You ever hear of Nuremberg?" I asked him.

Nick's eyebrows knotted. "Who the fuck is Nuremberg?"

"It, Nick. It. A place."

"Oh . . . yeah, right. Nur'mberg."

"A bunch of guys like you were there. They said what they did was orders. Nothin' personal. Orders."

"The fuck are ya talkin' about?"

"Sidney, Nick. I'm talkin' about Sidney. Was he orders?"

"The Jew was there! He got inna way!"

"So you whacked him," I said.

"He's a Jew, for chrissakes! Why d'ya give a shit?"

I felt my hand tighten around the gun and the slack come out of the trigger. He noticed it and pulled back. "Where's your gun?" I asked.

"What? Why?"

"Where is it?"

"Inna bag," he said, pointing to a small gym bag next to the couch.

I took his small revolver out of the bag and checked the cylinder. Fully loaded. Six shots. I put my gun in my waistband and pointed Nick's at him.

"What is this shit, Vesta? Whaddaya want?"

"A little conversation, Nick."

"About what? You know everythin' there is to know. Drago ordered us ta bomb Veal's joint, and—"

"You and Junior," I said, interrupting him.

"Right. Me 'n Junior."

"The other Nazi."

"So he hates Jews, so what?"

"Like you."

"Yeah, like me! What's the fuckin' point?"

"You killed one."

"Huh?"

"Sidney. Sidney Butcher. The kid who was with me on the library steps. He's dead. You killed him."

Nick didn't expect that, and it shook him. He looked at the gun and back to me. "Where's this goin', Vinny?" He thought using my first name would soften things a bit. "I told ya, Drago ordered the hit. We was supposed ta take ya out for a while. Nobody was supposed ta die. The Jew bought it. Whaddaya want from me?"

"Like I said, Nick, a little conversation. About the way you get to see the guy who wants to see you."

"What? Who?"

"The Reaper, Nick. The Grim Guy. He's waitin' to see you. The only question is how you're gonna get to him. It's your decision."

"The hell are ya talkin' about?"

"You, Nick. You're not gonna leave this room alive. You're gonna die. For Sidney. The only question is—how?"

It was hot and Nick was sweating, but now he started to tremble and he paled. He again looked at the gun and thrust out his hand. "No, Vinny, please—ya gotta listen. Don't shoot!"

"I'm not gonna shoot you, Nick."

"Huh?" said Nick, confusion spreading across his face.

"You're gonna shoot you."

"You're crazy!" said Nick.

"I'm glad you feel that way, Nick. Because then you'll believe what I have to tell you. You're gonna die. That's it. Now—either you can do it, or I can do it." I paused and smiled reassuringly. "If you do it, it's a bullet in your temple—quick, a simple suicide." I let my smile fade and paused again. I kept my voice casual—but cold. I'd seen a movie called *Black Magic* about a guy named Cagliostro. He was a hypnotist. Orson Welles had played the part, and I was imitating the calm, quiet voice he'd used. "But if I do it, it's gonna take a long time, Nick. First a shot through your left knee. Five minutes later, a shot through your right knee. Then a little higher. You ever think what it might be like to have your balls blown off? Then in about an hour or so, I'll put one in your belly and sit here until you rattle." I let it sink in and then asked, "So, Nick, what's it gonna be?"

It was working. Nick seemed frozen. The realization came slowly. He was going to die. And he was going to die screaming. Unless . . .

I flipped open the cylinder of Nick's revolver, shook out five bullets, and closed it. I then cocked the hammer with the remaining bullet in firing position. Nick watched every move. His eyes were glassy. He was mesmerized.

I got up and walked behind him. I took out a handkerchief and thoroughly wiped down the gun. "Okay, Nick, it's time to keep your appointment."

I pulled out my gun and held it against the back of his head. Then I reached over, took his hand, and put it on his gun. Nick took it, staring at the hand holding the gun as if it belonged to someone else.

He slowly raised the gun to his temple and pulled the trigger.

I checked the hallway for any curious neighbors who might have heard the shot, saw none, and took the stairs back to the rear entrance.

When I walked back out on Fourth Avenue, I saw Red, Benny, Boychick, and Louie leaning against the Ford, smoking cigarettes. They were expecting the gunshot and knew what it was. Anyone else who heard it probably thought it was a car backfiring. They saw me walking toward them, simultaneously dropped their cigarettes, and ground them under their soles.

"It's done," I said, and then added, "Sidney can rest in peace."

As usual, Boychick reacted first. His head snapped up and he said, "What?"

"Sidney's dead. Tonight, just before we got to the hospital. A blood clot."

Benny and Red exchanged a look. Louie shook his head, and Benny said, "Oh, man . . ." Red took a deep breath and let it out but said nothing.

I got into the backseat of the Ford. Boychick climbed behind the wheel, and Louie sidled into the passenger seat. Benny and Red went around the corner to pick up the Buick, and we all headed back to Benny's. No one uttered another word.

CHAPTER FIFTY-EIGHT

BO BARBERA DOUBLE-PARKED on Twelfth Avenue in front of my father's office at six forty-five. One block south, the *Queen Mary* was loading her passengers and there was a dockside bon voyage party in progress. Traffic cops did their best to keep things moving, but the entire pier area was heavily congested. A blizzard of streamers and confetti hovered above the dockside while a band played "Hail, Britannia." A row of limousines was double-parked on the street, and their occupants were gaily toasting the ship's departure with champagne flutes. Barbera once told me that my father had described the champagne drinkers as "café society." He said he wouldn't trade the whole bunch for a *sfogliatelle*.

Bo flipped down his visor. On it was taped a large card that read:

Official Business
NYPD

Half the wiseguys in New York had them because they were paying off half the cops. My father and Bo got out and entered the office. My father had sensed that Genovese was spinning out of control, and he wanted to alert Costello and Anastasia.

Beppo watched my father and Bo head for the office, then pulled around the corner and parked halfway down Fiftieth Street. In the backseat, Touch checked his .38, Carlo his silenced .22.

"You go in first," said Touch. "Take 'em both with the twenty-two. I won't shoot unless ya miss. Too many people ta hear the noise."

"Got it," said Carlo, and they both left the car.

My father entered his office, took off his hat, and went straight to the phone. He sat behind his desk and dialed Costello. Barbera sat on the edge of the desk, inadvertently blocking my father's view of the door.

"Mr. Costello, please . . . ," said my father. "I see. This is Gino Vesta. I'm at my office. Please have him call me when he gets in." He replaced the receiver and leaned back in the swivel chair. "Frank went down to the lobby for the paper. His butler said he'll be right back."

Barbera heard the door open behind him, and when he turned he froze. Carlo Ricci was in the doorway, leveling a silenced revolver, and Touch Grillo was standing behind him. Barbera heard *pfffft!—pfffft!* and the right side of his chest exploded. He crumpled on top of the desk and completely blocked Carlo's line of fire.

My father pulled the .45 out of his shoulder holster and was rising out of his chair to fire over the top of Barbera's body when Carlo fired three more shots. The first two hit Barbera. The third hit my father high in the neck. A geyser of blood spurted out, and he simultaneously grabbed his throat and squeezed the trigger. There was a deafening roar, and Carlo flew back into Touch with enough force to hurl them both to the floor.

Touch recovered quickly and dragged Carlo to his feet. Carlo was hit in his shoulder and was going into shock from the impact of the heavy slug. Touch was sure that someone on the crowded street had heard the roar of Gino's .45. He was also sure Gino was dead—he had seen the blood spurt from his neck. He threw the skinny man over his shoulder and bolted out of the office.

Several people on the street had actually heard the shot but had no idea where it came from. Others saw a huge man dash around the corner of Fiftieth Street carrying someone on his shoulder, but they were too involved in "farewell and Godspeed" to pay much attention. Touch got back to the car, unceremoniously tossed Carlo into the backseat, jumped in alongside Beppo, and said, "Go!"

Back on the pier, a band was still playing "Hail, Britannia."

When seven o'clock came and went and my father hadn't shown up at the clinic, Angelo became concerned. My father was never late. It was almost a phobia. He called Costello, who told him that Gino had called from his office but when Costello called back there was no answer. Angelo slammed down the phone and rushed out the door.

He drove up to the West Side piers, snaking the Chrysler through the crowd that was still celebrating the *Queen Mary*'s departure. Recognizing Barbera's car, he pulled up behind it and double-parked in front of my father's office. He flipped down his visor and revealed an "official business" card identical to the one on Barbera's visor. After he took a quick look inside Barbera's car, he went into the office.

When he opened the door, his jaw dropped. Barbera was splayed on top of the desk in a pool of blood. He was on his back, staring at the ceiling; the front of his white shirt was deep red, and his arms were stretched out. He looked as if he'd been crucified. A leg was visible on the floor behind the desk, and Angelo rushed across the room and saw my father crumpled on his back. There was a hole in his throat, and the floor behind his head was covered with blood from the exit wound. He had taken the bullet alongside his larynx, and it had come out the back of his neck. He felt for a pulse; it was there. My father was still alive but wouldn't be for long if the bleeding wasn't stopped. Angelo took out his handkerchief and stuffed it into the wound. My father moaned.

Angelo leaned closer. "Gino, can you hear me?"

My father opened his eyes and tried to focus.

"Hang on. I'll get help," said Angelo.

"Angelo . . ." My father beckoned him closer, and Angelo bent down to his face. "Grillo," he whispered, "with Carlo . . ." His eyes rolled back and he passed out.

Angelo reached for the phone and made three calls—the first to the clinic, the second to the twins, and the third to Frank Costello. He then cleaned up most of the blood and hid Barbera's body in my father's bathroom, to be dealt with later.

Ten minutes after Angelo's call, an ambulance from the clinic barreled up Twelfth Avenue and parted the revelers on the pier. It arrived with lights flashing and sirens screaming. Two white-clad attendants jumped out and ran into the office carrying a stretcher. A few minutes later, some of the revelers watched a "heart attack victim" being carried out on a stretcher. The covered body was placed in the ambulance, and once again the revelers parted as it sped away with lights flashing and sirens screaming.

The best surgeons had been alerted when Angelo called the clinic, and they were waiting when the ambulance got back. Angelo watched as they began their examination the instant the stretcher came through the door, continuing as they walked alongside the stretcher all the way into surgery. Angelo went to the coffee urn, filled a cup with coffee, and waited.

The twins showed up ten minutes later. Their faces still looked like Jackson Pollock prints, their temporary dental work was evident, and their eyes were so badly swollen that they were looking through slits. Angelo had to have realized they wouldn't be much help for what was coming.

"Christ, Angelo," Dino said through his puffed lips, "what happened?"

"Grillo and Ricci—in the office. Bo's dead, Gino's in surgery."

"How bad ith he?" asked Dino. His wired teeth gave him a lisp.

"Bad. He lost a lot of blood."

"Holy shit," said Matty. "Now what?"

"Costello wants it kept quiet. No one says a word, *capische?*"

"Doth Mickey know?" asked Dino.

"Not yet. You go pick her up and bring her here. Tell her nothing. Let the doctors handle it. Matty and I will pick up Barbera's body. On the way back we'll stop at Benny's place and tell Vinny."

"Thath it?" asked Dino, obviously surprised there was no retaliation plan.

"For now," said Angelo. "We meet back here in half an hour."

Angelo left with Matty. Dino went to pick up Mickey.

Costello dropped two Alka-Seltzer tablets into a glass and filled it with water. It was the second time he'd done it in the last half hour. He had a brutal case of agita, and it was tearing up his stomach. Angelo had called Costello, Costello had then called Anastasia—and Anastasia was not happy. At eight o'clock, "the Lord High Executioner" came thundering into Costello's den in a rage that only he could generate.

"They're dead, Frank!" Anastasia roared. "Every fucking last one of them!" He ticked them off on his fingers. "Grillo, Ricci, and Genovese! *Especially* Genovese! He's behind it! We know that! Fuck this 'proof' bullshit! I told Gino—I warned him: *We gotta whack him before he whacks us!* Now this!"

Costello thundered right back at him, "You think I don't feel the same way? *Think*, Al! Genovese spends half his life trying to set us up! Now he has! He *wants* us to move against him. He's *waiting* for us! We go after him without proof, we bring the whole goddamn organization down on us!"

Anastasia couldn't believe his ears. "We're just gonna sit by and let him get away with this?"

"No! But not now! Not when he's expecting it. And not when everyone will *believe* we went after him because Gino was hit. If we move, he'll say he had nothing to do with it. He'll say it was all Petrone. He's probably already figured a way to throw Grillo and Ricci to the Commission. They'll take the fall for Gino. *If* we move. But . . ." Costello paused to make his point. "If we *don't* move"—he jabbed his index finger at the floor to accentuate every word—"*this—never—happened!*"

"What?" Anastasia objected. "Gino's got a bullet in his neck and Barbera's dead!"

"True. But only *we* know that. No one else! Genovese can't say anything about it because he couldn't *know* about it unless he was behind it!" Costello sighed and slumped heavily into a chair. The strain had exhausted him.

"Frank, there's gotta be somethin' we can do."

"The something we do for now is nothing. Gino was taken to the clinic. Angelo will dispose of Barbera's body."

"I hate it! It's fuckin' spineless!" said Anastasia, and poured a large Scotch. He downed it in one slug.

"I hate it, too," Costello said wearily. "But we have no choice. We have to wait for our chance. It will come, Al, I promise you. But not now."

Anastasia threw up his hands in total frustration. "Fuck!" He went to the window, clasped his hands behind his back, and stared out over Central Park.

Costello let him fume for several moments, then said, "I need your word, Al. I know how close you are to Gino. For the moment, as far as anyone else is concerned, you're not even back from Italy. No one, not you or anyone else, moves without my go-ahead."

Anastasia turned, faced his old friend, and sighed. "You're askin' a lot."

"I know . . . Your word, Albert."

"Okay, you have it. But . . ." He pointed his finger at Costello. "I'm tellin' ya, he came after Gino and he'll come after us. It's only a matter of time."

Costello knew he was probably right.

He was.

My mother wasn't home when Dino went to pick her up at the tenement. He was knocking insistently on the door when Ira and Sarah Butcher came up the stairs. They had just been to a bar mitzvah in Queens and were nicely dressed. Ira, as always, was wearing his yarmulke, and Sarah had a shawl over her head in spite of the heat.

"Excuse me," said Mrs. Butcher, "are you looking for the Vestas?"

"Mrs.," said Dino, "you happen to know where she is?"

Mrs. Butcher nodded. "It's Thursday. She and Mrs. Maserelli go to the Rosary Society on Thursday."

Dino was probably thinking, *Why the hell didn't Angelo know that?* But he asked, "You happen to know where?"

"Well . . . ," Mrs. Butcher said tentatively. She didn't know this man and had an old country aversion to strangers.

The phone inside the Butchers' apartment began to ring.

"I'll get it," said Mr. Butcher. He unlocked the door and entered the apartment.

"Are you a friend of the family?" asked Mrs. Butcher.

Dino nodded and rattled off the names of the two families. "Gino, Mickey, Vinny—Angelo, Lena, and Attillio—Stuff."

Inside the apartment, Mr. Butcher could be heard answering the phone. "Yes . . . Ira Butcher, here . . . Ah! Dr. Singh, how are you? . . ."

Mrs. Butcher seemed satisfied with Dino's litany and said, "The Holy Cross sometimes, but tonight the St. Patrick's."

"Thanks. I appreciate it," said Dino, and dashed down the stairs.

When he got to the second landing, he thought he heard an anguished cry from above, but he was in a headlong dash to retrieve Mickey, so he kept going.

He sped across Forty-second Street and up Fifth Avenue, then double-parked in front of the cathedral between Fiftieth and Fifty-first.

The Rosary Society gathering at St. Patrick's was well attended, but Dino quickly located Mickey. He slipped into the pew and knelt next to her. Her head was bowed in prayer, so she didn't notice him. He leaned over and whispered loudly enough to be heard above the praying. "There's been an accident," he said.

"What? What accident?" asked Mickey, suddenly alarmed.

"Shhh!" hissed an older woman nearby.

"Shhh, you!" snapped Lena Maserelli, kneeling beside Mickey. "What's wrong?" she asked Dino.

"An accident," Dino repeated.

"Shhh!" hissed the same woman.

Lena turned back to her, raised her hand to her throat, and raked her fingers upward in a classic Italian rebuke. The woman recoiled, and Lena turned back toward Dino.

"Tell me!" Mickey ordered. "What is it?"

"Gino. He's at the clinic."

Both women immediately crossed themselves and stood up. They ignored the critical glances of surrounding worshippers and allowed Dino to lead them out of the church and back to the clinic.

Stuff and Bouncer were getting antsy. For almost two hours, they had tried to pass the time with a game of eight ball while they waited for word from somebody—Vinny, Gino, Angelo—*anybody* who would let them know what was going on. They finally broke out a deck of cards and started playing hearts. Stuff threw down the queen of spades, nailing Bouncer with thirteen points.

"Th-that's the th-third time in a row!" cried Bouncer. "How do you do it?"

Stuff curled his fingers, admired his fingernails and blew on them. "I cheat."

"Huh?" said Bouncer, taken aback.

"I'm a pianist. I have very accomplished fingers—so I cheat."

"You admit it?" asked Bouncer, astonished.

"Sure. But only when we don't play for money. We play for money—I don't cheat."

"Why?"

"Because that would be cheatin'."

"Sometimes you're w-wackier then R-Red, you know that?"

Boychick, Louie, and I walked in at ten after eight. There was an accident on the Manhattan Bridge, and it had taken us forty minutes to get back from Brooklyn. When we opened the door they all but jumped out of their seats. Red and Benny followed us in and went directly into the kitchen without saying a word to Stuff and Bouncer.

Stuff looked at me and turned up his palms. "What?" he asked.

"Colucci's dead," I said.

Stuff said, "Jesus," and crossed himself.

Red and Benny returned with three cans of beer and handed them to Boychick, Louie, and me. We popped the lids and took a long swig. When we lowered the cans, Stuff and Bouncer were still staring at us expectantly, awaiting details. There was no need to supply them, and I was about to say so when Angelo came through the open door and marched straight up to me without acknowledging anyone else. "Grillo and Ricci took a shot at your father," he said, eliminating any niceties. "He's at the clinic."

"Christ," I said. "How bad?"

"Bad. His neck. He's alive, but Barbera's dead."

I ran out the door.

*   *   *

We got to the clinic at eight-thirty. I rushed into the waiting room, followed by Angelo, Matty, and my crew. My mother and Lena were sitting in a small lounge area. When she saw me she jumped up, threw her arms around me, and buried her head in my chest. "Vincenzo . . . ," she said, sobbing.

"Mom, it's gonna be okay."

"They shot him," she said.

"I know," I said, and turned to Lena. "Any news?"

Lena shook her head. "He's still bein' operated."

I eased my mother's head away from my chest and took her face in my hands. "He's strong, Mom. He'll survive."

She nodded and wiped her eyes. I eased her back down on a couch and sat next to her. Matty paid his respects and then joined Dino at the coffee urn. Boychick, Stuff, Bouncer, and Louie took the last seats in the lounge area. Benny and Red sat on the floor. Angelo came over and took my mother's hand.

"Mickey," Angelo said contritely, "I'm sorry . . . I wasn't with him. I never should have let him talk me into—"

My mother looked up and shook her head. Her eyes were glistening. "No, Angelo . . . I'm sure it wasn't your fault."

I was as sure as she was. I patted Angelo on the shoulder and signaled Stuff to come with me over to the far corner.

"Sidney's dead," I said. "A blood clot from the beating. Tonight . . . just before we got to the hospital. Tell Bouncer." A look of anguish crossed his face, and he started to say something. I held up my hand and stopped him. "My mom can't handle this tonight. Have your mom tell mine in the morning."

He nodded and said, "Right."

Behind Stuff, I saw a tall, dapper man stride into the reception room. He was the mirror image of Vittorio De Sica and had an almost identical accent. He extended his hand to my mother as I walked back over to them.

"Ah, Mrs. Vesta . . . I'm Dr. Gennaro. Director and chief of staff."

She took his hand. "How is he?"

"Gino was shot in the neck. It's a very serious wound."

My mother's shoulders slumped and she crossed herself. "*Jesu Cristo . . .*"

Gennaro sat next to her. "He's lost a lot of blood, and there are lead fragments around his cervical vertebrae. It was a dum-dum bullet."

"And . . . ?"

"Dr. Altman's still operating. It will be at least another hour." He smiled and patted her hand. "I'll come back as soon as they're finished."

When he was gone, Angelo signaled the twins and they started out. I caught up with them at the door.

"Where're ya goin'?"

Angelo said, "Unfinished business."

"Grillo and Ricci," I said.

Angelo nodded.

"So there's gonna be a war . . ." It wasn't a question.

"No," said Angelo. "Costello wants to make like it never happened. He wants us to stand down."

"How?" I asked. "Barbera's dead and my father's on the operating table!"

"Hopefully Gino recovers," said Angelo. "Barbera disappears."

"And Genovese?"

"For the time bein', he's frozen. Costello and Anastasia'll have ta figure somethin' out . . . but Barbera's dead, and those two pricks tried to whack Gino. Costello or no Costello, they're history. But it'll be like he said—I'll make it like nothin' ever happened."

"I'm goin' with you."

"Fuck, no!" Angelo said, startled.

I pointed at the twins. "Look at them. They can hardly see. You might as well go after them alone."

"Your father will—"

"My father's on an operating table!" I took a deep breath. For the second time that night, I struggled to keep my voice calm.

"Colucci's dead," I said.

"Jesus Christ! Ya whacked 'im?"

"He whacked himself. It'll come off a suicide."

Angelo's eyes narrowed. "Cute."

I nodded. "And Sidney's dead."

"Christ, I'm sorry, kid. First Terry, now Sidney . . ."

"Yeah," I said. "And now you know why I want in. My guys and me. After all that's happened, you owe it to us."

"Shit!" Angelo spat out, and looked at Matty and Dino. Matty tilted his head sideways and shrugged. The move said, "He's right."

"You know where they are?" I asked.

"Their warehouse," said Angelo.

"How do you know?" I asked.

"I don't. It's what I'd do. They gotta figure when we find out they hit Gino, we'll come after them. Their logical headquarters is the warehouse. They'll go to the mattresses, but they ain't had time to call in their troops. If we move fast, we got the high ground."

I nodded. It made sense. And Angelo was right: We couldn't give them time to pull in their crew. I told Bouncer to wait for us and signaled the rest of the crew to follow me.

Touch slammed down the phone and swore to himself. It was the seventh call he'd made since he, Carlo, and Beppo had gotten back to Petrone's office. He had been trying to reach Genovese and some of the other members of his crew for almost two hours. At the funeral parlor Aldo Mari had told him that Genovese and several other men had left the wake around seven o'clock. He had tried Genovese at home, but he wasn't there. His wife speculated that he and his friends might be going out for an early dinner, but she didn't know where.

It probably never occurred to Touch that Genovese didn't want to be found. Costello was right: Genovese was setting up Touch to take the fall for killing my father. He would tell the Commission that Grillo and Ricci had held my father responsible for Petrone's death and Touch had retaliated. It was a logical accusation, and the Commission would buy it. There would be nothing to tie Genovese to my father's murder. Anastasia, of course, wouldn't care about tie-ins. He would come after Genovese anyway—which was exactly what Genovese wanted. What he couldn't have known was that Angelo would find Gino alive and would know who had shot him.

Carlo was still bleeding. He was on the couch on his left side with his legs drawn up in the fetal position. The .45 slug had entered his right shoulder below the collarbone and left via a plum-size hole in his back. Touch had stuffed a handkerchief into the wound, and Beppo had brought him a roll of duct tape from the warehouse floor. They had taped up his shoulder and stemmed the flow, but he was slowly bleeding out. Touch had given him half a dozen aspirin, which he'd washed down with a bottle of gin. The effort had eased the pain, but he was still moaning.

"Touch, please," he begged, "ya gotta get me a doctor."

"Hang in," soothed Touch, "the doctor's on his way—be here any minute."

It was a lie. After they hit Gino, Touch had taken Carlo directly to the office of their permanently retained doctor, but the son of a bitch was in surgery at Columbia Medical Center. Touch wasn't about to take Carlo to any goddamn hospital with a bullet hole in him, so he had driven back to the warehouse.

"I can't wait no more, Touch . . . everythin's gettin' fuzzy . . . I don't get help, I'm gonna die!"

"Shut up, for chrissake!" Touch growled. "Ya sound like a pussy! Ya ain't gonna die!"

Another lie—Carlo was getting dizzy from the loss of blood. He was right: If he didn't get help soon, he would die. Touch shrugged and dialed yet another restaurant where he thought he might locate Genovese.

No one had seen him.

Matty parked the van at the curb next to Petrone's warehouse. Boychick, Louie, and I pulled up behind it. Benny, Stuff, and Red parked across the street. The sun had set and the garment district streets were empty. Angelo and the twins got out of the van. Dino was carrying a partially concealed shotgun alongside his right leg.

"Wait here," I said to Boychick and Louie. I got out and joined Angelo and the twins at the curb.

Angelo looked at Matty and pointed to the small walk-in door next to the huge overhead roll-up. "See that door?" he asked.

"Yeah," said Matty.

"There's a buzzer," said Angelo, "and a peephole. When the guard opens it, reach in and grab him by the back of the neck and pull his face into the hole. I'll stick my gun in his mouth and tell him to open up."

"Got it," said Matty.

He turned to me. "You stay behind me, *capische?*"

"*Capisco.*"

Angelo and Matty strolled casually up to the walk-in door. Angelo flattened himself alongside the door and removed his automatic. He looked down and pointed at the sidewalk in front of the door. He tapped Matty's arm and asked, "What's it look like?"

"Blood," said Matty. "One of 'em got hit." He looked back up. "Gino?"

"Prob'ly," said Angelo. "His gun was out when I found him." He indicated the buzzer. "Go."

Matty pushed the button. After a brief pause, the peephole opened and Beppo was running off at the mouth before it was fully ajar.

"Yeah—whaddaya want? 'Cause we're closed—an' ain't doin' no bidness till tamorra when we'll be open at—"

Matty reached in, grabbed the back of Beppo's neck, and yanked his face into the opening. His forehead slammed into the back of the door, and he shrieked. Angelo shoved his gun into Beppo's mouth, stifling him.

"Open the door, or I open yer head," Angelo hissed.

Beppo's eyes bulged. He unlatched the door and wet his pants. Angelo pushed it open while Matty was still holding Beppo's neck. He swung with the door like a pinioned puppet.

Angelo, Dino, and I entered the warehouse. Matty released Beppo. He looked from Matty to Dino and back to Matty. He was so completely confused that he started babbling again.

"Jeez—what? I'm seein' doubles—what's goin' on? Who are yew guys—whaddaya want? I'm—"

Matty stuck his Beretta between Beppo's eyes and said, "Shut up . . . just—"

It didn't stop Beppo. He saw me and pointed. "Da nekid kid what Touch brung! It's me—Beppo! I brung ya lunch!" His eyes darted back and forth between the twins. "I wuz good ta 'im! C'mon, guys—take it easy—all I am is nobody—it ain't me ya want—I jus' work here—I don't know nothin'—I'm the driver—I drive—that's it, an'—"

Matty's hand shot out and clamped Beppo's throat. That stopped him. "Where are they?" he snarled.

Beppo gurgled out, "Uhuu-p th-there," and pointed toward the office.

"Show me," said Matty, and let go of Beppo's throat. Beppo rubbed his Adam's apple and immediately started to babble again. He couldn't help himself.

"Ain't no need ta get rough—I'm jus' a li'l guy what's tryin' a make a livin'—who don't know nothin'—ya know, a guy who jus wants ta mind his own bidness—and get along wit—"

Matty's hand again shot out and clamped Beppo's throat. "One more word . . . just one," he hissed, "and I'm gonna paint the wall with your brains."

That finally did it. Beppo shut up. I signaled Boychick, and he jumped out of the Ford, followed by Louie. Benny and Red got out of the Buick, and they all came to the door.

Angelo went back to the van and returned with a pair of shotguns. He handed one to Boychick and said, "You, Stuff, and Louie check out the warehouse in case there's anyone in back." The second shotgun went to Benny. "You and Red, wait outside and cover the door. Matty, Dino, and Vinny are with me." He turned to Beppo. "Okay, motor-mouth, lead on."

Beppo's head bounced up and down, and he led us through the garment racks and up the stairs. Angelo, Dino, and I had been there before and knew the layout of the swinging wall and hidden office. Matty didn't.

"When the wall opens," Angelo instructed Matty, "we all stand to one side. All anyone in there's gonna see is this clown." He indicated Beppo. "While their attention is on him, we jump in an' open up. Dino's shotgun first. Me'n Matty clean up after Dino lets go both barrels."

When we got to the bulletin board, Angelo faced me and stuck his finger in my chest. "You wait here!" he said in a stage whisper.

I grumbled something unintelligible.

"I didn't hear ya!" It was still a stage whisper, but it came out like a bark.

"Right . . . I stay here . . . I got it. I'm good."

Angelo snapped off a short nod of acceptance and turned to Beppo. He indicated the blue thumbtack. "Okay, motor-mouth—hit it. Stand there and say nothin'. *Capische?*"

Beppo's head bobbed up and down like a jackhammer. He was vibrating. He punched the thumbtack, and the wall started to swing. It was halfway open when Beppo could no longer control himself. He screamed out, "They made me, Touch! They got guns—they knew ya was here—I couldn't do nuttin'—I jus—"

Touch was still at the desk on the phone. He hadn't reacted when the wall started to swing open, but when Beppo began screaming he immediately pulled out his .38 and aimed at the door.

Dino whirled into the doorway behind Beppo and brought up his shotgun. Touch saw him and fired first, three quick shots. Two missed and one hit Beppo. It threw him back into Dino as he was squeezing the trigger. The shotgun barrel flew up, and both blasts hit the ceiling. Dino went down and was momentarily pinned under Beppo. Angelo and Matty dove into the room headfirst and hit the floor firing. Their first shots were high, and Touch had time to get off three of his own—his last three. He missed his fast-rolling targets, and his revolver clicked on empty chambers. Angelo stopped rolling and fired. Touch was lifted off his feet. His arms flew up. He slammed into the wall and slid down in slow motion.

I took out my snub-nose and peeked around the corner when the shooting stopped. Dino was still in the entrance, crawling out from under Beppo. I saw Angelo and Matty get up and move toward Touch. Behind them, Carlo was rising from his fetal position on the couch. He'd managed to get out his .22 when Angelo and Matty dove into the office. His hand was shaking as he struggled to point it at their backs. I aimed and squeezed off one round. It blew off Carlo's forehead.

Angelo turned and saw me next to the open wall, lowering my gun. He looked at Carlo and then back to me. "Ya said you'd wait outside."

I shrugged and gave him the same answer he'd given me a week earlier, in almost the same spot. "I lied."

Angelo smiled and squatted next to Touch. The twins and I walked over and hovered above them.

Miraculously, Touch was still alive. The lights were going out, but he managed a smile. "Fuck you, Angelo . . . I got yer boss."

"Sorry, Touch . . . he's still alive."

"Huh?" Touch groaned.

"He's still alive, asshole. Ya didn't finish it."

369

A look of absolute hatred came across Touch's face, and he tried to get up. As big and powerful as he was, it was one move he wasn't going to make. He slumped back against the wall and died. Angelo stood up and surveyed the carnage.

"Carlo's dead," said Dino. "Motor-mouth's out, but he's not hit bad."

Angelo turned to me. "Get the rest of your crew in here. We gotta clean this place up, get 'em all outta here, and get rid of the bodies. They gotta just disappear." He looked from me to each of the twins and said, "Like the hit on Gino—this never happened . . . *Capische?*"

We all nodded. "What about the hole in the ceiling?" I asked.

"Cudda happened when I blew up his desk. Everyone knows about that."

We set about the gruesome task. I retrieved the cleaning material from the closet where they had kept me prisoner. Boychick, Louie, Red, Stuff, and Benny joined me, and we scoured Gee-gee's office. The bloody throw rug was removed, and Carlo's blood was wiped off the leather couch without much trouble.

Angelo and the twins brought Beppo back to the clinic, where the doctors patched his shoulder wound and put him under guard. They brought back three body bags, and we loaded Touch, Carlo, and Bo Barbera into the bags. The whole operation would have been grisly if Louie hadn't added some unintentional humor. Typical of Louie, he refused to do any cleaning in his meticulous clothes, so he stripped down to his shorts, shoes, and garter-belted black socks. He was wielding a mop, but he still looked like something out of a porno film.

We carried the body bags out to the van, Angelo and the twins got into it, and they headed for the Lincoln Tunnel. The rest of us followed—Benny, Stuff, and Red in the Buick; Boychick, Louie, and me in the Ford.

*　　*　　*

Angelo and the twins were leading us back to the Secaucus Meadows, where they had buried the body of Junior Heinkle four days earlier. The Meadows was actually a rat-infested garbage dump, an enormous landfill project that would one day turn into the Meadowlands—site of a professional football stadium and home field of the New York Giants. Until then, it was one of the Mob's favorite burial grounds for bodies that had to disappear.

Matty pulled off the highway and onto the road the garbage trucks used to get to their unloading areas. It was pitch black. He drove the van deep into the dump and parked. We parked next to it, got out, and joined Angelo and the twins. The stench was overwhelming.

Matty opened the rear doors and asked, "Same spot as Junior?"

"For the two," said Angelo. "They deserve each other. Bo we put somewhere else."

We removed two bodies and a pair of shovels from the van. The twins picked up the bodies one at a time, by the feet and shoulders. They swung them back and forth and then threw them off the ledge that was the current extent of the landfill. The bodies dropped about ten feet to the bottom, and we covered them with a light coat of refuse shoveled from the top. It wouldn't take much. By eight o'clock the next morning, the trucks would arrive and start dumping tons of garbage over the edge. The rats would do the rest.

"That's it," said Angelo. "Find a place for Bo."

In the culture of the Mob, there was a vast difference between *amico* and *nemico*. Friends were brothers—enemies were scum. We went to a spot farther down the ledge and took Bo's body out of the bag. We bowed our heads, said a silent prayer, and gently rolled Bo over the edge. We shoveled a light blanket of garbage on our friend, climbed into the vehicles, and left the burial ground.

We all got back to the clinic at ten-thirty. I went to my mother and asked, "Any news?" She shook her head.

371

Lena said, "He's still bein' operated."

An hour later, a doctor came into the waiting area and walked up to Angelo. "The other man you brought in is awake . . . He'll be fine, but he never stops talking."

"Good," said Angelo, "let him talk to me." He left with the doctor and returned a half hour later. He had told Beppo that if he wanted to leave the clinic alive, he had best spit out everything that happened that day. He did.

It was almost midnight when Gennaro came out and made his announcement. "Gino is out of surgery. We believe it was successful, but the next few hours are critical."

My mother immediately got up and went to him. "When can I see him?" she asked. Her eyes were still red, but her voice was strong. The announcement seemed to have rejuvenated her.

"He should be awake by morning," said Gennaro. "We have a room for you if you wish to stay."

My mother nodded, and Lena said, "I stay with her."

Angelo and the twins told my mother they would return in the morning and said their good-byes. When I came to say good-bye, my mother grasped my arms, looked deeply into my eyes, and asked, "Is Genovese still alive?"

"What?" I gasped.

"Grillo and Ricci pull the triggers," she continued, "but Genovese gives the orders."

I almost choked. My mother had never given any indication that she even knew the *names* of those men, much less their relationships. She was the one who always insisted that my father was simply a tough union leader.

"Mom . . . ," I ventured.

"Your father told me . . . as long as Genovese lives there will be no peace."

I was again taken aback. I had no idea my father discussed these things with her. He never had before. It was an indication of how seriously he had taken Genovese's plot. He had obviously tried to prepare her for the possibility that something might happen to him. I saw no point in denying knowledge of the situation, but I tried to sidestep it for the moment. "We talked about it, Mom . . . but now what I think—"

"Kill him," she said. Her voice was as unemotional as I had ever heard it. Her eyes were steady. "Convince Angelo."

Again I tried to sidestep. "Mom, I—"

"Kill him before he kills your father."

In just a few hours, the sweet, soft-spoken woman I thought was in denial her entire life had become a cold-blooded Mob queen. I was speechless, and she was in no mood for an argument. Her eyes never left mine; they just continued to bore in. Finally I said, "Right . . . I'll talk to Angelo and be back in the morning." I gave her a hug and kissed her cheek. She hugged me back, but her eyes were cold.

Everyone left the clinic except Stuff, who paused to take Lena aside. "Ma, don't say anythin' to Mickey till tomorrow . . . but Sidney died a few hours ago."

Lena recoiled, crossed herself, and murmured. "*Madre di dio.*"

"Yeah," said Stuff. He hugged his mother and left.

Outside the building, a light breeze had dropped the temperature for the first time in weeks. There was no fog, and the Jersey shoreline was clearly visible. I leaned against the Ford and took out a Lucky. The gang shuffled into a semicircle around me and reached for their cigarette packs. Boychick held a match in his hand and flicked the tip with his thumbnail. It flared, and he held it out. I cupped a hand against the breeze, lit up, and inhaled deeply. The rest of the gang did the same.

Benny shook his head and said, "Seven days ago we hit the rail yard. One week. Now Junior, Gee-gee, Drago, Chucky, an' Terry—all dead

. . . Sidney, Barbera, an' Colucci—gone . . . Touch an' Carlo—history
. . . Man, we been worse than bubonic plague."

Boychick nodded thoughtfully and said, "Ya forgot my ol' man and
his dirtbag buddy, Carmine. They ain't been seen since Tuesday—
probably dead."

"You think?" asked Benny.

"Yeah," said Boychick. "Like Gino said—it figures." He took a long
drag on his cigarette and blew it out. "Funny, though. He used ta beat
the shit out of my mother, and now she's cryin' 'er eyes out 'cause he
disappeared." He shook his head. "And I'd like ta know what happened
to the son of a bitch, even though I hated 'im."

"You're lucky; your son of a bitch is gone," said Red. "I still got
mine."

I took a deep drag on my cigarette and slowly let it out. Benny was
right: It had been a disaster. Ten people were dead, there were two
probables, and my father was in critical condition. But Genovese, who
had caused it all, was still walking around untouched. I shook my head,
dropped my cigarette, and ground it out.

"When they have a service for Sidney, we'll be there."

They all murmured their assent, and we said our good-byes.

The river smelled of salt, and the night sky was ablaze. I looked up at
Sidney's "billion, billion stars." It seemed impossible that it was just
two days ago that he had asked, "Who could do that?"

Somewhere in the distance I heard church bells.

Midnight.

CHAPTER FIFTY-NINE
FRIDAY, SEPTEMBER 1

D R. GENNARO AND Dr. Altman monitored my father's condition throughout the night. At six in the morning they woke up my mother and told her that he had stabilized and was awake. He couldn't talk yet, but she could see him. She rushed in, took his hand, and dropped to her knees. She said a prayer, then rose and caressed his head. My father managed a smile of recognition before closing his eyes. He was heavily sedated and sank back into a deep sleep.

Lena came in with her hands clasped and tears of joy in her eyes. The two women hugged each other and quietly left the room. Once outside the door, Lena told my mother that Sidney had died. In little more than a minute, my mother went from a soaring high to a crushing low.

Lena said that she had heard that Jewish funerals took place very quickly. They asked Dr. Altman; he confirmed it and described shiva, which would take place immediately after the funeral.

The two women left the clinic and went to Lena's apartment. Lena baked bread. Mickey prepared lentils and boiled eggs. At nine o'clock they brought the food back to the Thirty-ninth Street tenement.

The Butchers' door was open, and there was a pair of shoes in the hallway. A man was setting up several chairs with short legs, and the living room mirror was covered. A table had been pushed against the far wall, and there was a burning candle on it. My mother and Lena placed the bread, eggs, and lentils next to the candle and left.

There was a cloudless sky over Union Field Cemetery at ten o'clock on Friday morning. An easterly breeze blew in from the Atlantic, and the humidity dropped to 30 percent. The heat wave of the past week was broken, and the temperature was a comfortable eighty-two degrees.

Over a hundred mourners filled and then overflowed the small chapel for Sidney's service. Ira and Sarah Butcher, relatives, members of the Butchers' synagogue, and Ira's fellow workers. My mother, the Maserellis, the Antonios, the Camillis, and the Icemen were all there. I had never seen Boychick, Stuff, Louie, Bouncer, Red, and Benny all wearing a tie at the same time. I didn't even know that Boychick, Red, and Benny owned black ties. They didn't; they had borrowed them from Louie.

Ira and Sarah Butcher looked exhausted. Their eyes were red, and their shoulders slumped. They had stayed with Sidney's body from the time it left Bellevue through the night and right up to the service.

The rabbi tore black ribbons and handed them to family members, who pinned them to their clothes. Psalms were recited, a brief eulogy, and then the memorial prayer, El Malei Rachamim, all in Hebrew. I thought it was all very simple, relatively brief, and beautiful. Sidney's uncles and two of his cousins lifted the traditional plain pine coffin and carried it to the grave site, followed by family and then friends. Along the way they stopped seven times, each time reciting Psalm 91. The coffin was lowered into the grave, and family members each threw a handful of dirt into the grave.

Mr. Butcher signaled me tó come to him. He bent and picked up a handful of dirt and placed it in my hand.

"He loved you," he said.

I nodded and let the dirt sift through my fingers into the grave.

Mourners filed in and out of the Thirty-ninth Street tenement throughout the rest of the day. It would go on for seven more days. Everyone brought food. The entire Sicilian contingent made a much appreciated shiva visit to the Butchers and then returned to the clinic.

My father was still in and out of a drugged sleep when we arrived, but he greeted us before Dr. Gennaro shooed everyone out. My father asked Gennaro to allow me to stay for a minute, and he grudgingly agreed. I sat next to the bed and took my father's hand.

"Vincenzo . . . ," he said. His voice was hushed and raspy, his grip weak. "Angelo told me about Colucci . . . I tried to stop it."

"I know," I said.

"You know what Costello wants?"

"Angelo told me."

"Your mother may disagree."

"She already has."

"V-cenz . . . I want you to do nothing. Your mother is angry. She'll get over it in time. Listen to Angelo."

"I will, Pop. You rest now. I'll handle Mom."

"*Bene,*" he said. He smiled and closed his eyes.

After saying good-bye to my mother, I went back to Benny's apartment with the rest of the crew. We each popped a can of beer, stripped off our jackets, and loosened our ties. One by one, we drifted silently around the oak-door coffee table and sat. A few small fragments of debris remained scattered around the room, and it still smelled of cordite. No one said anything—we all seemed to be contemplating our beer cans.

I finally broke the silence. "I got a letter," I said.

"Yeah?" said Boychick. "From who?"

"Franklin and Marshall," I answered. "Two weeks ago."

"Who're they?" he asked.

"It's a college. In Pennsylvania."

Everyone abruptly became alert. They exchanged looks and leaned forward.

"No shit?" asked Stuff. "Why'd they write you?"

"Mr. D'Augustino, my senior-year counselor, went there. He gave me an application. Just for the hell of it—I sent it in."

"And . . . ?" prompted Boychick.

"They accepted me."

Everyone's eyes again darted from one to the other. Louie let out a low whistle, and Bouncer's eyes popped.

"Ta college?" asked Boychick, as if it were a trip to Mars. "They accepted ya to go ta college!"

"Yeah," I said noncommittally. "Ain't that a bitch?"

Boychick was stunned. None of them had the slightest idea what to say next. Stuff finally recovered enough to ask, "What're you gonna do?"

"I haven't a fuckin' clue," I said.

"Actually thinkin' about it, though," said Benny, "that right?"

"You could say that. For a while now."

"Who knows about this?" Louie asked.

"No one. I didn't even tell Sidney." I smiled ruefully. "Sidney would have loved it."

"So will my old man," said Louie. "You go away to college, things are gonna change around here. He wanted us all to quit *before* things turned to shit."

"Maybe he'll get his wish," said Red.

"Think so?" asked Louie.

"Uh-huh. I got a letter, too."

"Who the hell wrote to you?" exclaimed Boychick.

"Uncle Sam," said Red. "I'm gonna get drafted."

"Christ!" said Boychick. "The whole fuckin' world's gone nuts! You're gettin' drafted, Vinny's thinkin' about college, Louie's ol' man wants us ta quit, and Bouncer's takin' *opera* lessons! What next?"

Stuff smiled and shrugged. "If it matters, I'm 4-F . . . overweight."

"What? They got enough blimps?" cracked Boychick.

"Again with the fat jokes," Stuff grumbled.

"You're right," Boychick said apologetically, "it ain't funny." He gulped a mouthful of beer and stared at the ceiling.

Everyone else took a swig and followed suit. It got quiet again. No one stated the obvious: It was over . . . the Icemen would probably be breaking up, and none of us would be able to prevent it.

Finally Boychick looked at his beer can and mused, "Lemme tell ya somethin', though. Even if we split up, ain't no one gonna replace us . . . we were the best."

I smiled and said, "None better."

Boychick broke into a wide grin and eased out his hand, palm down. "Let's do it . . ."

We all leaned forward over the oak-door coffee table, slowly placed our hands into the familiar stack, and froze it in place. Everyone was grinning from ear to ear.

It was Friday, September 1, 1950—the end of the Mafia Summer.

EPILOGUE

SEPTEMBER 1 – DECEMBER 31, 1950

I left Hell's Kitchen two weeks later. On September 15, I enrolled as a freshman at Franklin and Marshall College in Lancaster, Pennsylvania. My mother refused to accept my decision and did not talk to me for four months.

Boychick Delfina signed with a manager and turned pro. He won his first six fights—all by knockout and all before the fourth round. In late October, during the second round of his seventh fight, he broke his right hand. His left hook ended the fight in the next round, but they had to cut the glove off his right hand.

Benny Veal became Boychick's trainer. When Boychick broke his hand, he drifted between menial jobs while he waited for the hand to heal. It took longer than expected, and there were some who thought it would never be the devastating weapon it once was. Discouraged, Benny succumbed to an offer from another local gang and again took to the streets.

Stuff Maserelli bounced around playing piano in a variety of

Manhattan clubs for the better part of six weeks. In early November he auditioned for Artie Shaw and became the youngest member of one of the last of the Big Bands.

Louie Antonio went to work as a waiter for his father at the Copa. He did his first stand-up routine at a Mob party during Thanksgiving. By Christmas he was substituting as an opening act for a few lesser-name performers. He was billed as "Lou Anthony."

Bouncer Camilli lost his stutter when the gang dissolved. He continued his singing lessons, and in late November his father used his influence to have him hired as an "alternate" for the chorus at the Met. In December, to his surprise, they actually used him to carry a spear. The opera was *Aida*.

Red O'Mara came back to Manhattan for his Christmas leave after he had reported for boot camp in late September. He went with all of us to see Louie "Lou Anthony" Antonio perform at the Copa and Stuff Maserelli play with Artie Shaw. When he finished basic training, he was ordered to an infantry battalion to await further assignment.

My father recovered from his wounds and continued to rule a large section of New York's West Side docks, but he was happiest when he visited me on the campus of Franklin and Marshall College. On December 26 he was killed during an assassination attempt on Albert Anastasia. Five days later, on December 31, the "21" Club threw a New Year's Eve party that was attended by a fairly large number of lower-ranking wiseguys. Angelo Maserelli and the twins were parked outside the club on Fifty-second Street, waiting for the party to end. At four a.m. the men who assassinated my father came out of the club and were never seen again.

The first repercussions that resulted from Genovese's plot in the final days of August 1950 occurred eight months later, in April 1951. Albert Anastasia assassinated Vincent Mangano and took over as capo of the Mangano family. Like many before him, Vincent Mangano simply disappeared. His body was never found. His brother Philip's was—floating in Sheepshead Bay. Costello and Luciano were behind the assassinations. They needed Anastasia in the powerful position of capo of one of New York's five families in order to hold off the ambitions of Vito Genovese. With Anastasia firmly in control of the Mangano family, his alliance with Costello decisively cemented Costello's power—and held Genovese in check for six more years . . . until Genovese decided it was once again time to make a move. In 1957, almost seven years after his first attempt, Genovese engineered a conspiracy with Carlo Gambino, Anastasia's underboss, and Tommy Lucchese, the Bronx capo, convincing them that it was time for Costello to go.

When Costello returned to the Majestic Towers—his apartment on Central Park West—at about eleven p.m. on May 2, 1957, Vincent "the Chin" Gigante was lying in wait. Costello entered the lobby, and Gigante rushed in after him and shouted, "This is for you, Frank!" He fired—and missed. Costello had turned at the sound of his voice, and the bullet grazed his head. Costello was only wounded, but he had had enough. He asked and was allowed to retire. With Costello out of the picture, Anastasia was severely weakened.

Five months later Genovese made his next move, the assassination of Albert Anastasia, again conspiring with Anastasia's underboss, Carlo Gambino.

Anastasia was lying in a barber's chair being shaved in the Park Sheraton Hotel barbershop on October 25, 1957. Two gunmen entered the shop and poured bullets into his covered figure. He sprang out of the chair and tried to attack his assailants, never realizing he wasn't actually attacking them. He was attacking only their reflections in the mirror. The next round of shots went into his back and killed him. Genovese rewarded Carlo Gambino by making him capo of Anastasia's family.

With both Costello and Anastasia gone, Vito Genovese became the most powerful capo in the United States. The goal he had desired for over seven years was within his grasp—to be proclaimed *capo di tutti capi*. He convinced the other capos to hold a national meeting of La Cosa Nostra for just that purpose. The following month, on November 14, 1957, the meeting was held in Appalachia, at the New York estate of Joe Barbera, boss of the northeastern Pennsylvania crime family. Between one hundred and one hundred and twenty men attended.

It turned into a fiasco. As the bosses assembled and prepared for an elaborate outdoor barbecue, someone noticed New York State troopers taking down license plate numbers in the parking lot. The entire group panicked and fled into the woods. It was estimated that fifty or sixty escaped, but sixty-three were arrested, including Joseph Bonanno, Joe Profaci, Genovese, and Gambino. The repercussions were felt all the way down to the foot soldier level. The buffoonery was the worst part. The image of the Mob's leadership running through the woods like a pack of scared rabbits was humiliating.

In spite of this, Genovese attained his ultimate goal and became *capo di tutti capi* with Carlo Gambino as his underboss . . . but his reign would be brief.

Frank Costello knew that the image of Genovese was damaged. He had insisted on, and was responsible for, the Appalachian debacle.

In a final act of revenge—both ironic and brilliant—Costello conspired with Carlo Gambino, Meyer Lansky, and some of the older Mob bosses in a plot to bring down Genovese. In 1959, the conspirators had Gambino set up the ever greedy Genovese by bringing him into an irresistible drug deal. When Gambino had him fully committed, he tipped off the police, and Genovese was trapped. In what turned out to be poetic justice, he was tried, convicted, and sent to prison with a fifteen-year sentence because of a setup. Genovese's downfall was the result of a conspiracy that he himself had begun nine years earlier . . . during the last seven days of August 1950.

Carlo Gambino then began his rise. He became the most powerful

Mob leader in the country, and arguably in history: *capo di tutti capi*. He ruled La Cosa Nostra for twenty years of relative peace and quiet until his death, but in one of the few mistakes he ever made, he chose his brother-in-law Paul "Big Paulie" Castellano to succeed him over Neil Dellacroce, who was respected, admired, and wanted by most of the family.

The choice ignited another series of turf battles that led to Castellano's assassination and the rise of John Gotti. But the organization was greatly weakened, and La Cosa Nostra was never again the force it had been from the early thirties to the late seventies, almost half a century.

Lucky Luciano died of a heart attack in Rome, in 1960.
He was sixty-five.

Joe Profaci died of cancer in New York, in 1962.
He was sixty-six.

Thomas Lucchese died of cancer in New York, in 1967.
He was sixty-seven.

Vito Genovese died in Springfield Federal Prison, in 1969.
He was seventy-two.

Joe Adonis died of a heart attack in Milan, in 1972.
He was seventy.

Frank Costello died of natural causes in New York, in 1973.
He was eighty-two.

Carlo Gambino died of natural causes in New York, in 1976.
He was seventy-four.

Joseph Bonanno died of natural causes in Arizona, in 2002.
He was ninety-seven.

ACKNOWLEDGMENTS

First and foremost to Bob Smith, who got me to write a story that had been rattling around in my head for over forty years; and then to Ivan Reitman, who read the earliest draft and offered invaluable suggestions and encouragement. Next to Lady Luck, who placed three incomparable people directly in my path. The first, Fred Altman, my intrepid business manager, who read the first draft and immediately delivered it to the second: Ed Victor, the brilliant, internationally respected literary agent, who sent it to the third: the amazingly gifted Karen Rinaldi of Bloomsbury USA. It was Karen who introduced me to the exceptional talents of Lara Webb Carrigan, to whom I am eternally grateful for leading me through the pitfalls of a first novel and suggesting the pace and structure of the next draft. To Panio Gianopoulos, my editor at Bloomsbury, my deepest thanks for his unfailing help during a delightful round of e-mails and phone calls between London and Montecito as the novel took its final form. Finally, to the constantly available Internet, where I was able to garner those dates and facts that had faded from memory in the course of half a century, and with special thanks to the sites of Jerry Capeci, murderinc.com, and Mark and Kristi Fisher.

E. Duke Vincent, a native of New York and Bloomfield, New Jersey, graduated from Seton Hall University in February 1954. He was designated a naval aviator in 1955 and was selected to fly with the U.S. Navy Flight Demonstration Team, or the Blue Angels, for the 1960–1961 seasons. He flew the F9F-8P Cougar, from which the team was filmed for the NBC television series *The Blue Angels*, launching his interest in television. He resigned his commission in 1963 and went on to a successful career as a TV writer and producer. In 1977, he joined Aaron Spelling at Spelling Television, where he is currently executive producer and vice chairman. His credits include the series *Beverly Hills 90210, Melrose Place, Dynasty, Charmed*, and *7th Heaven* as well as TV movies, including the Emmy Award–winning *Day One* and *And the Band Played On*.

A NOTE ON THE TYPE

Linotype Garamond Three is based on seventeenth-century copies of Claude Garamond's types, cut by Jean Jannon. This version was designed for American Type Founders in 1917 by Morris Fuller Benton and Thomas Maitland Cleland, and adapted for mechanical composition by Linotype in 1936.

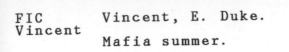